# A STUDY OF BLOOD AND ICHOR

KATIA BLACK

# AUTHOR NOTE

*The fragile lines that separate our realms are thin. I can hear the monsters from the other side—these demons, they whisper through the cracks between worlds. They promise to bring nightmares and otherworldly terrors upon us. They offer power to those who are fools enough to take it. They will only lie and steal your soul.*

*I pray to you, do not go knocking at the door when you do not know what might answer.*

- Erasmus Davio, The First Accounts of the Holy Order, 1616

# ONE

## AVA

The sour stench of ichor flooded my senses as I raced through the corridors of the Moreau Coven. It hung heavy in the air and on the fighting leathers of the witches and half-demon cambion hunters who had just returned from the field.

As familiar as I was with the scent of demon blood, it still didn't keep my gut from churning with unease, bordering on revulsion. I couldn't help but send up a silent thanks that my vocation kept me off the front lines. As a demonologist, my place was always behind the walls of the estate. I was a scholar, never a fighter. I was built for books and knowledge. Not bloodshed and ichor.

"Out of the way!" someone shouted at me as they shoved past.

The raid tonight on a demon nest had forced the infirmary beds to flood out into the hall. Soft cries, groans, and keening wails pierced my ears, every sound causing me to wince.

Healers leaned over the wounded with their elixirs and palms aglow with the warmth of their restorative magic and spells. The cambion fighters might recover well enough with the help of their demonic heritage, but we witches were mortal. Even in passing, the severity of many of their injuries was obvious, as judged by the deep lacerations through soft abdominal flesh, the torn and mangled limbs, the pools of blood—too much blood...I had to wonder how many of them would die tonight.

I couldn't squeeze past the bodies fast enough. My heart was in my throat, and my boots thudded against the worn carpets and cracked herringbone tiles as I flew through the rest of the east wing of the estate. Working my way down the grand staircase and into the foyer, only more blood and ichor greeted me.

Our coven, which usually felt like a safe house, looked like a war zone. A few weapons laid abandoned, surely left in the chaos to tend to the wounded. Fighting leathers had been discarded, some left in tattered ribbons amongst pools of crimson and tar-black blood that starkly contrasted the white of the marble floors. I took care not to track my steps through them as I pressed on toward the cellar stairs.

The itch of excitement had the tips of my fingers buzzing and my breath catching in my throat. Because beneath the underbelly of our coven's fortified walls, a demon had been captured.

It wasn't often that a live demon was brought in for my study anymore. Though they ran rampant in our world, having escaped from the dark rifts that separated their realm from ours, they were far too dangerous to be kept alive for longer than necessary. So, while to most, the very thought of a demon at all—let alone one being kept within our walls—was horrifying, to a studied demonologist like myself, my warped fascination of their kind only shot a thrill through me.

I paused at the base of the steps, my hand resting on the wooden door, and squeezed my eyes shut.

*Steady your heartbeat,* I told myself. *Clear your mind.*

Even with a decade of demonology study under my belt, no amount of training ever felt like enough when coming face to face with one of them. But as much as the prospect of it was damn-near petrifying, there was no denying the accompanying excitement that made my body practically hum with restless zeal.

Rolling my shoulders back, I pushed open the heavy door and strode into the entryway of the cellar. The familiar stale musk of wet rock and decay invaded my nostrils, and my footsteps echoed off the stone of the open chambered space.

Lena Moreau, the High Witch of our coven, stood tall with her back facing me and two other witches at her side. She was a striking image of authority when adorned in her official High Witch regalia. Her wavy golden hair spilled over her shoulders, which stood out against the cobalt-blue robe that pooled onto the floor around her. The silver rings adorning her slender fingers glinted in the flickering lights from the sconces along the old walls.

I had to force myself not to audibly groan when I noticed who escorted her. Thomas, I had been expecting. But I didn't miss the sharp glare that Luke gave me from halfway across the room, his stern features already set into a deep scowl from the sight of me alone.

"You're late, Ava," Lena said coldly at my approach.

Sometimes it was easy to forget that Lena was only fifteen years my senior. She was one of the youngest High Witches ever appointed within any coven, and a little over a decade in the position had not been kind to her, given the state of dark circles around her eyes and rather pallid complexion.

"Have you been briefed yet?" she asked me.

"No," I said. "I rushed down as soon as I heard."

Lena gnawed at the corner of her lip, a habit I'd quickly learned to mean she was fighting hard to bite back her annoyance.

"Our hunters subdued a demon during the raid and brought it here for interrogation. We currently have it contained in the Hull."

*The Hull?* It must be a very powerful demon if they had been forced to keep it there. The rest of the holding cages and cells below the estate were strong enough to keep most lesser demons suppressed, so The Hull was only used on the rarest occasions. I could only recall a handful of times during my assignment at Moreau that it had been necessary for more powerful higher demons.

"Thomas," Lena said, "make sure the wards are sufficient. No cracks, no weak spots. We don't want to risk the demon escaping...for all of our sakes." Her warning tone made my heart race faster. I reminded myself to tamp any anxiety before we confronted the demon.

*Show no weakness. Give them nothing that can be used against you.*

I repeated that mantra while I built up the walls of my mental shields that kept my thoughts and emotions contained, while also keeping the likelihood of a demon's prying claws out.

I made the mistake of catching Luke's hardened stare and glanced away before the look turned my stomach. If it weren't for the fact that he was Lena's attendant which forced him to be at her side for all hours of the day, I was sure that he'd rather be literally anywhere else if it only meant he wasn't forced to be in my presence. The feeling was decidedly mutual.

The High Witch's dark eyes fell upon me as she said, "Ava, you know the procedure. You are to observe only for this session."

"Yes, Lena," I affirmed, meeting her gaze.

She nodded and then turned to lead us past the other cells that lined the hall. A few guttural growls and scraping of claws from the lesser demons within darted around us as we walked past, but I kept my eyes trained ahead, focused on the looming doors of the Hull.

Lena shoved open the large iron doors. The hem of her robe trailed behind her, grazing the floor with a gentle hiss as she strode into the Hull with dominant authority commanding every step. I raised my chin in an attempt to exude even half the confidence she radiated.

I'd never liked this room, even in the few times I'd been inside. The circular chamber felt cavernous, too large and too empty. The open space always brought on a prickling sensation of anxiety that was impossible to ignore.

Our footsteps echoed around us, bouncing off the worn stone floor and up to the high, rounded ceiling. Suspended above the center of the room were three enormous rings—gold, iron, and silver—intertwined in an endless rotation and humming with power from the binding spells etched into their bands. The metal glinted off the light coming from the five bronze braziers lit around the edges of the room.

The hair on my arms stood on end, but it wasn't just from the magic emanating from the rings overhead. There was another force present—a power that radiated from the center of the room, both dark and ancient.

An icy chill ran down my spine, and my gaze flew to the tall figure standing shackled in the middle of a pentagram etched onto the floor.

The demon looked surprisingly human at first glance. There were no obvious indications of horns, no tail protruding from its backside, and no claws nor any other physical abnormalities that their kind commonly possessed. Its skin was slightly tanned, and strands of dark hair fell over its face as it stared at the floor with its hands clasped together at the waist. Someone had already bound each wrist in a set of iron manacles fitted with heavy chains that bound the demon to the floor and restricted its movement.

It was often the demons who appeared more human than monster that were the most dangerous. I kept that thought in the back of my mind as we approached it.

Lena stopped at the outer circle of the pentagram, leaving a healthy distance between herself and the first line of wards. She nodded to Thomas who broke away and circled the demon trap.

Lena clicked her tongue as if to catch its attention. "Hello, *demon.*"

Slowly, the demon lifted its head, and I stifled a gasp when I looked upon its face. Eyes of pure onyx peered back at Lena. The whites had been enveloped by fathomless dark voids so deep that they glinted whenever they caught the firelight from the braziers.

It was not merely a demon. No, the man who stood before us was *possessed*.

A sick twist of uncertainty formed in my gut.

Why hadn't Lena warned us? Warned *me*.

The demon curled the human male's lips into a wicked grin that was all teeth, directed at Lena. "Hello, *witch*," its voice purred, smooth as silk and laced with a malevolent hunger.

Thomas nodded his approval after finishing his inspection of the wards and Lena returned his motion. He took his place beside me, and I thought for a moment that I caught his hands trembling before he forced himself to still.

I looked back to the possessed man. He couldn't have been much older than me, mid to late twenties if I had to guess. Tattoos covered both his arms, starting at the wrist and stretching upward until they disappeared beneath the sleeves of his tight, black T-shirt. Above the neckline of his shirt, there was another tattoo that stood out from the rest—a V on the left side of his neck, a few inches below the edge of his sharp jawline.

"Has the High Witch come to finish me off then?" the demon asked playfully. Its voice sounded unnatural, almost warped as it came out of the human's mouth. Too low and too dark. "Or have you tasked one of your pupils with the deed?"

"You will be dealt with in due time," Lena promised.

"Oh, I should hope so. Please tell me what you have in mind. I want to know all of the viciously delightful ways you're going to make me suffer." The demon licked its lips and eyed Lena hungrily.

My mouth curled in disgust, but I forced myself to regain a neutral expression before the demon noticed.

*Show no weakness.*

I triple checked that my mental shields were still firmly in place.

"Release this human from your possession," Lena ordered.

"Rude of you to demand such a thing without even the proper manners." The demon raised its chin. "I don't think I will though. It's warm in here, and I've made myself very comfortable. I won't be going anywhere anytime soon."

Onyx black eyes flicked from Lena, to Luke, passing over Thomas, and then landed on me. They lingered for far longer than I would have liked, and my hackles rose in warning.

Primal instincts screamed for me to look away, but I continued to mask my horror, praying that I was feigning enough confidence to mirror Lena's stony demeanor. However, in the presence of this demon, it felt as if my mirror was nothing but an empty frame, allowing it to see right through me and glimpse the terrified, trembling girl behind it.

The demon let out a languid laugh. "On second thought, that one looks tempting." It cocked its head to one side as it studied me. "Perhaps I'll slip out of this vessel and into hers instead."

A sharp tongue peeked out from the corner of the human's mouth before it mused, "She looks delicious. Pretty too." The demon's head snapped toward Luke. "Tell me, mortal. How well did she fuck when she warmed your bed? What sweet little noises did she make when she—"

Heat rushed to my face, and I snapped, the words spilling out of me before I could stop them. "Shut your mouth, *demon*."

I knew that it was a mistake. Never before had a demon elicited that kind of response from me. Lena stiffened, and I knew that I would hear from her later—but not here.

The demon's attention glided back to me, satisfaction and awe reflected on the features of the human face it wore. Its lips parted slightly, and I was sure it was going to respond with another foul remark, but Lena cut in instead.

"Let us speak with the human you possess."

I was grateful when the demon finally pulled its attention away from me and back to her. "I'm afraid not, witch. He won't be coming out to play. He's a little shy, and to be honest, I'm much more fun anyway."

Lena's eyes narrowed as she concentrated her magic into an incantation I knew well. The familiar words flowed from her lips, and immediately, the human's body twitched in response as the demon within fought against her. I did not attempt to hide the smug, satisfied grin that formed at the corners of my mouth at the sight of its struggling.

The metal rings overhead spun faster, their soft vibrations quickly turning into a rapid whir. The chains rattled angrily, and the demon growled through gritted teeth while it strained against the magic as it attempted to maintain control of its vessel.

But however powerful the demon was, its strength had been severely diminished within our wards. The veins in its arms and neck bulged, its muscles vibrating with tension until the incantation finally finished and the human fell forward.

The wake of silence that followed was almost as unsettling as the demon's presence had been. For the moment, the demon would remain trapped in the dark recesses of the human's mind where Lena had driven it back, but it would resurface once it was able to regain some of its strength.

The man knelt with his head hung low, swaying slightly as he became reacquainted with his autonomy. His chest rose and fell with slow, heavy breaths. He looked like he might collapse onto the stone floor at any moment.

"What is your name?" Lena asked, her voice gentle but firm.

There was no response, only the sounds of him dragging air into his lungs and the crackling fire from the braziers echoed throughout the room.

"Your name," Lena repeated, sharper.

"Rory," the man said, his voice gravelly and hoarse compared to the smoothness of the demon's. He did not lift his head. "My name is Rory Masters."

Unease twinged in the back of my mind. I couldn't place why, but my gut was telling me something wasn't right. I wondered when the last time was that Rory had been in control of his body.

"Are you aware of what has happened to you?"

Still on his knees, Rory shifted his weight and placed a hand on the stone floor within the pentagram as if attempting to ground himself. His movements were slow and careful as he eased upright. That's when the wrongness struck me.

Rory was...calm. There were no pleas for help or mercy, no screams of terror or pain.

I had witnessed several possessions in my twenty-three years, and they had been mostly the same. The humans that had been turned into vessels for unspeakable horrors usually went mad after succumbing to a demon's presence. Many tended to claw at their skin, shredding straight through until they hit bone. Some gouged their eyes or dug at their eardrums until they bled. Once, I witnessed a young girl snap her own neck before we had a chance to exorcise the demon from her. Those screams that had turned her throat raw and bloody still haunted my nightmares.

But Rory showed no signs of any torment. He seemed almost resigned to his fate, kneeling there in the middle of the pentagram while a demon leeched off his soul, just beneath the surface of flesh and bone.

"You've been possessed by a demon and have been brought to our coven so we can help you."

Rory didn't respond, his silence testing Lena's already short patience. It was clearly not the sort of reaction she expected from him either.

"You are safe here, and we will do our best to take care of you in the meantime until we're able to perform an exorcism. The pentagram and wards are merely for your protection and ours." Lena said. Her bedside manner certainly left something to be desired.

I couldn't help but to feel a deep pity for Rory. He seemed so empty and broken in his silence.

"We will speak again soon," Lena said. She turned on her heel and made her way out of the Hull, giving me a hard glare as she passed.

I paused for a moment to give the man one last look, which was a mistake. Rory's piercing gray eyes lifted to meet mine, and my heartbeat faltered before racing into a gallop. Quickly averting my gaze, I followed Lena and the others into the hall. Relief flooded my chest the moment the heavy doors groaned shut behind us.

"Ava, my study. Now," Lena barked.

My cheeks burned as she led us out of the cellar and through the tight corridors to her study on the first floor of the estate.

Luke and Thomas broke away, the former ignoring my presence altogether, and the latter offering me an encouraging yet sympathetic look. I gave Thomas a tight-lipped smile in return before following Lena inside.

She didn't bother shutting her study doors after we entered, and I didn't dare close them myself unless I was asked. The High Witch illuminated the sconces with a flick of her wrist as she positioned herself behind her desk and placed both hands on the rich mahogany. "I have an assignment for you."

I was surprised she wasn't first breaking out into a lecture for my mouthing off to the demon before.

"For the next few weeks, I want you to spend time with the demon and the human. I am trusting your skills have improved since the last possession you oversaw. Study them. Get whatever information you can get out of it."

I caught myself anxiously chewing the inside of my cheek and chose to dig my nails into the soft flesh of my palms instead.

"What is it you think this demon knows?" I asked.

"I'm not sure yet," she admitted. "But it was found in highly infested territory where we've been receiving substantial reports that the demons are mounting an attack. We're not sure when or where, but we need numbers to present to the Council to corroborate the movements we've been observing. Something is stirring within their legions and none of the covens, not even D.A.R.C., are prepared for what they may be planning. So, I want you to glean as much information as possible from our prisoner."

"We shouldn't wait so long to attempt an exorcism though." Lena's glare turned sharp, but I pressed further. "It's cruel to leave him trapped with a demon for longer than necessary. We don't know how long he's been possessed for."

"I agree, it is. But in times like these, sacrifices must be made." She hung her head and pinched the bridge of her nose. "We lost more than we expected today. And even more returned wounded."

A part of me, the level-headed demonologist, knew Lena was right. New information could give us an upper hand in our fight against the demons. But the other, more sympathetic side of me, kept picturing Rory's face as he locked eyes with me.

My instinct to rescue him from the vile parasite inside him was impossible to ignore. No one deserved the fate of existing with a monster capable of controlling their every thought and action.

That existence was not living. It would be torture.

Lena knew that as well as I did, though nothing I could argue would be enough to convince her otherwise. The word of a High Witch was final and absolute, no matter how harsh their orders might be. Every witch in their covens was sworn to obey.

"I am allowing you daily one-on-one interactions with them," she continued. "And after each meeting, I want you to report back to me with the details."

I clenched and released my fists, a steadying pulse. "I understand, Lena," I answered, which earned me a pleased glint in her eyes.

"Good." She sat in the plush chair behind her desk and placed her glasses on the bridge of her nose—a sign that she was about to bury herself in her work. "It's getting late, and I'm sure you have plenty of work to finish before the evening is over. You may speak with the prisoner tomorrow once you are rested and all your other duties are fulfilled."

My mind reeled at the thought of facing the demon again. Sure, I was used to exorcising demons for study and researching everything I could about them. But using my skills in an interrogation setting? Not so much. How was I supposed to keep my composure when those obsidian eyes only served as a constant reminder of...

"Ava?"

"Yes?"

"Don't forget to keep your wits about you next time. You can't let the demon get under your skin as easily as it did today."

"I'm sorry," I blurted and tucked my chin.

"Don't be sorry. Just do better. Remember your training and why you are here in the first place." Lena bowed her head to the papers spread across her desk and waved me away. "That is all."

*Remember why you are here in the first place.*

She might as well have twisted a knife in my chest. Her choice of words had been intentional, a warning and accusation wrapped into one sharp blow.

The moment I cleared Lena's study, my shoulders slumped forward as I loosed a shaky breath.

I already couldn't stand the thought of losing Rory to the demon who'd latched itself onto his soul. There would be no room for failure. And the sooner I could get whatever information Lena needed out of the demon, the sooner I could save Rory. The task seemed simple enough, but I had a nagging suspicion that this demon would make sure it was nothing short of a challenge.

## RORY

I never wanted to die. Not really anyways.

Death felt imminent. Its presence was cloaked in every flickering shadow like a whispered breath in the air.

It had been weeks since I'd been in control. Or had it been longer than that? Sometimes, it felt like time passed differently with Vain. It was so hard to tell.

I felt so damn empty and cold. Being forced to the forefront was like being plunged into an ice bath or startling awake from a nightmare and not knowing how long I'd been asleep. When the witch in the blue robes first pulled me forward, the sensation had been so intense that I thought for a second I was about to be sick in front of them all.

Thank fuck that I hadn't.

There was nothing I hated more than being shoved back into the driver's seat against my will. Damn witches.

I shifted to a seated position on the stone floor and rested my elbows on my knees. I hadn't caught any of the witches' names. The light-haired one with the dark hooded eyes seemed to be their leader based on the way she held herself and the fact that Vain had called her "High Witch."

The male witch with the dark skin and buzzed hair had kept his face hard and unreadable like the High Witch. But the other male was more timid and more nervous, though he'd tried to hide it.

*See how the smaller one trembles when he thinks no one is looking?* Vain had chuckled through our bond. *He would be easy to break.*

*Careful,* I'd cautioned back mentally when his excitement nearly bubbled over.

Since becoming possessed, I'd learned demons were observant motherfuckers, Vain especially so. He was quick to notice qualities about others I was never sharp enough to pick up on. He also had a keen and uncanny ability to exploit those qualities either for his personal gain, or whether a particularly devilish mood struck his fancy.

When Vain scented the female witch with the coppery-red hair, she had smelled faintly of tea and eucalyptus. Her voice had an almost sweet and slightly raspy quality to it, and her curious honey eyes melted through to my soul as she stared, laying me bare for her to examine. There had been something behind those eyes that I hated. It had looked something like pity.

She had looked so temptingly soft too. Pretty enough to fuck.

I vigorously shook my head. Those were Vain's thoughts. *Not* mine. Right? It was hard to tell the difference when they seemed to blur together so often.

Sure, she was beautiful—stunning even—but *my* first thought surely hadn't been that I wanted to fuck her. And yet my thoughts wandered, imagining what it would be like if I did.

I raked my hands over my face, then attempted to smooth my hair out of my eyes—anything that might distract me and brush away the remnants of Vain's lust for the witch from my mind.

A gentle tug in my core caused me to still. It was a soft nudge, almost lazy, as if Vain was still waking from whatever spell the High Witch had used to force him under. Another tug came, more insistent and sharper than the first.

*Enjoying your time back in control, mortal?*

There was no mistaking the taunt in his tone. Vain knew how to push my buttons better than anyone. In fact, sometimes I swore he thrived off it.

"I fucking hate it," I responded. My voice sounded rough and unused, like I hadn't spoken in years.

I didn't need to speak out loud. I'm not sure why I did. Vain was like a constant headache that refused to go away. He was privy to every thought and emotion I had. Always watching, always listening. I'm not sure what it said about me that I found his presence oddly comforting.

"I forgot what it feels like to...feel. I feel everything."

If I was being honest, it was easier to let Vain control me. For the most part, it wasn't so bad, and frankly, I couldn't give a shit what the demon did with my body. I'd stopped caring a long time ago.

*You were thinking about the pretty one, weren't you?*

I let out a growl from deep within my chest before answering, "Stop it."

*She's mine.*

I practically shouted through the bond, *Will you shut up for once! I'm not in the mood.*

Vain's essence tightened inside me with sick, twisted pleasure, like a vicious and poisonous grin. But he let my outburst pass without retort, eventually filling the silence hovering between us with his soft melodic humming as he slowly regained his strength while I watched the smoke curl into the air above the flames licking up from the metal braziers surrounding the chamber. It felt more like a dungeon.

I was going to die in a dungeon.

Chuffing out a small laugh, I alternated between wringing my hands and running them up and down my arms, trying to soothe the anxiety rising like a wave in my chest. Fucking hell, I hadn't missed this at all.

*Are the witches going to kill us?* I asked Vain. I didn't mean to sound scared, but I did.

*Is that what you want?*

I thought for a moment and then responded, *No.*

*Then I won't allow it to come to that,* Vain said. *I'm forming a plan.*

Great, a fucking plan.

*You can thank me later when we're out of here, flesh puppet.*

I sighed and pressed my palms to my eyes until it hurt and the ache was no longer tolerable. I craved the darkness again, the desire accompanied by Vain's eager yearning through the bond as he coaxed himself back to the light, tempting me with the promise of sleep.

"It's all yours," I said aloud.

The demon wasted no time in tugging me further and further back into my mind, and I succumbed to him willingly as the void caressed me into the familiar warmth of darkness.

As I closed myself off, I couldn't shake the memory of the red-haired witch with the shining amber eyes. The vision of her penetrated even the recesses of my subconscious, and I couldn't stand to drive her out.

And all the while, Vain's smooth voice echoed, *Mine. Mine. Mine.*

# THREE

## AVA

Even shoved deep into my pockets, my hands trembled during the entire walk back to the dormitories in the east wing. My first encounter with the demon had left me shaken, which was not a good sign. Not to mention the incessant pounding in my head was more evidence that I had pushed far past my limits.

There was a heavy lull throughout the coven in the aftermath of the raid. Somber murmurs and hushed whispers followed me through the estate.

When I reached my door and grabbed the handle, I paused. Tinny pop music and muffled laughter floated from another room around the corner.

I rested my head against the door as I weighed my options.

I knew Remi would give me an elixir if I asked him for one. He might offer it begrudgingly, and I would still have to put up with his heated glare of resentment. But if Luke was with him...it was a lot to risk, but ultimately, I decided that a few minutes of suffering was better than the hours I'd lie awake in agony with a migraine.

Rounding the corner, the bitter scent of whatever elixir Remi brewed earlier grew heavier the closer I got to his open door. My chest ached at the familiar peals of his and Kalaei's laughter. As much as I hated to admit it, I did miss them.

When I reached the open door, Remi and Kalaei were drunkenly sprawled out in different positions on the floor. Remi was notably more wasted than Kalaei, and I wondered how long they had been at it if he was already this far gone.

It took them a moment to realize I was there, and their cheerful expressions fell immediately. Kalaei at least attempted a weak half-smile.

"Wha'd'you want?" Remi slurred. His brows knit together as he scowled up at me from the floor.

I gave a small wave, the only peaceful gesture I could think to offer. "Can I have an elixir for a headache?"

Remi's lips quirked as I watched him consider me, swirling the near-empty bottle of vodka between his fingers as he did.

"I've got cash," I said.

If there was one thing Remi definitely couldn't resist, it was a quick buck. With a deep sigh, he got to his feet, swaying as he made his way to the tall cabinet and began to rifle through the overflowing chaos of tinctures and brewing instruments set in delicate disarray along the shelves.

"You look good," Kalaei said to me, albeit a bit forced.

"Thanks," I said as I stepped a few feet into the room, arms crossed tightly against my chest. I didn't know what else to say.

*You too,* sounded too disingenuous. *How are you,* felt too awkward. *I miss how things used to be,* would have been pathetic even though it was true.

When Luke and I were together, things between the four of us had been easy. With them, I finally felt like I had a home at the Moreau Coven after all these years. We'd been inseparable once—a bunch of strays and misfits, just trying to find our place in the fucked-up world. But I'd blown a colossal hole through whatever friendship we'd had the moment I decided to raze my and Luke's relationship to the ground. Admittedly, I'd been cruel to him. Not that he hadn't also doled out his fair share of 'fuck you's in the process, but of course that didn't matter when no one took my side in the end.

"What's the occasion?" I asked.

Kalaei's mouth popped open, but Remi tossed his retort back before she could speak.

"Is the fact that we're still alive not enough reason to celebrate for you?" It felt like he'd tipped every consonant, every syllable, in venom.

*Ouch.*

I fully expected him to kick me out empty handed, but instead he plucked a vial from the drawer and teetered back over the mess of scrolls and bottles on the floor and pressed the elixir into my palm.

"I can pay you tomorrow," I said, wincing.

Remi rolled his eyes and gave a drawn-out sigh. "I don't want your money, Ava. Jus'go before—"

"What the hell?"

I spun to find Luke standing in the doorway, brows drawn together over narrowed eyes as he shot daggers at me. Before any of us could say anything, he turned and stormed away.

Remi's mouth had formed a silent O, and Kalaei's attention was fixated on the grooves of the floorboards, which had suddenly become the most interesting thing in the room.

"That's my cue," I said, giving them a small smile. Kalaei's mouth hung open as if she wanted to say something, but I didn't give her a chance. My skin was hot and itchy and the only thoughts I had right now were of avoiding Luke, knocking back the elixir, and nursing a hot cup of black tea before crawling into bed. I thanked Remi and ducked my head as I left.

I half-expected to find Luke waiting outside their room, but he wasn't there. My sigh of relief was short lived though, because when I rounded the corner, I found him guarding the door to mine.

He pushed off the wall and stood tall as I approached, his gaze just as threatening as it'd been earlier. "What were you thinking?"

I tossed my hair over my shoulder. "I don't know what you're talking about." I tried reaching for the handle, but Luke stepped into my path.

"Don't play dumb with me, Helacourt. Why'd you think it would be a good idea to be in my room?"

"It's not just *your* room, Luke. I needed something from Remi."

"I don't care what you needed. It doesn't give you the right—"

"You don't get to tell me what to do. You didn't get to before, and you sure as hell don't get to now."

I gripped the vial in my palms so tightly that I was afraid it might shatter. But even if it did and the glass shards were to dig their way under my flesh and stay there forever, I was sure I'd deserve that.

Luke opened his mouth, then shut it quickly. "Look..." His voice was laden with exhaustion. "I don't care that you're completely over us. It sucks, but I'm trying to move past it. So, I'd appreciate not having to run into you more than absolutely necessary."

I shouldn't have scoffed at him, but I did. "You know that's basically impossible."

"It's not. You stay in your lane. I'll stay in mine. We can be adults about this, right?"

"If that's your idea of handling a breakup like adults, then I've got a newsflash for you." I pressed a finger to his chest. It was closer than I had dared to get to him in a long time. "It's been over a month, and we're in the same damn coven. We sleep literally down the hall from each other. So, if it's too painful for your fragile ego to handle the sight of me in your day to day, then maybe you should request a transfer."

Luke's eyebrows shot up, and his lips pressed into a tight line. It was a look I had gotten used to—whenever I snapped at him without reason or started petty arguments in hopes that he might one day hate me. It was the same one as when I finally told him that we were done.

"Why are you still so adamant about pushing me away?"

"I'm not doing this with you right now," I said.

"I just don't understand why you want me to hate you."

Because it was easier for him to hate me. If he hated me, he could move on. He deserved more than I could ever give him. But I didn't have the strength to admit that to him. And even if I did, I knew Luke wouldn't accept it. He would try and fix things like he always did and convince me that we could work through anything.

He took a hesitant step closer, the edge in his tone softening as he continued. "You know, if I scared you too much with all that talk about marriage and wanting to start a family with you someday, all you had to do was say something. If I was moving too fast for you...I don't understand why we couldn't have just talked about it."

There had been a time where I'd considered being honest with Luke. A part of me knew he deserved that much. But I was a coward, and the truth was too painful for me to admit—that I could never be the one to satisfy him in those ways. It was neither the life I wanted, nor was it one I was even remotely capable of giving him. Telling him the truth meant I'd have to face his disappointment and the eventual bitterness of his resentment before he decided I was no longer worth his trouble. So, I'd broken things off before Luke had the chance, preferring to settle for his hostility and the contempt he threw into every glare. I'd much rather be hated than become another disappointment to someone else.

A pang of regret tinged with an all-too-familiar guilt shot through my chest before the words left my mouth. "I don't understand why you think I ever cared in the first place."

It was like a slap to the face, and I could see the exact moment my jab hit its mark in the way that Luke stiffened. He sucked in a sharp breath and leveled his gaze, assessing me. "Yeah, fuck my feelings, right?"

"Goodnight, Luke." I pushed past him and slammed the door in his face.

Leaning back against the wall, I squeezed my eyes shut and tried to ignore the heaviness settling in my chest. I should have gone to apologize to him. But he'd decided to be the asshole first, and confronting me had done nothing more than drag up past feelings I thought I had been doing a good job of tamping down until tonight.

*"You're a cold fucking bitch."* The truth of his words to me months ago didn't sting any less now than they did then. Pushing him away was easier. So much easier that I sometimes thought that disappointing and hurting people was the only thing I knew how to do well at all.

I stomped across the room and ripped the gold barrette and pin out of my hair before slamming them down onto my dresser. My hands curled into fists repeatedly until I saw the unopened envelope peeking out beneath a pile of books. I'd hidden it there for nearly a week and still hadn't mustered the courage to open it.

Apparently, all it took was a little anger to tip me over the edge. I tore through the light-brown paper and the red wax seal of my family's crest. Gingerly unfolding the letter in my shaking hands, I hadn't expected the paper inside to smell so strongly like home, rose from my mother's perfume and the bitter tobacco that my father occasionally smoked.

The ink was scratched angrily across the paper in my father's handwriting. I recognized it immediately as his, but also hadn't expected my mother to be the one to respond to my letter anyways. Not because she was too busy. She just couldn't be bothered to care. Not since the accident—since Sascha. I had accepted it a long time ago, but that didn't make it hurt any less.

*Ava,*

*Lena has continued to keep us updated on your progress at Moreau. From what she tells us, you've taken on the workload well, and she is confident that you are progressing at the rate we had hoped.*

*Your mother and I have discussed at length the prospect of you returning home as you requested in your last letter. However, we have decided that it is best for you to remain at the Moreau Coven. We can discuss the possibility of your eventual return when we deem it necessary for you to begin your High Witch training...*

I skimmed the last few paragraphs before my vision blurred. I wiped at my eyes with the back of my hand and then crumpled the paper into a tight ball, chucking it across the room before I threw myself onto my bed and hugged my pillow tightly to my chest.

It had been a moment of weakness, a pathetic lapse in judgment to send them that letter. The first in years. The mere thought that I had felt the need to ask for permission to return home accompanied with the rejection that I was neither needed nor wanted left a hot seed of anger burning a pit in my stomach. I was worth nothing but my name when the time came for me to continue as my family's legacy. I was nothing more than that. A vessel to carry on their line. And I wasn't even able to do that.

There was no denying that I would always be a dark stain on the Helacourt name. Recklessly summoning a demon that possessed and killed your sister wasn't exactly the kind of accident that could be forgiven.

I deserved nothing less than the bitter and angry makeshift excuse of a life I'd shaped around the shameful consequences that forever haunted me.

Maybe, I realized, it was pointless to try and escape them. Forgiveness wasn't meant for people like me. To live in a constant state of drowning in the depths of my guilt that had made a permanent home in the hollow crevices of my soul felt like an apt enough punishment.

# FOUR

## AVA

Standing before the doors of the Hull and holding my breath, I rested my hands against the cool iron to ground myself.

I was still suffering from the aftereffects of Remi's elixir I took last night. My limbs felt leaden, my brain foggy, and there was a lingering aftertaste of burnt willow bark that coated my tongue even hours after when I'd finished my morning classes.

I'd considered going to Lena's study and confessing that I was not cut out for this task and that she should find someone else. But deep down, I knew that wasn't true. She was the only witch in our coven who knew of my past, and she had still deemed me capable for this. And that was besides the fact that I was the only demonologist in the entire damn coven.

So why the hell was I nervous? I'd dealt with my fair share of all types of demons before. What made this one so different?

With a final inhale, I tucked away my doubts and threw up my mental shields. Rolling my shoulders back, I pushed open the heavy doors with as much of Lena's confidence that I could imitate.

I looked straight ahead to the figure within the warded pentagram in the center of the room. The demon was in control. It tracked my movements with an unnatural predatory precision and an intensity that left my skin teeming with goosebumps. A sharp prickling sensation raced up my spine and I forced myself not to shiver.

As much as I had tried to compose myself beforehand, now that I stood in its presence, I knew maintaining my cool, unbothered demeanor would not be as easy as I'd tried to convince myself.

I stopped a few feet away from the edge of the wards as Lena had done yesterday. Planting my feet, I stared back at the black-eyed demon who held my gaze with primal hunger and, to my surprise, a hint of curiosity.

It was waiting for me to speak first. Interesting.

I kept my voice steady. "What is your name, demon?"

"I have many names," it said. I had forgotten how unsettling the sound was when it spoke through Rory.

*Great.* Demons who favored cryptic words and played mind games were my least favorite.

"Then what do you call yourself?"

"Vain," the demon said. Its voice rumbled so deep that I swore it rattled my very bones.

My attention flicked to the V tattoo on the man's neck.

"And what do I have the pleasure of calling you, little witch?"

"You don't have the pleasure of anything." I attempted to keep my tone flat and even, rather than spitting out my words in disgust like I wanted. Lena's cautious warning echoed in my mind, so I focused on hardening my gaze and triple checking the strength of my mental shields.

*Show no weakness. Give them nothing that can be used against you.*

Vain let out a soft chuckle. "I'd kill for the pleasure of having you sitting bare on my lap."

I narrowed my eyes at it, a snarl itching to form on my upper lip. "You are a foul and vile creature."

White teeth glinted as the demon bared a devious smile. "And you are a delicious and wicked temptress. I find your eyes quite entrancing," it mused. "They look like the sweetest honey."

The demon's gaze raked over my body from head to toe, and I fought the urge to squirm, disgust settling sourly in my stomach.

I reached out toward the wards of the demon trap, and when I found the thread of magic I needed, I clawed my hand into a fist and watched with pleasure as the demon choked against my hold tightening around its neck.

"No more pleasantries," I said. "You will answer my questions. Clear?"

There was fire behind the demon's eyes as it burned its gaze into mine, hate and desire pooling together in the pitch-black. It blinked once, and I released my hold on the wards. Vain swallowed hard.

"How long have you possessed Rory," I asked.

"Years." That already wasn't good.

"How many?"

"I can't recall an exact time and date if that's what you're looking for, witch."

"An educated guess then," I said, doing my best not to sound impatient.

The demon paused. "Seven years, give or take."

I tried to not let the surprise show on my face. That many years for a possession was almost unheard of. How someone could survive that long with a demon latching onto their soul—it was unfathomable. The amount of torment Rory must have gone through...yet he hadn't shown an ounce of it when Lena had brought him to the forefront yesterday.

"You've possessed others before him?"

"Many."

I wondered how the demon's other victims had fared in its wake.

"So, you've been in our realm for a while?"

"Yes." The demon's lips curled up into a soft smile. "I'm quite fond of it."

"What rift did you crawl through to cross over from Gehenna?"

"So inquisitive..." the demon sang as it inspected the dirt underneath Rory's fingernails. "It's been too long. I don't remember."

I crossed my arms over my chest. "You don't remember a lot, do you?"

The demon peered at me through dark lashes, and my stomach lurched. I was grateful for the ward lines and magic that separated us. "Believe it or not, I don't have many fond memories of the demon realm. It's a time in my painfully long life I wish to forget."

I had no doubts that the demon told the truth. From what little we knew of their realm, some horrors were best kept unknown. Yet, I decided to taunt Vain by saying, "It can't be so bad for a creature like you. Or were you so intolerable that your own kind spat you out here?"

The demon laughed, low and dark. "Whatever your silly books have told you, I can promise Gehenna is worse than all of the stories combined." It paused for a moment and then continued. "You demonologists like to study us and think you understand what makes us tick, but all the worthless scribblings of yours and those who came before you won't tell you the truth."

I raised an incredulous brow. "And what truth is that?"

Vain leaned forward, eyes glinting. "Come closer, *mellilla*, and I'll show you."

I recognized the Latin immediately. A term of endearment that roughly translated to little honey. *Sweetheart*.

I ignored the demon's new pet name for me. I didn't want to show that it bothered me. And given what I knew about their gift for tongues, I was sure Vain knew about a thousand other languages to call me whatever name pleased it, and it would no doubt exhaust all of them if I let it.

"Keep playing games, demon, and see where it gets you."

"Oh, please, call me Vain. Demon is so degrading."

"I'll call you what you are," I spat.

The demon's eyes gleamed, bright as coals. "*Oh*," it purred. "I do like you very much." Its nostrils flared as it leaned forward. "There's something deliciously dark in you, witch."

I could admit this demon was captivating, both in its appearance and its velvety smooth words spun to ensnare me. But because it wore Rory's features, it was uncomfortable to look at it for too long. Its eyes were dark and soulless, and yet the rest of it looked so...unsettlingly human.

If not for the demon inside him, I might even say Rory was my type. He'd possessed a solemn and quiet presence when Lena had brought him forward yesterday. His physique was tall and lean, and there was a slight definition of his forearms hidden under the mural of tattoos. He had a classically attractive face with strong brows and dark hair—the kind I could imagine sinking my fingers into...

*No, shove those thoughts down.*

When I looked up, the demon was smiling at me as if it could read my mind. I swallowed hard, crossed my arms across my chest, and shifted my weight to one side. There would be time to question Vain about the dark plots the demons were stirring up later. I needed Vain out of my sight. My mask was slipping, and I didn't want to look into the demon's soulless eyes for another second. Not when they reminded me so much of Sascha...

"Let me speak with Rory."

"He isn't in the talking mood at the moment," Vain said with a smirk. "Am I boring you, witch? I thought we were having a lovely conversation."

"I'd like to hear Rory tell me himself." I tried not to clench my jaw so Vain wouldn't see how annoyed I was.

"You don't trust my word?" Vain feigned offense, raising one hand over Rory's heart.

"The word of a demon doesn't mean much to me," I said. "If you won't let Rory out, then I'll force him out myself."

The words of the incantation came to me with practiced fluency. Immediately, Vain's cool demeanor slipped. Its expression grew dark as its muscles spasmed and flinched at every syllable.

Before I could finish the second line of the spell, black eyes fell away like a curtain being drawn back and Rory's gray ones met mine, hard like a steel blade sharpened with rage.

"You pull me forward, and I'll make you regret it, witch." He spat the words, his voice rough.

That skin-prickling sensation at the back of my neck returned at the sight of him. His anger directed at me rather than Vain unsettled me to my core, almost more than the demon itself.

"What has Vain done to you?" I asked, barely a whisper as my eyes searched his for an answer.

"You're wasting your time," Rory said before the unforgiving black filled his eyes again, as if threatening to consume him entirely.

Vain's expression was that of a demon who had just won a small victory. It made me want to knock that stupid smirk clean off.

"What did you do to him?" I demanded, taking two steps closer to the edge of the ward lines.

"He's safe," Vain said, sounding bored. "Rory can come and go as he pleases. And he doesn't wish to speak with you at the moment."

I wanted to believe that Vain was lying. Demons usually did. But the anger that had flashed in Rory's eyes—anger he'd directed at *me*—had told me all the truth I needed to know, even though I couldn't wrap my head around it.

It was illogical.

"You're lying," I said. Raising one hand in front of me, my magic grasped at the restraints around the demon's wrists and ankles. With one quick turn of my wrist, I yanked at the chains and forced Vain to the floor. Sharp echoes of scraping metal filled the empty chamber, the suspended rings overhead resonating with the sounds.

The demon lay flat in the center of the pentagram. My magic kept the chains taut as I strode to the other end near Vain's head. The demon craned its neck off the floor, looked straight at me, and laughed.

I stepped alongside the outer ring of the wards, keeping as little distance as I dared from the dangerous edge. My heartbeat thundered in my ears. I relished the strained grimace working its way up the tight corners of Vain's eyes and the edges of its mouth.

"If I didn't know any better, I'd think you were enjoying this," Vain gritted through clenched teeth. The demon bucked against the restraints and flicked its tongue across cracked lips as its eyes tracked my movements.

"Do you like inflicting pain, Ava?" I froze. The demon spoke sweetly, almost tenderly, and I felt my traitorous heart flutter.

How had it learned my name? I only wondered for a brief moment before realizing—Luke.

*"How well did she fuck when she warmed your bed?"*

Luke's shields must have faltered yesterday when Vain made the comment that got under not only my skin, but likely his as well.

I extended three fingers toward the wards and swirled them in the air once. Vain roared in agony as Rory's body convulsed.

I needed to be precise and articulate with my spells. Weaving my magic into a balance of pain to hurt Vain, while inflicting the least amount of physical damage to Rory was an intricate dance. All the hexes I knew that were capable of breaking most demons would be far too risky to attempt unless I wanted to scar Rory for life. So, I settled on a minor torture charm that had served me well in the past.

I bit my bottom lip to keep myself from grinning ear to ear at Vain's screams. With another swirl of my fingers, I let the spell fall away, leaving the demon panting while still splayed out before me.

"You're a cruel little thing," Vain said through labored breaths.

I stopped in front of the demon as it craned its head toward me again. "I never claimed to play nice."

Vain winced, then its eyes softened. "Despite being the monster you think I am, would you believe me if I told you that it would be in all our best interests if you let me go?"

"If you're trying to compel me, it won't work." I motioned to the wards. "Your glamours hold no power while you're within the pentagram."

"I won't have to compel you to do anything," it said. "You'll soon be eager to obey all on your own."

A small laugh escaped my throat. "You are so desperate and pathetic, it's almost charming. After we've exorcised you from Rory, maybe I won't banish you straight back to Gehenna. I think you might deserve to be chained down here for eternity."

The demon growled but sounded more pleased than angry when it said, "You love degrading me, don't you?"

I stiffened but held my gaze. "Seems like you love it too."

The hardening bulge beneath Rory's dark jeans proved it. Was I sick for enjoying toying with Vain as much as I did?

"Can you blame me for indulging?" it said. "The thought of you taking me brings me the utmost pleasure."

"I would never give you the satisfaction," I said, thankful the demon couldn't see my toes curl inside my shoes.

"That sounds like a fun challenge. If you let me go, I can prove my worth to you."

"If you want me to let you go, then you're going to have to beg." The words were out of my mouth before I could stop them.

Vain's eyes widened. "*What?*"

What, indeed.

"You heard me." I crouched in front of the demon, my arm resting on one knee as I held its bemused stare. "Beg."

The demon laughed again, this time throwing its head back. The flash of teeth was nothing short of predatory. "Tempted, are we? Are you trying to turn me on?"

I ignored the question. "I can make your time here a living hell if I want to, worse than Gehenna itself. I can find ways to make you experience pain you've only imagined in your nightmares. I can break you. All you have to do is say one little word, and maybe then I'll consider holding back."

Vain was smiling, shooting me that adoring, malevolent gaze again through darkened eyes that I could only glimpse beneath the sweep of Rory's hair that fell forward. Ominous and alluring. Villainous and worshiping. That look alone could be my undoing.

"Please," Vain growled softly.

It was a fascinating thing to hear a demon submit as I held them prostrate. The sound of it was nearly intoxicating. I leaned in closer. "Again."

"*Please.*"

The space between my thighs throbbed at the sound of its velvety voice, shaking me out of my power-hungry haze.

What the hell was I doing? I was actually *enjoying* the feeling of a demon submitting to me. It felt...thrilling, dangerous. Exciting.

And I needed to stop before it got out of hand.

The demon hummed as it let out a long breath. "Would you like me to worship the ground at your feet, witch? Are you ready to be tempted with the promise of all that I could offer you?"

I froze, unable to find the words to object.

Vain smirked and said, "You are a curious thing, aren't you? It's going to be a delight when I finally have my way with you."

The Hull suddenly felt constricting like even the air itself was suffocating me. This had been a mistake. I had pushed too far with Vain, and what had started as nothing more than a curious experiment, now felt all too real.

I twisted my wrist and relieved the tension on the chains holding Vain. I heard them slink and rattle along the stones as the demon moved slowly to a standing position, but I had already turned and practically ran toward the exit.

"You can't run from me, mellilla," Vain called out. "I've only just begun to have my fun."

The demon's laughter trailed behind me even after the heavy doors slammed shut, a haunting echo I couldn't shake.

# FIVE

## AVA

My days shifted to a new routine. Mornings were filled with attending lectures or combing through my ever-growing collection of texts on possessions, and it was hard to keep a clear mind when I was barely able to hold down a shred of breakfast. I would return to the Hull in the afternoons, always steeling my nerves before facing off with Vain.

I made sure to go into each session with my mind heavily shielded, determined not to allow my control to slip, which I found to be a difficult task to manage around Vain. The demon was a shameless flirt, and its persistent advances became increasingly promiscuous over time. Our interactions were all the more aggravating due to the fact that Vain refused to cooperate with me, its responses to my interrogations ranging from severely uninterested, to vague enough to be exasperating.

The demon knew what it was doing; giving me just enough information to remain useful, but never providing the answers Lena was after, and I ended up leaving every session either drained of my magic or nursing a horrendous migraine. I was getting nowhere and running out of time.

On the rare days when I entered the Hull and found Rory in control, it was a small relief. He maintained a usually sullen and withdrawn demeanor and was never in control for long after I arrived. Sometimes, there were days he'd go without speaking to me, and even when he did, they were mostly clipped one-word responses. Still, I held desperately onto those small glimpses I caught of him, as if they were a lifeline.

Rory was wary. Distrusting. He reminded me of a skittish thing. It was in the way he flinched whenever the fire from the braziers would pop loudly. How he liked to tap out a nervous beat on his forearms. The quiet way he assessed me, pretending to be disinterested until his glare found my eyes and then quickly darted away.

Did he even want to be saved? A part of me had to wonder given his manner of detachment. How could I reach him when he'd sheltered himself behind the emotional walls he put in place between us? The way he chose to guard himself was so eerily familiar, and that only made me empathize with him more. Because I knew that any person who'd built their walls up so high and fortified them to that degree had something to protect.

I had no intention of bringing Rory's walls down. I only wished he would let me in, even if it was merely a fraction of an inch. At one point, I thought he might. I could sense the hesitancy in his eyes, the internal struggle whether or not to reach out toward the hand I'd left for him. But as the weeks wore on, the more I observed Rory pull further and further into himself, leaving more space for Vain to overtake him.

"Have you been eating?" I asked him one day, even though the answer was evident by the food pushed around the plate that he'd barely touched.

Rory didn't spare me a glance. With eyes trained to the floor, he sat with his arms set across his knees, his expression distant, bordering on annoyed.

"You're still set on ignoring me, then?"

No answer. If he would just look at me. If he'd at least say something...anything.

"Are you okay?"

That made him snap. His seething gaze flew to mine. "Do I look like I'm okay? I'm being held against my will by a coven of witches, locked in a torture chamber in your dank, dark basement that I'm most likely going to die in. So, I'm painfully aware of how fucking not okay I am. Thanks so much for checking in." His shoulders sank before he dipped his head to the floor again.

My mouth fell open, then shut quickly.

"You're not going to die," I told him.

Again, no response. I sighed and lowered myself to the ground to sit cross-legged in front of him.

"Please, talk to me, Rory." *Help me understand.*

His head tilted up a fraction, his gray eyes meeting mine through the fall of his dark hair. "Don't do this," he said.

"Do what?"

"Act like you care."

"It's my job to care."

Rory's features twinged, and it looked almost like he was fighting himself, letting the silence drag before he finally gave in and asked, "Why?"

"Because of all the possessions I've overseen, I've never witnessed a vessel where their resolve had all but disappeared. Why aren't you fighting back?"

Rory worked his stubbled jaw before tipping his gaze up toward the shadows of the arched ceiling. It almost looked as if he were searching for something within them. He remained decidedly quiet.

"Tell me about yourself," I asked him instead. I'd had little luck making any progress with Vain, but if there was a chance that I could with Rory, I had to at least try. Because he was finally *talking*. And I thought that had to count for something.

He sighed and met my gaze. "What do you want to know?" His words, while bitter, had me feeling hopeful for the first time in weeks.

I was suddenly at a loss. Of all the questions I wanted to ask him, none of my current options were great conversation openers. So as impersonal as it felt, I stuck with the basics to start.

"How old are you?"

Rory was slow to answer. "Twenty-eight."

"And where are you from?" I swore he almost rolled his eyes at me.

"New York."

"Do you have family there? Friends?"

His eyes turned to slits. "Do you mean if I have anyone who misses me?"

I nodded.

"No. Not anymore." His voice was thick and heavy with emotion, and I caught the movement of his Adam's apple as it bobbed in his throat. A shadow passed over his stormy gaze as he turned away from me.

*No, don't shut down on me. Don't—*

He'd just started to open up the smallest bit, and it felt as if he'd *wanted* to. But I'd pressed too hard.

"Whatever you have in mind for him today, don't be afraid to get a little rough," he said. "I can take it."

"Rory—"

But the unforgiving black had already seeped to the edges of his eyes. Vain stood slowly, the demon's attention locked sharply on me. I pushed myself up and took a tentative step back to create some distance between us.

"You look exceptionally tempting today, mellilla."

It was always a challenge attempting to mask my displeasure at Vain's arrival.

"I do commend your efforts with him," the demon continued. "I know how hesitant he is to be vulnerable with others."

"Are you planning on dodging my questions again today?" I asked, circling the pentagram.

Vain tilted its head to one side while he tracked me. "Darling, you know that depends entirely on what you ask of me."

My closeness to the wards made my teeth buzz. Even clenching my jaw tight didn't help soothe the discomfort of the magic.

"There was an attack yesterday," I started. The details were still a little fuzzy, but I relayed to Vain what I'd overheard Lena discussing earlier with one of D.A.R.C.'s priests. "It was a small horde, but still enough demons to overrun the Vittori Coven. All of the witches there were slaughtered."

The demon tossed me an uninterested glance. "Pity."

"Tell me something!" I shouted. "I know you have some information. I want names. Locations. Which greater demon do you serve?" I knew I was begging for scraps, but I would take anything at this point. Lena's growing impatience at my lack of results wasn't gaining me any favors with her either. Not to mention that my own frustrations festered more and more every day that I was forced to watch Rory's resolve wither away to almost nothing under Vain's control.

"As I've already told you, I don't meddle in the legion's affairs, and I serve no one but myself. There's nothing I can offer you."

"Bullshit! Our hunters found you locked in the middle of a pentagram deep in infested territory. Someone left you there like an offering, and I'd hedge my bets that you pissed them off." I ground my teeth together, blowing a hot exhale through my nose. "So, lie to me again. I dare you."

"I cannot," Vain said. "Honesty is one of my virtues."

Forming a fist, I drew upon my magic and curled it around the wards of the pentagram, my spell sending the demon straight to its knees. Vain bared Rory's teeth, muscles tensing and spasming against the shocks of pain I sent through its body. I would have let the demon suffer for far longer if I hadn't been worried about Rory's well-being.

*Please, forgive me,* I prayed silently, hoping that Rory might be able to read the apology in my eyes.

After a full minute, I released my hold on the magic, and Vain fell forward to the stones, bracing its impact at the last moment with both hands. The demon's body twitched in the aftershocks of the pain, and I fought to keep myself from feeling even a little sorry for it.

"You know, if you don't give me something useful, I can convince the High Witch to move up the timeline of your exorcism." Vain chuckled. "You think I'm bluffing?"

Vain lifted its head, the fervent expression it wore flaring with peaked interest. "Oh, I know you're not," the demon said between heaving breaths. "In fact, I'm counting on it."

Offering the demon a cloyingly sweet smile of my own, I did not attempt to mask the malice in my tone as I said, "Make no mistake, the moment we've exorcised you from him, I'll be the one to drive my blade straight through your black heart and banish what's left of your body back to Gehenna in pieces before you can do a damn thing about it."

I spun on my heels, fully intent on storming out of the Hull doors and straight into Lena's office.

"When you next see your High Witch, ask her how the first witches were born."

I stopped and my feet burned in place. "I'm not in the mood for riddles."

"It's no riddle. Humor me."

I pressed my eyes shut and bit the inside of my cheek. Vain was goading me, I knew it. I should have ignored the taunt. I should have walked away. In the end, I found it far more compelling to cast a half-glance over my shoulder to the demon who was still on its knees.

"When your kind first clawed its way through from Gehenna and opened the Great Rift between our realms, it caused a cataclysmic event. The expulsion of supernatural energy that was discharged from the rift transformed the surrounding areas and the people living there, granting the first witches their power."

Vain threw its head back and laughed. A real, true, and horrifying laugh. "Is that the lie they're feeding your kind these days?" Amusement glittered in the demon's obsidian eyes. "How interesting."

"I'm not playing your games, Vain."

"Ask your High Witch, then," it said. "Ask her how the first witches liked the taste of demon ichor."

It was a pathetic attempt at manipulation. In my career, I'd heard just about every fabrication or wild tale imaginable and from demons worse than the likes of Vain. And yet...its words gave me pause, a seed of doubt already niggling in the back of my mind at what it was trying to insinuate. I allowed the comment to fade to an errant thought, brushing off the demon's notions as quickly as they had appeared, and left Vain on its knees without another word as I strode out of the Hull.

I would not be taken for a fool.

As much as I desperately wanted to disregard the rules and attempt an exorcism on my own—to give Rory his freedom, to see that heavy weight fall off his shoulders and see him flooded with relief, with hope again—I knew I could not give that to him. Not yet. Not until the High Witch gave the order.

And every day I grew to hate Lena for it more and more.

She was convinced that Vain knew something useful about the demon's movements, something substantial that she could bring before the Council. So, no matter how hard I pressed Lena every day to allow the exorcism, she refused.

After today's particularly irritating session in the Hull, I sat in the High Witch's office, recounting the details to her as she stood in front of the singular window that overlooked the grounds and the view of the Smoky Mountains in the distance. She kept her hands laced behind her back, facing away from me while she listened.

"How long did you say that Rory has been possessed for?" Lena interjected.

"Seven years."

"That's almost unheard of," she mused. She half-turned toward me, her lips pressed together in a fine line. "I think it's time we switch to harsher methods with the demon. The spells you've been using to inflict pain are clearly not enough to motivate it to talk."

My expression twitched into confusion. "Are you asking me to resort to physical torture? To hurt Rory?"

Lena sounded annoyed that I was voicing even a remote level of concern. "That's exactly what I'm asking. The weaker the vessel, the weaker the demon inside will become."

I shook my head. "Lena, I don't think I can…"

"He's not Sascha," she said.

Hearing my sister's name was a shot to my chest. It forced the air from my lungs, allowing the guilt to sweep in to take its place. A vision of her with black eyes haloed in a swathe of red hair flashed behind my eyes. Lena was the only one who knew of the role I had in my sister's fate besides my parents. And I loathed how it felt as if she were holding it over my head like a dirty secret. A tool she could use to manipulate my will to hers.

I looked up and Lena had moved around her desk. She perched herself on the edge, her eyes softening slightly at the crinkled edges.

"When the demon is in control and you look at Rory, I know she's all you can see," she continued. "Ever since you came under my care and began your training, I've seen how every possession affects you. How each one feels personal to you. The weight of responsibility each one carries."

There was no room to disagree with her because she was right. I'd spent a little over half my life at the Moreau Coven training hard, learning everything I could about demons, studying their tricks and their weaknesses so I'd never repeat the same mistake again that I'd made with Sascha. So that every case of a possession that came through our coven's doors would have a chance. And that's why her asking me to go against my training—to hurt a human vessel instead of helping them...

"I can't do it, Lena."

"You can, and you will," she said sharply. "This is not a discussion. It is an order. Is that clear?"

I bit my tongue to restrain the defiance rising in my throat. As much as I wanted to voice my opposition, there would be no use.

"I understand," I finally said with a terse nod, then rose from my seat and turned to leave before she had the chance to dismiss me.

I cracked the door open, then stopped. Swallowing, I squeezed my eyes shut. I wasn't entirely sure what came over me or compelled me to ask, but the words flew out of my mouth before I could think better of it.

"Was it demons who created the first witches?"

The doorknob was wrenched from my grip, and the room trembled when the door slammed back into the frame. Immediately, I felt the heavy hum of magic push out along the boundaries of the room, sealing us in a silencing charm. My pulse jumped at the same time my stomach pitched.

"Where did you hear that?" she hissed, suddenly inches away, her fiery expression in stark opposition to the icy tone of her voice.

I stammered as she advanced on me, until I felt the wall dig against my back. "I didn't—"

"I know your father well enough that he wouldn't have told you before it was necessary for you to begin your ascension training. So, who did?" The High Witch's eyes narrowed to slits. "What has it been whispering to you?"

Shaking under her hard gaze, I forced my voice not to tremble before I said, "It's true then?"

Lena sighed and stepped back a few feet to give me space.

"Only the High Witches who sit on the Council are granted this knowledge. It's a secret we've kept for thousands of years since our origin, and for good reason. If D.A.R.C. ever discovered the truth, our alliance with them—which is already shaky at best—would be over, and they would wipe us out just as ruthlessly as they do with every other demon. So, you do not breathe a word of this to anyone. *Ever.*"

"I swear," I said, too rattled to say much else.

Pursing her lips, Lena turned and proceeded to fold herself back over her desk. She plucked up her glasses before placing them on the bridge of her nose before she said, "The exorcism will happen tonight."

Disbelief snagged in my chest, mixed with an overwhelming sense of relief.

"You're serious?"

Lena nodded. "The demon has exhausted its usefulness. And now that it has proven it has knowledge that threatens the safety of all witchkind, it is too dangerous to be kept here within our walls any longer." She steepled her fingers over the desk, and they trembled ever so slightly. "Return to the Hull," she instructed. "I'll join you within the hour. Make sure Rory is prepared before the exorcism. He should understand what he's in for."

In truth, there was only so much I could do to prepare him. A human vessel would either survive the aftermath of an exorcism, or they would die in the process of the separation. And there were too many factors that determined the outcome—the skill of the exorcist, how powerful the demon was, and even how deep their hold on the vessel had rooted.

But I was very much ready to rid Vain from this realm once and for all, and I could only hope that Rory would come out the other end unscathed.

# SIX

## RORY

It was easy to lose track of time in an empty chamber with nothing to occupy myself except for Vain's constant, restless presence. The only markers for time's passing were the bland, tasteless meals brought twice a day by one of the witches. And every few days, a pail of fresh water (not holy water to my surprise) would be sent down along with a worn cloth. Even the scruff on my jaw had come in as the days turned into what must have been weeks.

Ava seemed to visit every day, sometimes for hours, to ask Vain her questions. I didn't always care enough to stick around. She was nice to look at, but she was a stark reminder of the looming fate I knew would be coming for the both of us.

The shadows almost seemed closer as dread seeped from the dark edges of the chamber. It was only a matter of time before the witches decided they no longer had any use for us.

Waiting for the inevitable seemed a waste of the little energy I had, so I filled my days with dreamless sleep instead. In the recesses of my mind, there was nothing but an endless darkness. It made me wonder if death would be the same, an empty void of nothingness.

I figured I may as well get used to it, to prepare myself for when it finally came.

After Ava had left the chamber for the day, I allowed myself to drift into that darkness and the warmth of familiarity it brought me. Vain's presence cocooned around me, and I sank into him. Only when he let out a low rumble of approval did I stir awake.

"Hello again, mellilla."

The sound of Vain's crooning voice had me shooting back into my consciousness. It was too soon for her to be back. She never returned more than once in a day.

I watched through Vain's eyes as Ava approached the edge of the pentagram, her long coppery hair swishing across her back. His desire flared inside us, hot and bright and impossible to ignore.

Sometimes it felt as if there was no true separation between us at all anymore. Vain's emotions only seemed to fuel mine no matter how small they were. He could spur my irritation into rage in a millisecond or turn dislike into malice. And despite the little interest I had in Ava, Vain drove me to lust after her.

"Let me speak to him," she said to Vain.

"Skipping the niceties now, are we?"

She set her jaw in the way she did whenever Vain irritated her and she struggled not to show it. "I won't ask again, Vain."

The demon only raked his fingers through my hair and stared back at the witch, a challenge set in his gaze, and one that Ava took the opportunity to match.

Her lips parted, and the magic in her damned words threaded around my consciousness like a rope until they seized me and tugged. Tighter and tighter they wound, and soon each tug turned into a sharp yank pulling me forward.

Vain struggled against her, but he didn't hold out for very long. He was weak. Too long in this cage had drained his power, so much so that even I noticed his well had run significantly low.

The final pull yanked me forward, and I bounced back into the driver's seat. Every sensation ran over me like a tidal wave. My wrists and ankles ached, bruised and raw from the iron manacles that dug into my skin. The scent of smoke from the braziers coated my nostrils and throat, accompanied by traces of Ava's faint eucalyptus scent. Cool droplets of sweat clung to my brow and dripped from the ends of my hair.

It was all so overwhelming that I thought I might be sick.

*Vain,* I called out to him.

No answer. His presence was there, but significantly dimmed.

My eardrums buzzed as I prodded at him mentally until I became faintly aware that Ava was speaking to me.

"Rory? Rory, can you hear me?"

I glared at her, my jaw clenched tight. "I told you not to pull me out."

"Rory," Ava said again, this time with so much pity it was nearly unbearable.

"What do you want?" I winced when my voice broke, the words sounding raw as they tumbled out of me.

When she didn't answer right away, I looked at her—really looked—and that was a fucking mistake. God, it was a sin how gorgeous she was. How fuck-able her mouth looked with her lips slightly parted as she stared at me with those amber eyes that filled my head with sinful thoughts. And it didn't matter to me whether it was Vain's lust, my own, or some perverted combination of both that was driving me to want her. I craved every part of her. There was an ache to claim her. She was driving me fucking crazy, and I doubted she knew how much.

"Why don't you fight it?" she asked with a gentleness I did not deserve.

"Fight Vain?" I asked. She blinked in response. "Why should I?"

Ava looked at me as if she were trying to piece together an impossible puzzle, some unsolvable riddle where the answer sat just out of reach. Like I was nothing but an anomaly to her.

"Is that the lie Vain has been feeding you? That you're nothing without him?"

I scoffed and caught my hands moving over my arms subconsciously. "Contrary to popular belief, not all demons lie."

Her brows scrunched in a mix of confusion and anger, and I felt Vain begin to stir, his attention falling to parts of her he wanted to taste and devour. He squirmed within me like a ravenous dog waiting to be unleashed, and it took everything I had to get him to ease up, since his twisted desires were beginning to make my dick twitch and harden to an embarrassing point.

"Careful. If you keep making faces like that, you'll only get Vain more excited than he already is. He loves it when you get riled up."

"You can remind Vain that I have other ways of getting its attention." Her eyes flicked to the wards at my feet, the ones I knew she could manipulate to cause Vain a world of hurt. She liked to use them when he got too mouthy with her or when she needed to display some sense of control of the situation.

"Is that why you wore a low-cut top today?" I challenged with a quirked eyebrow.

Ava's attention dipped to the curves of her breasts peeking over the scooped collar of her tight light-blue shirt before snapping back to me, her eyes flaring a fiery gold. She was so easy to rile up—too easy.

A shiver of pleasure flooded through me as Vain regained his full awareness.

*Having fun with my pet?* he asked. I gave him a mental shove in return.

"I can promise that you and the demon were the last thing on my mind when I dressed myself."

I pursed my lips. "That's a shame. Vain says he likes that shirt on you though. I agree, it really accentuates your..." My eyes flicked to her cleavage, then back up to her face and found her mouth had turned downward into a scowl. "Assets."

The small smile I gave her caused her nose to wrinkle. She was cute when she got angry—beautiful actually. There was no mistaking the way she cast her eyes over my face, the way her attention lingered on my tattoos or the stretch of the shirt over my chest. And I thought I caught a hint of...

"Oh my god, are you blushing?"

The flush of Ava's cheeks deepened from pink to crimson in a heartbeat, her frown intensifying.

I couldn't believe she'd actually been checking me out. "I'm not blaming you," I said through a laugh. "I mean, I'm very aware of my irresistibly charming good looks."

It was such a damn shame she was probably going to kill us eventually.

As if reading my thoughts, she asked, "Do you want me to kill you?"

I let out a bemused laugh. "Vain was right about you. You really do get off on inflicting pain. Cruelty suits you, I guess."

The look she leveled on me was one of unbound fury, and the sadist in me wanted her to unleash it on me if only it meant I might find some comfort in the aftermath. But that fire in her expression guttered not a second later, and she let her gaze fall to her feet.

"We're attempting your exorcism tonight," she said softly.

My whole body pulsed with cold dread. I had known that the day would come eventually, but I didn't want to believe it was real.

"The High Witch will be here soon, and you should know that the process is not going to be easy. It will be painful, possibly excruciating, especially if the demon is unwilling to leave. But as awful as it may be for you, when it's done, Vain will be nothing more than a bad memory. Whatever happens after, I'll be here to help you through it. I'm here to face this with you."

I wanted to lash out at her and shove her self-righteousness back in her face. But Vain gently tempered my storm of emotions, quieting them with a simple thought.

*Let me speak with her.* It was a request, but Vain didn't wait for my answer. He yanked me back and pulled himself forward to face her.

"While Rory appreciates the warning, I'd like to offer you a deal."

Ava stiffened at his unwelcome resurgence. "Not interested," she said.

"I can make it worth your while. I can offer you a favor in return."

"I don't want or need your favor, demon."

"That's not true," Vain said sweetly. "Everyone has need of a favor. I just need to find your price."

*This is pointless, Vain. She'll never agree to it.*

*Patience,* Vain silenced me as he stared her down, cocking his head to one side. "From what I've sensed, you're full of ambition, driven by some need to please others, and yet...you push them away."

Ava bit back a snarl. "Stop."

"Does it exhaust you to have to guard your heart the way you do?" Vain continued. "Tell me, who was it that made you feel so unworthy of yourself? Of the ability to be loved? I know what you want, even though you're too afraid to acknowledge it."

"You don't know shit about what I want," she seethed at him through bared teeth, her voice hoarse and shaking.

I didn't know what exactly Vain had gleaned from her, but it was obvious he'd struck a chord.

"Let me pose a question to you," he said. "When your High Witch finds that she no longer has a use for us, what will she do?"

"She already determined you've expended your usefulness to this coven. That's why we're exorcising you."

"And when that doesn't work—"

"It *will* work."

Vain blinked slowly and gave her a slick smile. "Hypothetically, let's say it doesn't. I would imagine she'd find a more...unpleasant way of disposing of us."

Ava narrowed her eyes at him. "I couldn't give two shits about what happens to you."

"Perhaps. But that same sentiment doesn't apply to Rory, now does it?"

That made her pause. In her hesitation, I caught the motion of her throat bob twice before she collected a steadying breath.

"We're going to save Rory," Ava said, fueled by pure naïve determination. "We're exorcising you and then I'm going to make sure every last essence of you is destroyed and your corpse is withered away to dust."

The chains rattled as Vain extended his arms down to our sides, palms facing outward, and bent slightly at the waist in a show of humble resignation. "Feel free to return to me after your valiant attempt. My offer will stand. Since you say you want to save Rory's life, then it seems we have something in common. We'll table discussion of that favor for later."

"You're a pitiful excuse for a demon, Vain," Ava said. "I'll be glad to see you gone."

Vain only smiled at her, fading back to let me take control again just as the doors to the chamber swung open and the High Witch strode in like a vengeful storm.

Every nerve inside me went numb, and a cold realization struck me square in the chest.

*Don't leave me.* I hated how pathetically small I sounded as I pleaded for an outcome that was outside of our control. *I don't want you to go. Not yet.*

*I know.*

The High Witch stopped beside Ava, the gold thread embellishments on her ivory robe shimmering in the light from the braziers.

"It's good to see you're in control, Rory," she said. "I'm sure Ava has already told you about the exorcism. I want to make sure you understand the severity of the ritual before we get started."

I looked over to Ava, holding her stare in contempt before I shifted my attention back to the High Witch.

"Yeah, literally ripping a demon out of my body doesn't sound like it'll be a whole lot of fun."

"It will be very painful," the High Witch admitted and then clarified, "for you both."

It wasn't the idea of pain that scared me. No, it was the thought that even if I did somehow survive it, that I'd have to go on without Vain...it would be as if someone tore out my heart and expected me to go on without it. And that terrified me. More than anything.

Already knowing exactly where my thoughts had drifted, Vain's presence stroked down the walls of my mind, a soothing motion to keep my fears at bay. But even he couldn't stop my heart from jackhammering in my chest or the sharp prickling sensations running laps up my spine.

"It will help if you don't fight it."

"Just get it the fuck over with already." I gritted my teeth and stared straight into the witch's dull eyes, finding nothing behind them.

"Very well."

I expected her to be the one to begin the exorcism, but the High Witch nodded to Ava who stepped forward. I couldn't stop the bubble of laughter that came from my throat. It was fitting that it would be her. That she would be the one to end me.

She looked at me with eyes that were part-zealous, part-pleading, and maybe even apologetic. That's when I noticed the unmistakable tremble of her hands as she raised them in front of her.

I set my jaw and gave her a slight nod as if to say, *"If you're going to do it, just do it."*

Ava's lips moved slowly. Each word and every syllable she spoke left me trembling as I braced myself for the most excruciating pain I had ever felt in my entire life—a mind-shattering, world-ending torment—

But it didn't come.

I waited. And waited...

Ava's expression soured as she continued to speak the words of the incantation, though they lacked the same determination as when she had started.

"Am I...supposed to feel something?"

Ava paused.

"Keep going," the High Witch said from behind her.

So, she did, only with the same results.

I wasn't sure whether the witches were expecting me to writhe on the ground, scream at them in tongues, or puke up blood. But not a single muscle in my body did so much as twitch.

"Lena, it's not working."

The High Witch pushed Ava aside and lifted her hands toward the wards. Her magic sent me straight to the ground, the manacles around my ankles tightening as she drew on the chains and forced me to the floor until my head cracked against the stone.

Ava flinched but watched silently as the High Witch started to chant the incantations again. And again.

Still nothing.

There was no stopping the fit of laughter rising in my chest. I let it ripple out of me, uncontrollable and infectious enough that even Vain chuckled darkly alongside me through our bond. Relief flooded through me. I laughed so hard that I barely noticed when the restraints went slack, and when I glanced up, both witches' expressions had paled. They looked like they'd just seen a ghost.

Or a true monster.

"Ava," the High Witch murmured, her attention fixed on me with nothing less than vicious contempt. "Wait for me in my study."

Ava's eyes darted between us. "What do you—"

"Now!"

Ava flinched. "Yes, Lena," she muttered hurriedly, and then scurried away. She gave me one last worried glance before she let the doors ease shut behind her, leaving Vain and I to face the wrath of her High Witch alone.

# SEVEN

## AVA

My feet bounced in an erratic rhythm that matched my heart rate. I waited for what felt like an hour before I forced myself to stand and pace the room instead.

*Why was she taking so long? Why hadn't the exorcism worked?*

My thoughts spiraled, jumping from one question to another, juggling theories and probabilities. The exorcism shouldn't have failed. In fact, any exorcism where the demon was failed to be removed was entirely unprecedented. It didn't make sense.

The door to the study creaked open and my unease only heightened at the sight of Lena as she entered. She shut the door behind her, visibly shaken with a haunted glaze cast over her eyes and harsh worry lines creased between her brows. Saying nothing, she sank into the chair behind her desk and raked her shaking fingers through her disheveled crown of blonde hair. Lena waved an absent hand, and I felt her magic rush toward the edges of the room with the same deafening spell she'd used earlier.

That's when I caught the stain spotting the ivory of her robe. Crimson. Flecks of it, as well as thin red lines slashed across the fabric. I fought the urge to scream.

"I attempted the exorcism five more times." The tremble in her voice was unmistakable. "All different methods. Some of them...unsavory." Her lips went near-white as she drew them tight. "The demon will not come out."

"How?" I breathed. "How is this possible?"

"I don't know. I've tried everything. Absolutely everything. Nothing worked." Lena shook her head slightly, incredulous. "I-I've never seen anything like it before." She paused and took a long breath. "In all of your meetings with Vain, was there anything you gathered—any information that we may have overlooked that could suggest why this is happening?"

"No, nothing," I said. "I've given you every detail I've had from all my sessions." Everything except for the parts where I'd made Vain beg...and liked it. I also didn't dare mention the deal the demon had offered me earlier today, or how a small, irrational part of me had hesitated to wonder what would happen if I were to accept.

"I need you to think, Ava." Lena's tone was sharp as ever.

I took a deep breath and reanalyzed every session in my memory—all the notes I had taken, all the hours I had pored over the conundrum that was Rory, and the headache that was Vain. In the end, I came up with nothing.

No answers. Only more questions.

"Vain did mention that the exorcism wouldn't work. I don't know how it knew. I thought the demon was bluffing. But...it was right."

Lena sighed and unfurled her fingers to rub her temples.

"We may need to explore other options," Lena said, her voice dropping low.

"What other options do we have?"

She paused before locking her gaze with mine. "It can't be allowed to live."

"What are you saying?" I knew all too well what Lena was proposing. "The only way to kill the demon now would be—"

"To kill Rory in the process. We don't have another choice. If the demon cannot be expelled through exorcism, then a selenite blade is the only weapon we have to drive it out of Rory if we want any chance of killing it."

I couldn't believe the words I was hearing. It was just as Vain had predicted.

*"When your High Witch finds that she no longer has a use for us, what will she do?"*

My heart lurched. "There has to be another way. We shouldn't have to resort to killing an innocent man in the process." My mind was racing, caught between processing Lena's words and working through other possible solutions, only to come up empty-handed.

Lena clicked her tongue, then said, "That man is far from innocent. An innocent man would fight tooth and nail against the monster inside him. He and the demon are coexisting." She must have caught a hint of disbelief on my face because she went on more insistently. "You know that's the truth, Ava. You've seen it. If anything, we'd be doing him a favor. Freeing his soul would be a courtesy, maybe the only one we can give him now."

"There has to be another way. Lena, please—"

"*Enough.*" Her admonishment was razor-sharp.

The lump that formed in my throat ached as I struggled to tug it down.

"Rory is beyond saving. We've done all we can and exhausted all our options. We have done our due diligence, and now, we must fulfill our duty." The corners of her mouth tugged downward. "To want to save a mortal life is noble, Ava, but not at the cost of keeping a powerful demon alive. We live in a harsh world with only gray areas. No matter what we choose to do, there will always be casualties because of demons like Vain that force us to make terrible decisions every day. Don't ever forget who our enemy is—who the real monsters are."

I opened my mouth to object, to fight back, but shut it just as quickly.

Lena's mind was made up. I could see her fierce resolution etched on every crease of her mouth and the thin lines around her eyes. A High Witch's word was always final.

"When?" was all I could ask. Attempting anything more than a single syllable seemed impossible.

"Tomorrow morning," she said. "It's already late and I need time to prepare."

My stomach pitched, and I bowed my head.

Lena reached across the desk and gently squeezed my arm with a forced smile. "I know today has been hard. Go and get some rest. You'll need all your strength for tomorrow."

I muttered a quick goodnight and abruptly got up to leave.

My thoughts were at war with each other once again. Part of me knew Lena was right. Demons caused so much suffering in our world, and one less of them could mean thousands of lives saved in the long run. Yet, every time I thought of Rory, a cold ache shot through my chest, a sharp reminder that his life hung in the balance too.

When my thoughts drifted to Vain and those soulless, black eyes that allowed me a glimpse of the monster within, I hesitated.

*"I know what you want, even though you're too afraid to acknowledge it."*

I tried not to think about how the demon had acquainted itself with my darkest and most selfish desires, so I suppressed them all, shuddering inwardly.

I walked through the estate in a daze until I crossed the threshold of my room, slid the lock into place, and stripped off my clothes, leaving them in a trail toward my bathroom. The idea of sinking into a scalding hot bath sounded like exactly what I needed to clear my head.

I ran the faucet and stepped into the claw-foot tub, the enamel icy on my bare skin. Leaning back, I eyed the running water for a few moments, battling with my thoughts and the ache between my legs.

Perhaps the only way to expel the tempting thoughts Vain had planted in my head was to drive them out completely. With a sigh of resignation, I repositioned myself closer to the faucet and hooked my legs over the edge of the tub, then inched forward until the water rushed between my thighs. The pressure was immediate, and my eyes rolled back as I moved my hips underneath the stream, my body already melting into the sensations.

An image of Rory flashed behind my eyes with his mouth pressed to my neck, his breath hot and heavy against my skin.

I forced the vision away, but another one took its place just as quickly.

My fingers were threaded through a head of dark hair between my legs, a moan trapped in my throat as he flicked his tongue out over me as he drew me closer to the edge. But when his eyes slid up to meet mine, orbs of onyx looked back, heady and reverent.

Faster, I ground my hips. It shouldn't have felt so good. Nothing about imagining either of them should have spurred my carnal and twisted desires. And no matter how hard I tried to shove them down, they continued to resurface and swarm my mind like a virus until my body went rigid as the tension crested before shattering every last shred of dignity I had left.

My release left me panting, dazed, and just as confused as I'd been before. I sank underneath the water with my arms wrapped around my torso, wishing I could drown.

I had the same nightmare again.

Smoke and sulfur coat my tongue.

From below, it feels like the broken and uneven chalk lines of the pentagram drawn on the warped floorboards are mocking me.

The demon peers up at me, black eyes haloed by a curtain of copper curls. It draws my sister's lips back, curling them up into a sharp smile.

I whimper. The demon laughs.

"Such a weak mind," it says, twisting her small voice into something sinister and dark. "I fear I may have broken her."

A bone snaps, and I scream. Sascha's already awkward and gangly limbs suddenly contort. They jut out into wrong and unnatural angles as her bones continue to crack under the demon's perverted control.

*Banish it,* my thoughts scream. *Send it back!*

But I am hollow with fear. Dread. Guilt. Let them all consume me. For I'd rather be dead.

I shot out of bed in a cold sweat with my hand clawing at my throat as if to contain the scream lodged there that held the last of my resolve.

Before I fully understood what I was doing, I pulled on my sweats and padded through the empty halls of the estate until I was standing outside the doors of the Hull. The stone floor felt like ice underneath my bare feet, and I placed my palms against the smooth iron for what felt like minutes.

This was a bad idea. A really fucking bad one.

But in my gut, I knew it was the right one. At least that's what I tried to convince myself.

I eased the doors open and then pressed them shut with nothing more than a soft whine, one that I begged wouldn't alert anyone to my presence in the Hull at this hour.

I'd expected to find Vain standing there, waiting for me with a haughty expression. Instead, the demon sat on the floor, blood splattered across its bare chest and down at its feet. Crimson, mortal blood.

Deep purple and red welts marred Rory's cheekbones, the skin puffed up and pink. A half-crusted line of blood trailed from one corner of his mouth. But the wounds on his face were nothing compared to the long, jagged lashes across his torso and his back.

Rory's T-shirt had been shrugged off and hung around the end of his arms while Vain held a damp cloth in one scarred hand and dabbed at the raw flesh of Rory's wrists, the skin blistering and raw from the manacles around them.

Lena had mentioned that she had attempted more "unsavory methods" to try and exorcise Vain. But I hadn't thought she would ever resort to this level of torture.

The sight of Rory's blood spilled carelessly across the stones undid something in me. He was still a man, even with a demon wearing his skin. The slick distaste settling in my gut told me Lena had gone too far.

Witches were supposed to be the protectors—guardians. We were supposed to fight against the injustices and terrors demons brought to our realm, not stoop to their level.

Vain glanced up at my approach, nostrils flaring, then went back to tending to Rory's wounds with an almost motherly affection.

"You look flushed," the demon said playfully. "Did you think of me when you pleasured yourself earlier?"

I swallowed my retort and squared my shoulders as heat flooded my face.

"Is your offer still on the table?"

Vain perked up, black eyes flicking upwards and raking over my body in that sensual, lustful way I had grown accustomed to.

"It is."

"Then I've come to make a deal."

The damp, bloodied rag smacked onto the stones, and Vain rose to face me.

"Let's hear it."

If there was one indisputable truth that I knew above all else, it was that a demon should never be trusted. Their promises were veiled in deceits and half-truths. Taking anything they said at their word was a fool's game, a cursed vow that could rear its head at their whim.

Yet, there I was, about to break every rule in the damn book.

"Swear to me that what you said was true."

The demon's eyes gleamed. "Be a little more specific, mellilla. I say a lot of things."

I was suddenly hyperaware that my nipples were pebbled underneath the thin fabric of my shirt, not only from the cold in the air, but from Vain's seductive voice.

"You want to save Rory's life too."

"That was the truth. It still is."

The odds that Vain's words were a thinly veiled string of lies should have set off every alarm bell I had. Of course Vain would be desperate to save Rory. If Rory died, it would be a waste of a perfectly good vessel.

And yet, I couldn't shake the image of how Vain tended to Rory's wounds.

My mind spun, and I was left with more questions. None of the pieces of the puzzle were coming together. I was missing something and couldn't put my finger on it.

The demon cocked its head to the side, one brow twitching upward.

"Spit it out."

I dragged my bottom lip out from between my teeth. "I'll do it. I'll help you get out of here."

There was that wicked smile again. Vain bared Rory's teeth and said, "Glad we are on the same page for once."

"But I have rules."

The demon made a show of rolling its eyes. "Always some-thing," it muttered. With a dismissive wave of its hand, Vain sighed. "Your terms, then?"

"After we're out of here, you need to promise that you'll let me figure out a way to exorcise you."

Vain threw his head back, letting out a deep, throaty laugh that made my skin crawl. "Very tenacious of you, but I can promise you will find that to be most difficult."

I would grind my teeth to stumps by the time I was through with Vain. I was sure of it. "I'll find a way," I gritted out.

Something akin to admiration sparked in those dark eyes. "I'll allow you to exhaust yourself trying, if you must," Vain said. "However, it will cost extra."

*There it is.*

"What do you want?" Damn my voice for shaking.

"Oh, don't sound so afraid," Vain cooed. "I only desire the pleasure of your company."

"For how long?"

"For as long as you will have me."

The demon was offering a dangerous gamble. There was a trick hidden in its words, some deception I wasn't keen enough to pick up on.

*"For as long as you will have me."* That could mean many things and be taken a hundred different ways. And I had neither the time nor the patience to decipher them all.

I was desperate. And Vain knew it.

"If it helps, I would still owe you that favor I promised before as well."

I was half-tempted to outright decline the demon's favor, but seeing as I was already about to screw myself a million ways to Sunday, I held my tongue. Who knew if that favor might end up offering me my ticket out of this mess?

"I'll only accept if you give me your word. I need you to swear you will continue to let me do my job once we're out of here, and that you won't harm me."

Vain scoffed as if it were the most ridiculous request I could have made. "I wouldn't dream of hurting you."

"*Swear it,*" I hissed.

Black eyes narrowed, yet the demon kept that lazy smile trained on me. "I swear."

"The same goes for Rory."

"I swear."

The air between us hummed with a thick energy that curled around us like a living thing.

"Do we have a deal?" I asked.

"We do," the demon said.

I don't know what I had expected—some booming crack resonating through the room or a demonic sigil etched into my skin to signal the pact had been made, but my fate only sealed itself in deafening silence.

I took two steps forward, my face inches from the wards and the outer ring of the pentagram.

"Then help me save him."

Vain prowled toward me, and I had to crane my neck to look into the coal-black eyes of the demon I had recklessly decided to put my trust in.

"So, what is your grand escape plan?"

# EIGHT

## AVA

It only took me minutes to prepare once I returned to my room. A well-worn tan messenger bag was already stuffed full of books and supplies I had gathered. I'd made sure to tuck some spare selenite blades into the interior pockets for good measure, even though I had already secured one short knife to the tactical strap around my thigh, hidden beneath the hem of my dress. The material was a bit more form-fitting than I would have liked, but it was the far more practical option knowing I'd need something with enough stretch to give me the ability to move quickly and comfortably if we were going to be on the run.

After slipping into a pair of black combat boots, I twisted my hair up and back and stabbed the sharp, pointed end of the gold hair stick through the collection of strands with a shaky hand.

I gave myself no time to think or overanalyze the situation I'd put myself into, because I knew if I did, then I might just change my mind. As I threw the bag over my shoulder, I didn't bother closing the door behind me. As far as I was concerned, there was nothing left for me here.

Creeping silently through the estate, I hid along the shadowed corridors, fighting the urge to vomit as I descended into the cellar.

When I re-entered the Hull, Vain stood at attention, dark eyes tracking my every movement. It said nothing, which was unsettling, but I was at least thankful that it had pulled a T-shirt back on so I wasn't tempted to stare at Rory's bare chest.

I readjusted my shoulder bag and studied the series of spells that had been laid into the wards surrounding the pentagram on the floor. The magic in the symbols glowed a faint gold around the chalk line, and the power within them seemed to pulse in an unsteady rhythm, almost as if they were wary of my intentions.

A corner of my mouth quirked downward as I chewed the inside of my cheek in deep thought. I wasn't particularly gifted at wardwork, but the ones crafted along the stones would be simple enough to deconstruct.

The problem would lie in the levitating rings overhead and the stronger protective magic woven through the metal which only amplified their power. I decided those would have to be dealt with last, and unlocked Rory's shackles first with a few simple waves of my hand before I set myself to clearing away the wards on the floor.

The chains sang as they hit the stones, and Vain's sigh of relief was immediate. The demon rubbed at Rory's wrists as it watched me work to unravel the binding magic in the wards with a series of precise and intricate movements with my hands. One by one, the wards began to fall away, and the invisible barrier separating me from the demon grew thinner and thinner. Even the constant hum of magic that hung in the air weakened to a mere flicker until finally the last of the wards had dissolved.

Vain's vicious grin had widened to a point where it looked practically wolfish. I simply stared at the demon and swallowed. Its predatory gaze tracked the movement of my throat working, and its expression turned inquisitive before it asked, "Having second thoughts?"

I grimaced at Vain and then went back to studying the three rings spinning overhead, slow and lazy. Iron to bind, silver to wound, and gold to amplify the flow of magic. When intertwined and moving in sync with each other, their combined effects were enough to create a powerful trap, enough to ensnare even the most formidable demons. And it was far more experienced magic than I'd ever attempted to disrupt. If I could shift their alignment slightly or stop their rotation, even for a second, it would work.

Vain taunted again, "You're very much in over your head, aren't you?"

"Will you shut up so I can work?" I said in a clipped voice.

"Perhaps I could help?"

I gave a sidelong glance toward the demon. "I doubt you could help me."

"Don't be so cocky."

Ignoring its smug taunt, I threw my hands out and forced all the magic I had at the rings, but no matter how hard I pushed, they didn't budge. Beads of sweat formed across my brow, and I became more anxious with each passing minute that Lena would barge through the doors behind me.

I let my arms sag as I attempted to regain my strength and felt Vain's silent leering gaze burning a hole through me. In the sigh I heaved, I allowed myself to let go of the last shreds of my stubborn pride.

"How much power do you have now with the wards gone?" I asked in between heavy breaths.

The demon rolled its shoulders, seeming to test the well of its dark power.

"Not much."

"Enough to help me move those rings?"

"Perhaps. But, if I spend too much, I may not have enough left to shift out of here."

"Try."

Vain looked up at the darkened ceiling and focused on the rings as I lifted my hands again. Drawing on every last ounce of power within me, I swirled my wrists above my head. Alongside my own thread of magic, I swore I could feel the graze of Vain's power beside it. The sensation caused me to recoil sharply from its icy touch, but I didn't allow it to make me lose my focus.

With Vain's help, I grasped onto the enchantment woven into the rings and wrenched my fists apart as if I were pulling a string taut between them.

The rings stilled.

I'd sealed my fate in one movement, and my stomach dropped as the demon sprung free of its cage. Vain reached for my throat in one swift motion with an outstretched hand and then pulled me firmly to its chest with the other. Before I realized it, it yanked my hair and was holding the pointed tip of my hair stick to my jugular.

Vain could have killed me in an instant, but I could sense it toying with me, delighting my fear.

"So much for your word," I ground out through my teeth.

Vain wrenched my head around and forced me to look straight into its obsidian eyes, as if relishing in the last moments of my miserable, pathetic life before finishing me off.

"Do you feel foolish for putting your trust in a demon like me?"

"Go fuck yourself!" I spat. "If you're going to renege on our deal and kill me, then get it over with."

Vain kept my back pressed against Rory's chest. The smell of smoke and ash was heavy on his clothes. The demon leaned down to whisper into my ear, fingers squeezing around my neck slightly, and the scrape of a stubbled cheek against mine sent a shiver down my spine. "Oh, mellilla. I'm just making this look real."

The doors of the Hull burst open, and a flood of witches swarmed in. Vain whipped us around, still holding me with an iron-clad grip that didn't allow me to squirm away even an inch.

Lena led the charge, and from her wide eyes and blanched skin, it was obvious this was the last thing she had anticipated. Her hands twitched at her sides, but Vain tsked and shook its head.

"Ah, ah, witch. I wouldn't try anything if I were you." Vain pressed the gold pin harder against my throat, letting everyone see how the demon held my fragile, mortal life in its hands.

I shook in anticipation of that makeshift blade sinking into my neck and made peace with the fact that the sound of me choking on my blood might be the last thing I would ever hear. But if

Vain hadn't killed me yet, maybe it was possible the demon hadn't crossed me?

"Do it," I muttered so only Vain could hear the unspoken message: either kill me or get us out of here.

The demon grinned at the witches before they could raise their hands to form a single spell as a thick darkness of smoke and shadow swelled around Vain and swallowed us up. When I couldn't feel the ground beneath my feet anymore, my stomach lurched, and then we were hurtling suddenly through an expanse of endless night.

# NINE

## AVA

We landed on solid ground, and the world reappeared before my eyes. I tugged out of Vain's grasp and collapsed, my hands and knees connecting with warm, wet asphalt as I retched, and chunks of gravel dug into the flesh of my palms with each heave.

"I guess I should have warned you." Vain's shadowy voice stalked behind me. "The first shift is not an easy one."

When my stomach was completely empty, my eyes stung, and I slowly rose on wobbly legs to face Vain. The demon pressed a hand to the small of my back, a touch so different than the one that had held me minutes before. It was gentle...soothing even. I stepped out of reach.

"Where the hell did you bring us?" I choked out as I righted myself fully, attempting to get my bearings.

Vain had shifted us to the edge of a winding road in the middle of a thickly wooded area. I could barely see more than twenty feet in any direction thanks to the dense fog that wove through the trees and blanketed our surroundings in a dampened, eerie quiet. It was as if the nature around us had sensed the demon's arrival and was holding its breath in anticipation.

"I'm too weak to shift any farther than this. You can thank yourself and your High Witch for that." The demon's gaze remained fixed on the road. "Ideally, I would have taken us directly to one of my homes, but unfortunately, we'll have to make do here for now."

"And where exactly is here?"

"Somewhere in Tennessee if I remember correctly," Vain said absently, then smiled to itself.

We couldn't be far from the Moreau Coven, maybe less than a hundred miles if we had crossed the state border into the mountains like I guessed.

"This way," Vain said, then began walking ahead into the fog. "I'm starving."

Vain brushed past me, and I shuddered at the closeness of the demon—a puzzling, charismatic, terrifying demon—who somehow hadn't killed me...yet. It would have been so easy to do in the Hull, or even on the side of this dark mountain road in the middle of nowhere. But for some reason, it hadn't.

I jogged to catch up, not about to let Rory go. Vain kept a quick pace and it didn't take long for a burn to settle into my legs and my throat.

I'd never trained with the other witches in my coven. I never went into the field, so there hadn't been any point in learning alongside them as they honed their skills with blades and hand-to-hand combat. It had always been more important for me to keep my nose in my books. But now I was kicking myself for not building up my stamina.

Eventually, the glow of neon lights seeped through the fog, and a small diner came into view. Two cars and an eighteen-wheeler were parked in the front lot. Tiny slivers of movement flashed behind the windows.

I prepared myself for the inevitability that I would need to use all the power I had left to keep Vain in check. The demon was too unpredictable, and I still wasn't sure of all that Vain was capable of. I tried searching the demon's eyes for any hint of ill intent, but its expression was stony, giving nothing away.

When we reached the parking lot, Vain stopped. "I need to make a call first," the demon said and then veered toward the semitruck. I looked for anyone who might be nearby watching, but nobody was around to see. I followed Vain into the shadows.

It faced the side of the truck, which was crusted in gray muck and grime. It held a hand out, palm open to me. "I'll take that knife now."

"What knife?"

Vain gave me a sidelong glance. "Would you prefer that I took it from you instead?" it asked, annoyance clipped in every beat.

The thought of Vain running Rory's hands over the bare skin of my thigh left a heat in my lower belly I couldn't ignore.

"You promised you wouldn't hurt me, remember?"

"The knife isn't for you, mellilla."

I hiked up the hem of my dress and slipped the knife from its holster, watching Vain while I did. The demon's eyes roved up my leg until I shoved the skirt down and smacked the handle into Vain's waiting palm.

"Thank you," Vain said sweetly and then made a clean slice across its other hand, cupping the crimson blood as it pooled. It handed the knife back, then dipped two fingers into Rory's blood and drew a sigil on the side of the truck. Wide, sweeping strokes first formed a circle. Along the outer edge, Vain made smaller sketches of demonic runes, one on each compass point, connecting them with whorls and smaller symbols in between. By my study of it, it appeared to be a sigil for communication rather than for summoning, but my hackles rose all the same.

"What are you doing?" I asked.

"Phoning a friend. Unless you'd rather be stuck here?"

My grip on the knife tightened. "I swear if you're crossing me, I'll—"

Vain swung its head to me, one brow cocked, as if it knew as well as I did how limited my options were. "So mistrusting," it crooned.

With the sigil finished, Vain placed the bloodied hand to the center of the circle. Shutting its eyes, the words of the demon tongue spilled from its lips, too low and quick for me to make out. Vain hissed as it drew its hand away, and the bloody sigil ignited into flame until nothing but a stain of ash was left behind.

The demon stepped toward me but stopped, noticing how I took up the space between the truck and the car next to it.

Vain glared down at me, and I was struck by the size of Rory's body compared to mine. The glow of the neon from the diner sign overhead painted its figure in an eerie reddish incandescence. "Are you planning on stopping me?"

"What the hell are we doing here, Vain?"

"I told you, I'm hungry and craving waffles."

The demon snorted when my brows knit together, and brushed past me, heading toward the entrance.

"Wait," I whisper-hissed. "Your eyes."

Vain turned to look at me, palm resting on the handle, and I watched the black fade away until Rory's sharp gray eyes pierced mine.

"What about them?" Rory said and, not waiting for an answer, opened the door. I grumbled out a curse, swiped the blood off the knife, and shoved it back into the holster before following him inside.

"Two please," Rory said to the waitress behind the counter.

"Sure thing, sugar. Take a seat wherever you like." She motioned to the empty booths on either side of the diner.

There was only one other customer, a man bellied up to the counter with a hot drink and half-eaten sandwich. I caught myself letting out a small sigh of relief because at least there would be low casualties should Vain decide to wreak havoc for a little fun. I kept an immobilizing spell at the edge of my fingertips in case I needed to restrain the demon quickly.

Rory ambled over to the red and white striped booth tucked away in the furthest corner of the diner and sat opposite the bar so his back was facing away from the kitchen and the other customer. The plastic seat squeaked as I slid into the booth across from him.

Under the bright fluorescents, there was no obvious indication or even the slightest hint that a demon lay under Rory's surface. But *I* knew. It was hard—nearly impossible—to shake the image of those cold, black eyes. Vain was in there, and I swore I could practically feel the demon from within looking back.

"It's just me," Rory assured when he noticed me staring.

"That's not true," I muttered. "I know it's still in there."

"Fair point." Rory placed his hands on the table and laced his fingers together. "Why do you call Vain 'it'?"

"They're monsters, Rory." I forced my voice to almost a whisper because I noticed a woman walking toward our table.

The waitress had her pen poised above her little notepad, and a glossy pin on the breast pocket of her uniform read "Jessica". She eyed Rory's bruises warily. With the help of Vain's quick healing, the swelling had gone down significantly, but there were still a few unhealed scrapes and bits of discoloration.

Rory pasted a pleasant smile onto his face and ordered waffles and a coffee for himself, as well as a slice of apple pie at the recommendation of the waitress.

"Best pie in town." Jessica winked at him, and I couldn't help but sour at the gesture.

"And she'll have a coffee," he added, as if it were an afterthought.

"Tea," I bit back, a little too sharply.

Rory's forced smile for the waitress turned smug as he eyed me. "And a pie for her too."

"I'm not hungry," I muttered, but Jessica was already walking back to the kitchen and returned moments later with two steaming mugs and a dish stacked with little plastic pots of creamer.

"Will you stop staring at me, please?" Rory said when she was out of earshot. "You're freaking me out."

"I just watched a demon give you back control of your body, and you appear completely unfazed as if this is somehow normal."

Rory shrugged. "Define normal."

*Holy hell*, this man was nearly as infuriating Vain. And what was worse was that he knew just how much he was pushing my buttons too. The tiny crinkle at the corner of his eyes gave away how amusing he found my frustration.

"How can you be okay with a demon possessing you?"

Rory snatched one of the creamers and a packet of sugar, then dumped them into his coffee. "It's better than the alternative," he said as if I was supposed to accept that vague non-answer.

The smell of smoke from the braziers in the Hull clung to his skin, and every time he shifted in his seat, the scent wafted around me.

"Are you insane?"

"I don't think so."

"It's a *demon*, Rory. I've studied them my whole life. If you knew half the shit I did about them, you wouldn't be acting so indifferent right now."

"I know plenty about demons," he said and then took a tentative sip of his coffee before setting it back down. "Seven years, remember?"

I scoffed. "If that were true, you'd be begging me to exorcise it."

"Look, I'm very aware of my situation, sweetheart. I don't need another high and mighty lecture from you. Not right now." I caught a wince flash across his features after he snapped at me. With a sigh, Rory lowered his head and dug into his pockets. He slid my gold hair stick across the table. I shivered at the memory of Vain pressing the sharp tip against my throat, and I had to stop myself from rubbing at the skin there.

"Sorry about that, by the way. I told him not to be too rough."

"Thanks," I muttered as I snatched it up and pulled it under the table into my lap. I couldn't risk pulling out my knife in such a public setting, so having a semblance of something sharp in my hands calmed my nerves slightly.

Jessica returned with our food, and I didn't miss the way her wary eyes bounced between us, like she had either gleaned the animosity between me and Rory, or she could sense the same *otherness* about him that I did.

Only after she rushed away wordlessly did Rory speak again. "Vain says thank you for helping us escape."

"I didn't do it for him," I said. "I did it for you."

He ran his hand through his hair, pushing the dark strands out of his face. "Why the hell would you save me?"

My heart tugged at the unsaid words. *"I'm not worth saving."*

I swallowed and stared into my tea, lacing my hands around the mug as I tried to shove the image of Sascha from my mind. "I couldn't sit back and watch you die. Lena was prepared to kill you. She wanted *me* to kill you. I couldn't..."

Rory's mouth parted and then shut again. He picked up a fork and dug into his pie.

"And here I thought you were only interested in my charming personality," he said through a mouthful, then smirked. "Or you just wanted to get in my pants."

My hands shot out and clasped around Rory's wrist, careful to avoid the raw skin from the manacles. He flinched at first, but then relaxed into my touch.

"I did what I thought was right," I said. Knowing that I only had one good shot at it, I made sure to meet his eyes and hold his gaze so that he was less likely to notice the swirls of magic I had started to trace discreetly across his skin with my fingertips. "Vain's broken something inside you, Rory. And, for some reason, I think you feel like you need the demon to survive. But Vain is using you even if you can't admit it to yourself yet. It's the truth."

Rory's expression softened for a moment, but once I finished the last bit of the spell, he drew back, hissing and clutching at his left wrist. His fork clattered on the table.

Jessica whipped around for a moment, but then seemed to not think much of it because she returned her attention to her other customer at the counter.

Rory looked up slowly from the mark. A red band of sharp thorns encircled his left wrist that now matched the one etched into my own skin as well. His eyes turned to slits. The air in my lungs went cold, and my heartbeat hammered in my throat.

Maybe Vain wouldn't be the one to kill me after all. Rory's glare burned with murderous intent, appearing all too eager to do the deed himself.

"What did you do?" he snarled.

I leaned forward over the table. "It's not for you. It's for Vain. The demon knows what that mark means."

I wasn't about to take any more risks, not when I knew too little about what Vain was fully capable of. It was a fairly simple binding spell, one that wouldn't allow the bound to be more than a certain distance from its binder. The only catch was being too far apart would cause excruciating pain to not only Vain and Rory if they tried to escape, but to me as well. However, since Vain had given me its word that it wouldn't harm me, I had to hope that the demon wouldn't find a loophole to violate that part of our bargain.

Realization struck Rory, and the muscle in his jaw fluttered as he seethed.

"You are going to remove this mark right now, *witch*." The tattoos on his arms flexed as he shook. Whether it was all his rage or some of Vain's mixing with his own, I couldn't tell.

"I'm not going to let you out of my sight. Not after everything. Not until I've had a chance to exorcise Vain." I looked straight into Rory's eyes, knowing Vain was behind them and hanging on every word. "If you think I'll let you get away with Rory and renege on our deal, you're even stupider than I thought."

Vain's onyx eyes flashed, and I edged back into my seat. "I told you, my word is good."

The neon signs blinked outside the window, and the fluorescent lights overhead flickered at the demon's presence. Vain's power felt different when freed of the confines and magic of the Hull. It bounced around the diner like bolts of electricity, and my skin prickled in its wake.

"And I told you, I don't take the word of pathetic demons."

"Yet you're still the one who made a deal with me."

A terrible, crooked smile crept onto Rory's face, and I pressed further back into my seat. Vain was truly a nightmare in human flesh, and yet I was unable to look away.

"You may have made your mark on me, mellilla," Vain said. "But if you wish to test my thinning patience, then by all means, keep calling me pathetic. I can promise that your punishment will be slow and agonizing if you do. You can take my word on that." It was a threat and a promise, and each syllable made my skin crawl.

Vain's black eyes receded, and Rory's gray ones reappeared as quickly as they had vanished. The lights stopped flickering, but not before Jessica cast another furtive glance in our direction.

"I will never understand how you can stand that *thing* being inside of you."

"I'll only warn you once," Rory began as he picked up his silverware again. "If you respect me, then you're going to respect Vain too. He may be a demon, but that doesn't mean I'm going to allow you to treat him like he's somehow lesser."

"But it's a demon—"

Rory waggled the dull knife at me. "Manners, witch, or I'll put this through your pretty little throat."

I swallowed hard and took a deep breath. "*He's* a demon."

Rory lowered the knife and cut into his waffles. "I'm well aware," he said before he stuffed a decently sized bite into his mouth, nearly swallowing it whole. "I also don't expect you of all people to understand. Vain is…he's a part of me. It's kind of hard imagining my life without him."

"You know that's what a demon would want you to think, right? That you're too weak and worthless on your own, so your only option is to let them in and keep you hostage."

"So, you think I'm pathetic?"

"That's not what I said."

"It was implied."

I slumped back into the booth and tried not to roll my eyes at him. "It's Manipulation 101. Demons are selfish and cruel. They take what they want, even if that means hurting you in the process, and they'll chew you up and spit you out after they've taken everything from you. Vain is not your friend."

"I never said he was."

"You didn't have to."

It was my first attempt at trying to weasel out what I suspected might be the truth.

Rory huffed out a short laugh through his nose. "Look at that. A witch who thinks she's smart."

"You're almost as insufferable as Vain is, you know that?"

"The key word is *almost*," Rory said and then winked at me.

I wasn't hungry, but I refused to snap at him like a petulant child, so I resorted to shoveling a few bites of pie into my mouth instead. If this was apparently the best pie this town had to offer, then they had my deepest pity. Trying to swallow down the gummy filling and stale crust was similar to how I imagined eating glue and cardboard might be. Jessica was a goddamn liar.

"You're chewing angrily," Rory said in a sing-song voice.

"Shut up."

He laughed and shook his head. After Rory practically licked both plates clean and emptied his mug, he swiveled in his booth to glance around the diner, one arm propped up on the back of the booth.

"Vain says that there's a motel about ten miles down the road. We'll need somewhere to lay low until Alastair arrives with the jet."

My first question should have been, "You have a jet?" or "Who the hell is Alastair?", but instead I said, "There is no way we're walking ten miles down some dark, mountain road in the middle of the night."

Rory's eyes glinted when he looked back at me. "Who said anything about walking?"

When Jessica re-entered the kitchen, Rory sidled over to the lonely man at the bar.

"Excuse me, sir." Rory laid a hand on the man's shoulder. He turned with a grimace already set on his round face at a stranger's approach. "*I'd like your keys please.*"

It was so faint that I almost didn't hear it. The tone of his voice was all wrong—unnaturally and demonically wrong.

A shiver went straight down my spine, and the air around the diner vibrated with the power of the glamour as Vain compelled the human. Dread pooled in my stomach, but there was nothing I could do to stop him.

The man did not speak, only dug through his right pocket to pull out a set of jingling car keys and deposited them into Vain's open palm through a complacent glassy-eyed stare without a single objection.

Vain turned to me and smiled before Rory regained control. He dangled the keys in front of his face as if he were taunting me with my horrified scowl.

"Let's go for a ride, witch."

# TEN
## RORY

"You're delusional!"

"Look, I'm sorry you can't grasp the difference between stealing and borrowing," I said, raising my voice over the air rushing in through the windows of the pickup truck as we sped down the dark road.

"This is very obviously stealing!" Ava shouted.

I winced. "Will you give it a rest? All your yelling is giving me a headache."

*The feeling is very mutual,* Vain grumbled.

"You just let Vain glamour him."

I rolled my eyes and fisted the steering wheel tighter. "Again, it was a harmless glamour." Out of the corner of my vision I caught Ava's mouth pop open, ready to argue her point again, but I silenced her with a glaring look. "He will be fine. Once the glamour wears off, he's going to realize his truck is missing and, by some strange luck, he'll remember he left it parked in the motel lot down the road. And by the time he makes the trek back, he's going to find it right where we left it without a single scratch, and we'll already be long gone. No harm done in the end."

"Yeah, like anyone would convince themselves that a ten-mile, midnight stroll to some shithole diner was their own idea."

"You'd be surprised what some people will believe."

Ava shook her head. "Vain has got you so fucked in the head."

"I resent that," I said as the motel came into view. "I'll have you know, I'm the picture of mental health."

Vain scoffed, and I gave him the mental equivalent of a shove before I turned the truck into the lot and pulled into one of the last available spots.

Ava scowled and glared straight out the windshield, her arms tucked tightly across her chest. Her skin glowed a soft blue under the neon and fluorescent lights. Even with her hard exterior, she looked so soft. I was half-tempted to reach out and touch her.

The memory of Vain holding her against us as we escaped still burned fresh in my mind. She'd felt better than I'd imagined. Even though Vain had been in control, I had still felt the sensation of her underneath my hands, the smoothness of her skin, her erratic, shallow breaths ghosting over my flesh, the warm flash of her pulse.

*God*, I wanted to touch her again. I craved her in a way that caught me completely off guard. And no matter how hard I tried, I couldn't shake the feeling.

"Stay here. I'll check us in."

Ava stuffed a wad of cash into my palm. "No more glamours," she said.

"*Fine.*"

It took everything in me to keep from slamming the door shut as I exited the truck. Stomping up to the front desk, Vain stirred inside me at the sight of the short old woman behind it.

*Behave,* I growled through our bond.

He was itching to use another glamour for the hell of it. He'd gotten a taste for his power again and was begging for more.

*Just a small one,* he pleaded.

*Knock. It. Off.*

Vain slunk back reluctantly as I finished paying.

When I returned to the truck, I held up a singular room key and Ava narrowed her eyes on it.

"Where's the other one?" she asked.

"What do you mean?" I bit back the playful smirk at her confused expression.

"I thought you would get adjoining rooms."

"Well, they're booked, sweetheart. And a few hours stuck together in the same room isn't going to kill you." I raised my wrist and pointed at the angry red mark stamped around it. "Besides, I thought you didn't want me out of your sight."

Her eyes flared, and she muttered a string of colorful curses under her breath as she rolled the window back up. She slammed the door shut and walked behind me until we reached our room.

The overwhelming stench of stale cigarette smoke washed over us as soon as I opened the door. Ava wrinkled her nose as she brushed past me and gave the singular queen size bed a half-glance, then threw her bag onto the small coffee table in front of the couch and shut herself in the bathroom with another slam of the door.

*This couldn't have worked out better if I had tried,* Vain said, sounding more than pleased.

*Let's just hope she doesn't end up killing us in our sleep.*

*I can see the way she looks at you, Rory. She wouldn't risk hurting you. Me, on the other hand...*

Vain's curiosity dragged my eyes to Ava's bag.

*You're the worst, you know that?*

I tore it open and rifled through the contents. There wasn't anything in there I hadn't already expected, books and papers, some white chalk, and a few blades—all pretty standard, I assumed, for a demonologist.

When I heard rushing water from the bathroom sink, I shoved her bag back into place on the table and sat on the edge of the bed. Ava strode out with her arms crossed over her chest, still sporting that same scowl that appeared to be permanently etched onto her face. She jutted her hip out to one side as she glared.

*Let me have a turn,* Vain purred.

He crept into the forefront, and through Vain's eyes, I watched Ava's facial features twinge at the switch.

It was almost funny how hard she tried to hide her emotions from us, even though by this point I was familiar with most of her tells. I'd even grown particularly fond of the little nose wrinkles that appeared whenever she tried to hide a grimace.

"You still look angry with me," Vain said.

Even after all these years, it was still jarring sometimes to hear Vain speak through me. It was my voice, but not. When Vain spoke, his tone had a velvety-smooth dark edge to it that I didn't possess. And I could admit that hearing it sometimes scared me a little.

"I thought you might be a bit more frightened."

Ava squared her shoulders and said, "You don't scare me, Vain."

"You don't sound very sure of that, mellilla."

"You won't hurt me."

Vain tsked once and rose off the bed. His smirk grew wider when he took a predatory step toward Ava and she backed away. "You don't know the half of what I'm capable of."

Vain halted once she had backed herself into the wall. It would have been so easy for him to take her right then and there. His desire to claim her burned in my chest, yet there was a hesitation keeping him restrained that I couldn't place. Vain was a demon who took what he wanted, however and whenever he wanted it, so why the hell was he holding back?

*What are you doing?* I asked.

*Playing.*

*She's not a toy.*

He reached out and rested his knuckles under Ava's chin to tip it up delicately so she was forced to look up into our eyes. She was trying not to shake or show anything that would betray her fear.

She was strong. I'd give her that.

The sight of her nearly took my breath away. It was that fierce recklessness I couldn't help but admire as she stared into the face of the demon possessing me. Her pupils were dilated, but her brows were furrowed as she remained locked in Vain's stare. That tenacity, that spark and ambition she possessed, for a brief moment

I could glimpse what had emboldened her to free us in the first place.

Too bad for her, I didn't need her saving.

"I felt how your body reacted when I held that little excuse for a blade to your throat. You liked it. I wonder...did you wear it just in the hopes that I might use it against you?"

Ava's throat bobbed, drawing both Vain's and my attention to the pale skin, the delicate curve of her neck, and the jumping pulse point that was screaming at me to have my teeth scrape against it.

If I were in control, I was afraid that I wouldn't be able to stop myself. Even within the recesses of my mind, I was addicted to her. I wanted her touch, the very essence of her. I wanted everything just as badly as Vain did too.

"I want nothing to do with you," Ava said and then brushed past us. She eyed the couch, appearing to note the various stains with a grimace before settling on the bed. She pressed herself against the headboard as if to get as far away from Vain as was possible. Vain ignored her rejection and stalked toward her, relishing in how she squirmed as he approached.

"What the hell are you doing?"

"You exhaust me, witch," Vain sighed before yanking me forward to take back control.

I shook off the lingering remnants of the possession and flopped onto the bed beside her, causing Ava to yelp. After weeks of lying on that unforgiving stone floor, nothing felt better than this shitty motel mattress. It was heaven, minus Ava who was frowning down at me.

"You know there's a perfectly good couch you can take."

"If it's so good, why don't you take it?" Her scowl grew deeper, which I didn't think was possible. I chuckled. "That's what I thought. You're predictably stubborn."

Ava narrowed her eyes and said, "Don't presume to know me. You and Vain aren't much different after all."

I scoffed and set my jaw. "You're a hypocrite. You don't know anything about me either."

That seemed to shut her up. Ava looked away, and for a moment, I thought that she looked...sad?

I sighed. "Would it make you feel better if I gave you my word that I'll keep Vain away tonight?"

"You can't promise that. He's a *demon* who will do whatever he wants, whenever he wants. You'd not only be lying to me, but also to yourself if you think you can control him."

"You'd be surprised how persuasive I can be." The look she gave me was not one of confidence. "Fine. I'll sleep on the floor. I've gotten used to it." Ava winced.

"No. Just...don't try anything, okay?"

I reached behind my head and set a pillow in the center of the bed between us as a makeshift divider.

"No demons past this point. Promise."

Ava rolled her eyes. "I feel so much safer now, thank you."

I let out a short laugh, propped my hands behind my head, and shut my eyes.

*You sure she's not going to try and kill us in our sleep?* I checked in with Vain before nodding off.

His amusement was palpable. *I'd love to see her try.*

✵ ✵ ✵

I remained faintly aware of Ava shifting and fidgeting beside me as I faded in and out of sleep. She was probably too afraid to shut her eyes, too worried of Vain taking back control.

*She won't kill you,* Vain reassured me. *She cares too much.*

She was smart to be afraid though. If it was any other demon, they may not have thought twice about killing a witch and would've savored every moment while doing so.

Every time I turned over, Ava stiffened and held her breath. Sometimes when I opened my eyes, I could have sworn her piercing amber gaze met mine between the slivers of light that scattered into the room through the thin curtain.

Somewhere in the state of dreamlessness and consciousness though, a prickling awareness shot through me. I bolted up at the sudden shift in energy, my skin prickling as magic crackled through the air.

Ava's attention was fixed on a dark figure. They stood in front of the window, and what little light peeked through the curtains cast the stranger in a warped shadow.

Vain bristled with a nervous energy I matched.

"Ava, what the hell is this? What have you done?" The figure, a woman, spoke. She sounded young, maybe Ava's age.

"Kalaei—" Ava's voice trembled. "I—this is not what it looks like."

"You helped the demon escape..."

Ava stiffened. "Lena was going to kill Rory. I couldn't let her, not when there's a chance I can save him."

"What did the demon promise you?" Kalaei asked with sharp accusation.

"Kalaei—" Ava pleaded. Her mouth hung open slightly as her throat bobbed.

"Was it controlling you?"

Ava shook her head.

Kalaei's lips pressed together. "Then what the hell were you thinking?"

Ava flinched, and the corners of her eyes shifted for a split second to the coffee table in front of Kalaei.

"Where are you? We can send a group to rescue you and bring you home." Kalaei's eyes drifted to where Ava's had, a magazine laying across the surface of the table, and she squinted.

With Kalaei distracted, Ava wasted no time in throwing out her hands, a spell cast outward toward her figure which dissolved into nothing but air in an instant.

"What the hell was that?" I asked, my voice louder than I intended.

*Planeswalker,* Vain growled.

Ava jumped out of bed and flicked on the bedside lamp. She grabbed the magazine and shoved it in my face. The glossy cover sported a misty photo of the Smoky Mountains with the title, *Discovering the Best of Dead Oaks, Tennessee.*

"She knows where we are," Ava said.

"She can't know *exactly* where we are. There's no way she'd be able to tell which motel we're in."

Ava turned back to the coffee table and threw a small rectangle of cardstock onto the bed that showed the name of the motel, address and all.

"Shit."

Vain clawed his way into the driver's seat, and I was more than happy to take shotgun.

"There's a smaller coven not too far from here. Lena will send word and have them on top of us in no time." Ava paced while shooting furtive glances out the window. "Get us out of here. *Now,*" she commanded as she tugged the strap of her bag over one shoulder.

Vain reached deep for his power and assessed the amount of strength he had built up since the last shift. But even I could tell his reserves were still low.

"I don't have enough power to get us very far," he said. "Rory's body is too weak for my power to summon it any faster."

"So get out of him," she challenged with a raised brow.

I did the mental equivalent of rolling my eyes, and Vain subdued his chuckle of amusement. "Not going to happen. Nice try, though."

"Fine," Ava huffed. "Just get us somewhere, as far as you can. Anywhere is better than here where we're sitting ducks."

"Come here," Vain growled and grabbed Ava's arm, pulling her to our chest and placing his other hand against the nape of her neck.

Her hair felt soft between our fingers. Pressed that close, the faint eucalyptus scent of her overwhelmed me, and if we had the time, I could have counted every one of the freckles on her face.

Vain's grasp tightened around Ava, and he breathed against the shell of her ear, "Hold on."

The shift quickly enveloped us in shadow as the motel room folded away. Moments later, we were deposited into an empty field beside a private runway. Fat raindrops spattered onto the grass, and the air was so thick it felt like we were swimming in the humidity.

Vain kept Ava clutched tightly against our chest, almost as if he feared if he let go, she would be lost to him forever.

"Are you going to be sick again?" he asked.

Ava trembled in his grasp, but she said, "I don't think so. You can let go now."

Vain's reluctance mirrored my own. He obliged, but not after inhaling in one last deep breath of her scent.

Her quiet "thank you" sounded forced as she put some distance between herself and Vain. I caught a hint of Vain's surprise at her gratitude, but he stayed quiet, not ready to spoil what he considered a good thing.

A rural airstrip stretched out before us, and a small hangar and facility building no larger than a trailer stood a few hundred feet away.

Vain beckoned the witch as he started walking. "We can wait for the jet to arrive there."

"Wait." Ava hurried to catch up. She reached for Vain and moved her hands in the familiar way she did right before she would cast her magic.

Vain snatched her wrist and gave a low growl in warning. "No more spells...or tricks."

"It's not a trick. I want to ward us so Kalaei and the others can't astral project to us again. Or do you want them to keep tracking us?"

Vain narrowed his eyes.

"Do you trust me?" she asked.

"That remains to be seen," he said before he released his grip on her wrist.

"Turn around," she instructed.

He obeyed, and Ava placed her hand across the back of our neck. Warmth bloomed against the skin beneath Ava's palm. When she pulled her hand away, the heat of the magic faded, and she proceeded to repeat the same spell on herself.

We reached the facility building and found that it was empty, but it also happened to be locked.

"You're not going to shift us inside?"

Vain leaned against the side of the building as the rain came down harder, and he pretended to find something interesting on the pads of our fingers, swirling his thumb across them absently.

"I'm not about to waste my power just because you're uncomfortable."

"Well, when will your jet get here?" she asked.

"Can't say for certain," Vain said. "Could be a minute, could be an hour."

"Why do you even have a jet?"

Vain smiled at her. "For the same reason most other people do. I'm disgustingly rich. Besides, it does become convenient in situations such as these. And I am a creature that has become accustomed to such simple human comforts."

Ava unfolded her arms and brushed past us. "Whatever. I'm getting out of this rain," she said while tossing a sneer at Vain as she moved toward the locked door. She pressed her hand against the metal surface until I heard the mechanisms click. "You can stay out here and be miserable for all I care."

She pushed the door open and waltzed into the room. Vain's fevered attention hung on the curves of her waist and backside and how her fucking dress was plastered to her skin.

*You're pathetic,* I told him.

*And you're a hypocrite. You're looking too.*

Ava proceeded to plant her ass into a well-worn, brown leather couch.

"So, breaking and entering is acceptable for you, but compelling a human and stealing a car is crossing a line?"

"Shove it, Vain," the witch bit back, and Vain laughed.

It couldn't have been more than fifteen minutes before we heard the whir of a plane engine overhead.

Vain pushed off the wall and tipped his chin up at Ava. "Get up," he said.

We stepped back out into the night, and while the rain had subsided, the humid air was so thick it was nearly choking. A low mist curled around us as we watched the white jet approach the airstrip and land in front of the hangar.

Vain led the way, ensuring Ava still followed closely behind.

The jet's ramp descended, and Alastair's tall thin figure stepped out to greet us, pushing one hand through his shoulder-length blond hair.

"Thank you, Alastair," Vain said and clasped the demon's shoulder.

"Good to see you too, sir. You as well, Mr. Masters." Alastair said through a smile of pointed teeth and then gave a wink with only one set of his green eyes. He kept the other pairs of eyes on his face closed, the thin slits across his cheekbones and above his brows barely visible, more than likely in an attempt to not freak out the witch more than she already was.

*I knew he missed me,* I said to Vain, which prompted a soft smile to sprout at the corners of his mouth.

*Careful, mortal. He may even like you more than he does me.*

"Be gentle with this one," Vain warned Alastair, leaning in closer to him and motioning toward Ava. "She frightens easily."

The demon retracted his lips over his sharpened teeth and gave a gentle smile, then extended a hand to the witch.

"Alastair." He gave a small bend at the waist. "I'm at your service as well, Miss..."

Ava did not introduce herself, only looked down at the demon's extended hand in trepidation.

"You are in the presence of Helacourt royalty, Alastair," Vain said.

Recognition flared in his eyes. "A legacy witch? What in Lilith's name did you get yourself into?" Alastair said as he cocked one eyebrow up at Vain before turning back to Ava. "Well then, it certainly is a pleasure."

Alastair lowered his hand when he realized Ava wasn't going to extend the same courtesy, though he didn't look offended in the slightest. He motioned up the stairs. "Please, make yourself comfortable."

Vain half-turned and guided Ava around him with one hand pressed gently to the small of her back. She stiffened at his touch as he escorted her up the steps and into the cabin.

His eyes never left Ava once as she walked down the cream-colored carpet and planted herself in a seat toward the middle of the plane, facing away from us.

"Returning to New York, I presume?" Alastair asked after pulling up the ramp and sealing the door shut.

"Yes. The penthouse. The sooner we're in the air, the better."

"Of course, sir." Alastair nodded and then retreated to the cockpit.

Vain went to the bar and pressed the small button hidden in the glossy wood paneling to raise the console lined with crystal decanters. He pulled out one filled halfway with a warm amber spirit and poured a finger into a glass tumbler over ice.

*Ugh,* I groaned.

*What?*

*You know I hate that shit.*

Vain just lifted the glass to his lips and took a generous sip of bourbon, and I wished I had the ability to smack him.

As the plane rolled down the runway, he approached the witch while her back remained turned to us, and I didn't miss the way her body tensed when he neared.

"Care for a drink?"

Ava tucked her arms across her chest and stared out the window in pointed silence.

He took the seat across from her and tried meeting her gaze which she vehemently refused. Only when Vain began to levitate his glass above his palm and twirl it around as if he were performing a lazy parlor trick, did I notice Ava peeking an occasional glance from the corner of her eyes, but never quite giving us her full attention.

Her masked curiosity and predilection for malice towards him only served to amuse Vain to no end, and he remained delighted in the company of his newest obsession, no matter how far she kept herself at arms-length.

*You're preening,* I told him.

*And your jealousy is showing,* Vain retorted.

Vain sat back during takeoff and studied the witch as he sipped his drink. The color of Ava's eyes reminded me of the bourbon Vain swirled in his glass. I could probably drink myself away in her eyes as easily as I could a bottle as much as I wanted to despise both, but I felt unable to resist the temptation.

Her muscles were rigid as we ascended through the clouds, and it was only when the plane reached its cruising altitude that her shoulders relaxed, and her chest sank with a long exhale.

"Nervous flier?" Vain taunted.

Ava ignored him. "Didn't New York go dark years ago?" She asked.

Vain took another sip of bourbon, the ice clinking around in the glass. "Mostly, yes. Your kind still controls parts of the city but were forced to give up the rest when our numbers started to overwhelm them." Vain thumbed the rim of the glass and cocked his head to one side. "Was that witch back there a friend of yours?"

"Sort of, yeah," Ava said, then rubbed at her temples. "I was so stupid. I didn't think someone would try and astral project to find us. And now they all know I'm a traitor."

"They would have found out eventually."

Ava's eyes snapped to Vain for a split second before she turned back to the window. "I suppose they would have."

She fell silent for a long moment, chewing at her bottom lip.

"So, do you regret your choice?"

Ava paused before answering. "No."

"And what if you decide that Rory isn't worth the trouble of saving?"

Her glare was sharper than any blade. "Being able to save even one person is worth it."

Why the fuck did she care so much? I wasn't deserving of this woman's persistence.

"How very noble of you," Vain said. "I haven't known many witches in my lifetime that would have done the same in your position."

Ava's eyes guttered as she looked away. Her eyelids seemed heavy with traces of exhaustion.

Vain stood to refill his empty glass. "We should be landing in about two hours. Get some rest if you need it," he said over his shoulder.

Her response was cold and clipped. "I'm fine. Thanks for your concern."

Vain scoffed lightly and smirked to himself.

*What's the plan when we get back?* I asked him.

*What do you mean?*

If I could have rolled my eyes, I would have. Vain felt my irritation through the bond anyway. *You know exactly what I mean. I know you've got a revenge plan in mind for Eldin after the shit he pulled.*

A sick satisfaction bloomed in our chest. *Eager for blood, are we?* He poured another finger of bourbon into his glass. *We'll see where this takes us first. Then I'll decide.*

*We'll decide.*

Vain smirked again. *Of course. We.*

When Vain returned to his seat and looked at Ava, I was shocked to find her eyes shut and her head resting up against the window. She had her legs pulled up to her chest, and her skin was spotted with goosebumps.

Vain set his glass down and went into the small room in the back of the plane to grab a fuzzy blanket from the bed. He draped it over her carefully and tucked it in around her shoulders.

She stirred slightly at the touch but didn't wake, her breathing heavy. Apparently, her body had finally given in and decided her need to rest was more important than keeping one eye open.

I nudged him, throwing him out of his trance. *Stop staring at her, you creep.*

"Your loss," Vain replied aloud and then retreated to the bedroom. I wasn't about to turn down the promise of more sleep either. I curled up into my subconscious and allowed Vain to lull me into the dreamless dark.

# ELEVEN

## AVA

I jerked awake amid a bout of turbulence rocking the cabin. The lights had been dimmed, bathing the all-white interior in a soft glow from the hidden bands of LED backlighting throughout. To my surprise, there was a soft blanket wrapped around me, and whether it was Vain or Rory who had done it, my heart warmed traitorously at the thought. I peered over to the seat across from me, but neither of them was there. Not sensing them close by in the cabin either, I breathed a sigh of relief and sank deeper into my seat. Rubbing at the ache in my neck, I watched as the dazzling lights of the city below grew closer as the plane made its final descent.

I couldn't trust Vain—*shouldn't* trust him. He was still a demon after all, and no matter his dangerously deceptive charms, or the promises that he was good on his word, there was no way I'd ever be able to fully let my guard down around him. Saving Rory was my priority, and while Vain claimed we shared the same goal, there was no way to know for sure how genuine his true motives were.

As the wheels hit the tarmac, an interior door in the back of the cabin slid open, startling me from my thoughts. Vain sauntered out and ran his fingers through Rory's disheveled dark hair before looking straight at me. Against the low light of the cabin, he was every bit the preternatural hunter I feared, possessing an alluring and unnatural stillness. He melted into the shadows as if he were waiting for an opportune moment to strike. I shivered under his captivating gaze.

"Sleep well?" Vain's coal-black eyes drifted to the blanket I clutched to my chest.

I gave a disdainful huff and turned away from him, but not before I caught the flash of his signature smirk. He stalked into the cockpit as the plane parked in a private hangar. I shoved the blanket off, stood, and snatched my bag from my feet.

Both Vain and the demon pilot, Alastair, exited the cockpit together and released the exit door. Alastair descended the steps first, and Vain motioned me toward the exit with a slight tilt of his head.

My heart raced in my throat as I turned my back to Vain and descended the steps, fully aware of the predator sizing me up as he followed me down.

Alastair led us to a nearby black sedan, and I could have sworn that as we followed him, I saw a pair of bright green eyes flash open from the nape of his neck before they disappeared again. Maybe the lingering exhaustion was making me see things, but I couldn't shake the feeling it had been real. I shouldn't have been too shocked though, as it wasn't uncommon for some species of demons, even higher demons, to possess similar abnormal physical characteristics. And multiple sets of eyes were certainly further down on the list of possible least threatening traits.

Alastair held the door open for me and I slid into the back seat. Vain entered through the other side, taking the seat next to mine. A black leather center console divided the space between us, and I felt thankful for the distance it provided, however small it was. I wasn't used to the feeling of being in an enclosed space with a demon, let alone two of them.

The awkward silence resting between us made my skin itch, so I focused instead on the skyline as Alastair drove. We crossed a long bridge over a wide river, the lights from the skyscrapers casting the water in a twinkling glow, and for a moment, I forgot about all the possible dangers within the city—the demons and monsters that likely plagued the humans there. Larger metropolitan areas were prime breeding grounds for demonkind. The higher the human population, the more opportunity for demons to sow their chaos and feed off their fear.

"You talk in your sleep, you know?" Vain's smooth voice cut through the quiet.

I narrowed my eyes at him. "I do not."

He shrugged. "Just trying to make conversation."

"Well, you can stop. I don't have much interest in talking to you unless it's absolutely necessary."

As I looked away, I caught sight of Alastair's eyes in the rearview mirror bouncing between us. I quickly averted my gaze.

Vain sighed. "If you insist on being a bore, then—"

"You love listening to yourself talk, don't you?"

"I've been told my sultry voice and sharp tongue are some of my best features," Vain said as he leaned back against the headrest and winked at me.

I forced myself not to think of all the other ways Vain might use his sharp tongue besides his incessant, annoying remarks, and pressed myself further against the door, creating as much extra space as I could between us.

The car cruised to a slow speed as Alastair turned down a side-street before pulling into an underground garage.

Vain turned to me and said, "Welcome to your new home."

"Not my home," I snapped.

"Yes, well…temporary housing doesn't have quite the same ring to it." His expression brightened at my scowl. "Regardless, you will be my guest in this house, and I only wish for you to be comfortable while you are here."

"Trust me, it won't be a long stay. I'm done with you once I get the exorcism to work."

"Then I will enjoy your company for however long that might take you."

*For as long as you will have me.* His words from before echoed in my mind, and I shuddered at the memory.

"Yeah." I scoffed. "Right."

Vain exited the car and walked around to my door. When he opened it for me and extended his hand, I refused it and pulled myself out. That only made him grin wider.

Damn him and that smug fucking smile. Damn him for manipulating Rory's features so well.

"Thank you, Alastair," Vain said to the other demon before leading me toward an elevator in the middle of the garage.

"Anytime, sir." Alastair nodded and then returned to the car.

I pressed myself into the far corner of the elevator, and the brandished gold handrail dug into my back as I avoided Vain's gaze. He thumbed the topmost button and the elevator shot up at an alarming rate.

When the carriage stilled and the doors opened, Vain strode out without so much as a glance back at me. I stood there, frozen, my hands clamped on the cold metal bar behind me.

Once I crossed the threshold, there was no going back. This path I had chosen suddenly felt like it was more than I had originally bargained for.

"Reconsidering?" Vain called from within the next room.

I gritted my teeth and stepped into one of the most luxuriously styled penthouses I had ever seen. Nearly every surface was black, from the marble countertops flecked with gold, to the dark accent walls separating the rooms. Walking straight through the entryway led into an open concept living area decorated in opulent rugs, white couches, and modern light fixtures that hung from the high ceiling. Floor-to-ceiling windows spanned the length of the room, offering wide, unobstructed views of the city.

The city lights twinkled against the first hints of pink and indigo dawn that had started to paint the edges of the horizon in the distance. I couldn't help but to stand there in awe as I took it all in.

"You live here?"

"Were you expecting a dungeon?"

I frowned. "I don't know what I expected."

"This is just one of many homes I have. Though if you would prefer a dungeon, I believe my castle outside of Edinburgh might be better suited to your liking."

"You're insufferable," I said.

"Glad I'm not the only one who thinks that." A female voice sounded behind us from somewhere above.

My head snapped up toward the lofted space that overlooked the great room. Standing at the edge of the railing was a woman, around my age, shrouded in shadow.

"Who have you brought home this time?" she asked, tipping her chin at Vain.

"Play nice, Nesera," Vain sung.

The female curled her lips and flared her nostrils. "She smells like a witch." Nesera eased off the balcony then descended the stairs to greet us.

The closer she came, the more I could discern her features in the dim light. Her mousy brown hair brushed her shoulders, the color reminding me of Kalaei's. But poking out from the top of her head were two small black horns. She was either a demon or a cambion, at the very least then.

Four thin white scars marred her face in contrast against her warm, golden complexion. They cut through her left brow and down across her nose. And when she set her mouth into a bemused smile, the chrome ball piercing above her cupid's bow glinted back at me.

"You're up early," Vain said. "Were you worried about me?"

Nesera rolled her eyes. "The day I worry about you, is the day Gehenna freezes over."

"Not even a little bit?"

"I knew you'd find a way to escape eventually. Even if it did take you longer than expected." Nesera flicked her gaze to me. "I'm Nesera."

"Ava," I said. She didn't offer to extend her hand in greeting, and I didn't either. She came off a little wary, but not unkind.

"Things ran smoothly while I was preoccupied?" Vain asked her.

"Considering the building didn't burn down, I'd say so."

"And no trouble with the club?"

"Nothing I couldn't handle," Nesera said, then turned away. "I'll see you around then. Nice to meet you, witch."

She wandered toward the doorway that led to the kitchen and wrinkled her nose at Vain as she passed him. "Your meat suit stinks by the way."

I snorted at Vain's soured expression. "I like her," I said to him.

"Everyone does," he said through a scowl. "Come, I'll show you to your room."

He led me down a long hallway lined with expensive modern art pieces that hung in the recesses of the walls between the door frames. When we reached the end, Vain opened a door on the left, letting the soft morning light bleed into the hall.

"Make yourself comfortable and feel free to explore the rest of the penthouse at your leisure. If there's anything you need, Alastair or I will be around to provide it for you."

It felt like I should be thanking him, but I didn't want to make thanking a demon a habit of mine, so I kept my mouth firmly shut and nodded once.

Without another word, Vain turned and disappeared behind the door next to mine at the end of the hall. I slipped into my room and immediately locked myself inside.

Wasting no time, I secured every corner of the room with wards. I must have spent over an hour placing every combination of them I could think of. Ones for protection against astral projecting, spells that would confuse any sort of tracking, and most importantly, wards to keep demons out of my space. The ones along the threshold were ironclad, not even Vain would be able to cross them. The only drawback was that I'd need to strengthen them every day to maintain their effectiveness. It would be a drain on my magic, but it was a small price to pay for peace of mind.

My stomach growled once I had finished. I'd barely eaten since the night before. And though Vain had offered it, there was no way I was about to ask him or Alastair for anything.

I kept my hand against the doorknob for a long while, listening closely for any sounds beyond and catching only silence before I peeked out into the hallway. Finding no one lurking in the shadows, I slunk into the great room first, intending to creep directly through to the kitchen but the large windows caught my attention. At this elevation, Vain's penthouse rose high above the rest of the city, a palatial tower in the sky. The north-facing view offered a panoramic overlook of the long expanse of Central Park below and the Hudson, and it was nothing short of breathtaking. But it distracted me for longer than I should have allowed it to, so when my hackles rose with the sensation of a set of eyes watching me from behind, I whirled.

Nesera eyed me from the doorway to the kitchen with one arm slung across her chest, the other holding a half-eaten apple in her right hand.

"Sorry, I didn't mean to scare you," she said as she chewed, then chuckled as my shoulders sagged with relief. "Did you think I was Vain?"

"He does have a nasty habit of leering at me from across a room."

Nesera bit into her apple again, and my attention drifted up to the small horns crowning atop her head.

"Are you a demon?" I asked.

"Cambion," she replied simply. That settled my nerves a bit, knowing I had one less full-fledged demon to worry about here.

"And you live with him?"

"Yup. It's better than being one of D.A.R.C.'s little weapons they can order around as they please to fight their battles."

Unfortunately, I knew all too well how the mortal-led military front and their priests preferred to control their cambion soldiers like pawns in their war. And while I'd never worked directly along-side them, seeing as I was never ordered out into the field, I had still grown friendly with the few who had been stationed at the Moreau Coven.

Given their half-human, half-demon heritage, cambions were the perfect weapons—their supernatural strength and speed were unmatched, and their innate tracking capabilities allowed them to hunt demons better than anything else, making them valuable assets within our ranks. But not all cambions were willing to be controlled, and the ones that didn't side with our efforts aligned themselves with the demons, making them just as formidable enemies to encounter.

Nesera seemed intimidating in her own right, the kind of unassuming threat that was wrapped up in a quiet, demure package. And while I had a suspicion that Nesera was one of the good ones, I still held some caution due to her unknown potential.

"And you can come and go freely? Vain doesn't keep you here against your will?"

Nesera stifled a laugh. "No one makes me do anything that I don't want to do."

"He hasn't hurt you?" I couldn't stop myself from asking.

Nesera's mouth quirked downward, her tone immediately dismissive. "What? No. Vain has never laid a finger on me. Neither has Rory. Not that I would have minded." She smirked at the thought. "Lilith knows they've rejected enough of my advances."

She shrugged, then moved closer toward my direction. "Look, I don't know what situation you three have got going on, but you're under Vain's protection now. You'll be safe with him."

"What about you? Are you safe?"

Nesera clicked her tongue as she brushed past me. "As safe as I can be." Then the cambion shot me a wink and sauntered over to the elevator, the two curved blades slung across her back catching the sunlight and flashed like a warning.

⛧ ⛧ ⛧

I scurried back to my room with a handful of things I'd swiped from the kitchen: two apples, a bottle of what appeared to be the most expensive sparkling water on the planet, and a sweet pastry that had been sitting under a glass domed display on the counter. It was barely any sort of filling meal, but it was enough to sustain me through the afternoon of research I had planned.

I set to work, thumbing through my notes and written accounts on possessions from textbooks I'd smuggled with me to determine the best course of action to re-attempt an exorcism, all while struggling to theorize how my and Lena's attempts had all failed in the first place.

There were no written accounts I'd found in existence where an exorcism had ever failed, so the unprecedented nature of Rory's and Vain's situation left me baffled and unsure of myself for the first time in all my years of study. Over the course of endless hours of useless hypothesizing and an impending headache later, the only conclusion I'd come to was that in order to form a new plan, I would simply need to try again.

By the time I shoved my books away, it was nightfall, and it took me nearly another hour to steel my nerves before I decided to face Rory and Vain again.

I raised my knuckles an inch from their door at the end of the hall and hesitated, not sure who I would face. Holding my breath, I knocked once and then took a tentative step back.

Faint shuffling sounded from inside the room, but no answer came. I knocked again.

The muffled sounds of bare feet padded closer before the door opened and Rory peered through the crack. He stared down at me with glazed eyes. A crystal tumbler hung precariously from the tips of his fingers.

"Need something, witch?"

"Can I come in?"

His bored stare turned scrutinizing. "Why?"

"I need to attempt another exorcism on you tonight."

"So soon?"

At least it hadn't been an outright refusal. "If I'm going to find some way to exorcise Vain, then I need to do some research to figure out how to make it work."

Rory left the doorframe, retreating into the darkened bedroom. I followed hesitantly.

The decor in their bedroom matched mine, only theirs was larger and dressed in a bit more opulence with dark walls and tall windows adorned with heavy curtains. An oversized bed sat against the far wall facing the dazzling view of the city, and the rumpled black sheets spilled over the edge onto the hardwood floor.

Rory sat on the edge of a small sectional in the corner of the room and bent forward slightly to rest his elbows against his thighs. One side of his face was cast in shadow, the other bathed in the warm light from the gas fireplace set into the wall. It was difficult to ignore that he was practically shirtless when his robe fluttered open, granting me a view of his bare chest that revealed the faded lashes leftover from Lena's handiwork, and the sharp V that peeked out from the top of his low-slung lounge pants. I tore my gaze away and dug my toes into the fur rug at my feet.

"Well, get on with it." Rory gulped down the last of his drink. "Make it quick and painful for me."

My voice dropped low. "Rory, I'm not going to hurt you."

"Is that right?" His tone was scathing and accusatory, and I fought the urge to flinch.

"There are certain spells I can try. They can alleviate some of the pain that comes along with the exorcism so it won't be so excruciating for you."

"No. If you're going to do it," Rory said, his deep scowl and piercing gray eyes burning every inch of me in his hatred. "I want it to hurt."

My heart tightened. "You don't mean that," I said.

"You don't really know me, then." He slammed his empty glass down and it cracked hard against the table.

"You're right. I don't," I shot back, raising my voice. "It seems like I only know the Rory that's pathetically convinced he can't survive without a demon possessing him like nothing more than a cheap ride."

Rory shot up from the couch and stalked toward me. "And you're a witch with a savior complex who thinks it's her job to fix everything she touches." His jaw ticked once, then twice as he stared me down. "Let me be the one to clue you in and tell you the truth that no one else will. You're not capable of fixing *anything*. Not this. Not me. *Nothing*." His words slurred slightly as he seethed, but that didn't make the sharpness of them sting any less.

I backed away a step as my chest burned with anger. "You're a sad, pathetic asshole," I said, low and hushed.

"No, sweetheart. I'm a masochist."

I gritted my teeth. "Stop calling me that."

"What would you prefer me to call you, hmm?" I shivered as his voice dropped into a dangerous, low rasp. "Honey? Love? Darling?"

He advanced on me like a stalking wolf, his eyes unwavering from mine as I swallowed down my rising fear and edged away, half-expecting Vain to make an appearance at any moment.

"Or maybe those are all too nice for someone as cruel as you? Wicked Witch might suit you better or…Vain's little plaything?"

His hand twitched, almost as if he wanted to reach out to grab me. He was so close I could smell the alcohol wafting from him.

"You're drunk," I said.

He frowned and his eyes flashed with irritation. "Barely."

Rory was in no state to be exorcised, and I wasn't in the right mindset either as I struggled to keep my attention from dipping to his bare chest, and his heated glances kept making my face grow hot.

"Drink yourself into oblivion. I don't care." I turned to leave, but Rory's warm, calloused hand shot to my wrist, anchoring me in place.

He gave a slight tilt of his head as he scanned me. "Why is he so obsessed with you?" he whispered, so softly that I could barely hear him over my thundering heartbeat.

Gritting my teeth, I snarled at him. "Let me go."

"Make me," he challenged.

My hand wavered for a moment, but I remained frozen.

"You want to know what I think?" he asked. "At first, I thought that your interest in saving me was only because I thought you were so self-righteous and desperate to gain the approval from your peers. But I think I finally realized what really drives you."

Rory smirked, no doubt noticing the bob of my throat as I struggled to tamp down my emotions.

"I think you're lonely. You don't have anyone. You're just as broken inside as you believe I am. Do you often grow attached to others, thinking they might offer you the barest shreds of the attention you so desperately seem to crav—"

My free hand shot out and slapped him across the face before I could think better of it. The resounding crack was sharp, and the tips of my fingers tingled in the aftershock.

Regret pooled in me the second I jerked my hand away. I could barely breathe at the realization of what I had just done, in fear of how he might retaliate. Or how Vain might if he were to show himself.

The force had whipped Rory's head to the side. He turned his face back to me again slowly, eyes peeking through the tumble of his dark hair. The shadow of a crooked smile spread from the corner of his lips, his tongue darting out across them briefly.

"Did that feel good?" he asked. "Did you enjoy that split second where it felt like you were in control?"

Still breathless, I forced a whispered, "Yes."

"Good," he snarled, eyes darkening further. "I did too."

The full force of his body crashed into mine, pinning me against the wall. He cupped the nape of my neck and fisted my hair, causing me to suck in a breath through my teeth. His other arm slammed into the wall next to my face, and he enveloped his body around mine. Rory leaned in until we were nose to nose, his breath hot against my cheek. "I want you to fucking ruin me, Ava."

The sleeves of his robe had slunk up past his elbows, revealing the tattoos down his arms that rippled as his muscles strained. His mouth was dangerously close with lips parted slightly. Almost expectant.

I couldn't tear my eyes away from him. He was wild, completely unlike himself. If this was a shard of Vain's true nature mixing with Rory's, it was impossible to tell. Seconds passed as we shared breath after breath. My heart hammered in my chest erratically.

I hadn't meant for my attention to slip past his mouth, further down his chest until my whole body heated at the sight of the hard outline of him through his dark lounge pants, mere inches from grinding against me.

"Is this you talking, Rory? Or is it Vain?" I asked.

Rory didn't answer. His gaze slid down the length of my body. His cheeks were flushed, and based on his cocksure attitude, I gathered it wasn't due to any embarrassment on his part. A flash of teeth, then a soft laugh escaped him, smelling strongly of bourbon.

"I've seen how you look at me," he whispered. "If I were to slip my fingers between your legs right now, how wet would I find you are for me?"

He loosened the hand fisted in my hair and trailed it across my jawline, down my neck, then lingered on the side of my breast.

I would have been lying to myself if I said I didn't wish he would continue. But his drunkenness was a good enough reason as any to break this off, whatever *this* was becoming.

I planted my feet and pushed firmly against Rory's chest with both hands. He stumbled backward onto the floor and laid there for a moment, staring back at me with his robe splayed open, and his lips parted in what could have been either mild astonishment or lust.

"Have it your way, sweetheart," he hissed with syrupy sweet malice.

"Goodnight, Rory," I returned coldly as I stormed out.

I shut myself inside my room and I pressed my back against the door, wrapping my arms around myself as I tried to catch my breath, and fighting the small tremors after the encounter had left me thoroughly unsettled.

No amount of double and triple checking the strength of my protection wards was enough to calm my nerves. When I finally slipped into bed and curled myself beneath the cool sheets, I moved my hand down to touch myself, not at all surprised to find how soaked I truly was.

*Son of a bitch.*

# TWELVE

## RORY

Okay, maybe I was absolutely, beyond any shadow of a doubt, one hundred percent shitfaced.

I shut my eyes and sank into the feeling of the floor tilting beneath me, rocking like a ship at sea. I couldn't tell how long I stayed like that, exactly the way Ava had left me. Alone. A sprawled out, drunken mess of a human.

An asshole. That's what I was.

And I deserved nothing less than this.

I was thankful that at least Vain's roaring laughter had finally tapered off. He'd sounded nearly as drunk as I felt after Ava pushed me to the ground.

My head felt heavy with desire and lust. The bitter itch of frustration crawled like a virus under my skin, and it felt like a gaping hole had been shot straight through my chest. I'm not sure how long I laid there in the middle of the floor as I floated in and out of consciousness until a hand gripped my shoulder. I groaned at the touch and peeled my lids open. Six piercing green eyes swept over my face all at once as they leaned in close.

I startled back. "Jesus, Alastair!"

"I knocked," he said. "Neither of you were answering."

Breathing out heavily, I clutched at my bare chest, noticing the thin robe over my shoulders had fallen open at some point in my drunken stupor.

The memory of pinning Ava against the wall came rushing back to me. I cringed a little when I remembered my words to her. *"I want you to fucking ruin me."*

Had that been the alcohol talking? I guess being locked up for weeks while expectantly waiting to die had twisted me up inside and sent me to the dark places I hadn't visited in years. And though I knew that my inevitable end would come someday, the thought of dragging Ava down to my ruin with me had felt like a good idea in the heat of the moment.

Vain's lust for her had completely consumed me, to the point where I had wanted her more than anything in that moment. I'd wanted to see her come apart underneath me. To feel her. Taste her. Then let her destroy what little was left of me.

Alastair's eyes narrowed on me, noticing the hard-on tenting in my pants. He sketched a brow before asking, "Am I to believe you found your way to the floor like this on your own?"

My tongue felt heavy in my mouth as I rolled it behind my teeth. "Just help me up, please."

Alastair smirked and pulled me to my feet. "I can see why Vain is so smitten with her."

"Figures." I scoffed. "She's a pain in my ass."

"You do not share his same feelings towards her then?"

"I don't know. Maybe? I can't tell the difference anymore."

When Ava had stormed in demanding to exorcise Vain, a part of me had wanted to let her try. It would have been a fun show of watching her exhaust herself as she struggled with Vain to no avail.

"Has it gotten worse?" Alastair asked as he led me over to the bed.

Shutting my eyes when I laid down was a mistake. Fearing I might vomit, I kept them open instead, fixing on a single point on the ceiling in an attempt to steady the rest of the room around me.

"Yeah."

There was no use denying it. Not anymore.

I peered over at the demon, a sad and worried expression passing over his face.

"Vain," Alastair almost whispered, calling him to come forward.

Vain's presence slithered to the forefront of my mind to take over. He rolled his head across the pillow, peering up at Alastair through one half-lidded eye.

"What?" he grumbled, feeling the effects of the alcohol the same as I was. Unfortunately, his immortal powers weren't quite enough to stave off the very mortal effects of my drunkenness.

"Sir—" Alastair started, his mouth hanging open slightly at the pause.

"There's nothing that can be done, friend," Vain said to him.

Alastair nodded, his six eyes blinked slowly. "I'll bring some water," he said over his shoulder as he swept out of the room.

Vain relaxed into the mattress and groaned. "You drink too much," he drawled.

I didn't respond.

"Besides, I thought you hated bourbon."

When I remained quiet, he sighed and rubbed absently at his temples. "Tell me, was it your plan to punish me by downing four glasses? Or was it your sole intent to make you hate yourself in the morning?"

The sharpness of his words should have cut me, but I couldn't feel them. I didn't want to feel anything. I wanted to be swallowed up by the darkness, to be consumed completely by it until I was nothing at all. If it would be inevitable, then what was the point in fighting anymore? Why couldn't I just let go?

"Talk to me," Vain pleaded softly, staring up at the ceiling.

I sank deeper into my mind to try and shut him out—to shut everything out—but Vain ripped me forward instead.

I tore at the pillow with clawed fingers. "Fuck you!"

*Don't tempt me*, he purred back.

"Let me back in, Vain. Take over. *Please*, I don't want to...I can't..." I bit down hard on my lip to distract me from the lump lodged in my throat.

*You were sinking too deep where I couldn't feel you. I need you to stay close to the surface.*

The silence that hung between us was stifling, thick and heavy with all the words I couldn't say. With Vain, I didn't need to say them though. He already knew.

*I know that you are tired,* he said, and it took everything within me to choke back my sob. *You think that I don't feel how painful this is for you?*

It was true. Especially since the witches had held us in their prison for weeks, with death looming over our heads every day, that had forced something inside me to shift, something that I hadn't felt in a long time.

"I just don't see the point in fighting it anymore, Vain." I paused, allowing the words to sink in not only for him, but for me too.

*Do you want to die, Rory?*

He shouldn't have needed to ask. He should already feel the answer—know it as well as I did. But I could tell he wanted me to say it out loud. As if admitting the words beyond just my thoughts would somehow register differently.

"Sometimes, yes," I admitted. "There are times when it feels so inevitable and I convince myself it might not be so bad. But..."

*It's her, isn't it?*

"Yes." I choked on the word. I turned my face into the pillow and the room spun, so I shut my eyes. "Ava, she's—fuck she's frustrating and intoxicating. And...I've never felt more alive when I'm around her. She makes me want to fight this."

Vain was quiet, his presence calming. Leave it to a demon to force me to admit the truth of my feelings. I was at least self-aware enough to recognize that I'd been going through the motions for years now, strung along through life, content with being merely a passenger for Vain. And while he was a comforting and, more often, annoying co-pilot, he could only ease the emptiness inside me to a point.

It had been a long time since anyone had made me feel what Ava did. She'd sparked something in me that I couldn't deny any longer, but I still wasn't sure how to feel about it yet. Hell, I still didn't know why she even cared about me at all.

*You ask why she cares, and yet you never ask the same of me.*

I'd honestly never dared to ask Vain, though the thought had crossed my mind.

*Ask.*

"Why?" I braced myself for his answer.

*Because I see you, Rory Masters. And while you may have given up on yourself a long time ago, that doesn't mean that those around you have done the same.*

I swallowed, emotion tugging thickly in my throat.

"Are you the one that's making me feel this attraction to her?" I asked, needing to be sure. "Are your feelings for her why I feel the same way?"

*I think that is something you have to figure out for yourself.*

I sighed loudly and snapped my eyes open. I held up my middle finger in front of my face, staring at it. "You're worse than a fucking therapist, you know that?"

Vain chuckled darkly. *Do you remember what I told you when I first came to you?*

There was a lot that I remembered from that night—a lot I wished I could forget—and those memories remained as clear to me as they had been seven years ago. The blood-stained bathroom tiles, the icy chill in the air, the smoky scent of Vain's shadows curling around him as he stood over me, watching me die.

*I promised you one thing. That until your last breath, you would be mine until the end of your days. That you would never have to be alone again. Do you remember that?*

"I've never forgotten," I said, the words tugging sharply in my throat.

*You gave yourself to me. And I only ask that you hold on just a bit longer,* Vain said. *Allow me a little more time. Please.*

I tugged the comforter over me and appeased him with a quiet, "Okay."

*Do you trust me?*

A pause. "I trust you."

*Good,* he said. *You have no choice not to.*

"Asshole," I muttered and peered up only to find Alastair standing beside the bed holding a glass of water and an Advil. He set them down on the nightstand, one brow quirked as he looked down at me.

"Not you," I said to him. A small smile tugged at the corner of his mouth, but Alastair only rolled all of his six eyes and left before I could even offer him a thank you.

I swiped up the pill and downed the water in three swallows before curling back under the sheets and drifting off to the soft peals of Vain's laughter in the back of my mind.

# THIRTEEN

## AVA

As much as I would have preferred to hide in the safety of my bedroom all day, I couldn't stay in it forever. With any luck, I wanted to explore the penthouse without running into anyone.

But, when I finally did pluck up the courage to open the door, Vain was leaning against the opposite wall, his arms crossed over his chest while he glared at me with those deadly black eyes. His newly clean-shaven face was a stark contrast to the dark scruff I had grown accustomed to. And, to my relief, he was at least fully clothed.

"Are these wards going to be a new permanent feature in my home?" he asked, motioning down at the floor.

To my shock, I found myself relieved that Vain was in front of me and not Rory. If Rory was in control, I didn't think I could hide my embarrassment at the memory of last night.

"For as long as I'm here they will be."

"I'm glad to see you've gotten comfortable enough that you are already redecorating to your liking."

"What do you want, Vain?"

He pushed off the wall and leaned against the doorframe with fluid grace. He was toeing a dangerous line, so close to the wards at his feet, but his eyes never once left mine. "Why in all the infernal wastes would you think I must immediately want something of you?"

"Why else would you be waiting outside my door first thing in the morning?"

He smiled and said, "I have a proposition for you."

I cocked one eyebrow.

The demon extended a tattooed arm toward me. "Remove your mark from me."

"That sounds like an order, not a proposition."

A hint of annoyance twitched at the corners of his mouth and his nostrils flared. "Would you like something in return then?"

"You sound pretty desperate for a demon to resort to making more deals already."

"I mean it, Ava." A deep growl rumbled through his chest.

I scoffed. "You really think I'm going to give you a chance to get away?"

"I will repeat myself as many times as I need to until you understand. I gave my word. And I, as an honorable demon, do not back out on my word."

When I made no motion of conceding, Vain released a soft huff.

"An old friend is holding a gathering across the city. He and I have some...unfinished business to attend to, and I have no intention of bringing you along with me."

Whether he meant to or not, the way Vain said *friend* made it clear that they were definitely *not* friendly.

I pumped my eyebrows and gave my best sugary sweet smile. "Ooh, a party sounds fun. I'm in."

Vain took a slow, predatory step closer, and I prayed that the wards held firm. "This is me asking nicely. I won't be so nice if I have to ask again." The demon's voice had dropped dangerously low.

"You're not getting rid of me that easily."

"It is too dangerous, mellilla."

"Why?"

His gaze sharpened, and the way the muscles in his jaw tensed were more than enough indication of how much restraint he was forcing himself to maintain. "A demon nest isn't any place for a mortal, not even a witch."

"I'm used to handling your kind, remember?"

"Not in this way, you're not. I assume you're used to having the upper hand. You're used to being the one in control. You probably haven't dealt with more than a few demons at a time. I can assure you that you'd be far, far out of your league there. So, I will be going alone. I will not allow you to get hurt."

I jutted my chin and said, "Then it's a good thing you won't be leaving my side."

"Ava," Vain warned through another growl.

"I'm capable of handling myself perfectly well, thank you."

"Oh, I'm sure you're more than capable," the demon said. "Would you like me to show you how capable you are when I stop holding myself back? I'd be happy to demonstrate how truly in over your head you are."

The familiar cold pang of dread shot through my bones as my instincts tried to kick in, whispering to me that Vain was dangerous—a monster wearing a mortal's skin—but I tamped them down, unwilling to show him my fear.

"I'm coming. That's final."

Vain's face hardened and muttered a curse in the demon tongue that roughly translated to *difficult woman*. "There will be rules."

"Fine."

"You must listen to everything I tell you to do. No questions asked."

"Deal."

When had I become so emboldened to begin making reckless and careless deals with a demon? What sort of death wish did I have?

"If you're determined to be stubborn, I'll need to prepare some further precautions before this evening." The hard edge in his eyes melted. "Now, I'd like to show you something, if you'll allow me."

My curiosity got the better of me, and I nodded, unable to resist the tempting tone of his voice.

A pleasant smile inched across Vain's face. "Freshen up first. There are clothes for you in the closet adjoining your bathroom if you haven't found them already. They're mostly Nesera's, but she's similar to you in size, so there should be something in there that will fit. I'll return once you are ready."

"Is that your way of telling me I look terrible?"

"Would you like for me to tell you the truth or lie?"

I huffed, slamming the door in his face and storming into the bathroom, not giving him the option to tell me either.

I looked terrible. The mirror didn't lie to me. I stared at my reflection for longer than I cared to admit, barely recognizing the woman staring back.

*Traitor.*

My complexion was drained of all color, and my eyes were dry and bloodshot from exhaustion. Even my hair appeared to be a dull, knotted copper mess. Wild and unruly, and reminiscent of my sister's...

*Lonely. Broken.*

I stepped into the shower and scrubbed my skin raw until it turned pink. Until I couldn't bear the abrasive heat my scouring left behind.

*Your fault.*

*Your. Fault.*

The scalding water ran over me, and I let it wash away the last of my malignant thoughts until they were all but purged from the forefront of my mind. Brushed aside. But never truly gone.

After plaiting my hair down my back, I rummaged through the closet, a veritable trove of clothes of all different styles.

I pulled out a pair of too-large dark cargo pants that sagged off my hips slightly and a white long-sleeved shirt that hugged my torso. It wasn't perfect, but it was better than nothing, so it would have to do.

Vain was waiting patiently for me in the hallway when I reappeared. He led me through the penthouse and into the great room before sliding open a set of doors that gave way to a cozy and neatly organized study.

"My personal library is at your disposal. If you're insistent on looking for a way to exorcise me, I can promise you won't find the answers you're looking for here, but you're free to take whatever you'd like from my collection at your leisure."

Each wall was lined with shelves, all filled with hundreds of books. A large desk sat in one corner and a plush loveseat took up the opposite space.

When I glanced back up at Vain, one corner of his lips had quirked up into a soft smirk. "I'll make sure that breakfast is brought to you so you can spend your time here today if you choose," he said.

It was an unexpected gesture, more thoughtful than I assumed Vain was capable of. But before I could thank him, he'd turned away, shutting the doors on his way out.

Drawn to the shelves, I immediately began to familiarize myself with the titles. They didn't appear to be cataloged in any particular order. Some spines I recognized as the same demonic texts I had spent years studying at Moreau. Most of the others I didn't know. Many were even in other languages, some old, some current, some even written in the demon tongue.

I went to the desk with a decent pile stacked in my arms and found multiple plates of food waiting for me. I kicked myself for letting my guard down so much that I hadn't heard anyone enter the room behind me. No matter how hard Vain tried to convince me that he might contain some shred of virtue, he was still a demon. And I was still hopelessly mortal.

Yet, my mouth watered at the spread in front of me. One plate overflowed with grapes and berries and a second was heaped with glistening sausage links, smoked ham, and steaming scrambled eggs. There was salted butter to spread and a small jar of whipped honey to drizzle over freshly toasted bread and warm croissants. My heart skipped at the sight of a fresh pot of black tea.

How did he know that was my favorite?

I gorged myself on the feast, mulling over Vain's words with every bite. While he had assured me I wouldn't find any clues to help me perform a successful exorcism, I was convinced that he was lying. There had to be something in his collection to give me the answers I needed.

So, I became determined to prove the demon wrong.

The hours I spent hunched over Vain's desk poring over book after book left me with nothing to show for my efforts but a stiff neck and a dull ache behind my eyes. The damned demon had texts ranging from sigils and summoning spells, to tales and fables from Gehenna—the kinds of stories I imagined a demon child might be raised hearing. I was particularly engrossed in one, attempting to translate a tricky passage scribed in the demon tongue when I started.

"I'm quite fond of that one. I particularly like the part when the demoness strings up the devious lord by his entrails from the oldest banyan tree in the Bone Forest."

I looked up to meet Vain's sinful smirk. A lecherous and dangerous glint passed over his dark gaze as he stared at me from the open doorway.

"I take it you haven't found what you were looking for yet."

I scowled at the mocking tone laced through his words and slammed the book of demonic folklore shut.

"Are you trying to distract me, or did you want something?"

Vain pumped his eyebrows and glided into the room, dropping himself into the seat across the desk from me. "I've been lonely this afternoon without your pretty face to look upon."

My scowl deepened and Vain grinned wider.

"Yes," he purred. "That's the look I so dearly missed." He drummed his fingers over the desk, flashing the mark at me.

*Not going to happen, asshole.*

"I'm trying another exorcism."

Vain sketched a brow. "Right now?"

"Yes, *now*. Or did you forget the deal we made?"

My chair scraped loudly as I stood, and Vain tracked my every movement with intense precision. He set one ankle over his knee and propped his elbow on the arm of his chair, looking every bit like a king languishing upon his throne.

"Whenever you're ready," he taunted on a sigh.

I didn't give myself the chance to hesitate under his calculating stare. I let the words of the incantation flow through me with intention, my determination fueling their purpose, all the while holding the demon's blank stare. Word after word, line after line, even as the magic in them burned through me, Vain didn't so much as flinch. Not once.

"Don't be too hard on yourself," Vain said as I fought to catch my breath. "It's not for your lack of trying."

It was infuriating how much the exorcism had drained my well of magic when it hadn't seemed to affect Vain even a little. I bit back my retort and took my seat behind the desk again, my fingers clawed around another book to bury myself in. Anything if it took my attention away from the demon and his wicked smirk.

"Come now, don't be so hostile."

I slammed the book shut almost as quickly as I'd opened it. "If you're going to be insistent on constantly running your mouth, the least you could do is talk about something useful."

"I'll be whatever distraction you need me to be, darling." Vain reclined further into his seat and cocked his head to one side.

Ignoring the insinuation in his tone, I glared at him through my brows. "Tell me more about the first witches and how they were created," I said.

"I've already told you."

"You gave me the abridged version before. I want the full story. No vague answers this time. The whole truth."

The demon reached forward and plucked a stray blueberry off the tray of leftovers from breakfast and popped it into his mouth. "There are many versions of the legend," he started, "but the one that is most widely known amongst our kind is the one I will tell you."

I inched forward in my seat before I realized I'd done it.

"The first witches—before they called themselves that—were mere mortals tinkering with powers beyond their abilities. They had no magic when they sought to gain such power for themselves. They had too much pride, their greed and lust fueling them to breach the bounds of what shouldn't have been possible. They summoned forces far beyond their understanding or control, ultimately leading them to open the first rift between our two worlds, and it was the archdemons who answered their call."

"No," I interjected. "It was *your* kind that created the first rifts and broke through."

"You asked for the truth," he said. "So, I am giving it to you."

It was entirely possible the demon was lying. But when I remembered the horrified look on Lena's face when I'd mentioned what Vain had told me back in the Hull...I worked my jaw so tight that Vain apparently noticed and raised a brow.

"Is it that difficult for you to believe?"

"Which of the archdemons did the witches summon?"

"Sohlum, Vencula, and Ghen."

My blood stilled at the names of all three of them, but most of all Ghen's. His name was like a barb in my chest, and it took everything I had in me to claw it out before attempting to regain my composure.

"So, you've heard of them," Vain said.

I threw every bit of heated contempt I could into my glare, hoping it would be enough to sear right through him. "Of course I have." *I'm a demonologist for fuck's sake.* But I didn't say that part out loud.

I knew them all by name, as did all witches. They were no secret to us. The six archdemons were brutal legends. Dark gods, all of them the only direct sons and daughters of their queen mother, Lilith. Out of the three that Vain mentioned though, I was the least familiar with Vencula, but that was only because there were very few written accounts of him and his conquests. It was almost as if he'd been left out of their history entirely. Vanished or forgotten to time. No one knew. And so long as he never appeared or made himself known on our side of the rifts, no one cared.

"So, what happened?" I asked.

"The mortals asked for power, which of course the archdemons were willing to offer in exchange for something of value. One of them gave up their ability to feel any emotions, one became a demon's familiar, and the other gave up their soul. In exchange, the archdemons offered them their ichor, and when the mortals drank the demon blood, they were given power in return."

I furrowed my brow. "Demon ichor turns mortals into vampyrs though," I said.

"The ichor of higher and lesser demons can if consumed in excess, yes," he confirmed. "Their ichor only offers a minimal amount of power, and at a high risk. But an archdemon's ichor is pure power. It is the stuff of gods. The first witches were very powerful, but it seems that through the generations, your powers have become diluted."

I said nothing after that. It's not that I didn't believe him. Quite the opposite, actually. I could sense no tricks or lies in his words. Vain spoke so directly, that the truth coming from the mouth of a demon came as something of a shock.

Even remembering the look on Lena's face when she learned I had discovered the truth, and to realize that I had been misguided my entire life...it was a hard pill to swallow.

Vain ran a hand through Rory's hair, brushing the longer strands out of his face. "Our blood runs through your veins, witch. Whether you prefer to admit it or not. We made your kind what you are."

"That's it then?" I asked. "The whole truth?"

Vain nodded. "It is."

I snatched up another book off the desk and flipped open to a random page to absorb myself in the text.

"So does this mean you're done with me for now then?"

"I'm sure you can find your own way out," I snapped, not bothering to look up.

The demon hummed and rose from his chair.

"Before I leave, I thought I'd make you aware that your wards, while unnecessary, were a little worse for wear, so I took the liberty of...fixing them for you. Hope you don't mind."

And without another word, Vain slid out of the room, leaving me agape until the sounds of his footsteps faded away entirely.

I tore out of his study and ran back to my room. Being tucked away with my head in his books for the better part of the day, I hadn't noticed when the sun had set. The skyline was painted in brilliant red and warm orange, the fiery kind of hue that matched the ire burning in my chest.

Flinging open my door, I looked instantly to the wards I'd placed down the night before. The ones at the threshold of the doorframe had been all but wiped away, and the rest had deteriorated to nothing but dust, leaving the space wide open and vulnerable for any demon to walk through at their leisure. And the demon I'd least wanted to most of all had seemed to have done just that.

Two black boxes tied prettily with silver ribbon sat at the end of the bed. A small red card sat atop them, but I ignored it and went straight for the larger box first. I tugged the ribbon and then shimmied the lid off, my breath catching when I pulled out a scandalous black satin dress with a draped neckline, delicate thin straps, and a slit in the hem that rode up the thigh. Tossing the dress aside, I tore into the smaller box which revealed a set of Louboutin heels to accompany the ensemble. I tried not to dwell on the fact that each item had been picked for my exact measurements.

*Bastard!*

I cursed at myself under my breath for forgetting to strengthen the wards this morning. With a shaky exhale, I reached for the card and turned it over between my fingers.

*Mellilla,*
*10 p.m. Be ready.*
*Your favorite demon,*
*Vain*

Cocky asshole.

I threw the card onto the bed. Pursing my lips, I ran my fingers over the fabric of the dress. If Vain was dragging me into a demon nest, then I was sure there was some part he wanted me to play, and this outfit was only a piece of it. Whatever role he had for me, I hoped my mask of confidence wouldn't slip amidst a horde of demons.

I had a little more than an hour until Vain would come to collect me, so I reluctantly slipped into the dress, tugging it up so that it hung precariously from my shoulders. The straps were too thin for my liking—one careless slice would have the whole thing fluttering to the floor. Yet, when I stared at myself in the bathroom mirror, I couldn't deny the rest of the dress draped perfectly over my body, accentuating every curve. The heels on the other hand had to be at least three or four inches tall, and my calves screamed at me almost immediately after slipping them on. But just for a few hours tonight, I could endure them. I would have to.

"You're out of your mind for insisting to go along with him." Nesera's voice came from the bedroom. When I looked up, I caught a glimpse of her head poking around the corner in the mirror's reflection.

"I don't know, I think it was more reckless to help him escape in the first place."

Nesera grinned. "Don't blame yourself," she said as she strode into the bathroom. "He's always been a charmer."

The cambion watched as I fussed with my hair, and casually hopped up onto the counter. "A demon nest isn't exactly a place that's friendly to mortals. Even with Vain at your side, it's dangerous."

"I'll be fine," I said. "I know how to handle myself."

She shook her head and chuckled under her breath. "He told me you're a demonologist. That's why I can't understand why you'd make him take you to a damn nest. And I would go for some back up, but Vain's afraid there'll be too many demons who will recognize me."

I tugged my hair down from a high bun that wasn't sitting the way I wanted it to and looked at her. "Ones that might want you dead?"

"Yeah. More than a few," Nesera said as she picked at her nails.

"Does that mean Vain is protecting you too?" I dared to ask.

"I may be under his protection, but that doesn't mean I'm in need of protecting. If anything, they should be more afraid of me than I am of them."

I didn't doubt her. The cambion had a calm ruthlessness to her that I admired. She seemed like the type of merciless fighter who could take out more than a handful of demons all on her own and not even break a sweat.

Nesera tilted her head to one side and asked, "What kind of deal did you make with him?"

"How do you know I made a deal?"

She shrugged. "Because I also made one with him. Vain can never pass up a good deal. And I can only bet that a witch like yourself wouldn't have tagged along with him without one." A knowing smile crept onto her face, and the corners of her eyes crinkled. "So, what was it?"

I pressed my lips together and exhaled through my nose. "A very stupid deal."

Nesera gave a small laugh. "I can't tell if you're fascinated by demons or terrified of them."

"I wish I could tell the difference myself."

"My advice," she said, "don't fear them. Because that fear will only affect every decision you make. Feel the fear and own it, preferably before they can break you." Her fingers traced the scars across her face almost unconsciously before turning her head downward.

I felt tempted to ask Nesera about her deal and the obvious memory that had been dragged up, but I chose to keep those questions to myself and not press her any further.

I used a gold barrette to sweep the small sections that framed my face up while keeping the rest down. With one last look in the mirror, I decided this was the best it was going to get.

"Hold on," Nesera said and pushed herself off the counter. She went into the hall and returned a few moments later with a handful of palettes, brushes, pots, and tubes of various colors. "Is it cool if I add a few finishing touches? Really make it pop?" Then she added, "Not that yours looks bad. But the humans that are paraded around at these things are always a little more..."

"Sexed up?"

She winced. "For lack of a better term."

"Do your worst," I relented, and the cambion quickly got to work.

She stroked products through my brows, blended neutral shadows across my lids to accentuate my eye shape, and drew liner along my lashes, winging it out to my temples. Her final addition was to apply a deep burgundy color to my lips.

I felt as if I were looking at an alternate version of myself. It was remarkable how a little bit of product could wildly transform my face. My eyes had a cat-like appearance to them, and my lips looked fuller than normal, almost as if they were stained with blood.

Nesera smiled at her handiwork, and we walked out to the great room to find Rory waiting there and not Vain, like I'd expected. He was dressed sharply in head-to-toe black. Dark pants hugged his frame, and he had a jacket folded over one shoulder as he adjusted the cuffs of his long-sleeved dress shirt. On his left hand was a black leather glove, which hid the binding mark on his wrist I had given him, and the fingers of his right hand were adorned with an assortment of platinum rings.

When he looked up at us, his whole body went rigid, eyes widening as he took me in. Rory's mouth opened and closed. "You look..."

"Demon got your tongue, Masters?"

Rory clamped his mouth shut and reset his features into a mask of indifference. A stray lock of his dark hair fell forward over his eyes, and my fingers itched to brush it back neatly into place. He cleared his throat and absently tugged at his glove.

Nesera's eyes bounced between us, before pumping her eyebrows in Rory's direction and then slipped away after calling over her shoulder, "Have fun, kids!"

I turned back to Rory and gave the straps of my dress an anxious tug, trying to distract myself from how undeniably hot he looked in a suit.

"Is this outfit really necessary?" I asked. "I feel ridiculous."

"According to Vain, the demons at these gatherings flaunt their humans around like pets. So, if we want to blend in, it's either this or you can go nude. Your choice."

"So, I'm his pet then?"

Rory threw his hands up. "You said it, not me. You do look the part though. It's almost convincing."

"Almost?"

He smirked. "Don't worry. We're going to make sure you can fool every demon in the city when we're done."

I wasn't sure I liked the sound of that.

"Are you not afraid?" I asked him.

"I should be asking you that."

"I'm used to being surrounded by demons."

Rory took a tentative step forward. "It's okay to admit you're terrified," he said. "No matter how strong of a front you're putting on."

"It's not a front," I insisted.

Another step, and then Rory's eyes flicked over to black.

"Of course, it's not," the demon teased.

Narrowing my eyes at Vain, I asked, "Are we going to get on with this or what?"

"Patience, mellilla," he hummed and then made a come-hither motion with two fingers.

My skin buzzed as I glided up to him until we were toe to toe.

Vain turned his head slightly to the side to better display Rory's neck—the side that prominently showed off the dark V tattooed there.

"Do you know what this mark means?" he asked, pointing to it.

"Vain?" I guessed. "Because you're an insufferably vain asshole?"

"Your humor knows no bounds, my dear," Vain clipped. "It's a reminder to everyone that I *own* this body."

The demon's energy was palpable, heavy and ancient all at once. I felt as if I could barely take a full breath.

"Pull your hair back for me," he said, lowering his voice to a deep whisper.

Brushing them aside so my locks spilled down my mostly bare back, I watched as Vain slipped a short selenite knife from under the sleeve of his shirt. He reached his gloved hand to cup my jaw while he raised the blade to my throat, and I suppressed a shiver.

"What are you doing?"

"A necessary precaution," he said. "But I need your permission, as it goes against the terms of our deal."

"Are you asking me to let you hurt me?"

Vain let the question hang longer than was comfortable. "It will be a little more than a scratch. It is to keep you safe more than anything. Do you trust me?"

"Not in the slightest." I kept my focus on his eyes. They were so black I could almost see myself reflected back in them. "Do it," I said.

I hissed in a sharp breath through my teeth as the blade made a shallow slice across my bare skin in a V shape. The throb of pain ebbed quickly after.

Vain drew back, smiling softly. "And now, everyone will know that I own you too."

I should have yelled at him. Fought back or screamed obscenities until I was blue in the face. But the thought of being considered *his* shook me to my core, and a slow heat flooded my lower belly.

"It won't scar, I promise," he said, resecuring the knife up his sleeve before straightening the material back down.

"Are you arming yourself for a fight tonight?"

Vain's smile was deadly. "Darling, I always come prepared for war."

My focus flitted again to the V on Rory's neck. His was bold and dark in contrast to mine which I could feel was nothing more than a thin sharp line of red. A trickle of blood ghosted down my throat, and Vain swept it away with the pad of his thumb with a tenderness I did not expect from a demon. He drew the digit into his mouth, sucking it clean before reaching into my hair. He repinned my strands to one side so the mark he'd placed on my neck would remain on full display throughout the night.

"Now, when I show you off tonight in front of all the demons, they will see that you are mine—wholly and unequivocally *mine*—and none of them will dare lay a finger on you. Because they all know that no one touches Vain's property and lives."

"I am not your property."

"You will be," Vain said, "for tonight. I told you there would be rules. So, if you want any chance of leaving a demon nest unharmed, then you will do exactly as I say and play this role."

Vain's attention roamed down over other parts of me that should have left me feeling dirty and humiliated, but the shame never surfaced. "One more gift. And this one isn't nearly as unpleasant." He drew a thick chain of glittering diamonds from his pocket.

"Left hand, please," Vain requested as he held his own out toward me. The bracelet melted around my wrist, encircling my mark and hiding it from view.

"Don't pout," he said. "You should be grateful I didn't decide to leash you to me instead. Though, I admit, a collar of diamonds wrapped around your pretty little neck would look divine."

My lips curled into a snarl. "You disgust me."

"You never cease to enrapture me with your lies, mellilla."

I looked down at the upturned palm of Vain's gloved hand as he offered it to me.

"Come. We're fashionably late as it is."

# FOURTEEN

## AVA

I hated how used to shifting I had become. This time when Vain landed us on an empty street along the riverside, I didn't find the aftermath of it as jarring as the other times before. My feet felt steady underneath me, even in the high heels, and my stomach hadn't pitched like I expected it to.

A long row of townhouses stood eerily quiet and dark, except for one, opposite the river. A soft light burned in each window and faint music came from inside. Strings of lush, green ivy laced with soft, purple wisteria blooms crawled up along the white painted brick exterior.

I had imagined a demon nest to be in some crumbling, derelict warehouse they had claimed and turned rancid with their filth. But this house was the image of affluence, fit for an unholy prince and their minions.

Vain released me to shrug his jacket on before he slipped his hand back into mine, anchoring me to him as he faced me.

"I'm giving you one last chance to back out." He tugged down the edge of his glove, exposing the mark.

"Not going to happen."

Vain exhaled through his nose and yanked the glove back up, his gaze hardening. "In that case, you must do exactly as I say from here on out."

"Sure," I muttered as I rolled my eyes.

"This is not a game, Ava. Walking into a nest full of demons with you will be like waving meat in front of a starved harpy. You will be nothing but prey to them."

"Is that how *you* see me?" I asked, feeling bold. "As prey?"

Vain didn't answer, just stroked his thumb across the pad of my palm.

"You must act as if I've glamoured you. The minute we walk through those doors, you are my plaything. You will bend your will to me, and me alone, do you understand? Anything I say, whatever I tell you to do, you will obey. And you must remain by my side at all times." Vain's voice was smooth as silk, domineering and urgent, but also edged with caution.

Obedient. Submissive. That's how he expected me to play my part. Vain's glamoured whore.

"Must you treat me like a dog?"

Vain's eyes flared. "Do I make myself clear?"

"Crystal," I seethed at him as I gritted my teeth and dared myself not to meet his gaze. While I was pleased I'd forced Vain to bend to my will by bringing me along with him, his belittling demands left me simmering with contempt. He snatched my chin between his fingers and forced me to look up into his face.

"Say it again. But this time, make me believe it." Vain's voice turned thick with lust. "Convince me that I've glamoured you."

I forced my eyes to glaze over, as if I were truly under his wicked spell, pliant to his every will. "I promise to obey you, Vain. Only you."

"Very good, *pet*." The gleam in the demon's eyes turned wicked as he took a step closer. "You almost look eager enough to be fucked like my good little toy. Wouldn't you like that?"

His words shot a throbbing ache through me, and I attempted to mask it with a flippant eye roll, hating myself for wondering what he might feel like. "You're a vile, pathetic—"

Vain clicked his tongue. "Ah, ah. Try again. Show me how much you want me. Convince me."

There was no glamour behind his words, but the jolt they sent through my body affected me all the same. Keeping my eyes trained on his, I brought my hands to his abdomen and slowly inched them up his chest, my fingers skating over the warm silky fabric of his dress shirt and feeling the taut muscles underneath.

"Please," I whispered, the sound heady with desire, "fuck me."

Dropping my chin, Vain moved to cup my face in his palm, and I shivered. The smile he gave me in return was sinful, and I was painfully aware of the way my thighs slicked together when I shifted uncomfortably from one heel to the other.

"Such a good mortal," Vain said as his thumb swept over my cheek. "Now, let's go put on a show."

My skin prickled at the warm touch of his right hand as it settled against my lower back, guiding me up the steps of the townhouse and through the front door.

"Deep breaths, mellilla."

His words were useless because my lungs felt like they had turned to ice, with each breath shallower than the one before the moment I stepped a foot inside. I kept my head down as we entered into the crowded foyer, avoiding unnecessary eye contact with the demons mingling amongst one another. The energy and power crackling through the air set every hair on my body bristling with dread.

Every one of them seemed to be alerted to the presence of fresh, mortal blood at the same time. Dozens of heads swiveled in my direction as we passed, eyeing me hungrily, as if they craved my fragile mortality in one way or another; either to feed off of it, or to crush it helplessly between their claws. They roamed free of any wards or iron cages, laughing and howling amongst one another, and I was filled with a curious mix of both awe and terror.

Vain wrapped a possessive hand around my upper arm and led us through the crowded space. Whenever I got too close to another demon, he deftly maneuvered me so none ever came close to touching me.

Most of the ones I snuck glances at appeared to be higher demons, mostly humanoid in form but many bearing a common assortment of infernal attributes. One demoness with bright golden eyes and bronze skin moved gracefully between the other guests, carrying a thin champagne flute while keeping her leathery wings tucked tightly against her back, the hem of her red gown nipping at her heels and a thin spiked tail swishing lazily behind her.

I nearly avoided crushing it with my heels before almost bumping into a demon with a bulking figure and a wolfish snout. His dark blue fur bristled and he chuffed as we passed him and the bone-thin human man he kept on a short chain leash. The collar sagged around the man's neck as if it had grown loose over time, and his eyes held an emptiness I couldn't describe, heavy lids fluttering as he swayed in a trancelike state—glamoured.

Vain directed me behind the beast with a sharp tug at my waist. He seemed to be familiar with the layout as we worked our way through the crowd and up a flight of stairs. I made a detailed mental floor plan as we went, noting every possible exit since I worried whatever plan Vain had might go horribly south.

A very human scream tore from somewhere amidst the rolls of laughter and howling jeers, and it took everything in me not to flinch at the sound.

Lowering his head, Vain spoke softly into my ear when we reached the third floor. "You're calmer than I expected."

"What did you expect?"

Vain shrugged. "Most humans, even witches, startle easily around demons. Especially when there are this many in one place."

"You really don't know me at all then," I said, attempting to keep my voice down so as not to be overheard as we passed a demon crunching down on a severed femur between three rows of razor-sharp teeth, strings of sinew and flesh still hanging off the bone.

"That's right, I forgot how brilliant you are. You already know everything about our kind, so you don't fear anything."

"Don't mock me, asshole."

Vain shushed me and maneuvered us to an open door at the end of the hall. The warm summer breeze caused the gauzy curtains to flutter as we stepped past and onto a small private balcony. Vain removed his hand from my back, and I shivered in the absence of his warm touch. The night air felt cool against my skin, which only aided in reminding me of how much of my body was exposed for all the demons to gawk at.

"Are you going to tell me what we're really doing here?"

"I told you, I'm visiting a friend."

I looked to the courtyard below. The perfectly manicured trees and shrubs were strung up with twinkling lights, basking the whole yard in a gentle glow. I could barely make out the faint trickling sound of water splashing from a nearby fountain over the swell of stringed music echoing from an open window on a floor somewhere below us.

"I doubt you have any friends," I said, and Vain put a hand up to his chest in mock offense. "And you would only go out of your way for something if it was important. So, what is it you want, Vain?"

The demon leaned against the railing turning his head to the side as he cast his gaze toward the horizon where the lights of the city shone in the distance from across the river.

"I underestimated how perceptive you are," he said. "And because I pride myself for my continued honesty with you, I will be honest with you again now. Eldin used to be someone I considered a friend once. But as time is so often unkind to us in our immortal lives, we drifted apart a long time ago." There was a hint of sadness tugging at Vain's words, his tone flat and expressionless as he spoke.

"We reconnected not long ago over a shared interest in a particular item, a quite powerful one. Have you heard of the Grimoire of Aeternum?"

I shook my head.

"It's an infamous book. Most demons believe it to be no more than a legend, long thought lost to the eons. But Eldin and I found it. Only it just so happened that an archdemon had gone to great lengths to attain it for his prized collection. Looking back on it, I see how foolish it was of me to trust Eldin. The prick had always been greedier than myself, but I never thought he would betray me over it."

"He was the one who got you captured by those cambion hunters that brought you to the coven. He set you up?"

Vain white-knuckled the railing. The contempt over the betrayal was etched into every line on his face.

"So, we're here to take back a stupid book he stole from you? Or are you exacting your revenge on him too?"

"If revenge happens to be convenient, then yes. Whatever it takes to get the grimoire back."

"What's so important about it?" I asked. "Why go through all the trouble?"

Vain paused and pressed his lips together before he said, "Because it may be the only chance Rory has."

"What do you—"

"On the Mother herself," a smarmy voice called from somewhere behind us. "Decided to show your face again, Vain?"

I half-turned to peer past the sheer curtains. Stepping out, was a demon encased in human flesh with black eyes that matched Vain's. The male he possessed looked young, at least younger than me by a few years. His face was handsome and boyish, but his cheeks were hollowed and the red rings around his eyes reflected just how poorly the demon had been neglecting its vessel.

I managed to swallow down my horror as best I could while the demon's soulless eyes blinked back at me.

"And I see you found yourself a new vessel since we last crossed paths. I barely recognized you until your stench and that little mark you like to brand them with gave you away." The demon wriggled his vessel's nose and then jutted a sharp chin in my direction. "Who is this delicious treat you've brought for us?"

Vain clasped my arm above the elbow and tugged me closer to him. "She's not for sharing, Ilo," Vain said.

Ilo pouted. "Shame."

"Besides, it looks like you have your own pet to attend to. Or have you already grown bored of that one too?" Vain said through a snarl as he motioned toward a small cowering figure behind the demon.

I bit the inside of my cheek to keep my lips from curling upward in disgust as Ilo dragged the girl out. Vain must have felt my rage because his grip on my arm tightened.

The human couldn't have been older than nineteen. She shook next to Ilo as the demon stroked his hands over her bare skin. Her eyes remained pinned to the floor, but she shuddered and flinched at every movement he made.

Ilo had obviously attempted to make her a showpiece tonight. She'd been shoved into a tight pink dress, which matched the bubblegum strands streaked through her dirty-blonde hair. Her mascara was smudged down both hollow, bruised cheeks, the yellow and green marks barely hidden underneath the layers of concealer.

The need to comfort her strained inside my chest, aching to reach out, yet I couldn't do a damned thing to help her nor Ilo's possessed vessel. I fantasized about dragging Ilo into the Hull and exorcising him before tearing his demon body limb from vile limb, then burning his flesh until there was nothing left of him but sinew and ash.

My pulse thrummed thick and heavy in my veins, my blood practically boiling. Vain gently squeezed my arm in an attempt to assuage me.

The demon's grin widened as he appraised me. "I told you, possessing their bodies can be a fun distraction for a time, but nothing truly compares to the feeling of them underneath your own hands...so soft and delicate. Breakable." Ilo's lips curled, and his nostrils flared once, then twice as he eyed me. "Is she a—"

It only took me a second to realize that the demon was scenting me. I fought the urge to cringe backward as Ilo outstretched one hand toward my face before Vain knocked it away.

"She's an investment. One that is to remain untouched. Or did you forget that no one touches what is mine?"

Ilo's black eyes flicked to the mark Vain had cut into my neck, and his grin sagged. "I never thought you were the greedy type, Vain. It seems I was wrong."

"You'd do best not to forget it," Vain sneered as he steered us away. "Always a disappointment to see you, Ilo. Excuse us."

"The displeasure has been all mine," Ilo rasped.

I tried to give the girl a remorseful glance, but she didn't even look up at me. Vain stepped between me and the demon and dragged me roughly behind him, and I was still painfully aware of Ilo's raking glare on me as we worked back into the crowd.

Vain leaned in close and whispered, "I know what you're going to say."

I gritted my teeth, unable to fully shake the image of the girl's bruises or the state of Ilo's vessel. "You don't know the half of what I would like to say to you right now."

"I do. Unfortunately, this is not the time." Maybe it was the lack of oxygen from the ragged breaths I kept drawing in or the rush of blood pounding in my ears, but I could have sworn I heard a shadow of regret lacing Vain's tone.

Vain stopped in front of a shut door and casually leaned against it, facing me.

"Try not to look so angry with me, mellilla. As much as I love how it looks on you, I'd rather not draw any unwanted attention."

Then, turning the knob, Vain slipped into the room, pulling me along with him.

As my eyes adjusted to the low light, Vain moved past me and began to trace his hands along the mahogany paneled walls, tapping and pausing to press at random intervals like he was searching for something.

"Do you think the book is hidden in here?" I asked.

"It's one possibility, yes."

The clicks of my heels were dampened on the Persian rug as I crossed to the other end of the room where a large ornate desk sat. Each leg had been hand carved and ornamented with a detailed bust of a demon into the smooth dark wood. I stroked a hand along them all, taking in every detail as if they had been presented to me for study—the curled ram-like horns of one, the pointed tips of the harpy's wings on another, the jagged teeth and forked tongue of the third, and finally a coil of snakes spun atop the demon's head like a crown. I'd never observed such impressive demonic craftsmanship, and the art of it fascinated me more than I cared to admit.

I started pulling out the desk drawers to rifle through their contents, looking for anything that looked like it could be classified as a grimoire.

"The last thing I expected to do tonight was to be dragged along on a scavenger hunt."

"You like to complain a lot, don't you?"

Vain was turned away from me, still inspecting the walls with sharpened focus, so he couldn't see the glare I shot at him.

"Can you at least describe it for me, so I know what I'm looking for?"

"It's bound in black leather and has a red six-pointed star stamped into the cover. It looks old."

"Creepy, ancient, and demonic. Got it."

I moved to the right side of the desk to continue my search. Vain gave up his examination of the walls and began to move along the bookshelves behind me.

"Are you going to tell me how this grimoire is apparently Rory's only shot at surviving?"

"Not yet. You only need to know that it is, and leaving without it is not an option."

"I deserve more than that." I spun around to glare at him again, only to find him already towering over me, staring deep into my eyes, straight into my soul.

"You do," he said. "But I can't give you more. Only he can. And only if he chooses to."

A foreboding chill shot down my spine, and Vain returned his attention to the shelves, leaving me to wonder at his cryptic words.

The desk was a bust, so I moved my search to the farthest shelf away from Vain, pulling out every black book and inspecting the covers and the pages with no luck until we met in the middle.

"What if it's not here?"

"Then we look elsewhere. I'm not leaving without—"

"I should have known you'd find a way to free yourself sooner than expected." A low bone-chilling voice slithered out from behind us.

My muscles tensed and I slammed as much of my power as I could into reinforcing my mental shields. Glancing up warily at Vain, his face held no expression as he turned to the demon who had caught us red-handed. I didn't dare to look. The power radiating from him was the blood-curdling, hair-raising sort, enough to send any mortal into a fit of terror.

Vain slid his arm protectively across my stomach and pulled me closer to him.

"There's no mortal cage that can contain me for long, Eldin. I thought you were smarter than that."

The click of the demon's approaching footsteps sent my heart racing even with my back turned to him. Eldin's voice gurgled low in his throat as he spoke. "Found yourself a witch whore in the process, I see?"

Vain glanced down at me through cautious eyes. "I did," he said.

My tongue felt like ash in my mouth as I sensed the new demon's energy stalking closer.

"Well, let me have a look at her. I want to see what all the fuss is about."

I trembled, but Vain squeezed my waist once, a silent reassuring touch before he turned me around. His hold never faltered as he pulled my back firmly against his chest. Vain's other hand stroked down my arm as he presented me to the demon who had cornered us, and it took everything I had in me to choke back the scream clawing its way up my throat.

# FIFTEEN

## AVA

Eldin was a horror to look upon—the kind of demon I had only read about in books. Because if anyone ever crossed a demon like this in the flesh, it would be the last thing they saw before their gruesome ruin.

Long, snake-like tentacles slithered from the crown of the demon's head and coiled down past his broad muscled shoulders. Thinner tentacles sprouted out from the flesh below two dark nostril slits, shrouding what might have been the demon's mouth and falling like a curtain of snaking tendrils from chin to chest.

He stared at me as if he were trying to bore himself deep into my soul. Thin, elliptical shaped pupils encased in glowing red-orange irises, the color of embers from a dying fire, blinked back at me. He looked like he had clawed his way out of the deepest trench in the seas of Gehenna, and here he stood before us in a well-fitted dark gray suit. The humanness of it was jarring.

Eldin flicked a lit cigarette between his spindly roped fingers. He held it up and placed it between two of the tentacles shrouding his mouth, then took a long drag as he studied me. He was so close that I had to crane my neck to look into his face.

"She's not the sort of mortal I would have expected you to enjoy. Though I see the appeal." Eldin tilted his head to one side, the cherry flaring brightly as the demon took another drag of his cigarette. The smoke curled around his tentacles as he exhaled. "This one almost seems complacent and pathetic enough that you wouldn't need to compel her to do anything."

"Barely have to lift a finger," Vain said, every syllable clipped with animosity. My stomach flipped as I struggled to keep my glazed-over expression steady.

Eldin motioned to a pair of seats toward the center of the room. "Why don't you have a seat, old friend? Make yourself and your new pet comfortable."

The chair creaked beneath Eldin as he sat, his large, oppressive form squeezed in between the armrests. Vain took a seat in the chair closest to the door, and I stood attentively to the side of him, careful to keep my gaze down so as not to catch any more of Eldin's unwanted attention. I nearly jumped when Vain reached up to grab my chin and forced me to look into his obsidian eyes.

"Sit on the floor," he ordered, the command sharp.

My knees wobbled as I shifted my weight onto the floor beside him, but he halted me.

"No. Where I can see you. Between my legs."

I swallowed and moved in front of him, lowering myself between his spread knees and folding my legs to one side.

"Good mortal," Vain purred as he tucked a stray hair behind my ear to keep the V he had cut into my neck exposed to Eldin. Vain was playing a role just as I was, yet his was so convincing that it forced me to remember what he really was—what true monster that lay beneath Rory's skin.

I kept the empty, dreamy look behind my eyes so there would be no question that I was devoted to Vain in every way, helplessly entranced under his spell.

Eldin gave a small nod of approval and said, "You've leashed your little witch well." The scrape of a mental claw dragged against the walls of my shields, and the urge to scream bubbled up in my chest, but I held perfectly still. "Got her locked up tight too. I can't read her."

The demon's slitted eyes narrowed further, his tentacles flicking with the slightest unease. Did he know I wasn't really glamoured? Could he tell?

Eldin leaned forward until he was close enough that I could scent the salt and brimstone wafting from him. He stretched his long fingers toward a strand of hair that had fallen over my face.

Vain wound his hand around my neck and pulled me against him. "You touch her, and I won't hesitate to slice you up, starting with those tentacles of yours," he snarled. "She's *mine*. Isn't that right, mellilla?"

I tipped my head back to rest against the heat of his upper thigh, staring straight up into his soulless eyes. "Always, Vain. I'm your little whore forever."

A glint of surprise flickered across Vain's face for a brief moment, so quick I thought I almost imagined it, before he slipped his mask of indifference back on.

Eldin appeared amused and satisfied enough that he relaxed into his chair. "Very tightly leashed," he said. "You've trained her exceptionally well."

I gazed up into Vain's crooked, forced smile while he stroked my hair, occasionally twisting his fingers through the strands.

"She was difficult to break in the beginning. Certainly not willingly."

I had to wonder if a part of Vain was pleased seeing me this way. Docile and malleable. Nothing more than a pretty, breakable thing that he could play with and show off until he grew bored of me and tossed me aside. I tried to shake off those thoughts and instead continue to play my role under Eldin's watchful gaze.

Nuzzling my head against his lap, I nearly stilled when I felt his length, rigid and hard beneath my cheek. My whole body flushed. Vain shifted in his seat, the movement subtle as he continued stroking one hand through my hair.

"When you eventually grow tired of her, send her my way. I think I would enjoy her very much."

Vain's hand tightened around my throat, enough to display dominance in front of Eldin, but not enough to hurt me. My pulse fluttered beneath his grasp, and my breath hitched in my chest. There was no way he couldn't feel it—he knew just how his touch affected me.

I should have hated it, knowing how fragile I must feel to him. Knowing that he could snap my neck in an instant should he feel like it. And I should have loathed even more the thrill of arousal it sent rippling through me, accompanied by the sensation of a warm heat pooling between my thighs.

Eldin pressed his spindly hands together and set them in his lap as he relaxed into his chair. "Are you going to tell me what you're snooping for in my home?"

"I think we're past playing games, Eldin."

"Indeed," said the demon. "In that case, I should tell you I don't have it."

"You always were a bad liar."

"It's the truth," Eldin said, stubbing out his cigarette on the wooden table. "I never took it into my possession. Unfortunately, after you were captured, the rest of my plan didn't exactly go as smoothly as I had hoped. I lost the grimoire in the chaos, and last I heard, it's still safely locked up in that fortress of his."

"You take me for a fool, don't you?"

Eldin shrugged, appearing bored with the conversation. "Believe what you'd like. It makes no difference. But I'd prefer that you not turn over every corner of my home in a futile search. And I would so hate for you to waste your precious time."

When Eldin grinned—or what I mistook for a smile—his tentacles squirmed restlessly down his chest like worms burrowing beneath soil.

"That's very thoughtful of you, but—" Vain's body went rigid behind me, alerting me to something beyond the scope of my awareness. The fingers laced through my hair at the base of my skull tightened as if he were trying to warn me of it too. "I'll choose what to do with my own time."

Vain stood from his chair abruptly, yanking me up with him by my hair so hard that I heard my barrette clatter to the floor. I stifled a yelp and made a mental note to give him a swift, hard kick between the legs for it later.

"Enjoy the rest of the party," Eldin called out as Vain dragged us out of the study.

Vain released his grip on my hair and took hold of my bicep as soon as the doors shut behind us. I don't think he realized how forceful he was being with me. His attention seemed to be somewhere else entirely as he shifted his gaze nervously around us.

"Ow! Vain, you're hurting me."

His attention whipped to me, eyes softening with what I could only describe as desperation. His grip loosened slightly, but still firm enough that it felt like his fingertips might leave behind bruises. "Quickly. We're leaving."

Before we made it more than a few steps, Vain bristled, frozen where he stood in the middle of the room, staring straight ahead.

I tugged lightly on his arm. "Vain?"

I tried to follow his gaze to find what had caught his interest, but before I could, he yanked me around and dragged me behind him until we reached a secluded corner at the end of the hallway, partially out of sight from the attention of the other demons. His body snapped around mine like a whip, roughly pinning my back to the wall, and I hissed in a sharp breath. I wasn't sure if he realized how forceful he was being with me, and I was no longer in any mood to be handled like his toy.

"Whatever you do, do not catch his attention," he said, low and hushed.

"What the hell, Vain!"

Caging himself around me, he shot one hand out and planted it firmly to the wall next to my head as if he were trying to shield me from view. The other plucked my chin possessively between his gloved fingers.

"Listen. To. Me," Vain commanded, coal-black eyes burning. "I need you to trust me for once. I beg you."

In any other scenario, I would have been tempted to tease him for begging, but he was staring at me with such fierce intensity that my bones felt like they might catch fire. Every inch of my skin tightened under his dark gaze. My head hummed and the thrumming beat of my blood rushing through me felt like a warning buzzing in every fiber of my being.

Vain slammed into me, closing the small distance between us and crushing our bodies together until his lips were on mine, and he kissed me with a fervor I wasn't prepared for. I pushed against him, and he barely broke away.

"What the hell are you doing?" I hissed.

Vain's eyes had lost their lustful edge and appeared overly bright and alert. Every muscle in his body was taut. I never thought I would see him afraid of anything.

"Trying to blend in so we're not noticed."

"By who?"

"Ghen." My knees went weak, and my blood turned glacial. "He's here. If he sets his sights on us—"

The paralyzing fear in Vain's eyes, his hesitation...it all made sense. Even amongst their own kind, the archdemons were something to be feared. If Vain's own fear of Ghen had been immobilizing, then mine was nothing short of devastating.

"Then instead of kissing me, shift us out of here. Right now."

"I can't," he said, voice strained. "Not from within the house. Eldin has wards in place to prevent anyone from shifting directly in or out."

My heart plummeted.

Vain leaned in and pressed his forehead to mine. "Do as I say, mellilla. Please. So I can get us out of here together in one piece."

Maybe if I pretended Rory was in control, I could do it.

I tried, *really* tried, to force myself to stare at Vain and only see Rory—his sharp jawline, his soft lips, the faint pinpoints of freckles that crept up onto his cheekbones. The humanness of Rory was in every plane of his face, but where Rory's gray eyes should have been, there was nothing but Vain's fathomless black, and I was instantly pulled back to the reminder of the demon always lurking beneath Rory's skin.

I set my jaw. "Fine. Do it."

Vain unleashed himself, attacking my mouth with his. Instinct demanded me to recoil into the wall when I first felt his tongue slip out and trace along the seam of my lips, but the warmth and the taste of him was undoing something deep inside me that I was helpless to resist. He continued his insistent dance across my mouth until my jaw relaxed, and I allowed him in. His tongue parted my lips at the invitation, and I dug my fists into the silky material of his dress shirt, half-pushing, half-pulling as my mind warred with my heart.

The kiss was possessive and hungry, fierce and unforgiving in all the ways a demon could be. No matter how hard I tried, it was impossible to imagine I was kissing Rory instead. It was his body, his mouth, his lips. But this kiss was all Vain.

*Rory.*

My cheeks heated in shame as I imagined him locked in the confines of his mind, forced to sit back and watch as Vain claimed me.

Whatever Vain had said about the kiss being nothing more than an attempt to blend in, this felt no longer like pretending. It felt all too real.

His hand shifted toward the nape of my neck. Vain slowly threaded his fingers through my hair as if he were trying to tangle himself up in me any way he could. He tugged, firm yet gentle, forcing my head to tilt upward which allowed his mouth to claim me deeper, consuming nearly all of me. A low groan of pleasure crawled up from my chest and Vain's body tightened as he let out a deep and feral growl in return.

Under normal circumstances, the sound of it and the feeling of his chest rumbling against mine would have been enough to snap my last thread of self-control. I wanted to be wild and wholly at Vain's dark mercy. He wouldn't need to glamour me, not when I was already this undone by him.

"Resorting to hiding in the shadows, Vain?"

Vain stiffened, his muscles hard as granite beneath my hands at the sound of the thick and heavy voice that stirred the quiet. He pulled away, and I opened my eyes just as the archdemon, Ghen, appeared behind Vain's shoulder. And I knew then in that moment that there would be no masking the fear that overtook me.

"We have so much to discuss."

# SIXTEEN

## RORY

Even with Vain in control, I was acutely aware of how close Ava's body remained pressed tortuously close to ours. I couldn't shake the smell of her hair, her skin. Even the taste of her was still heady on our tongue. Vain looked down at her, and I watched as her pulse thrummed against her neck, nearly toe to toe with a fucking archdemon.

Her body was taut, and her pupils were blown wide as she looked at us.

*What the hell do we do, Vain?*

*Shut up. I'm thinking!*

But Vain's mind was blank. Ghen had left him stunned, cornered like a rat in a cage with nowhere to run. Nowhere to hide.

Vain pivoted a quarter turn toward the archdemon and said, "Yes, I suppose we do."

Ghen was domineering—all broad shoulders and corded muscles. His snow-white hair was slicked back, falling just past his shoulders, and his sharp, high cheekbones and strong dark brows gave off both an air of grace and an impervious ruthlessness. He was devastatingly handsome in a mystifying and deadly sort of way.

He radiated power—*was* power—all that energy pulsing off him felt vicious and unconquerable. Even Vain winced, shrinking back at the closeness and apparent force of him.

"Did I spoil your fun?" Ghen asked, his attention moving down to Ava's mark, the temporary brand that claimed her as Vain's.

"Wouldn't be the first thing of mine you've spoiled," Vain replied apathetically.

Ghen's eyes narrowed, a frigid disquiet hanging between us.

*I hope you know what you're doing*, I told him.

"Come with me," the archdemon demanded. "And let's find Eldin too, shall we? He should be around here somewhere."

*We. Are. Fucked.*

*Keep your incessant thoughts to yourself, or I'll shut you up myself.*

*Not if Ghen kills us first,* I said, tracking the span of Ghen's very large arms and his wide chest and trying not to imagine all the ways the archdemon could shatter me in his grip, even if Vain was in control.

Vain fumed with stubborn resolve. *That won't happen.*

Ava nipped closely at our heels like a nervous puppy as we followed Ghen in search of Eldin. I wanted to reach for her, to comfort her, but Vain refused, afraid that Ghen might use her against us should he notice our connection was more than just a demon and his pet. If he noticed that she wasn't really glamoured...

As much as I understood Vain's reasoning, I hated him for it all the same. She needed us. She needed *me.*

Rounding the corner, Eldin and Vain locked eyes, then the demon's undulating tentacles went limp at the sight of Ghen leading the charge toward him. He excused himself from one of his guests—a dark-skinned demon with flowing silver braids and six ivory spider-like legs protruding from her backside that curled over her chest like armor—and approached Ghen with trepidation.

Eldin set his half-empty champagne flute on the floating tray of a passing waiter, and I took notice of how his long fingers twitched as they moved back down to his sides before he bowed his head in greeting to Ghen. Because while Ghen was a disgraced archdemon, according to Vain, he was still an archdemon nonetheless.

"The three of us need to have a word in private, Eldin," Ghen said.

"Of course, my Lord. It's an honor to host one of the Arches. If I knew you were coming—"

"Save your pathetic groveling." Ghen rolled his eyes, his tone bordering on disinterest as he said, "False flattery isn't a good look on you."

Eldin cleared his throat, eyes darting toward an empty room across the hall. "We can speak privately in the den."

Vain followed Eldin and Ghen, but as soon as we reached the doorway, the archdemon turned and placed a large hand to Vain's chest. His eyes bored into ours and I found myself transfixed by the eons held within them, dusted with the constellations and galaxies swirled in his dark gaze.

"Your little whore will remain outside. I don't care how tight a leash you've strung her on."

"She's glamour—"

Ghen tsked and said, "No more tricks, Vain. The witch stays put."

Ava still held that forced blank stare. But, if I looked hard enough, I could almost see her pleading, silent screams beneath her mask, and that little spark of fear broke me more than I ever thought possible.

I willed Vain to reach out for her again, and thankfully he did. Careful to avoid Ghen's attention, he took Ava's hand in his and gave it one quick squeeze before tearing away from her and falling in line behind Eldin.

*She'll be fine,* Vain said in an attempt to reassure me. *She can hold her own.*

*Yeah, but for how long?*

Vain gave Ava one last look that offered both a promise and an apology before Ghen shut the door, severing our connection to her.

The archdemon made himself comfortable and went to the wet bar to pour himself a drink, the clear spirit flowing greedily. He took a long, languid sip from his glass before speaking in the harshness of the demon tongue, their language that I was only able to understand thanks to the bond I shared with Vain through the possession. "Say what you will about mortals, but I always found their spirits to be far superior to ours."

Eldin straightened the lapels of his long coat and busied himself by picking off stray bits of lint from the fabric. Vain leaned against the side of a cabinet near the door, as if he were trying to stay as close to Ava as possible even with a barrier between us.

Ghen reveled in the pointed silence like he owned it and regarded it with pride. "I'd like to clear the air and start by saying how disappointed I am in the lack of foresight by the both of you. You thought that I wouldn't find out it was the two of you who broke into my home to steal from me?"

"Is it stealing if it was never yours to begin with?" Vain shot back, the sharp bite of his words cutting across the room. Eldin flinched.

Breaking into a demon nest owned by one of the most powerful archdemons had been beyond stupid, even by Vain's standards. And what made it worse was the fact that Vain continued to wave his arrogance in Ghen's face even after the unsuccessful attempt that had resulted in our capture.

"I want it back," Ghen said to Vain.

"Want what back?"

Ghen's nails tinked against the edge of his glass as he clenched his jaw. "You don't understand all of the power that grimoire holds."

"I'm sure I don't. But I won't stand on trial for merely stepping a toe out of line. You still have your treasure. No harm done."

Vain opened the door a crack to leave, but the handle slipped out of his grasp and the wood boomed shut with such a force that rattled the whole house.

The archdemon glared as he lowered his arm. "Do not," he breathed, "lie to me." I could have sworn his irises flashed white. "We are not finished here."

Vain straightened as he faced Ghen. "I don't follow the orders of a disgraced demon."

Eldin hissed in a sharp breath through his tentacles.

*What the fuck, Vain.* Had he lost his damned mind? I wanted to cower under the archdemon's menacing sneer, but whenever Vain picked his battles, he never backed down. He lifted his chin defiantly as he stared Ghen down. It was as if all of Vain's fear had melted away, and nothing but fierce and stubborn resolve burned in its place.

"I am an *archdemon*. You owe me respect."

Vain scoffed. "I owe nothing to traitors."

Ghen cocked his head, one of his brows drawing upward at Vain's apparent audacious claim. "You think *I* am the traitor?"

"It's no secret you betrayed Lilith—and for what? Your greed? Your ambitions of power? *You* chose to disgrace yourself. Now, your house and all your spawn are in ruin while you scrape the mortal realm for a pathetic grasp at claiming it for your own, all because you couldn't stand the thought of bowing to anyone, not even your own queen. Your flesh and blood."

"Do not speak like you know me, *leech*," Ghen hissed, one eye twitching as he bit back a snarl. "Not all of us were meant to waste our eternity away in subservience. I was born to rise above those that were meant to follow—above my brothers and sisters. To lead." The archdemon stabbed a finger to his chest. "I've staked my claim here and I am creating a better home for us in this realm—one far better than Lilith would ever allow should She be released from Gehenna. That book, if placed into the wrong hands, has the power to set Her free. And if Lilith is released and crosses over into the mortal realm, then She will destroy everything we've built here. Everything *I* have built!" The archdemon's voice lifted to a roar, and his eyes flashed iridescent again like twin silver moons before they returned to normal.

Still, Vain did not back down, no matter how hard I pleaded with him otherwise. "But who are you to decide whether or not Lilith is freed? Who are you to make that choice for all our kind? She has been caged for long enough."

Ghen's eyes narrowed, and a flash of recognition sparked within them. "For someone who is known to claim they don't involve themselves nor care for the affairs of archdemons, you are contradicting yourself quite vehemently, Vain."

Vain swallowed, keeping his chin raised in defiance.

The archdemon's attention flicked between us and Eldin before he continued. "Now, I will only ask you both once. Which of you has the grimoire?"

Eldin shifted in his seat across the room, his fingers fidgety, tentacles twitchy, like how an anxious cat might flick its tail.

"*You bastard*," Vain breathed as he looked at the tentacled demon. "You did take it."

Vain crossed the room in a blur. He raised one arm, slamming Eldin against the wall. The surge of power lit up my nerves like a lightning bolt to my system. Every blood vessel, every hair, every molecule in me sang with Vain's power. It was addicting, especially when he lashed out in anger. It felt like the biggest hit of dopamine, of ecstasy. The pleasure was near soul-shattering.

Vain slipped out of using the demon tongue as he growled at Eldin through gritted teeth. "I hope it was fucking worth it, you snake."

He edged closer, leaning in to bask in the scent of Eldin's fear, gripping tightly onto the lapels of the demon's coat. I was faintly aware of a weight being dropped into the inner pocket lining of our jacket. Vain's eyes widened slightly before releasing Eldin and backing away.

"Restraint?" Ghen crooned. "How disappointing..." The curved bone-white tooth pendant that hung from his neck jumped against his chest as he laughed.

The archdemon took one last greedy gulp of his drink and then suspended the empty tumbler in the air above his palm before he let it drop with a crash. Crystal shards glittered across the floor.

"Where is it, Eldin?" Ghen asked. "I know you've hidden it close."

Eldin addressed the archdemon, but never took his eyes off Vain. "I did take it, but I don't have it anymore."

Ghen sniffed at the air, glass shards crunching under his shoes as he stalked closer. "Liar."

The archdemon's hand arced through the air, and Eldin released a strangled cry of pain as a severed tentacle splattered to the floor. It jumped and skittered as ichor pooled around it, making the most nauseating squelching sounds.

"My patience is not endless, though I will cut through every last appendage you have until you break if that's what it will take."

Eldin grimaced as ichor continued to ooze to his feet. He lifted his eyes to Ghen and spat, saliva and ichor spraying the archdemon's shoes. "I am no traitor to Lilith."

The dark brows over Ghen's equally dark eyes drew together, his sharp mouth turning up into a sneer.

"I will also not bow to an inferior who thinks himself a king," Eldin continued.

Another slice.

Eldin howled, clutching at a second gushing stump.

The archdemon advanced a step, his hand raised, ready to send out another cleaving blow. "You are a fool to give the Dark Mother such blind loyalty, Eldin."

"I'd rather be a fool than your hound," Eldin muttered. His eyes burned with the fire of the sun, and his voice rumbled low and dark in his chest. "Long has She suffered. And long may She reign." A silver tipped selenite blade flashed in Eldin's hand before he sliced across his own throat. Vain stumbled backward as Eldin gurgled on the tar-black ichor as it spilled from his open neck. The demon's tentacles still writhed, even after the last bit of light dimmed from his saurian eyes.

Disappointment glanced across Ghen's features as he rolled his jaw at the sight of the ichor pooling around Eldin's slumped body.

*Now would be a really good time to get the hell out of here,* I urged.

I never wished to be in control of my body more than in that moment. Our feet felt like they were burning straight through the floor, aching to run. But Vain refused to budge.

*What the hell, man? What are you doing?*

Still, Vain did not move.

Ghen sucked his teeth and then slowly raised his gaze to us, a stormy nebula swirled in his eyes.

Vain casually dug into the pockets of his jacket, his right hand wrapping around the round metal object he had stashed there "as a precaution", he'd told me earlier.

"Where is it?" Ghen hissed.

"I haven't the slightest idea, but I'm sure you'll find it eventually if you turn this whole place inside out…I'll leave you to it."

Ghen roared, outstretching one arm towards Vain. An invisible force slammed into our chest, throwing us backwards into the wall with a resounding crack. Vain scrambled to our feet, already anticipating another attack. As powerful as Vain was, his power was limited by him being restricted to my human body.

"And will you also be professing your loyalty to Lilith before I tear your pathetic little vessel to shreds?"

Vain let out a short cold laugh as he thumbed at the blood that had trailed out at the corner of our lips. "I hold no loyalty to Lilith or any of the Arches. Like you, I prefer not to bow to those I deem beneath me."

Ghen unleashed a treacherous wide-lipped smile. "It's a shame you've confined yourself to this pathetic form. I was hoping for a fair fight."

"At least this one is nice to look at," Vain sneered.

"For what it's worth, I much prefer your first iteration," Ghen said with a knowing glint in his eyes. "I know exactly who you are, *Vain*."

Vain straightened and grimaced at the archdemon. "Then let's stop pretending, shall we?"

Ghen lunged with inhuman speed, becoming nothing more than a blur of movement as he barreled toward us. I braced for the impact.

But it never came.

At the last possible second, Vain matched the archdemon's speed and sidestepped as if he had anticipated exactly how Ghen would move against him.

Vain was ready for the second attack when Ghen's power lashed out again. He rolled to dodge it, but Ghen was quicker. The archdemon redirected and slammed his energy into our chest, knocking us back and forcing all the air from our lungs.

The energy in the room sharpened as Ghen sent a cut made of shadow through the air, flying toward our head. I registered it all too slowly, but Vain reacted just fast enough for me to feel the edge of it graze our cheek, and I hissed internally at the stinging heat it left behind.

Ghen chuckled darkly as he reared his power back, strong enough that I could feel the force of it as it built within him—a climactic, crushing blow. Feet lifting off the floor, he flew across the room with a preternatural speed, a raging tempest which Vain met in force, bracing both arms in front of him.

Bulging black veins protruded against the pale skin of Ghen's temples. Vain ground our teeth together as he strained to hold the archdemon back, but I could feel his control slipping at the effort.

The archdemon smiled. "I don't know how I didn't see it until now. You certainly hid yourself well all this time."

"Or perhaps you were too proud to look." Vain groaned with the force of holding Ghen back. Contained in my body, he wasn't strong enough to hold out for much longer against the archdemon. And he knew it as well as I did.

Digging deep down into his well of power, Vain drew up enough to throw out a surge of energy that sent the archdemon stumbling backward halfway across the room.

Black flames tipped in shades of red ignited at Ghen's fingertips until they engulfed his hand and the fire had swelled into a brilliant orb, hot enough to melt the mortal flesh from my bones. Ghen hurled it toward Vain, who deftly dodged the attack, and the flaming ball sailed through the air and crashed into the curtains, sending them up in flames in an explosion of sparks and searing embers.

It was the distraction Vain needed. Reaching into his pocket, his hand closed around the cold metal of the grenade before he shot it straight at Ghen's feet where it exploded into a heavy battering of silver and selenite shards. Vain threw himself out of the worst of the blast, leaving the archdemon to choke and sputter as he inhaled the cloud of silver dust left behind that burned his lungs, followed by a roar that felt like it tore at the very fabric of reality.

Vain choked back a cough as he held his breath against the suffocating combination of the remnants left from the dust cloud and the billowing smoke as the black and red fire caught every surface like kindling.

The archdemon fell to his knees and Vain surged forward, driving the short selenite blade he'd hidden up his sleeve deep into Ghen's heart. It wasn't nearly enough to kill him—not that I was sure of anything that could kill an archdemon—but it could at the very least give us enough time to escape.

Vain shot toward the exit, daring one last look at Ghen who clutched at his chest, ichor flowing from the wounds left by the shrapnel and the blade.

"It won't take me long to find you," he rasped. "You run, and I will burn through everything and everyone in my way until I get to you."

With the echo of Ghen's words on his heels, Vain left the archdemon on the floor of the burning room behind him, and he ran.

Bursting into the hallway, the guests were frantic. Vain scanned the panicked crowd for Ava, but she was nowhere to be found. And the mark on our wrist...the mark was burning.

# SEVENTEEN

## AVA

I stood frozen outside that door for what felt like minutes, unable to move. Alone in a house full of demons, I felt cornered without Vain by my side, and all their stares were starting to make my skin crawl, and I was desperate to escape them.

My blood prickled as it tore through my veins, and every nerve under my flesh buzzed as my vision tunneled while I struggled to take in a full breath.

In our last look before the door shut between us, Vain's eyes had been pleading, almost seeming to say *"Everything will be alright. Do not move. I will find you."*

But everything was not alright. And I wanted to run.

Unlocking my legs, I fled through the crowd, not caring who watched as I narrowly missed stumbling into multiple demons, and found an empty bathroom to shut myself inside.

Wrapping my hands around the edge of the sink, I leaned into it and tried to ease the trembling in my core, reverberating off every bone in my body.

Ghen was here—an archdemon in the flesh. Every time I tried to swallow the panic, I gagged, my fear tasting like ash in my mouth.

"

*How could you do this?*

No.

*It should have been you.*

My grip on the sink tightened until the burning ache in my knuckles matched the pain in my chest. I braved a glance into the mirror, and my attention went to the V on my neck, the skin around it an irritated shade of pink.

What if he never came back for me? What if Ghen left him as nothing more than a mangled, bloody corpse? How was I going to get out of this?

Raucous laughter from outside made me lurch. I gripped the cool marble tighter as I continued to suck down breath after slow breath.

The door to the bathroom jerked open, and I jumped away. I raised my hands to attack, a hex sparking at my fingertips, half-expecting a demon, maybe even Ghen himself, to be the one barging through. But it was a human, a young woman who was just as painfully mortal as I was.

I recognized her as the same woman from earlier, the one Ilo had strung at his side to display proudly as his pet for the other ravenous demons in attendance. When she looked up and realized she wasn't alone, she jerked and scrambled for the door handle.

"Wait, wait! I'm not going to hurt you." I let my magic fall away and I reached for her.

The woman panted, but she stayed pressed against the door, cowering away from me. Her lips trembled, and her watery eyes seemed to plead with me through the blonde and bubblegum pink strands of her hair that had fallen out of her ponytail.

"Please, I can't take it anymore. If you're going to kill me, just do it. I'd rather die than be with him." Her wobbly legs gave out, and she slumped to the floor, sobbing.

I knelt in front of her and gently placed my hands on her bruise-covered arms. Angry red marks from claws and teeth scarred across her neck. She looked so young, so frail. Sallow cheeks and haunted eyes. Skin and bones. A sunken girl. A shell of who she had once been.

A hollow sense of gratitude burrowed deep in my chest for my luck that Vain was not the cruel and malevolent beast Ilo was.

"I won't kill you. I promise. I'm a witch. I can help you."

A sliver of distrust passed over her face when I'd said the word witch. Many humans had preconceived notions about us. Even as we fought to protect our world from the dark, unholy monsters that slipped in through the rifts, our power scared them because they couldn't understand it or where it came from. And now that I knew the truth myself—that our kind had been molded and formed from the very beings we fought—I couldn't exactly blame them.

"What's your name?" I asked, keeping my voice low and soft.

Her chin trembled again. "Dru."

"Dru," I repeated. "I'm Ava. Take deep breaths for me, okay, Dru?"

Her chest heaved, each breath strained in between her choking sobs. "Please, you don't know what it's like. I'd rather die. *I'd rather die.*"

I rested my hands on her shoulders and let her breathe as a plan stirred in my head. If Vain wasn't going to save me, then I would have to save myself. And I would save Dru.

"Listen to me, Dru. I'm going to get us out of here. But I need you to trust me. Can you do that?"

She furiously shook her head. "No, no, no. He'll find me. He always finds me." Tears welled in her eyes before breaking like a dam. They streamed down her cheeks as her jaw trembled. "I can't go through that again. Not again. Pleasepleose*please*, no."

"He won't. He *won't.*" I told her.

I reached down into my power, letting it swell within me as I let my hands hover in the air over Dru. My fingers felt clumsy as I controlled the magic and drew out a spell I hadn't practiced in years. Illusion charms weren't easy and required a skilled and steady hand to get just right, but I managed to manipulate the aura around Dru's form, coaxing the spell around her until she became a mirage-like figure in front of me. When she moved, the air shimmered, but she remained mostly imperceptible, save for the sound of her still-heavy breathing. Then I repeated the same spell on myself until the two of us were nearly undetectable. I just had to hope it would be enough to fool the demons.

"We're walking out of here together," I said. "You and me."

"I...I'm scared. There're too many demons here. It's im-im...it's impossible."

"Trust me. Everything is going to be fine."

The air around Dru quivered as I assumed she nodded.

"Hold on to me."

"Okay," Dru croaked and latched onto my wrist as we stood.

I took one last steady breath and eased the door open cautiously before stepping into the hallway. Maneuvering around the unsuspecting demons, we made our way toward the staircase, down and down until we reached the first floor.

Luckily, none of the demons seemed to notice our presence nor did we catch sight of Ilo searching for Dru. But I wasn't holding out hope that couldn't change. It was only a matter of time until the demon came looking.

The crowd was thick at the base of the stairs, making it impossible for us to worm our way through to the front door. Tugging Dru with me, we slunk between multiple groups of demons, holding our breaths the whole way until we reached the back door and slipped out into the night.

"Keep close," I whispered as we tiptoed across the patio along the shadows of a tall, manicured hedge. Once we cleared them, we slipped out of our heels and broke into a run toward a small park surrounded by a jogging path dotted with streetlamps and ginkgo trees. To the right, the street that ran along the river lay dark and empty. The silence was unnerving. The only sound was our labored breathing as we slumped against a tree trunk.

"We should keep moving," Dru gasped through her shaky breaths.

I could only nod as I gulped down more air, ignoring the twinging ache in my left hand as we jogged silently through the trees. A sharp pain lanced up my arm and it felt like barbed wire was digging into the skin around my wrist, stopping me dead in my tracks before I'd made it even a few feet.

The fucking mark.

I'd put too much distance between myself and Vain. Dru firmly tugged at my other arm, which she still clung to. "Come on, we have to keep going!"

If I could have removed the mark right there, I would have. But breaking the tether would require me to break Rory's mark at the same time. And without him here, it was impossible. I marveled at my own stupidity and stubbornness, but I refused to subject Dru to the same fate. There was still a chance for her to escape, and I would not drag her down with me.

"I'm sorry," I said, straining through the pain of the burning ache that was slowly radiating up my forearm. "I can't go any farther. You need to get past that tree line and run."

"No, don't leave me, please! I can't go alone!" Dru pleaded as she gripped my arm tighter than before. When I tried to push her off of me, she refused to budge.

"Dru, you have to run."

The back of my neck prickled and I spun around, squinting into the trees only to find nothing staring back. Still, I had a gnawing sensation that there were eyes watching us from the shadows, and that lingering unease sent goosebumps washing over every inch of my skin. What was worse was that all around us was nothing but dead silence, as if every living thing, even the air itself, was holding its breath. Quiet. Watching. Waiting.

"I can smell you, little witch," Ilo's slick voice called from somewhere behind us and we both jerked, tensing at the sound. "Your fear...it's intoxicating."

Dru let out a strangled cry next to me. I shushed her as I struggled to find her mouth to clamp my hand over it.

"Did you really think you could get away with stealing from me?" The demon tsked. "Very, very naughty."

I whipped my head around toward the sound of his voice, but Ilo wasn't there. The demon kept to the shadows, lurking in every corner of the dark as he sent out tendrils of dread to comb through the trees.

"There you are."

The demon came into view over Dru's shoulder with a vicious smile cut wide across his face. Not even Vain's eyes could compare to the dark black pits of Ilo's as he prowled closer, pinning me to the spot when he fixed them on me through my illusion charm. With a wave of his hand in front of my face, the charm melted off me, and I had never felt so bare in all my life.

Ilo squeezed the hollows of my cheeks with surprisingly claw-like fingers for a human vessel. They dug into my flesh like spears of ice.

"Vain always did have poor taste in pets," Ilo crooned. His wet tongue flashed across his lips, and my back pressed into the rough bark of the tree.

The ache of the mark on my wrist was a continuous burn. A desperate gnawing pang coursed through my body, with each pulse spreading further up my arm and across my chest as the tether between me and Vain stretched precariously thin. If pulled too far apart, this pain would destroy us both.

Vain would come. He would come for me.

As long as Ghen didn't destroy him first.

Dru cowered at my feet, and Ilo's head snapped to her at the sound of her muffled whimpers.

"Save your tears, little one. You'll cry for me later." He waved his other hand over the crown of Dru's head, and her obscuration charm fell away like sand, revealing her trembling form as she curled in on herself.

When Ilo spoke, I could feel the slick icy energy curling in the air around us, clinging to Dru most of all. A wave of nausea struck me at the realization. The demon was *creating* fear, then siphoning the elicited terror, feeding off it like a drug. It was no wonder Dru appeared so broken. I shuddered to imagine the horrible nightmares Ilo had forced Dru to endure, the unimaginable horrors he'd inflicted upon her both mentally and physically, all so he could use that fear he induced and take from her until she had nothing left to give.

"You've been very bad, Drusilla," Ilo rasped, leaning down to her. *"Tell me you love me, and maybe I'll forgive you."*

I could practically taste the glamour as it swirled past me and took hold of Dru. Her eyes became wide and glassy, and her sobs shoved themselves back down her throat as her body visibly re-laxed.

She leaned in towards the demon. Her voice went hollow, the sound tinny as she spoke. "I love you, Ilo."

"That's my good pet," the demon preened.

Ilo's head whipped around unnaturally fast as his attention flicked back to me. With the steeled grip of his fingers still digging into my cheeks, he turned my face to the left and then to the right as he studied me with an intense curiosity. I braced myself for a glamour to come my way next. I had been trained to resist demon glamours my whole life, but I knew I was susceptible to them eventually. I was still mortal after all.

An icy claw skittered across my mental walls, probing their strength, looking for any weakness.

"I was right." Ilo chuckled to himself. "I knew exactly who you were when I laid my eyes on you...*Helacourt*." He whispered my name into my face, and I was assaulted with the faintest tang of sulfur on his breath.

"Your name has quite a reputation amongst certain circles of ours," he continued. "The legacy witch who summoned one of the fiercest demons to ever walk the realms...I'm curious, what did you hope to gain by summoning him? Was it power you were after? Or were you simply trying to prove that you could?"

Ilo's fingers sharpened their grip on my face, and I hated the whimper that tore from my throat.

"Ahh, the latter, then." His eyes flicked down to my mouth, then crept back up to bore into mine. "You know he's here tonight, don't you? I wonder how thankful he might be if I were to hand you over to him. How grateful would he be to finally be able to finish with you what he started with your sister?"

Every last bit of air in my lungs turned to ice, and the world around me seemed to go still. It was as if I'd suddenly forgotten how to breathe.

"You wouldn't," I said with as much of a snarl as I could muster, trying to stall for as long as I could before Vain or someone—any-one—would arrive.

No one was coming.

I cringed against the whispers of fear trying to worm their way around my heart and seep into the edges of my mind.

The demon's smile was cruel. "No, you're right. Because I think I'd much rather keep such a pretty thing like you all for myself."

"If you do, you're dead," I said, hoping the demon wasn't able to detect the slight wobble that came out with it.

Ilo clicked his tongue, and then the tip of it flicked out across his lips. I caught another rotten whiff of his breath and cringed further back. "I do not fear Vain. Especially not when Ghen has his sights set on him. I would surmise he may even be dead already. So, I'm free to take that little taste of you I've been yearning for."

I shivered as he raked his knuckles down my cheek. With his dark gaze focused solely on my face, I took advantage of his dis-tracted attention and inched one hand up past the slit of my dress to reach for the selenite dagger I'd strapped around my thigh.

I gripped the handle tightly and arced the blade straight at the demon's neck. I knew that I should aim for the heart instead, but if

I could disable him, even for a second, I could attempt to exorcise Ilo from his vessel. I had to at least try.

But before my knife even came close to grazing him, Ilo knocked my hand away with a simple flick of his wrist, and the blade fell into the grass. The demon leaped on me, smashing his hands to my temples to invade my mind and bring my most suppressed nightmares to the forefront.

*The room is impossibly black. The darkness feels like its own entity. The shadows are alive. They feed off my fear as my heart leaps from my chest, a hollow ache clawing at my lungs. My blood pounds in my eardrums, nearly deafening me.*

*The darkness is hungry. And I let it out.*

*This wasn't supposed to happen. Not like this. Sascha. I need to find Sascha.*

*I don't dare speak. Not a single sound.*

*There is something else here with us now. Something not of this realm.*

*My feet feel as if they're anchored to the floor. My instincts scream at me to run, to get away. Fast.*

*But I can't leave her. I can feel that Sascha is still here. There's a prickling sensation at the back of my neck telling me that whatever else is here is close. I won't leave without her.*

*I claw my way through the darkness, one feather-light step at a time, reaching out for something, anything, anyone.*

*I'm acutely aware of the sound of my breathing as it comes out shaky through my nose. I'm so focused on it that I almost miss the low, dragging inhale from across the room.*

*My foot connects with a burned-out candle I had set around the chalk pentagram, and it topples over. I wince as it clatters and rolls away into the shadows.*

*I stumble toward the breathing and nearly fall to my knees when I make out Sascha's fiery red hair. She's facing away from me, and her arms are wrapped around her knees as she curls into herself.*

*The wave of relief is so sweeping that I don't notice the sense of wrongness surrounding her at first. Something is warped. Corrupted. But it's too late. I clasp onto her shoulder.*

*I turn Sascha to face me, and the demon inside her flashes me a wicked grin and obsidian eyes threaten to swallow me up.*

*The darkness consumed her. And it wants to take me next.*

I jolted back to my senses with a sputtering gasp. The trunk of the ginkgo tree sliced into my bare back and the stench of Ilo's rotten breath invaded my nostrils, clawing down my throat. The burning ache radiating from my mark was an insistent throbbing pulse that matched the racing beat of my heart. Ilo's wide slimy grin churned my stomach as the demon's fingers clutched both sides of my face.

He let out a contented exhale against my cheeks, and I gagged at the stench. "Your fear is *so* sweet. I will very much enjoy having you all to myself."

Ilo curled a hand around the nape of my neck as if I were a stray dog, then reached down with the other to yank Dru up by her ponytail. No magic I had left would have been strong enough to fight against him. I kicked his legs and clawed at his arms, but every blow felt weak, and Ilo chuckled darkly at my futile efforts.

He gripped me tight, and I could feel his power gathering, knowing exactly what he intended, and yet I was still unprepared for when it happened. In seconds, we shifted, and it felt as if my soul were being cleaved in two as the world fell away around us.

I couldn't tell when we landed, or where.

I had no sense of the ground beneath my feet or my surroundings. There was nothing except the mind-shattering pain ripping through my entire body.

The agony shredded through me, tearing me apart from the inside. I screamed.

It wasn't just my wrist. It was every inch of me. I was being set on fire. My bones hammered beneath my flesh like they were being pulverized to dust.

I wanted to die.

The only sounds I was aware of were my wailing cries and the blood whooshing loud against my eardrums.

The tether between Vain and I was hair-thin, stretched so far that I knew there was no chance of the connection holding for much longer. When it finally broke, it might very well kill us both.

"Shut up, you stupid cunt," Ilo hissed through my screams and then wrenched me off the ground as the tremors wracked my body. I writhed against his hold. "What the fuck is wrong with you?"

Dru's hands grasped for me as Ilo managed to yank me up.

I couldn't hold onto consciousness much longer. My vision was starting to go dark, and an icy numbness seeped into my bones, hollowing out my chest. I wanted it to end. I wanted it to stop.

A deafening crack sounded from behind us, breaking through my screams, followed by a wave of soothing calm that enveloped all my senses as if all the pain had been nothing more than a bad dream. It was like a band had snapped back into place, and I gasped. The dark fuzzy edges of my vision receded, and the seedy alleyway where Ilo had shifted us came into view.

Dru whimpered as she clawed her way over me before she buried herself against my chest.

A familiar energy radiated from somewhere close by. And for the first time, I was relieved to feel it. I craned my neck back to look toward the source. An imposing, dark figure stood in the mouth of the alley. Shadows, furious and deadly, whipped around him, licking at the ground like flames.

I only caught a glimpse of Ilo's shocked expression before Vain threw himself on the demon in a blur of movement, slamming him against a far wall with such force that a crack split through the brick facade. Vain snatched Ilo's throat and squeezed hard enough that the veins in his hand bulged.

"Only I," Vain spoke with a vicious snarl, "can leave a mark on that witch. *I* laid my claim to her. And you still touched what is *mine*."

Ilo trembled under Vain's grasp. "A mistake!" The demon pleaded. "It was a mistake, Vain."

"You mistake my warning as mercy." A low growl rumbled from deep within Vain's chest. "It is not. It is a promise of vengeance."

"Wait, wait. *Wait!*"

The voice that ripped out of Ilo's throat was...desperately raw and human and lacked that slick rasping quality from before. Ilo had handed control back to his vessel, and the young man's blue eyes searched Vain's for any shred of leniency.

"Please don't," he pleaded, lips trembling. "I don't want to die. Kill him. But please...don't kill me."

Vain's eyes narrowed on the human, but it felt as if he was looking straight through him. His hands shook as he fisted them in the young man's collar. "It's too late for you, boy. You're already dead."

The man paled before his eyes filled with black as Ilo wrenched back control of his vessel to fight Vain. But Vain's hands were already at the demon's throat, and the terrifying speed at which he clawed into the soft flesh was inhuman. Red blood spurted from Ilo's vessel as the demon's screams tore through the night. Teeth quickly replaced hands as Vain ripped into Ilo's jugular with all the preternatural strength and brutality he possessed.

There was no stopping him, not even when he dug deep into the man's chest with savage animalism, fury etched into every line of his face and glinting off his bared, bloody teeth.

I stared, awed at the pure violence of it. The monstrous cruelty. How in the moment, I couldn't see Rory at all. There was nothing human about him. All of the rage and the brutal tearing and ripping of flesh, that was all Vain.

All I could do was hold Dru to me, even after Ilo's vessel slumped down and the last bits of life in him drained at his feet in a river of crimson. Amidst the blood and bits of flesh, a dark smoke poured from the man's mangled corpse, slinking along the pavement until the dark shape coalesced into something material and Ilo's true form became visible.

I had to squint against the darkness to see him, and when I did, I immediately wished I hadn't.

Ilo looked like a creature born of midnight. It was impossible to make out any defining features of its face except for two unblinking, beady red eyes and a lipless mouth that cut across his face from ear to ear and displayed a row of serrated yellowed teeth. The demon's wiry arms clawed at the ground as he attempted to drag his body away, scraping through the pool of blood and sinew across the asphalt.

Vain's rage was like a living thing. His whole body shook with it as he plucked up the demon with one hand by the throat and held him high.

"*Pathetic,*" Vain snarled.

His other hand wrapped around the demon's forearm. Then he pulled. He pulled so hard that the pop reverberated in my eardrums as Ilo's arm ripped out of the socket and a rain of ichor spewed from the wound. Vain didn't stop there though. His insatiable need to hurt—to destroy—seemed to be an endless pit. With each tear and every rip of the demon's flesh, the glint in Vain's eyes only grew brighter.

Ilo's howls faded to gasping groans as his ichor sprayed everywhere, a few drops landing on my lips. Unconsciously, I swept my tongue across them and instantly regretted it the second I tasted the warm substance. The demon's ichor was sour and tasted more rotten than his breath. I wanted to gag to keep from swallowing.

But it was too late.

The ichor slid down my throat, and with it came a rush of power as it swelled and warmed in my chest. I had never felt anything like it before.

Ilo's body was nothing more than a carved-up slab of meat, a heap of sinew, scraps of bone, and a puddle of ichor.

Vain released what was left of the demon, and it smacked onto the ground with a heavy squelching sound.

His swirling mass of shadows dissipated before Vain crouched in front of me, onyx eyes coming into view. Splatters of blood and ichor lashed across his face, dripping off his chin as they traced his features in dark lines. I couldn't tell if I reached for him first or if he was the one who pulled me to him, but my face burrowed into his chest all the same. His arms gathered me up, holding me tightly against him.

"You came for me," I said, sighing into him.

Vain moved one hand from my back to cradle my head and lightly stroked my hair. "Perhaps you misunderstood me before, mellilla." He spoke with the velvety darkness I had once feared, but now couldn't have been more grateful to hear. "I will do anything to protect what is mine."

# EIGHTEEN

## AVA

Vain shifted us outside onto the rooftop balcony of the penthouse, still tangled in each other's arms with Dru by our side.

Alastair and Nesera rushed out toward us. Dru scrambled away from Alastair at the sight of him. I couldn't blame her for being so untrusting after having just escaped a demon like Ilo. Seeming to note her hesitation, Alastair let Nesera help her instead. She returned with a soft blanket and draped it around Dru's shoulders, telling her she'd help get her cleaned up and into some fresh clothes before walking her inside.

Alastair bent down next to me, and I became faintly aware that he was speaking. He sounded far away as he blinked at me with all three sets of emerald eyes. It was the first time they had all appeared open at once, and I found that I was fascinated by them more than I was startled. I nodded at him and allowed him to peel me off Vain and help me to stand.

"I'm okay," I muttered.

When I looked down, Vain was no longer in control. Rory knelt, shell-shocked, his eyes distant and hazy. His dark hair, which was still soaked and dripping with Ilo's ichor and his vessel's blood, fell over his face in shining ringlets.

"I'll help him," I told Alastair. "I need valerian, saffron, and chamomile...crushed amethyst too." I named off everything to draft a calming elixir. "Do you have all that?"

"If not, I can find some."

"As fast as you can, please," I said, voice straining. "He's in shock."

"I'll get what you need," Alastair said and retreated back inside.

I lowered myself to my knees in front of Rory and placed my hands on either side of his face, urging his eyes to meet mine.

"We're going to stand together, alright? Come on."

I guided Rory's hands to my forearms and lifted him by the sides of his abdomen until we were both more or less standing with his weight leaned against me.

"Damn you, Vain," I cursed under my breath as I guided Rory inside to the bathroom adjoining his room. How could he leave Rory in control after he had put them both through an ordeal like that? And what the hell had happened after Ghen pulled them aside?

I had to get Rory into the shower so he could wash the sickening smell of the ichor off him. The stench permeated the air, reminding me of Ilo's hot, rotten breath against my face.

"Can you get in by yourself?" I asked, turning the knobs. Hot water instantly streamed down from the large rain showerhead.

Rory merely nodded.

I tugged the jacket from his shoulders. There was an odd weight to it, and it fell to the floor with a soft, dampened thud. I turned away to find some spare towels and to allow him some privacy to strip the rest of his clothes by himself.

Vain's bathroom was obscenely large. I turned to the double vanity carved from a slab of black quartz and scoured the cabinets underneath. I grabbed a handful of fluffy towels and turned back to the shower only to find Rory sitting on the tiled floor directly under the showerhead, still fully clothed. His arms were propped on his knees, his head hung between them, allowing the steaming water to run over his neck.

I didn't ask for permission before entering the shower with him, the hot water instantly plastering the thin fabric of my dress to my skin.

Rory didn't object when I removed the tattered glove from his left hand or when I tugged the hem of his shirt and undid all the buttons to peel it away, exposing the slightly tanned skin of his chest and the dizzying number of tattoos crawling up both arms.

The water beneath him ran black, gray, and pink. Bits of flesh, both demon and human, slid down and settled above the drain. I nervously went to undo his belt, but as soon as my hand touched the buckle, he stiffened.

"I can do it." His voice sounded hoarse, similar to the first time I heard it in the Hull.

I leaned against the wall to give him some space as he struggled to peel off his slacks and boxer-briefs, finally shucking them off and wadding them into a sopping pile in one corner.

"Are you okay?" I asked.

A pause. "I should be asking you that."

"I'm fine."

Rory tipped his head back against the tiles with a *thunk*. I watched the rivulets of water trace the soft ringlets of his dark hair, across his cheeks, racing down his jawline, dripping onto his very bare chest. He kept his eyes closed as he breathed in deep amongst the wafts of steam, keeping both legs tucked into his chest which shielded his lower half from view.

After a minute of heavy silence, Rory tried uncapping the shampoo bottle next to his head, but his hands shook so violently, he lost his grip. The plastic clattered loudly, skittering across the floor.

"Fuck," he breathed out shakily. His Adam's apple bobbed as if he were trying to hold back a strangled sob.

"Let me," I said, more of a quiet request for permission than a statement.

Rory dipped his chin in silent agreement, still refusing to meet my gaze. I inched across the shower floor and shifted to my knees. I squeezed some shampoo into my palms and lathered it up, then began to massage the suds through his scalp with gentle fingers. The scent of spice and apples filled my nose, diluting the smell of the ichor. The water ran in varying shades of pink and gray, and I scrubbed and scoured until it finally ran clear.

"I was there for all of it." He mumbled the words so softly that I almost didn't realize he had spoken at all. I stopped moving and stared at him.

"What did you say?"

"I-I felt everything," he said. "I...killed him."

I squeezed my eyes shut at the memory of Vain tearing into Ilo's vessel. The human hadn't stood a chance.

"That wasn't you, Rory. That was Vain."

Rory lifted his gaze, his eyes sharpened with devastating anguish, and he clenched his hands into tight fists. "No, Ava. I...we both did. I wanted to kill him. *Fuck,* did I want to. And I'm not sorry about it."

The slight tremble in his voice broke me, his words leaving me speechless.

"The second that demon captured you and shifted you away, Vain and I felt it. The pain was...unbearable." A hard lump formed in my throat as Rory continued. "Vain found you thanks to the mark and when we saw you splayed on the ground with the demon forcing himself on you...I've never known anger like that before. Vain's rage consumed mine. I didn't care about Ilo's vessel. I wanted to tear them—both of them—apart. And I was happy to do it. I enjoyed the feeling of their flesh under my nails, their blood on my skin. Because he had hurt you. So, I wanted him to hurt."

"Rory..."

He rolled his head to the side and peered back at me through his hair.

"I don't feel guilty for it. I should. But I don't. The only thing we feel guilty about is putting you in danger in the first place. Vain can't even look you in the eyes because he feels so heavy with it."

Rory swallowed. "Vain is blaming himself. He doesn't want to see you hurt, Ava, ever again. And neither do I."

All of the words I wanted to say got caught in my mouth. "It's not either of your faults," I reassured him.

Rory wrapped one hand around my wrist. Bands of ichor were still encrusted under his fingernails, and I couldn't help but stare at where his knuckles had split from the repeated beatings Vain had delivered.

He brought his other hand up to my face in a gentle caress before his fingers combed through the wet strands of my hair. His eyes trailed across every inch of my face, and it felt almost as if he were looking at me for the first time.

"We thought we lost you. But it won't ever happen again. I promise."

The sincerity and desperation in his words held a weight I wasn't prepared for. He spoke like he...like he cared about me. My chest tightened suddenly, my expression stuttered. My lips parted, but no sound escaped them, so I pressed them shut again, completely unsure how to respond. What words could be enough when his admission wrenched at my heart, and the few inches of my skin that he touched felt as if he were igniting a fire in my blood?

Rory must have noticed my hesitation, because he cleared his throat and broke eye contact before releasing me. "I can finish up. You should go. Let Alastair know if you need anything."

"But your hands..." I reached for him again. "Let me bandage them."

Rory drew back. "They'll heal. Just go." His voice was cold. He dragged a hand down his face and hung his head again so the water made his hair into a dark curtain, shutting me out.

I rinsed the remaining suds from my hands and left him, not caring that I was still soaking wet and leaving a trail along the floor as I made my way back to my room.

My wrist ached, and the ghost of Rory's touch remained as a faint memory on my skin. Even his words had left me rattled, and I couldn't shake the echo of them, no matter how hard I tried.

✮  ✮  ✮

After pouring the steaming elixir into a mug, I passed it off to Alastair. "Bring this to him, please."

The demon blinked back at me, and it felt like each of his eyes held a different emotion. He hadn't left my side since the moment I'd stepped foot into the kitchen. He was quiet and attentive as he watched me work. "Ava, you're shaking. Are you sure you're alright?"

"I'm fine," I said too quickly. When I poured the next mug, I fought to keep my hands steady. "I'll take this one to her."

Sweeping past Alastair and out of the kitchen, I found Dru in one of the guest rooms and told her to drink. She was apprehensive at first, but once she'd swallowed the last few drops, she sank into the bed and drifted off quickly. I stayed with her for about an hour after that, just watching her and occasionally stroking her head to soothe her if I noticed her jerking in her sleep. It was the least I could do for her, and it still didn't feel like enough.

When I eventually returned to my room and crashed into bed, my sleep was fitful and restless. Flashes of the memories that Ilo had dragged up were still drifting on the surface of my mind, plaguing my dreams and my nightmares with unsettling clarity.

I woke in the middle of the night to a faint, haunting melody floating throughout the penthouse. Peeling my eyelids open, I squinted at the thin slivers of light peeking through a break in the heavy curtains. The echoes of the stringed music were rich and melancholy, and I laid there for a while just listening in the dark, my face cold as I shifted on the pillow which was still damp from the shower earlier.

With my nerves still frayed from my encounters with both Ilo and Ghen, I decided that I had no hope of falling back asleep, so instead, I slipped out into the hallway in an oversized T-shirt that hung past my thighs and made my way through the penthouse in search of the source of the music.

It didn't take me long to find it. Rory sat in the middle of the darkened great room, his chair facing the tall panoramic windows with a cello between his thighs. He was bare-chested, and a pair of gray sweatpants hung low on his hips. I kept my distance, not wanting him to notice me or stop in the middle of the beautiful song.

The melody was filled with immeasurable longing, deep and resonant. The tempo was slow, rising up into rich and powerful crescendos and then falling down into soft droning lulls. Each glance of the bow across the strings filled my chest with a familiar ache, and the vibrato that hung in the air whenever his wrist rocked against the neck of the cello made my heart swell. The bow slowed before it tapered off the strings and the final note echoed into silence. Rory's shoulders slumped forward, all the tension he'd been holding in his posture releasing at once.

"Rory?"

His head half-turned in my direction slowly, like he'd already sensed me before I had spoken. "How'd you know it was me and not Vain?"

"It's the way you hold yourself. You're more...relaxed. It's a subtle difference, but I think I can tell now."

Rory sighed softly through his nose. "Did I wake you?"

"Yes, but it was a beautiful song. I don't think I know it."

"You wouldn't. It's one of theirs." The way he said *theirs*, I understood he was referring to the demons. "Vain's fond of it. He hums it in my head all the time, so I play it sometimes. I think it's comforting to him."

I shifted my weight to my other foot. "I didn't know you played." I realized I didn't know a lot about Rory. And maybe I wouldn't mind learning more if he let me.

He rested the bow across his lap. "I used to play professionally before..."

Before he was possessed. Before Vain. The unspoken words cleaved through my chest.

"I didn't mean to interrupt you. I'll leave you to keep playing." I sounded like an idiot.

"No." Rory's voice stopped me in my tracks. "Stay."

I stood achingly still, unsure of myself, unsure of what he wanted.

He leaned the cello carefully onto its side on the floor next to him, then curled a finger at me. "C'mere."

My heart practically leaped from my chest, but I moved toward him hesitantly. I paused beside him, and he looked up at me, his eyes so piercing in the darkness that they caught me off guard. Rory patted his thigh, indicating for me to sit.

I sat with my legs between both of his, and the heat that radiated off him through his sweatpants warmed the bareness of my legs. Goosebumps washed over me as Rory moved to wrap one arm across the small of my back and let it rest against my waist.

I took his hand in mine and raised it to inspect the ridges of each knuckle. He was right; the wounds were little more than bruised and inflamed skin, the cracks had stitched together almost entirely after only a few short hours, no doubt thanks to Vain's supernatural healing. But the further I traced up his arm, I hesitated when I grazed the uneven, textured ridges running across the skin beneath his tattoos. One, two, four, seven. Bisecting them was one line that ran especially long, the skin more raised than all the others.

My fingers stilled and I stopped counting. My heart sank low in my chest as I realized I may have crossed some line by revealing something so deeply personal that I had no right knowing.

"It's okay," Rory said gently. "That was from a long time ago."

Releasing my lower lip from between my teeth, and in an effort to change the subject, I asked, "Did you...choose the tattoos?"

"No, Vain had them done. I didn't even know that he had gotten them until I came back into control one day and they were just there."

Rory spoke about it so casually as if it didn't bother him at all. But if I put myself in his position, there was nothing that terrified me more than becoming conscious in my body only to discover someone had had their way with it.

"At first, I thought he did them because maybe he liked the pain. But now I think he knew how much I hated looking at the scars, so he turned them into something I could learn to live with—showing me that I didn't have to love them, but it also didn't make me any less because of them." He laughed softly to himself. "I never pictured myself as a full sleeve guy."

"You pull them off well," I said.

We stared at the city skyline and as time passed my heartbeat grew less pounding, even as Rory's hand continued to brush at my waist.

"How is Dru?" he asked.

"As good as she can be, I think," I said. "She'll be okay."

"What you did to help her was brave."

His words caught me off guard. "I thought you were going to call it stupid."

"Maybe I'm getting used to all the stupid ideas you have," he said, biting back a small laugh. "But it was brave, Ava."

Worrying my lip between my teeth, I said, "I should have been able to help them all. There were more people I—"

"Don't go down that road." Rory's hand at my waist stroked up and down, a gentle, soothing motion. "If you think about all the things you could have done differently, it will only do more harm than good. You did your best."

I could feel his eyes on me, steadily searching my face as I stared into the distance.

"My best is never good enough." My eyes welled with tears as I turned away from him. Rory didn't need to see me this way. Not to mention, crying in front of him meant crying in front of Vain too. And I wasn't ready for my vulnerabilities to be laid bare for him to witness.

Rory caught my chin in his other hand and forced me to fix my eyes on his. The piney scent of rosin clung to his fingertips, and I found myself inhaling deeply as I leaned into his touch. He looked at me with such emotion that my whole chest ached, wishing to close the gap between us and wrap myself up in him.

My heart raced, and I wondered if Rory's did the same.

"You are enough," he whispered. "More than enough."

Our faces were no more than a hand's breadth apart, and I was transfixed by the uneasy tug in his throat as he swallowed, his lips set slightly apart.

"Ava, what I said to you the other night...about you not being able to fix anything. I was angry...and drunk. I didn't mean it. I didn't mean any of it. I'm sorry."

"But you were still right. I can't fix everything."

"No one expects you to." His thumb lightly swept across my jaw. "Why go through all of this? Why do you care so much?"

"I'm the reason my sister is dead." My breath hitched the moment the words escaped my lips. My eyelids fluttered closed to fight back the tears. "I've always been fascinated by demons, ever since I was young. As a kid, I was overambitious and deluded myself into believing I could contain one to study it and prove to my parents I could be just as powerful as they were. But I had no right to play around with dark magic."

When I reopened my eyes, Rory was staring at me with an unmatched intensity burning in his irises.

"The demon possessed my sister before my parents were able to exorcise it from her, but they were too late. She didn't survive." My lower lip trembled as I struggled to push away the memories that haunted my nightmares, the horrors that stared back at me whenever I closed my eyes. "I see her in you, Rory. I see her in all of them...every possession I've ever been assigned to. And each of them breaks me a little more, especially the ones I can't save."

Rory let my admission hang between us. His only response was the light trace of his thumb across my jaw.

I hesitated before asking, "What does it feel like when Vain is in control?"

Rory paused, then said, "On a good day, it's like I'm strapped into the passenger seat of a car and he's behind the wheel. On my bad days it feels like I'm at the end of a long tunnel, and the black is closing in around me with only a pinprick of light to focus on in the distance. But I can always feel him with me. He never makes me do anything I don't want to do. His wants are my wants. And mine are his."

He tucked a strand of hair behind my ear, his knuckles glancing over my skin, a touch so soft I nearly melted into him.

"And what do you want, Rory? Not what Vain wants, but you."

The distance between us was so small that I could feel his shallow and uneven breaths against my cheek as he studied my face.

"Right now? I want to feel something. I want to know what it feels like to have *my* lips on yours. Not Vain's. I want to know how you feel under my hands and not his. I want to know if this is real." His hand cupped my jaw, and he drew me closer to him. Rory kept his eyes locked on mine, a dangerous yearning set in his gaze. "What do you want, Ava?"

When I stared into his eyes, noting the tender strokes of his thumb against my cheek and how his touch ignited the blood thrumming through my veins, it was easy to forget the demon that lay beneath his surface. I knew all too well the pitch-black that swam behind Rory's stormy gray. And yet, I didn't want to care. There was a compulsion gnawing in my chest that I was no longer willing to ignore the more I studied the curve of his mouth, the creases between his dark brows, and the strain feathering the muscles of his jaw.

I was done pretending.

"You."

His lips parted, and my eyes tracked the movement. "Can I kiss you?"

I didn't remember saying yes; I think I nodded or mumbled an acknowledgment. I must have, because Rory guided me forward to close the already small distance between us. His lips brushed my mouth with a softness I wasn't expecting from him. My skin prickled, and I shivered at the touch. He seemed tentative, a little hesitant even, almost as if he were afraid of breaking me. I reciprocated each movement of his mouth against mine, a careful dance. Tracing my tongue along the seam of his lips, I sighed into him when he slid his tongue against mine. The taste of him was intoxicating.

In each breath, I inhaled the warm, spiced scent of him mixed with a hint of apples from the shampoo still clinging to him. I sank my fingers into his hair, tangling them through the strands as I pressed my body closer to his, further deepening the kiss.

Rory matched my enthusiasm with an insistent need all his own, his fingertips digging into my hips like a pulse that echoed his desperate heartbeat. There was a warmth to his touch, a balance of eager sureness and wavering hesitancy. His hands quickly turned greedy. The one at my hip fluttered over the fabric of my T-shirt and skimmed down until he met the bare skin of my thigh.

Heat pooled between my legs, and I wondered if Rory could feel it through his sweatpants.

"You shouldn't feel this good," he whispered against my swollen lips. "Why the *fuck* do you feel so good?"

My answer came out as a groan against his mouth which only drove him to take from me with a far wilder kind of desperation.

He pulled back an inch, panting, his eyes full of pure lust. "Fuck it," he growled. "I want to do a whole hell of a lot more than kiss you right now."

Rory gripped my hips and shifted me into his lap so that I sat facing away from him with my back against his chest. With my legs hooked over his knees, Rory knocked them open, spreading me wide.

I gasped as his mouth worked across my jaw and then to the sensitive skin at my neck. The sharp graze of teeth and the warm flutter of his tongue sent a wave of goosebumps to pepper my flesh underneath his touch.

Each breath I drew in was dizzying and full of unrestrained desire.

His hand traveled up underneath the hem of my T-shirt and tentatively grazed the underside of my breasts, and when I sucked in a surprised breath, he drew back slightly.

"Do you want me to stop?" he asked.

"No," I rasped.

He cupped one breast in the palm of his left hand, teasing the nipple with the swirl of his thumb while his other hand wandered further and further up my thighs until he was met with the slick heat that had already left my panties soaked.

"Fuck, you're wet," he breathed out heavily against my skin.

Rory pressed against my clit through the fabric, and I moaned as his fingers made tight circles over the aching bundle of nerves. He kept a patient pace until I was squirming against him, silently begging for more.

It was impossible not to notice the hard length of him beneath me, and I could feel Rory stiffen every time I shifted over him, the restrained groans vibrating in his chest as he bit them back.

He methodically hooked his finger into the fabric over my core and tugged it aside.

With one finger, he dragged it slowly up through me, swirling it lazily as he explored his way back up to my clit, still throbbing for more of his attention. The whimper he dragged from me turned into a heady sigh as I closed my eyes and ground myself against Rory's hand.

As he continued to explore the blazing heat below my waist, his other hand drifted past my breasts and reached up through the collar of my shirt until it settled gently at the base of my throat.

Our breaths were heavy and hot, mingling together as I leaned back against his chest, feeling the rise and fall of it as he continued to stroke me over and over until my legs were tense and trembling.

"Look at you shaking for me." He dragged my earlobe through his teeth, and I shuddered, pressing further into his lap and feeling him achingly hard for me. "You're close, huh? Am I going to make you come?"

"*Rory,*" I gasped as he slid one finger inside me, dipping it in and out slowly while he worked my clit with his thumb.

The hand at my throat remained steady, and I found myself giving into the feeling of his possessive touch more than I cared to admit. Maybe if it was Vain's hand wrapped around my neck, I might have felt some unease. But with Rory, there was a tenderness I found a level of comfort and safety in.

Rory's finger pumped in and out of me, eventually adding another and spreading me wider. He crooked them inside, finding the textured spot that had me writhing on top of him until my whole body was singing for him and weeping at his touch.

I bit down on my lower lip, attempting to muffle my cries.

"No, no," he panted against my ear. The hand at my throat dragged upward, his fingers sliding past my lips to hook my mouth open. "I want to hear every fucking moan. All for me. It's all for me."

Rory's teeth grazed and nipped at my neck, sending me past my breaking point. I cried out as my climax ripped through my body. A satisfied groan eased from his chest as I continued to rock and grind against his palm, riding out my release until my inner walls ceased spasming around his fingers. My head felt light, spinning even after the final wave crested, and I slumped against his chest, panting hard.

"I've got you," he whispered into my hair. "Come on." He planted a short kiss to my temple and lifted me up in his arms as if I weighed nothing to him. "Let's get you into bed."

I was too spent to put up a fight. He carried me down the hall to my room and set me down gently onto the mattress and pulled the duvet over my shoulders. Rory loomed over me, a hazy figure made of shadow as he bent down to brush my hair back.

His lips grazed my forehead as he whispered, "Goodnight, Ava."

Unable to battle the heavy weight of exhaustion anymore, I fell into dreams filled with demons dancing to a melody of strings, a haunting lullaby.

# NINETEEN

## RORY

*You smell like cunt.*

I shot out of bed from the shock of Vain's voice in my head piercing the silence. Groaning, I threw myself face-first into the pillows, wishing I could slam the snooze button on him. Unfortunately, demons didn't respect the snooze button.

"Is it too much to ask for a few extra hours of peace and quiet?" I grumbled into the pillow.

*Get up, or I'll do it for you.*

I groaned again. *Two minutes, please.*

*You wouldn't be so exhausted if you hadn't stayed up fucking her last night.*

The memory flooded back to me as I winced at the crudeness of his words.

At the mere mention of Ava, my dick was rock-hard. To be honest, I don't think I had stopped being hard since the moment my hands had started roving over her perfect body in my lap. I pressed my hips into the mattress at the reminder of her soft skin, her wetness pooling at my touch, and the scent of her hair when she leaned into me as she came on my fingers.

*You're so pathetically obsessed with her.*

*You're one to talk,* I countered.

If I had a death wish, maybe I would have told Vain he sounded jealous. I held my tongue instead. I knew better than to rile him up when he was already in a sour mood.

He was still shaking off the last bits of his rage from last night. The moment he saw Ava struggling beneath Ilo, Vain had transformed into a storm of fury unlike any I had ever felt before. In the swell of all that anger and vengeance, something inside me had unleashed itself as well, and I became every bit the monster alongside him.

I'd never killed anyone before, not even a demon. And while Vain would never admit it, I knew he had made an effort not to kill anyone for my sake.

But Ilo had been different.

I had craved his blood on my hands. I had found a warped sense of pleasure at the sound of his screams. I hadn't cared about the human vessel in the way. I'd barely given it a second thought to be honest, even though I should have. Looking into his watery blue eyes, I should have seen myself reflected in them, but I only saw the demon cowering beneath. And at that point, I was too far gone to think rationally—to think of mercy.

All the blood and all the ichor that had sprayed through the air and covered our skin, I swore I could still smell the soured, metallic tang of it in the back of my throat in every breath I took. In that moment, it felt right. Killing. Ripping. Destroying.

There had been no other option but violence. I had wanted—no, needed—to protect what I felt was mine. *Ours.*

Maybe it was all the years of being possessed that had turned me feral. Obsessive.

But the minute Vain shifted us back to the penthouse, the gravity of it all hit me like a freight train.

Ava had been taken—almost killed.

My head swam with the possibilities of what could have been, and Vain had shut down on me. He'd retreated into my subconscious with all his shame and rage for failing her. He had refused to let her see that part of him and he'd gone to great lengths to keep it from me as well. And I was still angry with him for abandoning me last night and for deciding to show up only when he damned well felt like it.

Only Ava had been there to pull me out of the shock. I'd often wondered why it was she possessed the need to fix everything around her that she felt was broken, but after her confession about her sister, I think I finally understood why.

I used to think her need to fix me was her most annoying trait, but last night it had been a blessing. Somehow, she had known exactly what I needed to ground me and remind me of who I was.

I was no monster. I was no demon.

I was just Rory.

The problem was, I could barely remember what it felt like to be *just* me. Vain had become such an integral part of me, like he was an extension of my soul, so intertwined that there were days when it felt like I could barely distinguish between us.

I ground my hips into the mattress again, and Vain let out a groan alongside mine, so loud it reverberated through to my core.

The demon shot forward, taking control.

*What the hell are you doing?*

But I knew full well what Vain intended because he'd already flipped over onto his back and fisted a hand around my cock, tugging at it. Teasing.

*Finishing what you started.*

I shuddered internally at his touch. The way he jerked our shaft in slow, unhurried movements had my very essence quivering. I was so painfully hard that my whole body ached.

"Tell me how you want it." Vain brought a hand up and spit before sliding his slick palm over the head and squeezing hard.

*Fast,* I answered, and it sounded like a gasp even in my mind.

Vain hummed thoughtfully. "Shame. I think I'd rather take my time."

His grip tightened before I could object, and he tugged his fist from crown to base, pulling a moan from me that traveled down the bond like a rippling wave and echoed from our chest.

It was pointless to fight him, not that I could anyways. Vain knew my body irritatingly well, almost as well as he understood my mind. More often, we'd started to exist in moments where it felt as if we were one, and there wasn't a single barrier that stood between us.

We became one body, one entity. One soul. My hand was his. This body was mine—ours—his to control and do with as he pleased.

And I let him. Because I was a desperate man.

*Harder,* I pleaded with him through the bond. He smirked and clenched his fist over our cock, every long and slow stroke bringing us both closer to the precipice of a rapturous bliss.

As he controlled every firm caress of my hand, Vain forced images of Ava into my mind that he knew would make me lose the last shreds of self-control I had left, like that tight fucking dress that had practically been painted onto her curves, her thighs deliciously spilling from the hem.

He showed me all the things I had tried so hard not to imagine too, particularly her soft luscious lips wrapping themselves around our shaft, the warm wetness of her tongue flicking out and lapping at all we had to give her.

Even the memory of her last night, her breathless whimpers and the rasping sounds of her losing herself all over my fingers...that thought combined with Vain's vice-like grip as he pumped our cock—faster, harder—I fucking lost it.

With my hand completely left at Vain's mercy, I came in thick, heavy ribbons that coated my stomach, and he let out a groan that tore through our chest and echoed my internal moans I casted down the bond.

He sagged against the mattress and looked at the glistening mess he'd made of us with twisted satisfaction.

*You're a fucking sadist,* I said.

"Don't pretend you don't fucking like it." Vain's smirk was practically audible and then he slipped away, handing back control. *Now, get up. We have work to do.*

I grumbled. "Sure, leave me in charge to clean up your mess."

*Technically, yours.*

"Shut up."

Vain growled in warning, but I rolled my eyes and swung out of bed, going straight to the bathroom. I needed a cold shower to snap me awake and ground myself back into my body, and maybe also to get rid of my raging hard on that was already aching for another release not at Vain's hands.

The pile of wet clothes from last night rested in one corner of the shower, and even though the black material hid the stains from the ichor, nothing would be able to get rid of the stench. I stepped out and wrapped a fresh towel around my waist before scooping up the ruined clothes and chucking them into the bin to throw out later. But when I snatched the black jacket from the floor, there was a weight to it that triggered a memory of Eldin slipping something into the inner pocket.

I rooted inside them until I found it, and I somehow knew exactly what I would pull out as soon as my fingers touched the smooth leather.

It was as if it were made out of white-hot flame, and I couldn't drop it quickly enough. The grimoire flopped onto the tiles, and I cringed away from it. Its essence was all wrong, like corruption had ingrained itself into the ink and pages. And there was a sentience surrounding it too, almost like the book itself was breathing, sucking all the air from the room until I felt as if I were suffocating in its presence.

*Stop being so dramatic.*

I backed up to the vanity and white-knuckled the edge so hard that if Vain were in control, he might have cracked the stone in half. "Why the hell did Eldin give you that thing?"

Together, we stared down at the book on the floor.

*I don't know,* Vain said. *Perhaps he decided he'd rather have it in anyone else's hands but Ghen's.*

"Ghen seemed to know you. What the hell was that about?"

*That's a longer story than we have time for.*

I shook my head. "Whatever. But I don't want to fucking touch that thing again."

*Fine,* Vain said, a pith of annoyance blooming from deep within him before he slithered to the forefront. He grabbed the leather-bound book and tested the weight of it in his hands. I shivered and drew back further into myself so the dark energy wouldn't affect me as much.

*What the hell is in that thing?*

"More than your pathetically mortal brain could begin to understand. And honestly, you're better off not knowing."

*Don't pull that shit with me,* I shot back at him. *Not after everything we've been through.*

That earned me a warning growl. I sighed.

*What do you think Eldin wanted it for? Why keep it from Ghen?*

Vain tsked before speaking down the bond again. *I'm not sure yet. He could have had any number of uses for it.*

He thumbed through the wafer-thin pages, skimming the contents, and deciphering what he could from the handwritten ink that occasionally bled through multiple pages. Demonic symbols and words appeared in different levels of legibility covering nearly every blank space, and even though I was able to understand their language, the words on the page still made little sense. A lot of it read like gibberish or the ravings of a mad lunatic.

Vain found the passages he was looking for, his finger trailing over the ancient and long forbidden magic that I could glean was unlike anything I had seen before or even imagined was possible.

My attention snagged on a block of text as I skimmed ahead, the words sending my stomach to my feet.

*Vain...no.*

"If Ava is willing—"

*You are not dragging her into this. Not like this.*

"It is the only way," he said.

But the cost of this magic...it was too much. *I don't care. I would never ask that of her. Not of anyone.*

"You can't ask me to give up on you—"

*I'm not asking!* I shot back firmly. *I'm telling you. We'll find another way.*

The longer Vain kept our hands on the grimoire, the more the sentient energy radiating from within seemed to grow stronger. Whatever this book was, it deserved to be locked up in a fucking tomb, deep in the crust of the earth so no one could lay a hand on it ever again.

*Vain...you can't say a word to her.*

He clutched the grimoire tightly in his fist. "Are you asking me to lie to her?"

*I'm telling you to omit the truth.*

"Rory." My name rumbled from his chest like it was a warning. "Eventually, she will need to know."

*I'll tell her when I decide,* I said. *But we're not doing it like this. This isn't the way.*

Vain didn't press again. He silently let the towel around our waist fall before he padded into the bedroom and went straight to the hidden panel next to the nightstand, revealing the safe tucked behind it. A wooden box sat inside, and the intricate locking mechanisms clicked open in response to Vain's touch. He tossed the book into it without a word and threw the locks closed with the snap of a finger. Whatever wards or charms he had in place, they did a good job at blocking the grimoire's malignant energy, and the absence of it immediately cured the prickling sense of unease that had been building inside me since the first moment I'd touched it.

"Don't be relieved yet, mortal," Vain said as he regarded our reflection in the mirror, his black eyes searing straight through me and reminding me of the dark beast who'd made a home beneath my skin and in my soul. "I haven't finished with you yet."

# TWENTY

## AVA

My head jerked up from the desk in Vain's library, disorganized stacks of various texts splayed out in chaotic disarray. After shaking away fuzzy remnants of sleep, I wiped at a small trail of drool from the corner of my mouth. I couldn't be sure when I'd drifted off, but based on the books in front of me, it had been somewhere in between researching how one might strengthen the potency of holy water and the exorcism techniques used by the Vatican in the early 1700s.

Between brewing a new batch of calming elixir for Dru, sitting with her to keep her company through the morning, and continuing my research in the library for the better half of the afternoon, I was drained.

Dru had refused anyone's company besides me and Nesera, though she was still somewhat hesitant with the cambion. In the time that I spent with her, I could tell she was wary, even a little skittish, and I did my best to make her as comfortable as possible while she was here.

Nothing lifted my spirits more than the moment I watched the first smile light up her entire face. When she'd finally opened up and started telling me about her family, specifically her two older brothers back home, it was clear how she adored them, and I knew she could have gone on about them for hours if I let her.

Once she took the elixir, eventually her eyes grew heavy before she quickly fell into a deep sleep. Dru needed to rest, and the calming brew would keep her down the rest of the day and into the night, keeping the worst of her nightmares at bay.

There was a soft rapping sound and I looked up to find Rory leaning up against the doorframe, tattooed arms crossed over his chest. He wore a light smile that I found myself wanting to kiss right off his face.

*Infernal hell.* I really was in over my head.

"How the hell do you read all day?"

Were it not for his bright gray eyes, I would have thought I was looking at Vain with his dark and lustful gaze.

Was he thinking about last night like I was? Had it been a mistake? A one-off encounter we'd only been driven to act on due to a near-death experience coupled with our lonely, desperate need for some sort of connection? A part of me hoped that wasn't the case. And even though I knew it was dangerous to entangle myself with Rory when Vain was still a constant presence lingering underneath his surface, I couldn't shake my desire for him that continued to creep into my the crevices of my soul, seeking to bury itself there and turn me into some lust-crazed thing.

Something had shifted between us, and I knew there would be no going back to how things had been before. How could it when he had drawn out my desire and tempted me so sweetly with his words, his lips, his fingers...

I cleared my throat and attempted to smooth my hair, which I was sure looked like a frazzled mess, and desperately hoped he wasn't able to tell I had drooled on Vain's desk. "How the hell do you walk around with a literal demon possessing your soul all day?"

His sinful smirk turned into a full grin at that. "Touché."

"Rory…" I started, but paused, finding that I was still unsure of the new dynamic we'd found ourselves in. "Were you and Vain able to get the grimoire?" I hadn't asked him before only because there had been no opportune moment that presented itself after everything that happened last night.

There was a slight tick in Rory's jaw before he answered. "No."

"But Vain said—"

"It doesn't matter what he said, Ava." I didn't like how his tone took on a stern edge.

"No," I cut in sharply. "You're not doing this. Do not push me away like that."

The way that his posture straightened and brows rose, I could tell that I'd actually shocked him.

I dragged in a breath and then sighed. "Look, I'm not sure what Vain was alluding to before about the grimoire being your only chance, but I need you to know that whatever it is you think you need to protect me from, you don't have to. You can tell me. I only want to help you. You know that, right?"

"Yeah," Rory murmured. He looked down at his feet and stroked one hand over his forearm. I decided not to press him too hard, knowing his likelihood to shut down in the past.

"What happened with Ghen?" I asked.

"It wasn't anything Vain couldn't handle," he answered quickly, like he couldn't have been more relieved at the change in topic. A muscle feathered in his jaw, and I narrowed my eyes on him.

"What aren't you telling me?"

Rory's attention flicked to the floor again before coming back to me. "All Ghen wanted was the grimoire. Eldin refused to hand it over, so the archdemon killed him. Vain was able to sneak away during their fight. That's all that happened."

"But the grimoire—"

"Is not important. I told you, we'll find another way."

"But what if it's the only way to save you? None of my attempts so far have even come close to working. What if—"

Rory pushed off the doorframe and was across the room in three long strides, emotion warring over his features. He pulled my face between both hands and stared down at me through dark creased brows.

"You are worth more than any book, Ava." His gray eyes were overly bright, but I thought I caught a dark cloud pass over them for the briefest moment before the look was gone. "We'll find another way."

The way his voice shook with determination had me nodding between his palms. "Okay," I said.

"Okay." Rory released me, dropping his shoulders and giving me a soft, tight-lipped smile.

"Are we safe?" I couldn't stop myself from asking. There was a gnawing sense of unease seeping into my very bones that I hadn't been able to shake since the confrontation with Ghen. Perhaps I was simply overthinking things by giving into my anxieties, but regardless, I wanted to be sure.

"Yes. Vain even strengthened the wards around the penthouse this morning as a precaution. He'll make sure no one can hurt you again."

"I don't need protection," I said.

"I know that," he said. "But it's impossible for me to convince him otherwise once he's got his mind set on something." Rory dragged one hand through his hair and pinched the corner of his bottom lip between his teeth. "But anyways, I actually came to see if you could use a break. Have a little fun? Something that hopefully won't bore you to sleep again."

Dammit, he had been able to tell I'd dozed off. I narrowed my eyes at him. "What kind of fun?"

"Just trust me," he said, extending a hand out to me.

The elevator doors slid open onto one of the lower floors of the building, and my ears immediately thrummed to a heavy beat of synth and bass. Pulsing streams of light scattered through the dimly lit space as we stepped out onto a balcony that overlooked a dance floor below. Bodies writhed and swayed together, sweat-licked skin brushing and joining and moving as one. The energy in the room was electric. Fevered and intoxicating. I couldn't help but stare down into the crowd as I pressed myself to Rory's side.

"Don't tell me Vain owns a nightclub too."

"Okay, I won't tell you," he said, and then winked.

I straightened out my black cotton dress subconsciously, suddenly feeling underdressed for this kind of setting.

As if sensing my concern, Rory laced his fingers through mine and gave my hand an encouraging squeeze. "You look fine," he said.

"Just fine?"

"More than fine. You're beautiful." His eyes softened, and the warm smile he gave just before he leaned in to plant a kiss between my brows sent my pulse racing. "Come on, they're waiting for us in the lounge."

With his hand still wrapped around mine, Rory led me down the spiral staircase and onto the dance floor, weaving us through the crowd. There were couples grinding together to the tantric beat of the music that blared, and plenty more sprawled lazily across plush jewel toned couches or perched on bar seats as they swirled multicolored cocktails in their glasses. From the occasional glimpses I caught of horns and wingtips interspersed through the mass of bodies, there appeared to be a curious mix of demons amongst the humans who danced alongside them, free of any worry or fear. A far different scene compared to the gathering at the demon nest last night.

My chest felt tight as we pressed through the crowd, and I only felt as if I could breathe again when we reached a roped off VIP area that led to a private space at the back of the club.

Alastair stood behind the long bar on the back wall, in the middle of fixing a drink in a crystal tumbler. I spied Nesera at the opposite end flirting with two human men who stood between her and appeared to be nothing short of transfixed by her. Her red dress swished around her thighs as she twirled for them, and I noted how their attention kept dipping to her legs and back up toward the plunging neckline that perfectly accentuated her full breasts. My eyes were particularly drawn to her horns, tipped in gold and jeweled embellishments strung together with thin chains that hung above the crown of her head.

If I didn't know better, I would say that she was a demoness—a queen leading mortals to ruin for her own pleasure.

The men weren't glamoured in the slightest, and I realized she might have some succubus blood in her demonic heritage if she was driving these men to such levels of obsession. She beamed at each of them coyly, all while giving each of them little glancing and teasing touches. I felt a flush of embarrassment for staring too long, and wondered if she was having the same effect on me as well. I forced myself to avert my eyes and join Rory at the bar a few seats down.

"This is...fancy," I said.

Rory leaned back against the edge of the bar, a warm smile softening his features.

"Someone is here for Vain," Alastair said to Rory as I took a seat. It sounded almost like a warning.

"Save a dance for me when we get back?" Rory winked at me again before his gray eyes flicked to Vain's black in a heartbeat. I wasn't sure if I would ever get used to that.

"I'll handle it," Vain said and then turned away without even a glance in my direction before making his way back out of the lounge and onto the thrum of the dance floor.

"Can I make you a drink?" Alastair asked. A golden amulet hung low on his chest, etched with a familiar sigil I recognized as the same one Vain had used on the side of that truck the night we'd escaped the Moreau Coven.

"Surprise me," I told him.

Alastair grinned and each set of his left eyes winked at me in unison before he got to work mixing a variety of spirits into a tumbler, running the oils of a twisted orange rind along the rim of the glass, and finally garnishing it with a sprig of fresh rosemary. When he slid it toward me, the open eye on the back of his hand blinked up at me expectantly.

I took a sip and almost melted into my seat. It was the perfect balance of bitter and sweet, the aromatics of the garnish complimenting the flavors of the spirits perfectly. The heat of the alcohol left a trail of warmth radiating down my throat that settled into my stomach with every sip.

"I'll bet you never met a demon who could fix a drink that well before."

"I can't say that I have," I said. "So, you're not just Vain's personal chauffeur but his bartender too?" I winced as the words left my mouth. They sounded ruder than I'd meant them to be.

Alastair appeared unfazed. "I'm whatever Vain needs me to be. I've pledged myself to his service."

"Why?"

"I owe him everything. Offering myself to him until the end of my days was the least I could do in return."

He turned away, and I braved another glance in Nesera's direction, noting a flare of jealousy in one of the men's eyes as she doted more heavily on the other. But as soon as the half-demon turned back toward him, his stance relaxed and his face brightened like the sun at her smile. Nesera trailed her fingers teasingly down the man's chest while she giggled at something the other said against her ear.

"Are we all the monsters you believed us to be, Ava?" Alastair asked.

His question knocked me out of Nesera's trance, and I wasn't quite sure how to answer him. I spun my glass around on the countertop between my fingertips.

"I'm still trying to figure that out," I said and then took another sip.

Alastair finished pouring a new drink, I assumed for Vain, and set it on the counter beside mine. "I understand how hard it must be for you to have to shift this view of us that you've undoubtedly held your entire life," he said. "But not all demons are monstrous."

"But many are."

"Are there not humans that display similar monstrous qualities you attribute to our kind?" he asked. In my silence, he offered me a soft smile. "The actions of the many do not define the nature of the whole."

There was a resounding crack of a fist colliding with bone that made both our heads whip over toward Nesera's direction.

The two men who'd been fawning over her had pulled away from the bar and were trading punches. The one with dark hair gave a two-handed shove to the bearded blond who was nursing his jaw with one hand.

Nesera sat back, elbows braced against the bar as she looked on with a satisfied grin. She lifted her glass in the air and let out a cheerful whoop of excitement as the bearded man charged the other. His fist flew into his opponent's cheek, while the trading punch went high, straight above the other man's eye.

Alastair and I both raised an eyebrow. He shrugged in response.

"They'll tire themselves out eventually."

"Does this happen a lot?"

Another shrug. "I'm not one to judge, so long as nobody breaks or bleeds on anything. I won't be the one to clean up that mess."

Both men grunted as fists continued to fly. I was so captivated watching them stumble and spar that I barely noticed when Vain entered back into the VIP area and approached behind me.

"So glad I didn't miss this," Vain muttered, grinning as he brought his glass to his lips. The rigidity in his stance caught my attention, and there was a wavering shift behind his eyes before he tried to mask it.

"Okay, boys, that's enough," Nesera said after she knocked the rest of her drink back in one gulp. She slid off her seat and went over to the bruised and bloodied men. Grabbing one of them in each hand, she practically dragged them with her out of the lounge and onto the dance floor, their eyes immediately softening at her touch.

"I take it you're enjoying yourself?" Vain asked.

"Where were you last night?" I looked into his bemused expression, not really sure what else I had been expecting to find there.

"You're upset with me."

"How come you get to decide when it's convenient for you to show yourself? Rory needed you after what you did, and you were just...gone."

"He seemed to get on quite well without me," he said with a knowing glint in his eye as he looked me up and down.

"That's not what I meant." I clenched my jaw and punched a finger to his chest. "You left him to deal with all that trauma on his own."

"I was—"

"You killed him! He was just a kid, Vain. I could have exorcised Ilo from him and you just—"

"He was already dead," he interjected. "Whether you exorcised the demon or not, that boy's outcome would have been the same. I did what I had to do to protect you."

"Only you used Rory to do it. And *he's* the one who had to bear the consequences of *your* violence."

Vain pressed his lips together into a tight line. "I didn't mean—"

"And how do you expect me to cut loose when all I think about every day is how to exorcise you from Rory? And now on top of that, I'm trying not to die at the hands of demons and a fucking archdemon in the process. How can you expect me to enjoy myself?" My tone was just as harsh as I meant it to be. I was done holding back.

Vain's nostrils flared as he scrutinized me, curiosity furrowing his brows together. "Are you not happy, mellilla?"

"Stop calling me that," I blurted and Vain actually flinched. "I know what you're doing. You're trying to get into my head and distract me. I'm going to exorcise you from Rory. *I'm* going to save him."

I was letting my pent-up anger and frustration get the better of me, and I knew that if I ended up pushing Vain too far that I would be toeing a very dangerous, possibly deadly, line. Something was already digging under his skin, and I was only adding salt to his festering wound.

Vain set his drink down and rolled his lips between his teeth. "What's gotten into you?"

"I could ask you the same."

"Stop deflecting."

"Who did you meet with just now that got you unnerved?"

Vain laughed. "It seems you know me better than I thought, *witch*." He spoke the last word sharply. He hadn't called me that in a long time. "One of Ilo's crew came for a visit."

That couldn't be good.

"Were they here for Dru?"

"They asked for you, actually."

Confusion set between my brows as I paused. "Me?"

"Yes," Vain sighed. "But you don't need to worry about it."

"Not worry?" I parroted his words. "How am I supposed to not worry when you tell me there are demons at your doorstep asking about me? What did they want?"

Vain shrugged.

"You didn't ask?"

"It would have made no difference. Regardless, they won't be coming back again."

"Were you planning on telling me at all if I hadn't asked?"

"I thought it of little importance seeing as you are safe as long as you are in my home. No one will be able to touch you here."

"Do you expect me to stay here forever?"

"That's not what I said."

"But that's the truth, isn't it?"

Vain pressed his eyes shut and pinched his lips together before snapping both back open again. "That is not what we agreed to in our deal. I only asked for the pleasure of your company for as long as you would have me."

"But I'm really just a pet to you, aren't I?"

"Ava—" Vain started, his voice low and hushed as his eyes softened. He reached out to me, but I brushed him aside with one hand.

"This is not my home," I snapped. "This will *never* be my home. And I won't let you string me along like I'm nothing but a dog you keep on a short leash. Go fuck yourself, Vain."

I was grateful my voice hadn't wavered once. Smug satisfaction flooded my chest at the ire burning in Vain's soulless black eyes. At the same time, that anger he refused to vocalize set a pang of dread deep down in my gut.

"Thank you for the drink, Alastair," I said without another look in Vain's direction, then stormed out of the lounge, hoping I had wiped the smirk clean off his arrogant face.

# TWENTY-ONE

## AVA

Anger seared through my chest as I worked my way through the pulsing crowd back toward the elevator so I could escape to the penthouse. I still held onto a sliver of satisfaction whenever I remembered the sour look on Vain's face before I had turned away. That look had been better than anything.

I climbed the staircase and was almost at the elevator when the sounds of muffled grunts came from nearby. I slowed to a stop outside a door that had been left open a small crack, and eyed the plaque labeled "Employees Only" before inching closer to peek inside.

The supply closet appeared to double as a storage room. Spare furniture sets, loveseats, barstools, rugs, and lighting fixtures were scattered about among the piles of soaps, mops, and cleaning products stuffed into buckets or along the cluttered shelves.

Again, the faint smacking sounds came from further back in the room, accompanied that time by a strangled moan. I strained my eyes as they adjusted to the shadows, and I held my gasp as I caught sight of the dark shapes moving through the shelves.

Three of them were tangled together on top of a velvet couch, bare skin flushed and slicked in sweat. Nesera moaned again, the sound ringing out louder this time. She was lying between the two men from earlier. The one who had thrown the first punch and had been left with a bruised cheek lay beneath her. She whimpered as she writhed on top of him while the other man with the bloodied lip thrust into her hard from behind at the same time.

Her long nails dug into the man's chest below her as Nesera bent forward, taking them both deeper. Each moan rasped as they escaped her throat between every gasping breath.

I shouldn't have watched. I should have turned away and went straight for the elevator, but I couldn't look away from the pure ecstasy that tugged at the cambion's lips and the corners of her eyes as they rolled back.

The man behind Nesera gripped the fabric of the dress bunched around her waist as he rammed himself again and again into her ass. His hands scraped up her back until they were fisted around the gold chain that dangled between her horns, holding them like reins. He yanked on them, pulling her head back and sending her over the edge in turn.

Nesera's eyes went half-lidded, and her mouth dropped open as she rode the initial waves of her orgasm. And when the man yanked again, her eyes shot open and locked straight onto mine. Her expression held no flush of shame or embarrassment. Instead, her smile only grew wider at the sight of me watching her come, and it took everything in me to tear myself away.

I whirled to escape toward the elevator, but I was immediately met with a hard wall of muscle. Vain had put himself squarely in my path, his chest blocking me from reaching the exit. How long had he been standing there? And how much had he seen?

"You're quite flustered," he teased.

*Oh, he had seen plenty.* I was too taken aback to speak.

"Did you like what you saw?"

There was no point in answering him. I had no doubt he could tell how turned on I was. I was sure every emotion was written plainly on my face. He might as well have been able to read my mind.

Maybe it was because I was still so aroused, but I couldn't help but notice the angles of Rory's face as Vain's dark eyes peered down at me, our chests nearly pressed together. But when I moved to sidestep around him in the hallway, he prowled closer, advancing on me slowly until my back was pressed against a door opposite the closet.

"Rory convinced me I should come and apologize to you, but now I'm wondering if there's another way I might beg for your forgiveness." The glint in his eyes was unmistakable. "And if I remember correctly, you do so love to hear me beg."

"You don't have to," I whispered.

"I *want* to."

I swallowed hard, and my skin prickled against Vain's dark energy wrapping itself around me as I stared up at him. Vain brushed a hand against my waist as he opened the door. I took the opportunity to back into the room and make space between us, even though I was only cornering myself again.

The office we stepped into was mostly dark, and only the sconces on the wall kept the shadows at bay with their soft warm glow. Vain closed the door behind him, not taking his eyes off me once. I backed away slowly while ignoring the inexplicable pull toward him. My body ached at the distance between us, but I reminded myself that he was not Rory. The demon was on the hunt.

He rolled up the sleeves of Rory's sweater while he advanced, step after slow predatory step.

"Don't act so frightened," Vain said with a grin.

I staggered backward again. "You're not compelling me, are you?"

"I don't need to compel you, mellilla." He chuckled darkly and then slowly traced his tongue over his lower lip. "I could have my way with you now, and you wouldn't lift a finger to stop me. Not because I could overpower or glamour you, but because you want this. And you would enjoy it."

"Get out of my head."

"I'm not in your head, Ava. You're projecting." Vain leaned in until I could feel the heat of his breath against my cheek. "And you're very, *very* loud."

The demon was right. In my panicked, lust-filled state, I had let my mental shields falter without realizing, allowing Vain to hear all my most primal and carnal desires.

I had let myself get far too comfortable around them both. It was surprisingly easy when all of Vain's darkness was constantly masked by Rory's charming looks and unassuming nature. They'd both lulled me into a warped sense of safety that was quickly becoming dangerous.

And while the thought terrified me that they might just become my undoing, there was a part of me that didn't want to care. Because the way Vain looked at me was not something I had ever seen from him before. His eyes held a gentle, adoring hunger, and his movements were languid as he stalked ever closer to me.

A demon of pure lust. That's what he was. How had I not noticed it before?

My voice was barely a whisper. "*Shit*. Are you an incubus?" I asked, staring up at him.

"Would that change anything for you if I was?"

"It would explain a lot," I said, hating the slight tremble that came with it which was impossible to hide, especially from him.

I took another tentative step backward and knocked into a low table, which made me stumble back onto a velvet chaise lounge. Vain moved impossibly fast, his body curving over mine with his hands braced next to either side of my face.

"Look at you," he breathed while tucking a strand of hair behind my ear with the same reverent touch that Rory possessed last night when he had me on his lap. "What a needy little mess you are for me. I don't need to be inside your head in order to read your thoughts and know your desires. I can see them all written on you now. It's in the flush of your skin, the way you quiver when my voice brushes against your ear and sends a shiver down your spine. The way your pupils are dilated. How your breathing has shallowed."

I trembled beneath him, feeling confused and delirious with a kind of fevered excitement I'd never experienced before in my life.

Vain leaned in close to the hollow of my throat and breathed in deeply. "I can even smell the arousal on your skin. And you smell so *fucking* good, Ava. I like to imagine you taste even better."

When he drew himself back up, his attention roamed to the heavy rise and fall of my chest and the neckline of my dress that came to a sharp point between my breasts. The way Vain's eyes glanced back up and lingered on my lips, I thought he might kiss me.

"What are you doing?" I whispered.

Vain smirked. "I find it interesting how you're not stopping me," he said as he grazed one hand along my neck. His thumb lingered over the marked V that had already scabbed over before traveling further down my body.

I glared up at him. "Even if I told you to stop, I doubt you would."

"You're welcome to test that little theory anytime you'd like, darling." His hand paused at my waist when he found the delicate sash that tied my dress in place. "You can tell me to stop. Or you can give in."

The problem was, I didn't want him to stop. But I kept that mortifying admission to myself. Understanding that I could say no at any time gave me some sense of security and allowed me to give in to the thrill of seeing just how far I would let this go.

Vain tugged at the sash and the fabric fell away to my sides. The second the cool air hit my bare skin, my nipples pebbled underneath the mesh of my bra.

"So beautiful," he whispered, leaning in. Vain traced the length of my neck with his lips and kissed along my collarbone. Tugging the cups of my bra down so that my breasts popped free, he wasted no time settling his mouth around each nipple, swirling his tongue, and sucking tenderly. The slight graze of his teeth had me arching into his body without permission. Every inch of skin he settled his mouth against lit up like a fire, leaving a trail of heat down over my stomach until he settled his head between my legs.

I thought I would have felt more exposed, lying so defenseless before him with just a thin strip of fabric between us. But I secretly loved the way his rapturous eyes enthralled me. It felt like he was seeing all of me, without reproach and lacking all judgment, and I feared it was something I could become addicted to if I wasn't careful.

Vain paused, his eyes trailing back up the length of my body as if in awe, before settling his gaze back to mine. With every sensual graze of his hands across my skin, his expression darkened further, even as he hooked his fingers through the thin fabric of my panties and slid them down my legs.

Shifting to anchor himself in the space between my legs, he gripped my thighs, his hands pulsing with excitement, and my clit throbbed in turn. He was so close that I could feel the teasing heat of his breath as he leaned in further, mere inches away from where I wanted him the most.

Our eyes remained locked in a delicate trance as Vain lowered his mouth to the inner flesh of my thighs and nipped at the sensitive skin.

I gasped, and Vain growled with pleasure.

He trailed three more tender kisses on either side of me, each tempting press moving closer to my center as he continued to test my line, the one I was becoming less sure of by the second, if it even existed at all anymore.

"Spread your legs," he ordered.

I obeyed.

"Wider."

"Please," I said, my voice trembling.

"Say my name when you beg me again." He ran his tongue along the curve of my hip. "I want you to hear yourself, knowing that it's me you're asking for."

"Please, *Vain*." His name felt like glass in my throat. Like poison on my tongue. It was wrong—*so wrong*—what I was doing. What I was allowing *him* to do.

His eyes burned into mine as he watched me from below. "Again."

"You're a fucking bastard, Vain—"

The demon unleashed himself on me before the words had fully left my lips. He dove in and lapped at me hungrily, attacking with his tongue before he sucked my clit into his mouth.

The sounds that escaped me were nothing short of degrading, strangled whimpers and unintelligible words as the pleasure quickly took its hold. Shock waves lit up my spine with every passing swirl of his wicked tongue. His rhythmic strokes wound me up tighter and tighter until I feared I might snap.

He would break me. Destroy me entirely if I let him.

"You taste so fucking good." Vain groaned against me, his words vibrating through my core. His tongue made one long, sweeping stroke, dragging it up through my arousal and flicking again at my clit with a devious grin. "Tell me, how does it feel to have a demon between your legs devouring you?"

There were no words to describe it. Vain's touch, his mouth, his tongue, his words...they all overwhelmed me to a near-devastating point.

"Vain," I panted, "*please.*"

There was a pulse in his jaw and then Vain cocked his head to the side before the darkness pulled away from his eyes and Rory's gray came to the forefront.

"My fucking turn," he rasped, and then Rory dipped his head back down to consume me completely.

Rory's hunger was gentler than Vain's, his mouth softer and more patient as he took his time with me. It seemed that I could tell the two of them apart in more ways than one now.

As if Rory could sense how close Vain had brought me to the edge, he drew his tongue along every nerve with languid precision, like he was trying to savor me for as long as he could. I didn't want it to end, but I also had never wanted to come so badly in my whole life.

Whenever Rory's tongue flicked back up toward my clit, he would suck it gingerly into his mouth before drawing away again, leaving me shaking and whimpering for more. My eyes rolled back as I dug my heels into the muscles of his back. My hips rocked forward of their own volition, and a breathy moan escaped my lips.

Rory emitted a deep guttural groan. "*God*, yeah, grind yourself against my face like that. Show us how bad you want it."

My soul nearly left my body the moment his tongue dipped inside. My hips lifted off the seat, and I cried out, eyes slamming shut. When I opened them again, Vain was back in control. He gripped me tight, using the hand splayed across my stomach to reach down and pull my hood taut before he suctioned his mouth to me and sucked hungrily. His teeth grazed my clit, and I was so sensitive I nearly screamed as I threw both my hands to the back of his head and dug my fingers into his dark hair.

I lost count of how many times Rory and Vain switched back and forth, driving me closer and closer to my release, until I was grinding against their mouth and panting hard. I called out both of their names, but I wasn't able to keep track of who was in control anymore.

"Please," I began to beg. "Please, please."

I was so desperately close that I squirmed beneath them so hard that they had to brace my hips down firmly.

"Which one of us will you come for?" one of them asked, but it was impossible to tell who said it.

"You beg so sweetly for us."

"Maybe we should make her beg a little harder."

*No, no, no!*

My head buzzed, and the insistent tingles at the base of my spine were beginning to bloom the longer they held me on the edge.

"No, I think she's ready, aren't you, mellilla? I want to hear your sweet moans as you come on our tongue."

Vain's words undid me, and my orgasm hit me hard, a full body crash of sensations and pleasure as my hips lifted off the cushions, and I cried out in ecstasy. They continued to give and take control from each other, using Rory's mouth to drag every last pulsing tremor from my body.

"That's it."

"Ride it out."

Each of them murmured to me, but their voices were dampened due to my pulse thudding loudly against my eardrums. I collapsed against the cushions and sucked air into my lungs like I had forgotten how to breathe.

When I reopened my eyes, Vain stared back at me, his body braced over mine.

"Look at the mess you've made of us," he purred, licking my come off Rory's lips. With a swipe of his thumb across his glistening chin, he gathered up what remained and placed the digit against my lips. I sucked greedily, and a dark grin crept up at one corner of his wicked mouth.

"*Good mortal*," he said, a deep rumbling sound.

Vain's words sang in my chest, and it was in that exact moment I knew I was ruined for him—for both of them, possibly forever.

# TWENTY-TWO

## AVA

Dru left the next day.

Alastair flew her home to her family in Illinois because she'd refused Vain's offer to shift her back. She was still distrusting of demons, but she had accepted Alastair's help as he was the only one who could fly a plane and she was desperate to be reunited with her mom and brothers, who she hadn't seen in months.

Before she left, I offered to help take some of her memories to ease the nightmares and pain of everything she had experienced with Ilo, but she refused.

"I don't want to forget," she'd said. "If I do, I might end up making the same mistakes that got me here in the first place."

I couldn't fault her for her decision, because I would have done the same if I was in her position and given the same choice.

I gave her a reassuring hug before she and Alastair drove off for the airport, leaving me in the penthouse alone with Vain and Nesera.

After last night, I couldn't look Nesera in the eyes, and I feared the same might be true for Vain and Rory. So instead of facing them like any normal mature person, I sequestered myself in Vain's library to avoid them altogether.

Trying to concentrate on anything was a challenge. My thoughts circled around last night and the way Vain and Rory had drawn out my basest desires with little effort. My body hummed remembering the way they pinned me down and held onto my hips. The brush of their mouth, the smooth rumble of Vain's voice.

I pressed my thighs together beneath the desk and shifted in my seat. The memory was enough to make me wet all over again. I was already craving them—

*What the hell are you doing?*

Both of them were quickly becoming a force that was growing harder for me to ignore by the day. What they offered me was nothing more than a distraction I couldn't afford to entertain. They were becoming my weakness. There was no denying my attraction to Rory, but as much as I found myself wanting him, I could not allow myself to fall for him. Because falling for him meant I'd be falling for Vain as well.

How had the lines between them both become so blurred over time?

Lusting after Vain felt instinctively wrong. And yet, he had rooted himself into the darkest corners of my mind and, somehow, my heart. Vain, no matter how alluring, was still a demon, and that fact alone should have been all the reason I needed to stop whatever this was becoming before it was too late.

I could never trust him. It was too dangerous to allow him such power over me, and so until I could find a way to exorcise him from Rory, I decided it was best to keep a level head and not be driven by my emotions and insatiable lust I'd developed for them. I would need to push them both away, no matter how much it might hurt me—or hurt Rory.

The problem was, I was still no closer to unraveling the mystery of Vain and how to exorcise him. It felt like there had to be some solution, a piece to the puzzle I wasn't seeing. The idea of the answer being just out of my reach was nothing short of infuriating, and as the hours droned on, my mood soured abysmally.

While I sipped at my tea that had long gone cold, I flipped mindlessly through the pages of the book in front of me, noticing the splotches of ink on the handwritten pages, and I was struck by how much it resembled the shade of pitch-black ichor.

*Ichor*.

I pressed my fingers to my lips, recalling the taste of Ilo's ichor on my tongue and the power I felt as its energy surged through my body.

*Power*.

Perhaps that was the key. Maybe I simply wasn't strong enough, but if I could become stronger...

I shot up and ran into the great room, finding Rory sprawled out on the couch with a book raised over his head.

"My shoes aren't *on* your couch. They're hanging *over* your couch," I caught him saying to no one in particular, so I knew that he must have been talking with Vain. Rory flicked his gaze over the edge of his book with one brow quirked as I scrambled into the room.

"I have something that might work," I said, sounding more out of breath than I felt.

"What might work?"

"I think I know how to exorcise Vain."

Rory unfurrowed his brows before Vain took control. I swallowed hard at the switch. I had been unprepared for him to appear so suddenly.

His voice was ice cold. "You still wish to get rid of me?"

I ignored him, because I didn't know if I could answer him truthfully and I couldn't risk him sensing a lie, no matter how hard I'd tried to convince myself it wasn't. "I need demon blood. Ichor."

Vain didn't utter a word, but I could still see the surprise reach his eyes as he studied me intently. He knew exactly why I intended to use it. He wasn't a fool.

He cocked his head to one side and said, "Last I heard, your silly little witch Council forbade the use of ichor nearly three centuries ago."

"That doesn't matter."

His mouth quirked to one side. "Quite the rule breaker..." He paused, but after a moment, Vain said, "No."

"I know you think it's probably dangerous, but—"

"It *is* dangerous. And it's not up for discussion."

I bit my tongue and took a breath to keep from lashing out at him. I wanted to keep Vain calm and not send him into a rage. "This was our deal. I give you my company and you'll let me find a way to exorcise you. I'm not giving up on Rory. We tried your way.

But since whatever plan you had for the grimoire got us nowhere, now we're going to try mine."

He took a deep breath and held it for a moment before he said, "Do you even understand what you're asking of me to allow you to do this?"

"I'll turn in my favor if I have to. Or are you afraid this might actually work?"

Vain scoffed and then grumbled curtly. "I *know* it won't work. That is not the issue."

"Then what is? Because you look scared to me."

Vain's already dark eyes seemed to darken further. He pulled himself off the couch and advanced on me in one graceful motion. Suddenly, I was looking up into his face as he eyed me through narrowed slits.

"Demons don't fear anything, mellilla. But I can admit that I have one fear. And that is losing either of you. I almost lost you once, and I promised that I would never allow it to happen again." I could have sworn I heard a slight tremble in his voice, but I waved the thought off as Vain inched closer. "You're aware of what ichor can do to a mortal. So please, convince me that you're not foolish enough to attempt this."

"I know what I'm doing," I said, squaring my shoulders. "When you killed Ilo, I accidentally had a taste. It wasn't much, but I felt the extra power it gave me. I just need a small amount. I swear. That was the problem all this time. I haven't been powerful enough to exorcise you before. No one was."

Vain sighed and shoved his hands into the pockets of his dark slacks. "Ava, you are powerful already. Most exceptionally so."

It sounded like he was trying to give me a compliment if I didn't know any better. That or he was just an excellent manipulator, which, of course, all demons were, so I settled on it being the latter.

"I thought you were a demon of your word," I said, jutting my chin up at him. "If you're reneging on our deal, then say so."

It was a low blow to insult his honor, but it was the last card I had. So far, Vain had kept all his promises, and he seemed to take pride in that fact.

The demon pressed his lips together and sighed deeply through his nose. "I have conditions."

I tried not to break a smile. "Fine."

"I mean it, Ava. I will let you amuse yourself with this little experiment, but the moment I feel it is getting out of hand, it stops."

"Deal."

"Now, unfortunately, the ichor won't be easy to obtain since Alastair is away and cannot give his willingly. We'll have to wait for Nesera to collect a sample for you."

"I can wait," I said, deeming the conversation over. But as I turned away to retreat back into Vain's library, he reached out and grabbed my wrist.

"Ah, ah," he tutted. "That's not all."

I narrowed my eyes. "I'm not removing the mark, Vain."

"I wasn't going to ask you to. Though I do find it curious how adamant you are about keeping it. Is it your way of claiming me?

Or have you not removed it yet because you're afraid if I were to escape, then you'd be left all alone, and I'd become another name added to the list of those that have abandoned you?"

I had to fight to keep my expression neutral. "We're not talking about this." Not with him. Not now, not ever.

Vain blinked. "As you wish. However, I did want to speak with you about last night."

It was impossible to look him in the eyes, so I stared down to where he'd wrapped his hand around my mark. "What is there to talk about?"

"You had some very choice words for me."

I stopped myself from releasing a whoosh of breath, thankful he only wanted to discuss our argument and not the heady display of arousal I wanted so desperately to push from my memory.

"What of them? I said everything I needed to say to you."

"And I did not."

He closed the distance between us until we were practically chest to chest and the force of him made my skin buzz.

"You are beautiful when you get angry with me, mellilla."

I kept my eyes fixed on our hands, down to the floor—anywhere but Vain's smoldering gaze. And though I held onto the strong desire to punch the audible smirk clean off his face, that feeling was overshadowed every time I remembered the touch of his hands and of Rory's mouth as they devoured me until my body sang for them.

"Look at me," he said, his voice low as he tipped my chin up with the ginger caress of his long fingers.

It was painful letting him search my face as if he were looking into my soul. I didn't dare to move an inch as he took me in with a tortured longing etched onto his features.

Since when had Vain become so easy for me to read? I had never encountered a demon who laid out their desires so plainly and openly. But, in many ways, Vain was still an enigma. Maybe he always would be.

"You lied to me yesterday," he said.

"No, I didn't."

"Don't try to cover a lie with another, Ava. You lied when you told me I had leashed you like a dog. That I had made you my pet."

"Was that a lie?" I challenged.

"It was. The truth is, that you are not the one that's leashed. You are the one who has leashed me."

The hand still clamped around my wrist said otherwise, until I realized that Vain's grip was shaky at best, like he was clinging to me for dear life, afraid to let go.

"Stop looking at me like that," I said, barely a whisper.

"Like what?"

*Like you care about me.* His expression was so far from lust. It had shifted to something deeper. Something I couldn't bring myself to measure.

Love?

Vain's lips twitched, and I realized my mistake. I had let my mental shields falter in a lapsing moment of shock.

"To call it love would be doing my feelings a grave disservice."

I couldn't breathe as he studied me, his obsidian eyes so piercing that my skin prickled uncomfortably under his gaze.

"My darkness calls to yours." He edged closer. "Your blood sings to mine. Tell me you don't feel it. Tell me that it doesn't stir some twisted, dark piece of your soul, and I'll walk away. I'll break our bargain."

The words of rejection lingered at the tip of my tongue, but I couldn't force them out because I knew that they would be a lie. And it would be so easy for Vain to scent it.

I hated how right he was. How it felt like there was some part of me that had never truly been able to deny him, even given everything that he was. Vain was *everything* that I should despise and seek to destroy. And yet, it turned out this demon was far different than I had ever imagined him to be. He was...surprisingly complex—multifaceted. Kind in some ways, even thoughtful, while still being a ruthless beast and devious manipulator in others. But was I so starved for any sort of affection that I was willing to throw myself at the first thing that offered it to me?

No. I couldn't allow that—I wouldn't.

"I can't deny it," I admitted quietly. "But that doesn't mean I will ever fully give in to you. You've never had me. And you never will."

His thumb brushed back and forth over my wrist. "Why do you continue to push me away?" he asked. "Who was it that made you feel like you were unworthy of being loved?" When I didn't answer, Vain's lips twitched a fraction. "Perhaps it's best you never tell me.

Because I'm not sure I could keep myself from destroying anyone who has ever made you feel as if you were never enough."

"*That* is exactly why," I hissed. "Because beneath all your silver-tongued confessions and promises, you're still just a monster hiding beneath Rory's skin that does nothing but prey on the weak and hurt people."

Vain's brows shot up. "A monster?" he echoed. "You truly think that low of me?"

I felt his energy spike to an ominous level. Perhaps it had been a mistake to say it, given that he towered over me and held me in place.

"Let me go," I whispered.

He did not.

"I only ask that you listen to what I have to say," he said, leaning in slightly until I could feel the heat radiating off him. "I see you, Ava. I see *all* of you. You do not have to hide any part of yourself with me. All of the desperate and depraved pieces of your heart, the power and longing you feel in your soul. All of your strength, all of your darkness...I see it all, and feel like I am starving for you to see your own worth in the same way that I do." His throat worked before he continued. "You have settled into every fiber of my being like an all-consuming ache that has only grown since the first moment I laid my eyes on you, and I would be remiss if I did not disclose to you the true depths of my desires."

Vain's words made my head spin, and I was strangely grateful he was still keeping hold of my wrist like an anchor to steady me. Yet, at the same time, a small desperate part of me wanted to run from him and whatever confession this was. It felt all too real. And I wasn't sure that I was ready to entertain any more of what he had to say.

I could have sworn I heard his breath hitch in his throat. "I would give you the world if you asked it of me, mellilla. I would bear the weight of your grief, worship your strength, even all your hatred and cruelty if it meant that you could stand unburdened in your power. All of that would be the least I could offer you, and yet, I feel it still wouldn't ever be enough."

Every belief I had about demonkind rushed through my head, a dizzying mess of everything I'd been taught. It should be obvious that Vain's words were nothing more than intricate lies spun to imitate truth. He spoke with such intensity and raw desire, but demons lied. So why was I tempted to believe him?

"How can you feel all that? You're just a demon."

I half expected Vain to laugh, but his expression remained stoic as he stared at me. "You call yourself a demonologist, yet you don't truly know anything about our kind at all."

"I know enough," I said. They were the only words I could manage that I knew wouldn't become lodged in my throat.

His face inched forward, close enough that it would have been so easy to kiss him. I hated that I still wanted him. I hated how the warm fan of his breath across my cheeks made me breathless. Hated the inexplicable pull to bury myself in his chest like he was the only safe place in the world I could exist.

"And yet you still hesitate," he said on a whisper. "Is that because perhaps you are beginning to realize that I'm not the villain you first took me for?"

I glared up at him through my brows, our foreheads nearly touching. "No matter what you are...you will always be nothing to me."

Somehow saying those words didn't feel nearly as good as I wanted them to. Maybe it was because as they left my mouth, all I could imagine was Rory's consciousness swimming behind Vain's black eyes and knowing he heard them all—that he was a witness to my cruelty and the hurt I intended to inflict by actively trying to push them away.

Vain dropped his hand from my chin, but I didn't lower my gaze even after he released me.

"If that is how you truly feel, so be it," he said. "Just know that no matter how your little experiment goes, if by some miracle you were able to drive me out and banish me, my feelings for you would still not have changed. And I would crawl back to you both every single time."

Then without another word, Vain stalked out of the room, leaving me reeling in his wake.

# TWENTY-THREE

## RORY

The demon thrashed against the restraints, jaws snapping at the air as it struggled to free itself from the obsidian slab.

It had only been a few hours since Vain had asked Nesera for a sample of ichor, and she returned with a bound and unconscious demon slung over her shoulders, appearing to not have even broken a sweat over the encounter.

"You owe me," she had said before leaving to deposit the demon in the storeroom a floor below the penthouse.

Vain and I both grumbled at the thought of owing Nesera anything while we waited for Ava to join us.

He was looking forward to this. I, on the other hand, was not nearly as excited at the idea of being near ichor again anytime soon. The smell of it had almost made me sick the last time.

*You're being dramatic again,* Vain said. *It's not that bad.*

"You can only say that because you're used to the stuff."

The demon, which was apparently classified as a simulacrum, appeared more beast than human. The proportions of its body were all wrong—legs and arms longer than the rest of it, an emaciated torso, hollowed cheeks that were so sunken in that the bones protruded to sharp points beneath the gray skin.

My palms slicked with sweat each time the demon rattled against the chains, and I was sure it would break free and unleash itself on me, driven by nothing but primal hunger.

The door eased open quietly as Ava let herself into the storeroom. Vain's essence fluttered inside me at the sight of her, or was that my own heart reacting? Did it even fucking matter anymore?

She'd somehow managed to root herself a place within my soul, right alongside Vain. Just as deep, and just as profound. There was no longer any question or doubt in my mind that my feelings for her were not just Vain's that warped my own.

But something had changed in her, like a complete shift had happened overnight. Earlier today, I could feel her pulling away—could see the hesitancy in her eyes. And the hurt of it stung more than I cared to admit. Especially because I couldn't understand why.

Watching her cross the room, the hem of her dark green dress kissed just above her bare knees, and I wanted to rip it to shreds and throw myself at her like a feral—

*Would you cut it out and stop thinking so loud?* I hissed through the bond. *Stop being so fucking horny and control yourself dammit!*

Vain squirmed inside me. *Give yourself some credit. That wasn't all me.*

And I hated how right he was. He was trying to make me fucking lose it in front of her, and I had to discreetly adjust myself before pushing off the stack of wooden crates.

The room was nothing more than four concrete walls and piles of crates stacked on top of each other with no order to them.

The obsidian slab with the demon shackled atop it was tucked away near the back with a singular fluorescent lamp hanging from the ceiling above it. The simulacrum squinted against the bright light as it writhed with newfound vigor at the sound of Ava's approaching footsteps.

"What is this?" Ava asked, waving her hand at the slab. "I asked for a sample of ichor, not a full-blown demon."

I raised both my hands. "Don't look at me."

Vain pushed himself to the forefront, offering her a soft smile. "Obtaining the sample is half the fun."

Ava crossed her arms and scowled at him. "You're sick."

"No, I just know how to have a good time."

"Semantics," she groaned and then stalked past Vain toward the slab. Her head tilted slightly as she approached it, her studious gaze trailing along the demon's odd and gangling form. The simulacrum snarled louder, a low gurgling growl that rumbled through its body.

According to Vain, these demons, while mostly humanoid in form, were born and bred to kill. They survived solely off the emotions of mortals and would leave them as nothing more than hollow husks of their former selves by the time they were through.

Every snap of teeth flung strings of foaming saliva from its mouth. Its yellow catlike eyes bulged from its skull.

"I'm laying out my conditions," Vain said from behind her as he rolled up the long sleeves of his white shirt to our elbows.

Ava didn't spare him a single glance. "Okay."

"When I tell you to stop, you stop. I will not interfere with your amusing little exorcism attempt, but I will not allow you to run yourself into the ground over it either. If I think you've ingested too much ichor or it's running through your system too quickly, then I will force you to end the session."

"Fine."

"Do you even realize the risks you are taking here?"

She whipped around, eyes flashing with irritation. "I know the risks of consuming too much."

Vain dipped his head and let out an exasperated sigh. *Stubborn thing,* he thought.

"Come." Vain walked up to a chest set atop a stack of crates. It was a large black leather box with a set of complicated gold locks sealing it shut. Vain pressed a hand to the locks, and they threw themselves open automatically.

Ava stepped up beside him as he raised the lid to reveal all manner of weapons—the sharpest knives and long blades forged of the purest silver and selenite, iron chains fitted with razor-sharp prongs, a crossbow with explosive selenite bolts, and polished manacles and collars for binding—a demon hunter's dream cache in a single box.

Ava's gaze trailed over the weapons, landing on the large glass bottle filled to the brim with a clear liquid.

"Is that—"

"Holy water. An extra measure of precaution should we need to expel the ichor from your body quickly."

"You thought of everything, didn't you?"

"I like to plan ahead for every possible outcome. One of my better qualities, I'm afraid."

Ava sneered at him. "You really are vain."

"I never claimed to be humble," he said with a smile.

"You're insufferable."

Vain inhaled slowly, in part to let the insult wash over him, but also attempting to scent out the lie. "Ah, you don't really believe that, Ava. Tell me, what would be so bad about accepting your desire for me?"

A hard frown set across her features as she glanced up at him. "You're a *demon*."

"My, you're perceptive."

"Shut up. You know what I mean," she snapped, her tone as sharp as the blade she ran her fingers over.

Vain's voice dropped dangerously low as he asked, "What changed, mellilla?"

Yesterday she had allowed Vain closer to her than she ever had, and now she acted as if she wanted nothing to do with him.

*She regrets it.*

*No,* Vain said. *She's afraid.*

Vain didn't look away from her as he let his question hang in the air between them. Ava's throat bobbed, but she refused to meet his hardened gaze.

"There's no shame in admitting you're fascinated by me or that you want me as badly as you want Rory."

"You don't understand," Ava blurted.

"I understand perfectly."

The closeness of her was too much to bear. The familiar scent of her, the way her eyes swept over every inch of our face while she attempted to mask her feelings. If I were in control, I would have kissed her right then. I would have wrapped myself up in her and never let her go. Fuck, I wanted that so bad.

But I wasn't in control.

Vain cupped the side of her face, forcing her eyes to his. Ava became so still; it was as if her entire body had turned to stone.

I could practically see her struggling to make sense of her own thoughts. I knew she was seeing Vain, but it felt like she was trying to see me too. It always felt like she was searching for me. I used to hate that look. Now I craved it.

"I see the way you respond to my touch. To my voice. You can't stand that you find yourself attracted to me. But there's no shame in it."

Her breath trembled. "Stop it."

"Stop what?"

"Trying to manipulate me."

Vain shook his head. "I have never once," he said and absently stroked his thumb across her jawline, her skin smooth and soft under his touch. "I know what your heart desires, what you long for and crave. And I also know that it hurts you to hear the truth."

Her eyes flickered before she shied away from him. "Can we get this over with, please?" It felt like she was trying to shut Vain out—to shut the both of us out. And I didn't like the sting of it one bit. She snatched up a short selenite blade and stalked over to the simulacrum demon with a fire in her eyes I hadn't seen the likes of since the day we met.

The demon grew increasingly rabid the closer she edged to the slab. Its gaping maw clicked shut repeatedly as it strained its neck toward her arm, which was only a few feet from its face.

Ava lifted the point of the blade to the demon's throat and the creature stopped moving, eyes ravenous. A knowing glint passed over its eyes and its forked tongue swept out over pointed teeth before hissing at her. The chilling sound sent a shiver through me, straight to my bones.

"Mmmmh. Sweet, mortal blood."

"That's a weak attempt at flirting your way out of this, don't you think?" Vain said, totally bemused as he crossed his arms over his chest.

The demon's head snapped to Vain, slivered eyes narrowing. "Traitor! You think when she is done with me that she won't also rip you to shreds?"

"I highly doubt it. I'm going to enjoy watching her break *you* though," Vain said to the demon who snarled in return.

"You enjoy seeing your own kind slayed at the hands of inferior mortals? We are meant to slaughter and rule their kind, not to align with them."

"I don't align myself with either side. I prefer the role of an objective outsider."

The demon jerked its attention back to Ava, nostrils flaring before its lips curled back and bared an entire row of teeth. A knowing look passed over the demon's eyes before its voice twisted, morphing into something...other.

"You were a pathetic mistake. Stupid, stupid girl. How could you be so foolish?" The demon's voice had turned strangely feminine, almost like it was taking on the voice of someone else entirely.

It looked like Ava stopped breathing. Every part of her appeared frozen except for her chin that wobbled, and the muscle in her jaw flexed as she clenched her teeth.

The demon took on a different voice next—a man's. "Our family name will forever be tainted because of what you have done."

"Shut up," Ava muttered.

But the demon did not stop. The simulacrum had somehow gleaned its way through whatever mental walls Ava had tried to put up and was on a war path.

"It's your fault she's dead! We will never forgive you for what you've done. You are worthless! You are nothing!" It hurled her deepest regrets and most shameful memories at her through rasping shrieks that grew louder and louder with each word. "You are our greatest disappointment."

Ava didn't blink. If she did, the tears welling in her eyes would have broken free. She white-knuckled the blade in her fist.

"It should have been you! IT SHOULD HAVE BEEN YOU!"

"Stop it!" Ava roared with the fury of a thousand demons as she unleashed herself on the creature, and even from where we stood, I could tell that this was not just about wanting ichor anymore. There was a fire in her eyes, a burning retribution fueling her as she drove her blade into the flesh of the demon's stomach. Again, and again.

It keened an unearthly howl that pierced the room. Ava grimaced as she continued her assault, drawing long cuts down the length of the simulacrum's limbs that sank to the bone. There was no mercy left in her eyes, only pain, and she threw it all into each downward strike of her blade into the demon's chest.

Ichor, hot and black, pooled into the troughs carved along the edges of the slab and ran in a slow, steady stream toward the shallow well at the demon's feet. My cock twitched, straining against the front of our jeans to the point where it had started to become painful.

*How the fuck are you getting off on this?*

A sick sense of pride welled in Vain as he watched Ava from across the slab. He delighted in her determination as she broke the demon within an inch of its pathetic life.

The simulacrum slung curses and obscenities at her, both in English and the harshness of the demon tongue with every slice she made. But Ava's rage was an unstoppable force.

Her blade came down on the demon's throat again and again and again. The only sounds it made were wet gurgling noises as ichor spurted out from the arteries between mangled gray flesh.

Ava hacked at it until its neck fell to the side, and she sliced through the vertebrae, severing the demon's head clean off. It tumbled to the floor with a heavy, wet smack.

Her chest rose and fell heavily while she stared at the butchered mess she'd made of the demon. The ichor had painted her hands black, same with the knife she still held clamped in her shaking fist. With one last stab, she planted the blade deep in the demon's chest and left it there, the ichor-slicked handle glinting in the light.

After wiping her hands clean, Ava moved silently around to the well at the base of the slab where the ichor had pooled. She picked up a small glass Vain had set there and dipped it through the thick substance, filling it nearly to the brim.

"That's too much," Vain said.

"Relax," she told him. "I only need to drink about half of it."

Ava tipped her head back and, true to her word, only swallowed half of the ichor in the glass before slamming it back down. A strangled gasp escaped her throat, and then she was coughing, clutching at her neck as if she might claw herself open. My natural instinct was to rush to her side, but Vain remained firmly in place as he watched her struggle.

When the last of her retching subsided, Ava wiped at her mouth with the back of her arm and shut her eyes. She inhaled sharply, her hands curling into fists and then flexing at her sides before her eyes popped open, and she stared Vain down with a tenacity that rivaled any I'd seen from her before.

"Do your worst then, witch," Vain taunted.

A hint of a smirk formed on her lips, then she started murmuring the same incantation I recognized from all the times before whenever she attempted an exorcism.

The only difference was that this time...I could feel it.

I could *feel* the words attempting to latch on to Vain and rip him from my body. They lashed out like whips curling around the corners of Vain's essence but couldn't quite hold. Regardless, it was enough to make me nervous.

*I thought you said this had no chance of working.*

Vain grimaced through it, snarling whenever the incantation snared him like barbed wire being dragged over our bond.

"Stop fighting, Vain," Ava called, her chest heaving.

Vain couldn't help but grin back at her. "It's alright to admit when you're wrong, mellilla."

"I don't give up that easily," she said quietly and then reached for the glass vial again, still half-full of ichor.

"Ava…" Vain's voice dropped low in warning.

She shot him a hardened look. Defiant until the very end. "It's not that much."

"I have seen mortals become vampyrs over less."

"I'm strong enough."

Vain surged forward before she could wrap her hand around the vial, unsheathing the knife strapped beneath our shirt and deftly maneuvered behind her. He pulled her back against him, one arm pinned over her chest as he held her by her throat and pressed the tip of the blade against her neck in one fluid motion.

"This all feels very familiar, doesn't it, mellilla?"

*Don't you dare fucking hurt her,* I warned him.

*I won't. I just need to scare her a little.*

*I think you've proved your point,* I said. *Enough.*

Ava's pulse pounded underneath Vain's hand at the base of her throat. He angled the blade with the right amount of pressure to not break the skin, but just enough to keep her docile.

"I would strongly caution you to reconsider," he whispered against the shell of her ear with that sinful voice of his that might have caused her to melt if we were in any other situation.

"Back off, Vain," Ava growled.

By the time Vain noticed what she was doing with her hands below her waist, it was already too late. Her fingertips came together, sending a force of magic shooting outwards. Vain stumbled backward before another blow quickly followed and slammed him against the opposite wall.

"Ava!" Vain shouted as he scrambled to reach her, but she was already tipping her head back and gulping down the remaining ichor left in the vial, choking on it as she swallowed every last drop.

The vial hit the floor and shattered, the glass shards spraying at her feet.

Ava threw Vain against the wall again, pinning him with his feet lifted inches off the ground. The force of her magic was crushing, so powerful that Vain struggled to use his power against hers. Even her glare was lethal.

"On second thought," she mused before her lips curled upwards into a cloyingly sweet smile. "Get on your knees."

She curled her outstretched hand into a fist and our knees cracked sharply against the floor when we went down.

She kept one arm extended as she repeated the words of the exorcism again, each syllable sharpened with the fervor of her newfound power. Vain fought against the bindings of her magic despite him becoming more and more aroused by the display of her power. I had no control over my own dick as it strained against our pants.

*Maybe if you wanted to fight her as badly as you wanted to fuck her, then you'd be able to break free and actually stop her.*

*Don't tell me you're not having fun*, he said.

*She's going to end up killing herself over us, Vain!*

Ava wobbled slightly on her feet but steadied herself against the obsidian slab where the simulacrum's tortured body still lay. She kept one arm outstretched, keeping Vain anchored to the ground, but her shoulders slumped the moment the incantation ended, and Vain remained unscathed. The arm she'd propped on the slab shook as she attempted to hold herself up.

"Why won't you leave?" she yelled.

"Now do you see that there is nothing you can do to get rid of me, Ava? I am constant and eternal. And your adorable little attempt at matching my power is now over."

If she could have felt the churning swell of Vain's power, she would have been afraid—terrified, even—but she merely shrugged as she stared back into the eyes of the demon who sought to claim her. "You don't look all that powerful to me when I have you on your knees."

"You wicked little temptress." Vain smiled. "You're enjoying this aren't you?"

He let his energy surge within me, and it was like throwing kerosene on a burning pyre. It was then that I understood, everything up until this point had been a game to Vain. He had allowed her to think she had the upper hand, knowing she could never recreate even a fraction of his power.

Vain eased himself up off the ground, sifting through Ava's magic bindings as if they were sand. She stumbled back, then scrambled to throw her magic toward him again. But Vain advanced on her, step after slow step like a wolf on the prowl. Every spell and every hex she shot at us dusted away to nothing while Vain continued his patient and steady hunt. His malicious grin only grew wider as he closed the distance.

Vain stopped at the open trunk of weapons and plucked up the holy water, swirling the clear liquid around in the elegant crystal bottle.

"You're going to drink this," he said, "and then we can forget this ever happened. Drink, and I won't punish you when you're done."

A bubble of nervous laughter rose from Ava's chest as she continued backing away from him.

"You wouldn't," she said.

"Try me."

Vain uncorked the bottle and rushed at Ava until he had her pressed against the wall.

He tipped her chin up and raised the holy water to her lips. "Drink," he ordered.

She locked her eyes with his, her gaze piercing as she took the water past her lips but didn't swallow. Instead, she sprayed it back into his face and then shot another force of her magic at him.

The blow threw us back a couple of feet and knocked the bottle from Vain's hands. Bits of glass and holy water exploded across the floor. Ava grinned.

Vain wiped a hand down across our face in a weak attempt at tempering the anger slowly rising inside him.

*There goes your brilliant fucking backup plan,* I muttered.

His icy rage blended with mild amusement, and heady arousal flooded my senses as Vain reared up, ready to pounce.

"That was a fun game—you pretending you were in control. Now, it's my turn."

And then the demon launched his attack.

# TWENTY-FOUR

## AVA

Vain lunged at me with unnatural speed. Even with the amount of ichor raging through my veins like wildfire, it still didn't offer me enough agility to escape him. If anything, my weak attempt had done nothing but prove the extent of Vain's near-boundless power.

He slammed into me so hard that the tattoos on his arms rippled as he pinned me against the wall. A blazing heat flared in Vain's eyes as he searched mine.

Pressed together, we were a silent storm, a battle of sharp breaths as we shared the same air, inches apart, and I swore I could hear the hammering pulse of blood rushing through both our veins.

Then, in an instant, Vain's mouth was on mine, attacking with the same fervor and hunger as before when he had gone down on me in the club. Our teeth clashed and our tongues tangled as we fought for dominance. Vain bit my lower lip hard, until I tasted the bitter metallic tang of my blood, and then he swallowed my tongue as if he were trying to suck the ichor straight out of my body.

The simulacrum's ichor roiled within me like a surging wave on the verge of cresting. It swirled in my core right below my chest, its power continually filling the well inside me. At first, it had been overwhelming. But I hungered for more just as strongly as I craved more of Vain's touch.

Like I was addicted to them both.

Vain moved one hand to the base of my skull and laced my hair through his fist, which allowed him access to control where he wanted me and to delve further into my mouth, deepening the kiss. He gave my hair a sharp tug as he broke away to explore my neck with teeth and tongue, letting out low panting groans as he did.

I sighed at the feeling of his mouth on my skin and the hard length of his cock through the fabric of our clothes as he pressed his body against mine. His other hand trailed along my hips and over my breasts while he licked at my neck, kissing me feverishly, as if he wouldn't be satisfied until he had overtaken every inch of me. Every moment of it was blissful anguish, so much so that I ached for him.

Vain tore at my dress, the fabric giving away easily and exposing the delicate undergarments beneath. Those came away too as he clawed them from my body with little effort. Heat flushed my chest. He hoisted me up with my back pressed against the wall, and I wrapped my legs around his waist.

"You are far more tempting than any mortal should be," he groaned.

Leaning his head down, he pulled my breasts into his mouth, and I gasped as he sucked and swirled his tongue around my nipples, occasionally sinking his teeth into my flesh hard enough to leave red marks behind.

With his hips aligned perfectly with mine, I could feel his cock twitch when I pressed myself against him, seeking any friction he could give me. Vain lifted his head to recapture my mouth, and I ground myself into him again, a heady moan escaping my lips, one which he returned in earnest.

His onyx eyes seemed insatiable as he searched mine.

"Is this what you meant when you said you were going to punish me?" I asked breathlessly against his mouth.

There was that wicked smirk of his again. With a glint in his eyes, he said, "No, mellilla. But I'm sure you'll be begging me for it very soon."

Then, in one swift motion, Vain hoisted me up higher, hooking the backs of my knees over his shoulders so his face was pressed against my lower half, and his tongue flicked out over my throbbing clit.

The sound he tore out of me sounded almost like a scream, and I slammed one hand into the wall behind me and latched the other into his hair to keep his mouth locked in place, as he worked his tongue through me. Up and down, he stroked and teased and sucked, again and again until I was crying out for more.

My throat ached, already craving the taste of more ichor. I could see it still pooled in the divots of the slab, nearly overflowing with the black liquid.

*Drip.*

My throat bobbed.

*Drip.*

My muscles strained against the urge to surge forward and suck up every last drop. Only Vain's wild hunger as he took from me kept me rooted where I was.

Edging me closer to orgasm with every sweep of his tongue, he built me up and up until I was shaking and the tingles at the base of my spine turned insistent, ready to explode through my body at any moment.

Vain held me on that border between devastating pleasure and torment for too long, only granting me relief when he slipped a finger inside and curled it toward my most sensitive spot, and I was completely gone. My thighs clenched around his face so tightly that I wondered if he was able to breathe as I shattered.

He gave me no reprieve as he continued to suck and lap at me greedily through the overwhelming rush of pleasure. It felt as if he was savoring every shudder he tore from my body. Memorizing the taste of my come. He groaned against my flesh, the sound traveling up my body, vibrating through to my very soul.

When he had pulled the last pulsing tremors from me, Vain lifted me off his shoulders and lowered me to the ground while keeping my back pressed to the wall. He slid one hand back down between my thighs and cupped me there. I rocked lazily against it, still dazed from that fresh wave of pleasure.

His lips found mine again, this time with a slower yet more punishing need. The taste of him and myself mixing together on our tongues made my head swim with an agonizing desire.

I couldn't get enough. I wanted more.

Through heavy lids, my attention flicked over Vain's shoulder toward the mangled demon on the slab, and I imagined the taste of its still-warm ichor coating the back of my parched throat.

Just one taste. *One more taste.*

Vain's black eyes narrowed on me and his grip on the back of my neck tightened. "Don't you *fucking* dare."

A storm of shadow amassed around us, and I felt the floor fall away beneath me as Vain shifted us back up to his bedroom in the penthouse.

Hot, seething anger flashed through my body. I wanted to shout at him, to push him away, but I surprised even myself when I instead shoved my hand beneath the seam of his pants and wrapped it firmly around his hard cock.

Vain's eyes went wide, and it was the first time he had smirked where I didn't want to wipe it clean off his face. No, I wanted that smirk to devour me. Body and soul.

"You wicked little witch."

He invaded my mouth again with his tongue, only breaking away briefly when he wrested his white shirt over his head while I fumbled with the zipper of his pants. I pulled them down with me as I dropped to my knees, and his cock sprang free inches from my face. My tongue swept up from the thick base to the tip like I was starving for him.

Keeping my eyes locked on his, I watched his muscles tense as my tongue swirled around his head. The heady taste of him, the spicy musk that was both mortal and something distantly *other*, invaded all my senses and sent a warm jolt through me. Vain's lips parted, and he let out a shaky breath when I lapped at the heavy bead of pre-cum that had pooled at his tip.

His jaw ticked and he clenched his teeth. "So, *so* wicked."

I eased forward, my lips pushing over the head as I took him into my mouth, savoring the sharp, salty taste.

By the way his hands flew to the back of my head to grip my hair, his sharp intake of breath and the way the muscles in his thighs tensed as I swallowed him greedily, I didn't think he had been ready for me at all—not so unleashed and eager.

I kept one hand cupped around the back of his thigh, the other holding him at the base to guide him in and out as I hollowed my cheeks. I swirled my tongue around him as I stroked his shaft with one hand and my mouth, in and out, increasing the suction each time. I was sure if he pushed himself any deeper, I would struggle to breathe.

"I always thought you had the prettiest lips when you argued with me, but they look even better when they're wrapped around Rory's cock."

I pulled my mouth off him and tilted my head up. "I want him to look at me."

Vain flinched, and I caught the movement of his jaw ticking as I knew it would. It was the confirmation I needed that Rory was still in there, and he was watching from behind those black soulless pits of the demon's eyes.

Vain drew his lips into a thin line and a possessiveness flared across his features as he growled low and deep. "That's not going to happen, mellilla. As much as you both might want it to. You're all mine right now."

He gave me no chance to argue. Without even having to touch me, Vain threw me backward, one slight flick of his wrist commanding my body to slide up his bedroom wall as if he were pulling me by some invisible tether. No matter how hard I strained against the force locking my ankles and my wrists in place, I was helpless to stop it. Even with the ichor still pumping through my system, I couldn't stop *him*.

"Vain—" I was quickly silenced by another turn of his wrist, spinning me upside down so my face was level with his cock.

"All *mine*," he purred as he eased forward. His mouth settled onto my pussy at the same time the head of his cock met my lips. He pressed his hands into my hips, gripping me savagely, and worked his tongue against me in all the ways he had learned my body responded to him each time before.

The velvet smooth skin of his shaft slid past my lips. With each thrust, I relaxed my throat and took him deeper.

Vain was stripping away the last of my resolve little by little, taking everything I had, and I was giving it to him. He seemed intent on claiming every piece of me. And it didn't scare me anymore to know that I wanted him to.

I wanted him—all of him. But I wanted Rory too. Hell, I had Rory now, but it was the demon possessed part of him, and I desired the man within just as ardently.

Vain's fervor was unrelenting, and I was dripping—soaked from how he pulled every ounce of pleasure from my body. He fucked me with his tongue until I could feel the combination of our wetness trailing down my stomach and over my breasts, all while he pumped himself in and out of my mouth.

"Vain," I choked out against the head of his cock. "I don't think I can—" I couldn't form sentences anymore. My head swam with pleasure, dizzy from the blood rushing to my head in the inverted position. "I need...I can't..." Vain had brought me so close to the release my body so desperately craved again, but I wasn't sure how much longer I could hold on without passing out.

I was faintly aware of sliding further up the wall as Vain levitated us together toward the ceiling. When we stopped moving, I opened my eyes and looked through the break in his legs, noticing his bed was directly below us. Relief swept through me as the blood left my head and the heavy sensation ebbed, but I felt as if I could barely take a full breath, even as Vain's thrusts into my mouth had slowed.

My vision darkened at the corners of my eyes and slowly filled my vision, threatening to drag me down into the hazy black.

"Stay with me," he murmured in between rolling his tongue over my aching clit and then sucking it back between his lips. "Don't hold back."

His fingers sought entry, pushing into me so deep and I clenched around them. He held me on the verge of breaking. The breath I held was caught in my lungs, my mouth hanging open in a silent cry as my muscles tensed moments before I tipped over the edge and my orgasm tore through me, merciless to stop it.

Vain popped free of my mouth as I came, a shout ripping from my chest. I jerked against the weight of him over top of me, but he seemed intent on dragging out my pleasure as he continued to curl his fingers inward, even as I spasmed around him.

When the last of the shivers wracked from my body, I felt as if I was on the verge of losing consciousness. The invisible shackles holding me loosened, and then Vain floated us down from the ceiling before setting us onto his bed. I felt heavy and drunk, and my head buzzed with a dizzying high I felt incapable of ever coming down from.

Vain's body covered mine and I was acutely aware of his hard length of resting against my entrance. He held his two glistening fingers to my face, then rested them against my lips. "Taste how sweet you are for me, mellilla."

I obeyed by sucking them into my mouth hungrily. My tongue swirled around and in between, enjoying the taste of myself. I wanted to lick every last drop from them like I was my own personal drug, a heady elixir of my wanton, craven desires.

"Good mortal," Vain hummed. A warped sense of pride hooked in my chest at his praise.

He dragged his mouth over my body, peppering my skin with kisses, quick nips of his teeth and warm wet lashes of his tongue before recapturing my mouth with an insatiable hunger. For a moment, it was easy to forget that Vain was the one in control. I found myself slipping into the comfort of Rory's scent, the feel of him under my hands, and imagining that it was him who oversaw my pleasure. But the reminder of everything Rory was, and everything he was not, was apparent in his eyes—Vain's eyes.

"I want Rory," I gasped against his mouth. Vain drew back, his eyes hollow and assessing. The muscle in his jaw ticked once, and then a second time. "I. Want. Rory."

"You do not know what you're asking," Vain said. He took my wrists and pinned them above my head, his grip around them tightening as he pressed my body deeper into the mattress. "I will claim you first. I will worship you, Ava... your body, your soul..."

"Is that your attempt at begging?"

His lips turned nearly white as he pressed them together. The searing breath he exhaled through his nose brushed my cheek as I looked up into his face.

Rory's face.

"I'm calling in my favor," I told him softly. A tear stung my cheek briefly before it melted into the sheets.

"You wouldn't dare," the demon snarled.

I may have been manic with lust, but I at least had enough sense left in me to know that I needed Rory to have a choice in this. He deserved that much. It was his body after all.

"I want him. Now."

Something guttered within his gaze before Vain tore his eyes from mine.

"Consider our debt settled then," he said. "I hope, for your sake, he makes himself worthy of you." Then the pools of black receded from his eyes, revealing Rory's piercing gray.

Rory softened his grip on my wrists and eased off my chest, enough that I was no longer suffocated by the weight of his body.

"I need to know that you want this, Rory," I said, reaching to cup his cheek. His skin felt cool beneath my palm. "Not because Vain wants this. But because you do."

Lowering his forehead down to mine, he whispered, "You think I don't?" He traced light kisses down across my collarbone and back up my neck. When his lips grazed against the shell of my ear, he rasped, "It's all I've wanted for so long."

I shuddered, and Rory's hips eased forward. His cock glided against me easily, sliding up and down and grinding against my clit until I was shaking for him.

I let out a soft whimper. "Tell me again."

Rory lifted his head from the base of my throat and stared back at me. "I want this," he said. "I want *you*."

Relief flooded through me, and I allowed myself to settle into his touch.

"Then take me," I breathed. His mouth was dangerously close to mine, and the heat radiating off his body was scorching. "Please."

The smirk he gave me could have easily rivaled Vain's. "Look who's begging now," he teased and ground his length against my clit again, the lust in his eyes undeniable. "How could you think I haven't thought about fucking you senseless since the first moment I saw you? Holding your body like this in my hands—having you underneath me...it's more perfect than I ever imagined."

Rory's words sent a throbbing jolt through me. He crushed his lips against mine, and we became a rush of heat and labored breaths. Our tongues melded, and I laced my fingers through his hair in the way I had dreamed of doing for so long, to pull him impossibly closer.

"Ava," Rory whispered, the sound oddly strained. He dragged his lips from mine, down to the sensitive skin of my neck, pulling a moan from me. "Vain may have made you come first tonight, but that was my mouth—" he kissed me again, "and my hands—" and again, "that made you scream. And right now, you're all fucking mine."

Rory's cock pressed at my entrance, and with a gasp, he pushed in, just to the tip at first, before thrusting deep inside. I arched off the bed, and my toes curled in the sheets as I gouged my nails into his back. "Oh, fuck!"

Rory hissed and then let out a deep groan, sending a long shiver down my spine. He kept himself buried to the hilt, allowing me to adjust to the size of him. I knew he would feel good, but I never imagined it would be this fucking good.

My whole body tensed as he drew out completely, before driving back in again in one hard stroke. There was no way to hold back my trembling whimper as I threw my hands into the pillows behind me, clutching onto them for dear life.

"Don't fight it," Rory said, his voice soft and a little shaky, like he was barely holding himself together. "Relax, sweetheart."

He ran one hand through my hair and then down the length of my body, and I commanded my muscles to relax just as he'd asked.

His cock pulsed inside me, and my inner walls clamped around him in answer.

His thrusts turned to even, measured strokes that had me melting into him more than I ever thought possible. My body shook each time he hit that spot inside, and my toes curled into the sheets. He was building me up slowly, with torturous care and precision, but I was insatiable, desperate for everything he had to give me.

Rory raised himself to his knees, angling my hips up as he pulled me with him so that my legs fell to either side of him. As if he knew what I wanted without even having to ask. With his fingers digging into my hips, Rory fucked me fast and hard. I nearly screamed as he drove into me. The sight of him pumping in and out with such vicious enthusiasm was enough to send me hurtling straight to the edge. Clenching around him, I bit my bottom lip hard enough that my mouth filled with the bitter iron taste of blood.

"Fuck, Ava," Rory groaned as he continued his steady, pounding rhythm into me. "Do you know what you're doing to me?" His eyes were hooded, drunk on the sensations of our bodies coming together over and over again. "You're making it so hard for me to want to ever give him back control."

"Rory, please don't stop," I begged him. The tingling sensations were building quickly at the base of my spine, and my whole body flushed with warmth. I wound my legs tighter around his waist.

"You're trembling." He smirked. "Are you going to come for me?"

I nodded, unable to make another sound.

"Come on, sweetheart. Give me one orgasm that's just mine. That's all fucking *mine.*"

I shuddered, my body tensing as my mouth parted in sheer bliss. Close. I was so close.

"Come all over my cock, Ava." Every snap of his hips was forceful and demanding as he drove us both toward our climax. "That's it," he panted. "Come for me right fucking now. *Come for me.*"

Rory's words unleashed me. My whole body hummed, and I came shouting his name.

"That's a good girl. That's a good *fucking* girl," he forced through gritted teeth as he continued his punishing thrusts. He sounded as if he was just on the verge of coming apart.

My inner walls clenched and pulsed around him until he couldn't hold out any longer and he tumbled down after me, groaning as he gave me everything he had.

The last shudder tore through him, and he let out a shaking "*fuuuuck*" as a feral smile slid over his face.

Beads of sweat dotted his hairline, and he slicked back the loose strands that kept tumbling over his eyes. I stared at him and marveled at the rise and fall of his hard chest and down to the veins and rigid muscles of arms. He collapsed on top of me, his forearms braced on either side of my head, as he studied my face.

"I think I could stay like this for a long time," he finally said with a small, surprised laugh.

I managed a contented hum, and Rory leaned down to kiss me again. His tongue delved between my parted lips, searching and tender while he continued to roll his hips lazily into mine.

"Thank you," he murmured, trailing his lips across my jaw.

I arched into him, tightening my grip on his hair as my eyelids fluttered. "For what?"

"For not giving up on me." There was a thick strain in his voice that gave me pause. I pulled back to stare up into his face, but the heavy emotion I thought I felt from him was already gone, and in its place was a spark of playfulness dancing behind his eyes.

"I really took it out of you, huh?" Rory teased, dragging his thumb over my brow as he cradled my cheek in his palm. He swept his tongue across his shit-eating grin and rose from the bed. "Lie still. I'll be right back."

I made the mistake of shifting my hips and was met with the sensation of his cum trickling out from between my legs. Rory returned seconds later with a warm cloth and helped to clean me up.

The room swam around me as I lay on the bed beside him. He moved under the sheets and pulled me to him, my bare ass tucked against him as he wrapped me in his arms. Nestling his face into the crook of my neck, he brushed open mouthed kisses along my skin, his breath warm and his lips soft.

I thought I heard Rory murmur "I'm sorry", but the sound was too muffled, and I was already drifting off with his arms wrapped around me as he held my body to his. And I never wanted him to let me go.

# TWENTY-FIVE

## AVA

I woke with Rory's warm body pressed behind mine, enveloping me in a strong embrace. I exhaled deeply, comforted by his touch and the smell of him. I cracked a small smile when he shifted against me, slowly stirring awake.

His lips pressed against the curve of my ear, and he whispered, "Good morning, mellilla. Did you miss me?"

The hair on the back of my neck stood and an icy shiver shot through me. I tore myself away from him, scrambling from beneath the sheets, and I jumped out of the bed to escape him.

Vain threw his head back and laughed, baring a smile that was all teeth. His black eyes raked up and down my body, feasting on every exposed inch. "Why so frightened? You know I prefer it when you fight back. You're so deliciously good at it too."

I had known my choice to push Vain away last night was going to have consequences when he eventually took back control. A vengeful demon fueled by lust and spite was a dangerous thing, and I could see the promise of that consequence swirling just beneath the surface of Vain's calm demeanor. But faced with him again, I was surprised to find that there was still a ghost of the desire I'd felt for him last night.

I'd thought the lust had been fueled, at least in part, by the ichor. But even in the aftermath of that frenzy, I could still feel that same glimmer of desire low in my gut, tempting me. What if it had been something more?

"Where is he?" I asked.

"Rory needed his beauty rest. Now, come be angry with me in bed." When I didn't move, he laughed and gave me another wide, toothy grin. "Honestly, mellilla. I won't hurt you."

Normally, I would have believed him. The demon hadn't gone back on his word once. But it was hard to imagine him holding to that promise when he was eyeing me with such vicious hunger.

"You said you would punish me…"

"I did."

"And will it be worse because I used my favor to deny you for Rory?"

Vain waved a hand dismissively. "Think of it not so much of a punishment as it will be a lesson. You made your decision. I respect that. But I must know, if given the option, would you deny me again, Ava?"

I swallowed hard. My voice came out weaker than I intended. "I should."

"Ah, you feel ashamed?" Of course, he could tell.

"I'm not sure what to feel."

I shouldn't want him. I *knew* I shouldn't want him. And yet I couldn't deny how I felt—how the demon made me feel.

Vain eased back into the pillows while keeping his dark gaze on me as he said, "You do not need to feel shame because you want what you've been convinced you shouldn't have. By denying your-self your true desires, you are only denying yourself happiness." He licked his lips and then his gaze turned molten. "Darkness calls to darkness. You've always felt a pull to it—an insatiable, obsessive need to seek it out and discover what it might have to offer you. It's alright to admit it."

When I didn't answer, Vain cocked his head slightly. "You're still unsure of me? Even now?"

I shook my head, folding my arms tightly across my chest. "It's not that. I'm just not sure how..."

There were a lot of things I was unsure of, and even more that I struggled with how to vocalize. How to give myself to him fully without fear. How it would change everything I had once believed about him—about all his kind. And how to learn to be okay with it. It overwhelmed me to the point of fear, and I froze, unable to move or speak.

"Then allow me to show you," Vain said.

I let out a shaky breath and said, "Okay."

One moment I was staring straight at Vain lying amongst the sheets, a slick smile creeping up the corners of his mouth. The next, shadows poured into the room, enveloping everything around me in pure darkness. I could barely make out my hand in front of my face as I scrambled to hold onto something—anything.

"Don't be afraid of the dark." Vain's voice cut through the shadows, and I jumped. He sounded like he was all around me, his words echoing from every direction. "Just listen to my voice."

Wispy tendrils, soft as silk, curled and brushed against my skin and then would dissipate before reforming elsewhere and licking at me again.

"Even though you're so pretty when you're frightened."

My heart skittered knowing he could see me, vulnerable, naked, and trembling within his shadows.

"I love seeing the way your pulse flutters against your neck." Vain's voice was velvet soft and just out of reach, sounding close and far away simultaneously.

His next words sounded as if they came from directly over my shoulder. "Even your breathing has shallowed as you try to anticipate me."

I whirled to face him, but he wasn't there.

Vain laughed and it echoed around me. "Such a nervous little mortal. I am so very eager to have my turn with you."

I felt like little more than prey as he toyed with me.

The next whisper that brushed against my ears elicited a shiver from my body. "Touch yourself for me, mellilla."

Vain had seen all of me already, but still I shied away on instinct, attempting to cover myself with my hands.

"Ah, ah," he tutted. "No hiding from me. I want to see everything. It's all mine."

The encouraging caress of a shadow curled across the underside of my breasts, then flicked out over my nipples, which had already hardened into firm peaks.

"Touch there."

My hands wavered before I cupped my breasts and rolled my nipples between my fingers. I shut my eyes and breathed in and out, slow and heavy as I let the darkness guide me.

"Good," Vain purred.

Another shadow trailed down my abdomen before settling at the apex between my thighs. I dragged in a shaky breath, trying to hold back a moan from escaping past my lips.

"Here," he instructed.

This time I didn't hesitate. I kept one hand cupped on my breast while the other moved to rest against my aching clit.

"I want you to show me how you like it." Even in the pitch-black, I could hear his wicked grin in every syllable as he spoke.

The shadows gathered at my back like a gentle embrace, and I settled into them, allowing them to sweep me off my feet so that I laid on top of them as I touched myself for Vain.

The air vibrated with a low rumbling sound as I pressed hard against my hand, working myself in slow, tight circles.

I let a moan spill out of me, the sound catching in my throat as a pounding heat rose within my core. Phantom wisps glanced and teased along my collarbone, caressing the sensitive skin of my throat. More shadows curled around my thighs, gently squeezing and holding me in place as my movements picked up and my body grew more needy by the second.

"Do you like touching yourself for me?"

"Yes," I rasped. Not being able to see him, yet knowing he was there, hidden by shadows, watching my every move...it ignited a wicked desire deep in my bones, my blood. I arched my back against Vain's bed of shadows and tipped my head back as I slipped a finger inside, but the curl of a dark wispy tendril around my wrist dragged my hand away.

"Don't be greedy, mellilla. I haven't told you to touch there yet."

My eyes shot open, and I gasped. Vain stood over me, his body hovering over mine as he watched my obscene display with distinct pleasure. He appeared to be one with the shadows that wound themselves around his naked form, almost as if they were as alive as he was.

"Patience," he said and tugged my hand back toward my clit before the shadows enveloped him again, and I was left searching again for the demon in the darkness.

I whined at the near agonizing ache of being empty. His denial left me needy, the desperation causing my breasts to swell. My pussy clenched, the muscles tensing as I circled my clit. I both hated Vain and needed him simultaneously.

My hips nearly jumped up off the shadows at the sweep of Vain's warm tongue upward through my folds, then licking back down before plunging into me.

His mouth was pure sin, and I never wanted him to stop.

"Don't you dare stop touching yourself."

Every other sense felt heightened in the dark. Even the lightest of Vain's touches lit up my nerves like wildfire, and my blood crackled with electricity that ran through me and left me a disastrous, needy mess for him.

I was wound so tight, my muscles vibrated as I shook, and I feared I might snap at any moment. But each time I neared my climax, Vain would pull back and tear my hand away from my clit, leaving me crying out, aching, and needing to come.

Over and over again, we did that dance, toeing a dangerously thin line between pleasure and the torturous ache of him denying me everything I wanted. If he'd sought to purge every last one of my doubts—any hesitations I once had—he was succeeding.

I wanted it all. I wanted *him*.

Every time Vain denied me, he left me gasping and my mewling pleas sounded desperate and pathetic in my ears. I thought I caught a hint of a faint laugh escape him, his breath fluttering over my core. He was ruining me and reveling in every second of it.

"You don't get to come yet. Only when I say you can."

He knew how I lusted for him—his touch, his body, his mouth. All of him. I wanted every last sinful, depraved part of this demon. His continued groans and soft laughter against my pussy as he edged me only made the ache worse.

"It's okay for you to say it," he said before he sucked my clit back into his mouth. "There's no need to deny it anymore. Haven't you gone long enough refusing your desire for me."

I squeezed my eyes shut and felt something break in my chest. That small crack in my armor Vain had so acutely chipped away at since the beginning, I had felt it growing over time. Ignoring it and pretending it simply didn't exist had been useless. Trying to mend the fissures and rebuild my walls had proved futile. Denying him was no longer an option. Not when my soul sang for him, called to his darkness like a moth to flame.

"I want you, Vain."

My words coaxed him from the darkness. Vain emerged from the shadows as if he were born of them. The sight of him was mesmerizing, the combined image of Vain's dark power and Rory's beauty stunned me as I took him in. He leaned over me and caged me with his body. The faint stubble along Rory's cheek scratched against my jaw as his lips pressed to the shell of ear. "Again."

"I want you. Please, Vain."

He pulled back enough to flash me a grin that had my heart turning over and the last of my resolve dusting away to ash. His nostrils flared as he drew in a slow and satisfied breath "Have I ever told you how much pleasure it brings me to hear those words come from your lips." His eyes darkened further. "Beg me again."

"Please." I shuddered. "Please, I *need* you."

Taking my chin between his thumb and forefinger, Vain held my gaze with an unmatched intensity. A stare that could bring mortals and gods alike to their knees. "Look at me."

It felt as if I was seeing Vain through new eyes. Beyond the sparse constellation of freckles stippled faintly over Rory's cheekbones and along his jaw, his full lips and defined arch of his cupid's bow, the fall of dark hair over his forehead that just barely curled at the ends—beyond the humanness that was Rory, I stared into Vain's onyx eyes and felt as if I was truly seeing him for what he was for the very first time—a demon of infinite darkness and eternal lust, veiled in secrets and shadows.

There was a haunting danger in his essence that drew me to him. I wanted to drown in him. I would let his darkness overtake me, wanting nothing more than to be swathed in the safety it offered. He might easily have been the most terrifyingly beautiful thing I had ever seen, and I found that I couldn't look away.

Vain kept my chin tipped upward as we stared silently at one another, and tears filled with awe stung at the corner of my eyes while the tip of his cock nudged at my dripping entrance, begging him to press into me.

He swept my tears away with his thumb, and his gaze softened the moment he noticed I'd eased into his touch, accepting him for everything he was and everything I was no longer ashamed of wanting.

Together, we laid atop his shadows, and he held me with such reverence and lust as he drove his cock into me, hard and slow. I clawed at his shoulders and dug my heels into his waist as he slid in fully. Pressing his chest to mine, Vain lowered his face until our foreheads met, our breaths hot and heavy against the others cheeks.

The sounds of our flesh meeting with each thrust tightened the knot in my core, and I knew it would only take a few more strokes before I couldn't hold myself together anymore. I was a whimpering, quivering mess beneath him, begging Vain within an inch of my life to let me finish.

Caressing my cheek in his palm, he held my gaze as he spoke with unwavering control. "Look at me when you come, Ava. I want to watch you fall apart for me."

His thrusts were relentless, and then my whole world crashed around me, my release wrecking me. Mind, body, and soul.

I clenched around Vain as he offered me no mercy. He fucked me fast and hard through it all. Even after I started to come down from my release, Vain lanced himself in and out, his pace only slowing after he had dragged the last of my orgasm from me, and I crumpled against his shadows, feeling drugged and heavy.

He pressed a light kiss to the corners of my mouth as he fucked me with a newfound gentleness I wasn't used to from him. I pulled him down to press his mouth to mine fully, feeling drunk with the taste of him. A jolt of pleasure shot through me and settled in my core as he parted my lips with his tongue and explored my mouth while he sifted his fingers through my hair, his nails scraping gently against my scalp.

With his mouth still molded to mine, Vain rolled us so I straddled him, his cock still buried deep inside. I rolled my hips forward, barely an inch, but it was enough to force a low growl of pleasure from Vain, which reverberated through his chest into mine. He looked up at me with a delicious, satisfied grin before his black eyes fell to where we were joined.

"I love how you look grinding on his cock," Vain said, his voice low and gravelly.

He looked so good below me, lips slightly swollen and set apart as if he were in awe, and his eyes darkened further than I thought possible.

"Use me," he said, sounding like a command and a plea all at once.

I slid along his length in slow, languid motions, rolling my hips over him as I ground deep and taking great pleasure in the sharp hissing sounds of Vain's ragged breathing. Finding a steady rhythm, I rocked against him, each stroke taking him deeper and driving me wild every time he nudged that sweet, sensitive spot that had me keening into Vain's shadows.

He grabbed my hips, and the muscles in his arms flexed as he held me firmly. Vain wasn't taking control. He was losing himself in me as much as I was with him. The sight of this fearsome demon being completely wrecked beneath me was nearly enough to send me over the edge again. Vain was allowing me to ruin him completely.

This was power.

His shadows licked around us in a wild frenzy that matched our movements. I clawed at his chest in a desperate attempt to latch onto something—anything—before I was cresting again and then breaking as I rode him through another brutal orgasm.

My eyes shot open, and I saw stars—literal stars. Their light pierced through Vain's shadows and illuminated us in a silvery glow. The way they shimmered and danced around us almost re-minded me of Vain's eyes when the light would hit them just right. I peered down at him, finding his obsidian eyes glinting back at me, tempting and wicked.

And mine.

The muscle in his jaw feathered, and the veins in Vain's neck pulsed as he groaned through clenched teeth. "Fuck!"

Vain roared as he came, spilling himself inside me and leaving me wild and breathless all over again. I rolled my hips over and over until I took everything from him, and he shuddered with a trembling breath.

I stayed seated firmly against his still-hard cock when he pulled himself up, dark eyes never once leaving mine as he wrapped his arms around me. As he kissed across my collarbone and throat, his shadows fell away, and the bright morning light spilled in through the bedroom windows, blanketing my bare skin in its warmth.

We sat tangled on the fur rug we'd found ourselves on after the shadows had dissipated, holding each other in silence. Vain ran a hand through his hair, pushing the stray locks off of his face with a cocky swagger and then brushed the loose strands of mine behind my ears before resting his palm at the base of my throat. He kept the pressure light, somewhere between greedy and possessive.

"Now," Vain said, low and full of promise. "Now you belong to both of us."

# TWENTY-SIX

## AVA

After we stepped out of a long shower together, Vain left to make breakfast while I dove back into his bed and refused to move a muscle under the cool, silken sheets that smelled like a combination of both him and Rory. Warm and smoky. Bright and sweet.

The mouth-watering scent of sautéed onions and garlic wafted through the penthouse and a gentle sizzling echoed from the kitchen. As I laid there in his bed, I watched the dust motes dance lazily in between the golden rays of the morning sun. I had once told Vain that this would never be my home, but I had never felt more at home than I did in that moment.

I had spent the majority of my life at the Moreau Coven, living among my peers, some of whom I once considered to be my family, but I never truly felt like I fit in like the rest of them. I had sought out their approval but never received the love I desired or needed. Not from them. And certainly not from my real family.

But, somehow, I had found some sense of belonging with Rory and Vain.

When they returned to the bedroom, Rory was in control, bare chested with a pair of dark sweatpants slung low across his hips as he balanced a platter of food and two mugs on a wooden tray table.

He beamed at me as he set it down. "Unfortunately, you drank all the tea, so you'll have to settle for coffee."

"Coffee is fine," I said, returning a grin.

The dish he set between us was four poached eggs set atop a red, peppery sauce, garnished with salty crumbles of feta cheese. There were even toasted slices of bread to dip into the sauce and the golden runny yolks. The moment the first bite hit my tongue, I nearly came again.

"How are you feeling?" Rory asked after finishing up what he had claimed as his half. He rested on his side, head propped up with one arm as he sipped at his coffee.

"Good," I said, offering him a soft smile. "A little sore, but I feel better than I've felt in a while."

"And what about the ichor? Are you still feeling the effects of that?"

I flexed the fingers of my right hand and assessed the fuzzy remnants of the power that still lingered after.

"It's just barely there," I said, then noticed the slight hesitation in his expression. "Don't worry, I'm okay." I took another bite and hummed before changing the subject. "I didn't realize Vain was this good of a cook."

Rory chuckled. "Bold of you to assume I didn't contribute anything to the cooking. What if I told you I was the one who made breakfast?"

Given the mischievous glint in Rory's eyes, I already knew the answer. "I'd say you're a pretty liar."

We both laughed.

I pushed the tray away and laid down on my stomach beside him with my arms cradled beneath the pillow. He stroked a wisp of hair behind my ear, his touch warm and endearing.

"Look, I feel like an idiot for not asking earlier. But are you...taking anything?" he asked.

"No," I said.

"Shit." He shook his head. "I wasn't thinking. I shouldn't—Vain shouldn't have..."

"Rory, it's..." I paused and tugged away from his touch. "We won't have to worry about it."

I almost couldn't bear to look at him. But when I did, his gaze was soft, searching yet understanding somehow.

"My last partner...he wanted a family. But I knew I didn't want that. I can't, even if I did—Rory, I can't...I can't get pregnant."

How could I even begin to explain to him? I used to think that I was broken and that no one would ever truly want me. The rejection I feared—the pity—it was the reason I had never even told Luke. I couldn't bear the thought of catching that hurt in his eyes as I dashed his hopes in an instant. Instead, I'd left him and made him hate me. It had been easier that way, for the both of us, at least that's what I'd tried to convince myself. But really, it had just been easier for me.

But there was nothing like that rejection I feared in Rory's eyes. The way he looked at me, his eyes so full of understanding and lacking any judgment, I could have cried.

"Hey, hey." He thumbed his palm across my cheek. "You don't have to explain, not to me, not to anyone. You hear me?"

He cradled me to his chest, one hand stroking my hair. Lying together in the comfortable silence, I felt grateful for his presence. For once, I didn't feel the need to run.

"What are you thinking about?" he asked, and I peered up to look at him.

"Nothing."

Rory hadn't missed the way I'd said it too quickly, his brow quirking upward in response. "What's wrong?"

I considered avoiding his question altogether, but my boldness got the better of me.

"Do you ever miss it being just you?"

A shadow of concern passed behind his eyes at the question, and he paused briefly to consider it. "I think I used to. But honestly, I barely remember what it felt like without Vain." He turned his gaze to the ceiling. "I haven't dreamed in seven years. If I had to miss anything, that may be it. But I know that I can never go back to how things were before. And I'm okay with that."

I pulled my bottom lip from between my teeth. "It doesn't have to be that way though."

"Ava." Rory's eyelids twinged shut before he scraped a hand down his face. "Please..."

"I can help you," I insisted. "I don't want Vain gone. But if I can exorcise him—can separate the two of you—then you can live your own life. You can be your own person again."

"Ava, stop," he said. "I need you to get those ideas out of your head. They're fantasies. It's never going to happen."

"Why not? Why don't you want him gone?" My voice sounded hollow, shaky.

"You—" Rory stopped and exhaled loudly. "You wouldn't understand." I could tell he was biting back his frustration and yet I wanted to push him. I wanted to understand. I *needed* to.

"Do you love him?" I asked, all too quietly.

Rory's gray eyes found mine, unblinking and earnest. "Yes," he said. "For a long time now. And you can't exorcise Vain because I don't want him gone." His voice was sharp, his words laced with the truth I had already guessed.

His shoulders slumped, and he reached for me. One palm rested against the side of my cheek as he sighed through his nose. "I don't need you to fix me, Ava. I never did. I'm already on borrowed time."

All the air whooshed from my lungs. I sat up slowly and Rory's hand fell away from my face, the spot quickly turning cold in the absence of his touch.

"What the hell does that mean?"

He cast his attention down to the sheets, unable to meet my cautious gaze.

"I-I shouldn't be alive... Vain is the only reason I'm not dead. He...fuck." He released a shaky exhale as he scrubbed his hand down over his face again, biting back a choked sob.

Rory's hands brushed over his tattoos. "Have you ever made a mistake?" he asked after a moment. "One you couldn't take back and instantly regretted?"

I wanted to tell him that yes, I had. And I was all too familiar with the feeling. I knew it intimately. But it didn't seem right to interject as I watched him struggle to find his words, his throat bobbing with every apprehensive swallow.

"I used to cut myself. I did it for years, but there was one night that was really, really bad and I...I spiraled. I went too far. I regretted it immediately, but it was too late...I was dying, and I didn't want to. I knew I wasn't ready. Vain was my second chance. He saved me by offering me a choice to act as a vessel for him in exchange for my life." Rory looked up at me, and I caught the tears swimming in his eyes. "He's so strong though, Ava. And I don't know how much longer my mind will last. Vain says most vessels don't take well to possessions. After a time, it warps their minds until there's nothing left of themselves and the demon fully takes over. And I can already feel myself slipping."

He took my hand in his, but I felt nothing.

"You can't fix me, Ava. Either way, I'm already dead. I don't know what I did to deserve for you to care this much about me, but just know that I'm sorry. I'm so, so sorry."

Before I could reach for him or utter a single word, Rory re-treated into himself and allowed Vain to come forward. The demon stared back at me with a pained expression, so hollow and haunting, it tugged at the creases between his brows.

"Tell him to come back," I said, knowing Rory could still hear me and see me pleading. "We're not done talking about this."

"Ava, please—"

"I need to hear it from him!"

Vain blew out a sigh, then pressed his lips together. "Listen to me, Ava. What Rory said was true. An exorcism cannot be successful if the host vessel refuses to let go. You could never exorcise me from him because he never wanted me gone in the first place."

I shook my head. "That's not possible." But it was. How else could I explain it? How many theories had I sought out and exhausted only to fail at every one?

"Rory let me in. He accepted me into his body, and I have protected him for seven years. I am the only thing keeping him alive now."

I froze again. "What does that mean?"

Vain glanced down at Rory's arms. "I healed him the moment I possessed him. These wounds were once a death sentence. If I were to extract myself from him, he would return to the state I found him in when he was very nearly dead. These cuts were too deep for too long. The moment I leave his body, they will reopen and he will bleed out in seconds. But even if he could be healed physically, nothing could repair the scars the possession would leave on his mind afterward. Because our bond has only strengthened after all these years, Rory wouldn't survive the separation."

It felt as if a knife had been plunged through my chest, and Vain was the one twisting the blade, tearing my heart to shreds.

I clenched my teeth until my jaw ached. "So, you're possessing him and eating away at his mind and his soul until there's nothing fucking left of him?"

Vain's eyes softened yet held a warning in them. "I cannot control it. It is not my intention, but the force of my nature."

"Did you know?" I whispered loud enough that I knew Rory would hear it. But he didn't pull himself forward.

Vain blinked once. "He knew. He knew the risks from the beginning."

I shoved his chest with both hands. "Shut up! Rory, tell me yourself, you coward!" My voice broke as I yelled, but it was no use.

"I did tell you that you wouldn't be able to exorcise me, mellilla. You knew from the start."

"*Don't,*" I snarled, my fists clenched in the sheets. I'd been so sure it had been a grand lie, some trick or riddle I might be able to solve. I wasn't sure what hurt more; knowing Vain had never once lied to me, or realizing that I had been too stubborn to see the truth.

Rory and Vain coexisted as one. There would always be a wrongness, an unnatural peculiarity to their bond no matter how hard I tried to look past it. Rory would never know the quiet of his own mind without Vain again. He would wrestle the demon for control until Vain overtook him completely and all that remained of him was a hollow shell, and he was nothing more than a ghost. From the start, I'd never had any real chance of saving him.

A wave of nausea struck me, and I suddenly felt flushed, my skin clammy as I struggled to swallow. Even my limbs shook as I moved to get up from the bed. Vain's hand shot out and encircled my wrist, keeping me locked in place. "I'm sorry, mellilla. Truly, I am."

I looked deep into Vain's eyes, searching fervently for any sign of gray. Finding them empty, I yanked my hand from Vain's grasp and moved toward the door, not caring that I would be walking into the hallway completely naked. Vain's bedroom suddenly felt claustrophobic. The walls swam, the floor underneath my bare feet wobbling. I wanted out.

My head pounded, and every breath shattered in my lungs as a hopeless ache settled in the pit of my stomach. I stumbled a few feet away from the door and Vain appeared beside me in an instant, his arms braced against my waist to steady me. He spoke, but the words were muffled against the buzz in my eardrums. As his lips moved, his eyes shifted from black to gray, back and forth, the sight making me dizzy. I couldn't make sense of either of them.

My heart and mind raced. But as I tried to shove myself away from them, my legs gave out from underneath me and tremors began to wrack through my body. The edges of my vision darkened, and the last thing I remembered was one of them catching me before I collapsed to the ground.

# TWENTY-SEVEN
## RORY

"She's not going to turn, is she?"

*I don't know,* Vain said after considering for a long moment. *If she were, then I think it would have happened by now.*

Vain had done everything in his power to flush as much of the remaining ichor out of Ava's body as he could. Once she had stopped seizing, he forced her to throw up twice, leaving a dark stain behind on the floor of our bedroom. It hadn't looked like much, but it was enough that we hoped that whatever was left in her wasn't enough to turn her.

I'd carried her into her bed, and Vain had hooked Ava up to an IV to detox her system and keep her stabilized. For two days she remained unconscious.

Each time we would check on her I leaned in and pulled back her lips, afraid I would find her canines had turned into deadly fangs. But no matter how often Vain tried to convince me otherwise, I never believed that she would be okay.

*There's not much more we can do for her now but to wait. Holy water is rare to come by.*

Ava had destroyed the only bottle of holy water that Vain owned, and it would be useless to try to find and acquire more now. Even if by some small miracle we got our hands on a bottle, it would be too late either way. Ava would either have turned or recovered on her own. All we could do was wait.

I sat in her room with her and forced myself to endure the weight of my guilt as I monitored the uneven rise and fall of her chest. The way her eyes danced beneath closed lids. The beads of sweat dotting her flushed cheeks and her brow before soaking into her hair.

Every day, her fever came and went suddenly, and Vain and I brought cold compresses and soft towels to keep it at bay. There were even points when she would slip in and out of consciousness where paranoia took over and Ava would scream out the same name.

"Sascha! Sascha!"

Over and over, she screamed and thrashed while attempting to rip the IV out of her arm. And every time, Vain would go to her side and press two fingers to her temple to subdue her into an unconscious state again. It was the only time he had ever allowed himself to use his power on her mind, and he silently hoped she might one day forgive him for it.

Not only had the demon's ichor brought her to the brink of turning into a monster herself, but I remembered the tortured look in Ava's eyes when the simulacrum had slung all of those horrible taunting insults at her. I wondered if those dark memories were still haunting her in her fitful sleep.

Sometimes in the night, I would crawl under the covers behind her and hold her in my arms as the chills wracked her body so hard that her teeth chattered. I didn't know if it helped her or if she was even aware of my presence, but it made me feel better knowing she was safe. Our skin touching and our breaths mingling was enough for me. And when I wasn't with her, every second apart felt too far, too long.

I couldn't remember feeling that way about anyone in my whole miserable life. No one had come close to the way this woman made me feel—except for maybe Vain.

She had changed us both, for better or for worse.

Ava was ours. She would never be just mine. A part of her would always belong to Vain. And I didn't mind. Maybe it was due to the fact that Vain felt more like an extension of myself than anything—the darker side of me that resided deep inside my own soul. We would care for her until the day I no longer could, until there was nothing left of me but the demon that remained.

"Sir, you need to rest," Alastair said to Vain the night he returned from helping Dru get back to her family. But Vain and I had refused sleep. We barely even ate since neither of us had the stomach for it. I couldn't have felt more useless sitting there, waiting for Ava to wake—or turn.

It was worse for Vain, the powerlessness he felt, his crushing guilt sat like a cold stone in our chest. It was almost too much for me to bear.

The thought of living without Vain had become a foreign concept to me, and the thought of living without Ava had become similarly incomprehensible.

Did that make me pathetic?

*You know I love how pathetic and needy you are.*

"You're not helping," I grumbled aloud at him as I ran my hands over my arms and let the longer front ends of my hair hang over my eyes to shadow my expression, not that anyone could see. Vain could mock me all he wanted but it didn't change the fact that he felt the same way about her as I did.

I wanted her to wake up. I needed to look into her eyes and hold her in my arms and tell her she was okay. I would never forget how she had looked through Vain, right into my soul, as she slammed her fists against his chest, her pain and betrayal painted on her features after he'd laid out the hard truth that neither of us had told her after all this time. Whenever she woke, I could only hope she might forgive me.

I hoped she could forgive *us*.

# TWENTY-EIGHT

## AVA

I had known the risks, but I had taken them anyway.

Having a dangerous fascination with demons myself, I understood how humans became so easily entranced by them. But even in all my years of study, I had never fully understood the obsession a mortal could develop with demon ichor, especially consuming it to the point where it would turn them into a monster worse than the demon themselves.

When consumed in excess, a demon's ichor could turn even the most gentlehearted human into a blood crazed killer—a vampyr which craved and feasted on demon ichor and human blood for survival. Once turned, they became ravenous, too quick and cunning, insatiable and destructive, and far too feral and unpredictable to be kept alive, making them rare but deadly predators to both mortals and demons alike.

The laws forbidding the consumption of ichor were clear, and I'd always understood them. But being under the influence of a demon's blood, I finally understood the extent of the hunger—the obsession. The full-body craving and the primal need to sate myself to the point of overindulgence was unlike anything I had experienced before. The desire for more—for power—felt all-consuming.

I swam in and out of consciousness, only vaguely aware of where I was or how long I'd been out. There were moments when I could have sworn I woke with a warm body pressed against my back while the room spun around me. Dampened, mumbled voices cut in and out through my half-lucid state and my nightmares. Sometimes when my eyelids twitched to flutter open, I could have sworn Rory's dark figure sat across from me, watching me intently. Other times, Vain's smooth, low voice whispered to me from afar in words too hushed for me to make out.

I desperately wanted to reach out to them, to lift my hand up or call out their names. But my limbs felt like they were encased in stone, my tongue leaden in my mouth. I had no choice but to lie there in the dark with nothing but the terrors of my mind, waiting for fate to decide my consequence.

In my nightmares, I saw her face. In the void, I heard her screams. Never had they felt so tangible before. So real. And I was doomed to re-live the memory of Sascha dying over and over. The scent of sulfur in the air, the dark, hollow eyes of the demon that stared back at me, wearing her face, warping her smile into a sinister thing. There was no escaping the painful visions my unconscious mind subjected me to. If the ichor didn't destroy me, then surely my lingering guilt would tear me apart in the end.

A piercing chill shot through my chest, and I sprung up, gasping and sputtering for air. The sheets around me were cold and wet. Sweat ran down my temples, my arms, every inch of me. A numb ache rushed through my body, and my throat felt raw when I swallowed.

Rory darted to my side, his panicked eyes sweeping over me. As I violently shook, he held down my arms, his hands hard and soothing. I hadn't even noticed I'd been clawing at myself until I looked down and noticed the lines of scratches marring my pale arms and the scrapes over my chest leading up towards my neck. There was an IV sticking out of my forearm that shifted uncomfortably under my skin whenever I moved.

"Hey, hey, it's okay. You're okay. Ava, look at me," Rory said, taking my face between his hands. He pushed the sweat-slicked strands of hair clinging to my skin out of my face, brushing them behind my ears. His touch was ice cold and soothed my fevered skin. "You're okay," he repeated, over and over. "I'm here, Ava."

I threw my arms around him and clung to him tightly. He stroked one hand down my back, the other cradling my head as he rocked us, all the while holding me close.

My throat, my teeth, my bones all ached. Even my blood felt heavy in my veins as the withdrawal from the ichor lingered.

"It hurts." The words sounded foreign as I strained to get them out.

Rory stroked my hair as he shushed me. "I know. I know it hurts," he said. "I know, sweetheart."

I hadn't turned. I was alive.

Rory held me, and I sighed into him, calmed by his familiar scent as my breathing slowed. I broke away and met his troubled gaze.

"Why didn't you tell me?" I asked. His hand slid down my temple to cradle my cheek in his palm. "This whole time I was fighting for you, and you never had any chance. Why not just tell me?"

"I was afraid," he whispered, and my throat immediately choked up with emotion. "I was afraid that if you realized that I was a lost cause, then you would leave. It was stupid and selfish of me to keep it from you, I know that. But I wasn't ready to let you go." Rory swallowed, his Adam's apple bobbing sharply with the motion. "Trust me, Vain tried to convince me that I should tell you. But I just couldn't. I know that I should have, and I'm sorry. I'm so, so sorry, Ava."

His eyes flickered downward, but I drew his watery gaze back up to mine. "You were *never* a lost cause."

"I thought we lost you," he breathed. Drawing my hand up to his lips, he pressed a kiss to my knuckles. "I would have never forgiven myself if something had happened to you."

A warmth pulled in my chest as I stared at him. And even as I knew that there may never be any hope left of saving him as I once intended, I felt contented in the realization that what we had—the three of us together—was enough. No matter how long Rory had, until there was nothing left of his mind and all that remained was Vain, I was ready to spend every last second of that time appreciating every moment.

I'd never known a happiness quite like this before them. There'd never been a sense of acceptance and belonging like what they offered. And for once in my miserable life, I didn't want to push it away any longer. I deserved to be happy. I *deserved* to feel wanted. To be loved.

To even call it love was terrifying, but there was no denying the emotion that stirred in me was exactly that. Ignoring it was no longer an option.

I opened my mouth, struggling to form the words I so desperately needed to say to alleviate the knot twisting in my heart, but a deafening boom crashed through the penthouse before I could, and it felt as if the entire foundation of the building shook with the sound. A scream tore from my throat instead, and Rory threw his body overtop of mine, tucking me tightly to his chest.

Both of us jerked as another boom and then another sounded again in violent rhythmic succession. The air crackled and I could feel the threads of magic and the energy of the wards shattering with every tremor that rocked around us.

Rory pulled his face out of the crook of my neck, and his eyes filled to black.

"Vain, what's happening?"

He stared down at me, our foreheads pressed together and our racing heartbeats keeping pace with each other. Our attention shifted at the same time when Nesera whipped around the corner and flew into the room, decked to the nines in her fighting leathers and her scimitars fisted in both hands.

"He's here," she yelled over the thunderous roar of another ominous crack that tore at the wards. "He's almost broken through them all."

Vain looked back at me, and I recognized the panic shimmering behind his eyes in a way I had only seen once before.

"Ava, what was the name of the demon you summoned that killed your sister?"

I grew faint all over again. "Vain, I—"

"Did you ever properly banish them after they were summoned?"

"He wasn't—" I stammered. "I couldn't—"

He clasped both hands around my arms and gripped them tightly. "Were you the one who banished him?"

"No!"

"Who was the demon?" he demanded. "Tell me his name."

I held the answer at the tip of my tongue, but I could see in Vain's eyes that he already knew the demon's name long before I said it.

"Ghen."

She shook her head. "I'm fine." Her attention flickered to a spot over our shoulder and her eyes widened. Vain swung his head back to look in the same direction.

Ghen hovered in the air, his form barely more than a dark shape on the terrace. He was somehow much larger than I remembered. The wind whipped his silver hair around him like a storm, and I swore his eyes burned a hot white as his figure floated closer. When he slowly dropped to the terrace, the energy around us went electric. Every footfall the archdemon made in our direction felt as if the ground were shaking, like he was putting every ounce of power that he had into each step.

When the glow of his eyes faded, he was still every bit the unnerving, dark omen that shot a lance of fear straight through my chest. His energy was a palpable, living thing, inescapable and present in every atom in the air that Vain breathed into our lungs.

Vain rose and brought Ava up with us, maneuvering her body behind ours and keeping one hand wrapped back around her waist as he faced Ghen.

From across the room, Alastair and Nesera stood as well, the former extracting long, thick shards of glass from his body, his wounds stitching back together almost immediately, and the latter holding a wide stance as she drew her scimitars, appearing steadier on her feet than she had been a minute before.

The archdemon stalked a slow, wide circle around us with a crooked smile eased across his perfectly sculpted face that felt very much like a threat. His searing gaze never left ours, and Vain stared him down with equal hostility on his part, like they were two predators, each sizing the other up.

"There you are, brother." The archdemon's voice, sharp and smooth, rumbled as he crossed the threshold into the penthouse, glass shards crunching underneath his shoes.

*Brother?*

Vain winced, and in my periphery, I caught the motion of Nesera's head tilt to the side, one quizzical brow raised which would have matched my exact expression if I were the one in control.

*Is he lying?* I asked him.

And he actually hesitated before answering, "No."

I felt Ava stiffen behind us, but she remained decidedly quiet.

There was barely time for the thought—let alone the implication—to register.

Vain tipped his head up and watched as Ghen brushed stray bits of debris from the lapels of his long, elegant coat that appeared to be more of a formal piece of armor than anything. The wide shoulders flared upward, the points tipped in gold accents which matched the markings ingrained into the gray fabric that shimmered with a semi-metallic quality. Whenever the ends of the heavy coat brushed his ankles, it emitted a muted jangling noise with every step.

Vain growled low. "You are not welcome here."

The archdemon clicked his tongue. "So it would seem," he mused. "You went to great lengths in an effort to keep me out. One might wonder what you're so determined to protect up here in your little tower."

"Just take the grimoire," Vain said. "Take it and leave."

"I'll take back what I'm owed after I've run through every last one of your little pets." The archdemon's smile grew malicious. "Perhaps I'll even force you to watch the light leave their eyes, one by one. I think I'll leave the witch for last too. It would be so fitting, wouldn't it?"

Vain snarled. "You will not touch them."

"Hiding under my nose," Ghen admonished with a shake of his head as he continued circling us. "Did you really think I wouldn't eventually realize who you were under all those mortal masks you so desperately clung to like they were your armor?" The archdemon appeared to stand almost impossibly taller, leveling us with a look that could have brought cities to their knees. "Do you think you can somehow fix them? Because they cannot redeem you, brother. They will not absolve you of what you are."

Ghen took another slow step closer and Vain pulled back to maintain the distance between us. Cocking his head to the side, the archdemon peered around our body to where Ava stood.

"There's the little summoner bitch," he purred with malintent. "Did you even recognize me when I was not wearing the skin of your sister? Though, I suppose, a witch never truly forgets their first, isn't that right?"

Ava whimpered behind us, and Vain's glare turned scorching.

"I'll admit, it took me longer to recognize *you*," Ghen continued as he stared at her, his grin nothing short of predatory. "But it was the scent of your fear that eventually jogged my memory." His nostrils flared as he breathed in deep. "It seems all that guilt you've harbored after all these years has done nothing but fester inside you, leaving a deliciously dark stain on your soul. I'll even admit, I'm a bit prideful of the fact that I'm the cause of it."

Vain's grip tightened on Ava's waist, and I caught the faintest whisper escaping her lips, the magic in the near-silent words floating past our ears like a soft breath. They did not escape Ghen's ears though. He paused mid-stride and narrowed his eyes on her.

"*Shut up.*" The glamour took hold of Ava immediately and silenced her as her posture went rigid.

From the shadows, a long blade glinted behind Ghen. Nesera's form peeled through the darkened room as she took the opportunity of the archdemon's distracted attention to leap out and attack. Her scimitars poised above her head, Nesera drove them straight for the archdemon's exposed neck at a speed I almost couldn't register. Ghen's body turned into a blur at the same moment, and the split second before impact, he sidestepped so Nesera's blades bounced off the armor of his coat.

Every lunge Nesera made after still failed to strike the archdemon. She danced circles around him, her face twisted into a fierce promise of violence, all while her attacks glanced through the air, never quite finding purchase in Ghen's flesh.

As Ghen whirled to avoid another of her assaults, his foot snared on a ring of golden chains worming up through the floor. Across the room, Alastair's eyes flared like blazing jewels. With his palm upturned, he commanded the glowing chains which shot out like whips at the archdemon, and they coiled themselves around Ghen's legs and arms like a leashing of snakes.

Ghen roared against them, his teeth bared in a sharp grimace as Alastair forced him to his knees. A growl crawled up his throat as Nesera continued her assault on him, but each time she sliced at his exposed skin, the dark gashes knit back together extraordinarily fast, even though her blades were forged from the purest silver and selenite.

Vain surged forward, his shadows swirling around us like a midnight storm. They pooled down his arm and coalesced into a sharpened blade, so dark it appeared to be made of night itself. He collided with Ghen and plunged the makeshift blade straight through the archdemon's armor. It sank deep into his chest, and when Vain gave the hilt a sharp twist, it emitted a sickening crunch right before he yanked the blade free.

Ichor flowed from the wound in a heavy black channel, streaming down the front of the Ghen's chest and seeping into the strange material of his armor.

Again, Vain drove his shadow blade through the archdemon. Then again. And again. But Ghen only laughed while rocking back on his heels as he took blow after unforgiving blow.

"You know this only ends once I've cut through every last weakness you hold so dear," Ghen taunted in the demon tongue through a low chuckle.

A hum rose in the air again, that same thrumming warning. It radiated outward from Ghen and grew quickly with such a force that there was no time to brace for the surge before it exploded outward from him. The force launched our body off the ground, and Vain and I saw stars before we even connected hard with the far wall. Vain collapsed against it with a groan before lifting his head to survey the damage.

Bits of glass and debris rained down around us. Both Alastair's and Nesera's bodies lay crumpled together on the opposite end of the room. Vain scanned frantically in search of Ava. She laid at the edge of the terrace, one side of her face resting against the floor while she remained under the thrall of Ghen's glamour, her eyes still wide and glassy.

*Shake out of it.* I chanted like a prayer, as if she'd somehow be able to hear me. *Get up. Get up!*

Ghen rose from his knees and lifted one hand above his head. Red-black flames flickered to life at his fingertips, and he cast them to the ground in a tall ring around where Nesera and Alastair still lay bruised and battered.

"And now to deal with you, brother." The archdemon sighed as he stalked forward with one arm outstretched and sent an invisible force slamming into our chest that felt like a crushing weight, keeping us pinned in place and unable to move.

Ghen crouched low in front of us, his sneer softer than the one Vain wore. He plucked up our chin in one large hand and pivoted my face from side to side, his lip curling as he appraised us with apparent disgust.

"Just when I thought you couldn't become any more pathetic, demeaning yourself and tarnishing our name by throwing yourself in alliance with these pests, you decide that confining yourself to their weak mortal forms is somehow a more suitable way to exist. I will never understand what you see in them and why you are determined to let them make you weak when you could be so much more." Ghen leaned in close until we could feel his breath heat our face. "You've always rejected your nature, Vencula. Why?"

Vain took a breath before answering, the words coming out through a snarl. "I know what I am."

"I don't think you do," Ghen replied with a shake of his head. He still spoke in their language, the words sharp and guttural which felt like an assault all on their own. "We were built to break them. To control. To rule. We are better than them in every way. But by denying that truth, you deign yourself to be weaker than they are. Perhaps all you need is another reminder of our place...starting with her, I think."

Ghen stood sharply, and the invisible restraints around us tightened. No matter how hard Vain struggled against them, there was no breaking through the archdemon's hold. He wasn't nearly powerful enough confined in my mortal body. And that understanding gutted me more than anything.

*Move, damnit!* I yelled down our bond. *Get up! Do something!*

But Vain was already throwing everything he had—every last drop of power in his reserve—into fighting back, and we could do nothing but watch as Ghen strode across the room and lifted Ava into the air like she was a boneless puppet held up by invisible strings. His flames reappeared, licking up one arm and illuminating Ava's face in an eerie red glow. When he dragged the back of his other hand down the side of her face, Ava's eyes shot wide open as she finally broke out of the glamour. Her chest jerked with every quick and shallow breath. Her fingers and toes twitched the higher she rose into the air.

"Ava!" Vain cried out, but the sound was strangled and fragile.

Her eyes—those petrified amber eyes—locked onto ours, and I couldn't stand just how fucking powerless I felt in that moment.

"Which would you prefer..." Ghen asked from over his shoulder. "Would you rather watch her bleed out? Or burn?"

No, not like this. There was no universe where I would let us watch Ava die—not at the hands of this monster. Not at all.

I dug deep within me, clawing at every last part of my soul and pulling for every shred of power I had until I was the one in control.

It was pure instinct that drove me. I threw myself at the demon, moving faster than should have been possible. If I was siphoning off some of Vain's power or if I was running purely off my own adrenaline, I didn't know, but the force of the impact as I slammed into Ghen's chest and knocked him to the ground was earth-shattering. My bones vibrated as my body curved over his. Compared to his size, I'd never felt so small, and yet, in this position looking down at him, I'd also never felt more powerful.

The night air whipped around us alongside Vain's shadows. I pulled them from me, wielding them as if they were my own, like they had always been mine and they sang to me just as naturally as they did for him.

It truly felt as if we were merged. With our essences co-mingling together, we were a shared force, stronger than we'd ever been. But mortal bodies were never truly meant to harness the power of gods.

As he stared up into our eyes, Ghen laughed. "Oh, how adorably pathetic. I can tell he's already broken you, boy. And yet you still cling to him as if he were your divine savior."

"He never broke me," I said. It sounded like my voice, but darker, something sinister twisting the words as I spoke. "I was already broken when he found me."

The shadows that curled around my fist formed into a sharp blade. I stabbed it straight into the side of Ghen's neck, the muscles and veins beneath his skin bulging as ichor bubbled to the surface when I pulled it out and proceeded to drag it across his throat until I could feel the tendons shredding and the blade scraping to the bone underneath.

The archdemon gargled and sputtered as ichor began to overflow from each cut I made and it bubbled out from the corners of his mouth until it dripped down his chin and over my hands. Ghen's power ebbed under my fingers, as if it were recoiling from me and attempting to bury itself like a wounded animal.

I struck harder, cut deeper.

I wasn't going to stop until I could feel the life leave Ghen's body. Until I'd drained him of everything that he was and there was nothing left of him to be able to hurt us—any of us—anymore.

The archdemon's eyelids fluttered, his body spasming beneath ours in one final shudder of life. And then a punch rocked through me, barreling straight into my chest which stole all the air from my lungs.

I gasped, but the sound was sharp and rattled softly in my chest. Every breath sounded wrong. Rasping and wet.

I peered down to see Ghen's fist connecting to the middle of my chest, the golden hilt of a knife protruding from his grip. And then I realized that the blade was *inside* me. That cold realization struck me with such an intensity that only then did I register the hot searing pain that radiated from that point in my chest and shot outward to every nerve in my system until it felt as if my entire body was screaming with pain.

When I looked back to Ghen's face, he wore a vicious smile, and not an ounce of weakness graced his striking features. The wounds I'd inflicted on his neck were sealing themselves before my eyes, every scrap of skin, every tendon and muscle reforming anew.

Ghen ripped the blade from my chest, and I screamed. Pain seared through me like a wave of white-hot fire. The archdemon threw me off his chest and I landed facedown on the ground.

My muscles groaned when I lifted my head. Standing over me, Ghen wiped his ichor and my blood off his coat with a few quick flicks of his wrist.

Ava was screaming from somewhere. I couldn't move anymore to see. Everything was too heavy—too cold. Glacial rivers plotted an unrelenting course through my body, and the chill of icy claws raking their way up my spine left my bones shivering.

"Human vessels are so messy, aren't they?" Ghen said, tossing me a look of mild amusement before he turned back toward Ava.

I gathered what little energy I had left to brace myself up on my forearms. Nesera and Alastair were still trapped within the confines of Ghen's demonic flames, the fire singeing them as they watched on through horrified and helpless looks.

Ghen stood over Ava and lifted her up by her hair like she was a doll. She looked so small in his grasp. She had nothing left to give to fight him...and neither did I.

*Vain...*

*You will heal,* he said quickly, already trying to dismiss my thought before I could finish it.

I shook my head—or tried to at least. *You and I both know it won't be quick enough.*

*Rory.* The pain in his voice was evident. He knew what had to be done as much as I did. But the bastard was hesitating when we didn't have the time. *You're sure?* he asked.

I caught Ava's gaze, lifting my head with every bit of strength I had, determined to look into her eyes with my own and have her see *me* one last time. Her chin wobbled and she mouthed "no". And then she was yelling it, screaming as much as she could scream with an archdemon's hands closing around her neck.

*If she means half as much to you as she does to me, then you get the hell out right now. Do you understand me?*

My face was hot with the tears I hadn't even registered until they ran in tracks stinging down my cheeks.

Vain still hesitated. It was as if he were trying to memorize us in that exact moment. The last breath we would share, the last thoughts, the rhythm of my heartbeat or the warmth of my body. I could feel him struggling for something. Maybe the last words he wanted to say or trying to find a way to dull the pain I would feel.

But I was done waiting.

*Get out!* I yelled. *NOW!*

I roared and dug deep into myself, finding Vain in the dark corners, webbed in between the cracks in my soul. I clawed at them and tore him out myself. I tore him out until there was nothing left of me but the fractured and broken pieces of my own soul.

Ava's screams echoed my own as the pain consumed me. All of the crevices left empty in the absence of him were nothing more than sunken, hollow pits, and that familiar darkness rushed in to fill the spaces. This time, the void came back to greet me with open arms, welcoming me into its punishing embrace.

My vision swam with the last sight of Ava, a scream tearing from her lips before she faded away from view entirely, and the last words I heard were Vain's.

"Thank you."

# THIRTY

## VAIN

Nothing could have prepared me for the shock of re-emerging into my true form again. After seven years, which was a mere blink in my immortal existence, I'd forgotten what it felt like. The surge of power coursing through my own veins, amplified a hundred-fold, was exhilarating and freeing. I'd forgotten how steady my heartbeat was and how quiet my mind felt after years of sharing a body, a mind, a soul with another. There was a quiet relief that came with it, and yet that feeling was overshadowed by the most tortuous ache imaginable.

I could feel a warm wetness pooling at my bare feet, and registered that it was Rory's blood, but I couldn't bring myself to look at him. I wasn't sure I could bear it. The only blood I wanted to see was the black of Ghen's ichor seeping between my fingers until he lay in shreds beneath me. And I would rip him apart again and again, forever until the end of time, if it meant bringing him the same level of pain he'd inflicted on me.

Red-black flames sparked at my fingertips, twin to Ghen's. They licked up my arms like a wildfire, like vengeance. I think I had missed the feeling of them most of all.

Ghen spun slowly, appearing not at all shocked by my reappearance.

I let my fire and my shadows envelop me completely until I became a whirlwind of them. A looming siege of destruction.

"A fair fight?" he taunted with a smirk. "Are you so ready to reacquaint yourself with defeat at my hands after all this time?"

I did not have a shred of grace left in me to offer my brother a response. Not when my power rose within me like a surging wave, and not when my hands found themselves wrapped around Ghen's neck. Not when I became every bit the monster the world would believe me to be.

My wrath was like a war drum in my head, accompanying the sounds of shredding muscle, the slick pull of tendons and the spray of ichor as we clashed. No matter how many blows we traded or how many times we tore into each other, there was no end to the cycle of the wounds we would inflict, only for them to heal moments later.

"You should know better than that." Ghen laughed even as my shadows coiled around his throat. "We cannot be killed. We are as eternally cursed as our mother Herself. We can go at this until the end of time, brother, but it will always end the same. You will watch them die, and I will leave you broken until you come to understand your place. We are gods. And again, you have proved that these mortals are nothing but your weakness."

"If they are my weakness," I said, "then I never wish to find the strength to deny myself of them."

Ghen sneered, nothing but sheer and utter disgust twisting his features into something unrecognizable. "Then you will continue to be nothing but a disgrace to us all."

"Ghen!"

His head whipped over toward the sound of Ava's voice at the same time mine did. She knelt on the ground beside Rory, her eyes burning red with tears not yet fallen, her hands coated in his blood, and her body curled over a sigil she'd drawn on the smooth concrete tiles.

It was Ghen's sigil she'd painted in Rory's blood, surrounded by the deep magic of a banishment spell. The achingly familiar whorls and symbols of the demon tongue sparked a hint of pride within me.

Ava caught my eyes, and I flashed her a nod. She was strong enough. She had been strong enough to summon him then, even as a child. She could banish him now.

She threw her hands down to the sigil and I gripped onto Ghen, keeping his hands bound behind him and my knee shoved into his back to lock him in place. Ava's hair flared around her like a great pyre, kicked up by the wind and the magic she commanded. She was the striking image of retribution. An avenging witch.

When Ava spoke, her words were commanding, every syllable harsh and every consonant tipped in striking clarity. "Hear me archdemon, Ghen, son of Lilith, I banish you from this realm so that Gehenna may welcome you back home."

The bloody sigil began to glow, and a crack cleaved through the night, a rift opening at Ghen's feet. A great wind howled through the realms with a mighty scream, but Ava's words remained clear and booming as she continued with the banishment.

As mighty as my brother might be, no demon, not even one of the Arches, could resist the magic.

"I cast you out, unholy demon, creature of the cursed night."

Ghen snarled, a loud and strangled cry ripping from his throat. He struggled against my hold, but I remained firm. When I peered down, the rift had ensnared him, tugging him through the mouth of the great dark hole, inch by slow inch.

"I command you, son of the Dark One, to return to the cursed lands beyond the rifts. I banish you!"

Ghen reared back, his slitted eyes boring into mine beneath twisted dark brows. "When our mother is freed and comes to reclaim this world, I hope that you have made peace with your choices, brother."

I sunk my fingers into his shoulder, my grip clawing into his flesh as I leaned forward to whisper against his ear. "You can send Her my regards, then."

Then with a forceful shove, I thrust Ghen the rest of the way through the rift until the very last of him had been swallowed whole and all that remained were the echoes of the warm air breathing from Gehenna into the mortal realm.

Slowly, the crack between the realms sewed itself back together, mending the gap Ava had made. She kept her hands pressed to the bloody patio tiles even after the rift had closed and the sigil beneath her had burned away until nothing but the remnant of ashes was left behind.

Only then did I let my gaze fall to Rory's body which lay at her side, and my breath caught in my throat at the sight of him. His blood appeared to have run rivers down his arms, those painfully long gashes laid open and as fresh as the day they were made.

Ava dragged herself to him, closing the inches between them and placing her hands on his chest, as if hopeful she might find a heartbeat. But we both knew there was none.

He had chosen his fate, and still I wasn't sure if I was strong enough to let him go. Because truthfully, I believed that I needed him, maybe just as much as he had once needed me.

A soft "no, no, no" rushed out of Ava's mouth on a hushed breath, her fingers shaking as she stroked them through Rory's hair and swept them over his cheekbones. The tears that had pooled in her soft amber eyes spilled down over the freckles dotting her cheeks.

I thought I had understood it before, but only now seemed to realize the true hold she had over me—how much I had allowed her in and permitted such a being to ruin me completely. This mortal woman—this witch—I had wanted her from the moment I laid eyes on her. I could crave her for eternity and never be sated.

With her, just as it had been with Rory, all my faults and offenses of my past faded to no more than mere specks in the vast memory of my painfully long and horrid existence I so eagerly wished to forget.

They could have asked anything of me, and I would have done it. I would have given them the world if they wanted.

I stepped toward Ava quietly, fearful that I might catch her flinch at the sound of my approach.

Would she be too afraid to look me in the eyes? Would she even want to?

I made peace with the fact that she might wish to have nothing to do with me ever again should she choose. But I would not allow her to grieve alone.

My fingers twitched when I reached out and laid my hand against the back of her neck. I fully expected her to draw away or to run from me now that she understood what I was. But nothing prepared me for the feeling of her sinking back into my touch, as if she wanted it to envelop every part of her, whether she realized it or not. That simple, unspoken answer was enough for me.

And so we stared down at Rory together, sharing no words—nothing but the touch between us and the insurmountable grief that had burrowed itself into both of our hearts.

# THIRTY-ONE

## AVA

It felt like a hollow chasm had split my chest wide open. My entire body was numb.

I knelt beside Rory, my fists clawed into the fabric of his shirt. His skin was still warm.

When I looked down, the binding marks that had once been woven around our wrists were gone, and my hands were coated with his blood.

There was *so* much blood.

His arms were slick with it, and it had stained the stone patio beneath him crimson.

The echoes of my screams and Rory's pulsed in my eardrums, and I couldn't shake the image of Vain being ripped out of him, leaving Rory lifeless on the ground. My heart clenched when I pictured the look on his face, somehow knowing that it had been Rory's choice—that he'd sacrificed himself to give Vain a chance to save us. It was a chance I didn't feel deserving of, and that's what hurt most of all.

I had caused this. I had led Ghen straight to us. Because of me, Rory was dead. I'd been just as powerless to save him as I had been unable to save my sister.

I don't know how long I sat there like that, limbs heavy, just...staring at him, my heart shattered into millions of pieces. Everything around me felt distant, nothing more than muffled sounds ringing in my ears. The warmth that had been curled around my neck pulled away, leaving my skin cold. It was jarring enough to pull me from my daze.

Turning to stare up at Vain, I watched as Alastair approached him, melancholy, and handed Vain a thin charcoal-colored robe. Vain was completely unclothed, not a mark on his pale skin to be seen on his sculpted figure. He shrugged the robe over his broad shoulders, tying it loosely at the waist where I could still see the smooth, muscled planes of his chest and torso.

It was impossible to tear my gaze from him. Vain dragged a hand through his short icy blond hair and swept the longer strands in front to one side as he stared at me with dark eyes. The color of his irises appeared black, but in the right light they swam with color like an ever-shifting aurora against a midnight sky. There was something darkly ethereal about him, and though I could feel a cursed essence looming underneath his surface that made my skin buzz with an instinctive warning, I did not cower before him.

He was too beautiful to be mistaken for a human. He may have been the most breathtaking demon I'd ever seen.

"Is this a glamour you're making me see? Or are you real?"

"I am very real. No tricks, no glamours." Vain's voice was so deep it was almost unnerving. He still had that same velvety smoothness as when he had possessed Rory. But it wasn't Rory's voice anymore. It would never be his voice again.

Towering over me, Vain's gaze softened as he reached down and offered his hand to help me off the blood-stained ground. "Come with me, mellilla."

I was reluctant to leave Rory's side, but Vain insisted gently, so I took his hand. Even at my full height, I only came up to his chest in his new form. He had to be at least a full head taller than Rory.

With a wave of Vain's hand over me, Rory's blood vanished from my skin and clothes. The crystal-like shards scattered across every surface rose and reformed until each pane of glass appeared brand new. Every act felt as if Vain were wiping away the stain that Ghen had left behind, but even after all traces of him were gone, there was still one scar that remained that couldn't be ignored.

Vain knelt and lifted Rory's body, limp and lifeless, into his arms. Wordlessly, we walked through the penthouse together and brought him to one of the spare rooms. Vain set him down on the bed, and for a moment, I could have fooled myself into thinking that Rory was merely asleep—that his eyes might open at any moment, and he would look back at me and smile.

We left him there in that room and shut the door behind us.

Nesera and Alastair broke off into one of the other rooms, and Vain led me down the hall to his bedroom in more silence.

A large black stain greeted us on the rug when we entered, and I wasn't prepared for the swell of emotions that barreled through me and the memories that came with it. The remnant taste of ichor lingered at the tip of my tongue and stopped me dead in my tracks, but Vain gently laced his fingers through mine and led me across the room toward his bed.

It was odd how Vain should have felt like a stranger to me, but he didn't. I knew his heart as he knew mine. The demon was the same as he'd always been, even though his appearance had changed.

I sat myself on the edge of his bed and Vain knelt in front of me. My limbs buzzed, the tingling numbness spreading higher and higher until I felt it tighten around my lungs. Everything felt light and sharp.

"You need to breathe, Ava," he said, stroking a hand down one side of my face. "Breathe for me."

I followed his slow, deep breaths, mimicking them until the pressure in my chest receded. Squeezing my eyes shut, I took one last shaky inhale before I re-opened them and stared at Vain. He was so close, and so unlike what I could have ever imagined.

"You're...an archdemon."

"Yes," he said, as if it were the simplest answer in the world.

"Vain..."

"Is not my true name. It is the one I gave myself," he said and laced the fingers of his other hand through mine. "I once told you that I am a demon of many names. But my first and true name given to me by my mother, is Vencula."

A dizzying wave crashed into me, and I became breathless all over again.

Vain's thumb swept over my cheek. "Breathe," he said again, little more than a gentle whisper.

My lips parted before I quickly clamped them shut again. Every time I tried to force words past my lips, I ended up choking them back. "I have...so many questions."

"Ask anything of me, my love. Anything, and I will answer it."

A sob cracked through my chest. Without ever realizing it, whatever mark summoning Ghen all those years ago had left on my soul had only worked to break me down over time, whittling away at my self-worth and allowing every regret I harbored to tear me apart from the inside. He had taken so much from me. Not only Sascha, but now Rory too had become nothing but collateral in the archdemon's devastating wake. And no matter which way I looked at it, I kept tracing every fault line back to me.

"He's dead because of me."

I tried to bury my face in my hands, but Vain's grip was iron-clad. He tightened a fist at my nape, tugging at my hair to keep my head up, and the dull pain was a surprising distraction from the cleaving ache in my chest threatening to split me in two.

"None of this," he said, "is your fault, Ava." Vain sighed out through his nose, his gaze flickering briefly before coming back to mine. "My brother made a promise long ago that I would never know peace in this world or ours. We never quite saw eye to eye on many things, and our vehement dissension on mortal life proved to be the driving force of our division, one that devolved our bitter rivalry into that of all-out war."

Vain's hand tightened in mine, and I squeezed back. He paused, hesitating before he continued.

"When the first witches summoned us into this realm and we were met for the first time with mortal life—so fragile and precious—all Ghen could see was human weakness. A thing to exploit. He saw all mortals as beneath him, something to rule over and control. Whereas I could look at any human and see the vitality in them, their lust for life. Even all the heartache, all your wicked wants and desires. I saw your kind for what you are, fallible and imperfect creatures. And I celebrated it. To me, there is nothing more wondrous. Nothing as beautiful."

The reverence in Vain's voice was heady. He spoke about humanity with an almost breathless amazement, like we were something to be worshiped and cherished. Such an odd notion to hear come from the lips of an archdemon.

"When I took one of the first witches as my familiar, binding their soul to mine, Ghen decided my fascination with humankind was a weakness. He took it as a reprehensible offense against demonkind. But I was happy. My brother allowed my affections for my familiar to bloom into something so profound, so that when he did destroy the one thing that I had truly come to care for in my pitiful existence, he made sure it hurt me more than anything, to the point where it nearly destroyed me."

I realized his hand in mine was shaking, so I steadied it by clasping my other palm on top of it.

"His greatest malefaction led us to war, one which my brother won. Ghen either thought me dead, or presumed he'd buried any hope of me resurfacing after my defeat. He'd broken me in more ways than I could have fathomed, and so I hid. I slipped into your realm and took a long series of mortal vessels to conceal my true form. I have lived thousands of lives, enough to last me for eternity. But I am done running."

Vain's throat bobbed before his grip tightened in mine. "Now that whatever connection between you and Ghen has been severed, I will make sure he can never find you again, not even when he does eventually come crawling back through one of the rifts. I will never rest in order to keep you safe. That is my promise to you, Ava."

There'd been a time once where I would have never believed a demon's promise, not trusting it could be anything other than a lie or some sort of manipulation. But I'd been so wrong. When Vain looked at me, there was nothing but pure, unconditional devotion swimming in his eyes.

"Who else knew about you?" I asked.

"Only Alastair. But that is only because the cunning bastard already had his suspicions and worked the truth out of me one night when I had gotten my vessel particularly drunk, and so I may have been a bit more forthcoming than I meant to with certain details that gave away my identity. But I entrusted no one else with my secrets. Not even Rory knew. I wanted to shield him from the pain of that knowledge for as long as I could."

Vain's hand left my nape and he swept a finger across my cheek, catching my tears that had fallen while he'd spoken. The mention of Rory had my sobs breaking free all over again, and I was unable to control the emotion barreling out of me. It was all too much at once, I felt so heavy with grief and guilt that I never felt as if I might know the true feeling of happiness again.

Vain held me to his chest and allowed me to cry until I was sick of it. Until every last piece of me was spent and I felt a space hollow out in my chest, large enough where it felt like I could breathe again.

The silk of his robe was wet with my tears when I finally stopped crying. He placed a gentle kiss to my forehead and rose to step up to the wall by his bedside table. With a wave of his hand, he revealed a hidden panel that held a small safe inside that was fitted with all manner of magical locks. The small door swung open, and he pulled out a wooden box with wrought iron fastenings clamped over the lid. The mechanisms of the locks clicked open with a snap of his fingers, and then Vain reached in and presented a book to me.

It was obviously very old, given the worn state of the dark leather bound over the cover, with a series of demonic symbols etched down the spine and a red six-pointed star carved on the front. I recognized it immediately from the heavy weight of its presence and the power of what it contained. Without even having to touch it, the sinister ancient magic within seeped out like it was a living, breathing thing, and I recoiled away from it on instinct.

"How? When did you—" I started.

"Eldin slipped it into my pocket at the party to keep it out of Ghen's hands."

I stood slowly, staring up at him, my head spinning. "So, you had it? All this time?"

Vain said nothing, and my confusion quickly morphed to something hot and bitter inside me. "Why didn't we use it then?" My voice rose as I fought to keep the hot tears welling in my eyes from spilling over again. "If we could have saved him earlier..." I choked on the rest of my words and Vain squeezed my hand once, like a silent acknowledgment.

"It was not that simple," he said.

I looked at him, completely puzzled, and then back down to the grimoire. Even as he offered it out to me, I did not reach for it. The very thought of touching it repulsed me and made my skin crawl with unease.

Seeming to sense my hesitancy, Vain flipped through the dark grimoire with careful, long fingers, then presented a set of pages to me. The writing was in the demon tongue, albeit a much older dialect than the one I was used to. Some of the words didn't come to me easily, while others were simpler to pick apart through context.

*Ritual. Soul. Blood magic. Binding.*

The more I read, the passages came together slowly piece by piece. The crude hand-drawn diagrams and scribbled notes in the margins indicated a complex series of spell work, but one word I couldn't translate kept appearing. When I finally broke the roots of it down, at last everything clicked into place.

*Resurrection.*

The dark energy swirling around the ancient tome as if it had a life of its own finally made sense. I edged away from the book further. My breathing stilled and I looked up to Vain who had been staring at me, studying my expression with sad, curious eyes.

"This is...necromancy."

"Not quite," he said. "Necromancy reanimates the body without a soul attached, or in some cases, only a shard of the soul may remain. But this spell is supposed to ensure that the body, mind, and soul remain intact. The newly dead may become whole again."

There was a reason necromancy was forbidden. The consequences for bringing back the dead in such a twisted and evil state were more severe than all other dark magics.

All dark magic came with a cost. But even if the ritual wasn't full-blown necromancy, resurrection was still a risk.

Vain's eyes gleamed with a mesmerizing iridescence. Up close, his irises shifted like colors on the surface of an oil slick. Deep purples and bright reds undulated with flashes of gold and silver. They glinted with grief and a small shimmer of hope.

"What's stopping you from doing it? If you're so powerful, why don't you help him?" I demanded while choking down my sobs. "I'm not strong enough. You've seen it yourself. This is powerful dark magic, Vain. I'm not—I would need your ichor to even attempt something like this."

Vain set the book on the nightstand and took a cautious step toward me. He held my face between his hands, forcing me to meet his gaze. "You are more than strong and capable enough to do anything, Ava. You don't need me or my ichor. But my powers do have their limits, and this magic demands more cost than what I could give alone. It requires a measure of equal worth. A soul."

My hand shook as I pressed it to my trembling lips. "He knew what it would cost and told you not to tell me, didn't he?"

Vain nodded.

"So, this is really possible?"

"It is."

I shook my head and clenched my jaw to stop my chin from wobbling. "Even if I could, I don't have the ingredients necessary to do this spell."

"I have them," Vain said.

"What? How?" My skin prickled as the realization struck me.

"I knew that his death was inevitable, as did he. So, I prepared for it." Vain shut his eyes and dragged in a breath before he continued. "I could not bear the thought of him dying."

"Why?" I asked. The idea that a demon—an archdemon at that—could feel in such a way for a mortal soul was still so incomprehensible to me.

Vain shrugged, a strikingly human gesture. "I am not without my faults. I fell for him the same as you did."

The pain gleaming in Vain's eyes forced me to look away and concentrate on anywhere but him. I looked back down at the pages of the grimoire, taking in all I could of the spell until the words made my head spin.

*Blood exchange. Soul-bound.*

"It's a binding ritual?"

"A soul for a soul." He nodded, and I took two wobbling steps backwards away from that damned book. Away from Vain.

"It is your choice. I cannot..." he paused. "I will not force you. I know the ritual ceremony itself is...intensely intimate, and not one to be taken lightly."

Heat rushed to my cheeks, and my mind raced at what was being offered to me; binding my soul to a demon—to an archdemon—to complete a spell that might bring Rory back, resurrecting him by the means of the darkest magic I had ever seen. And my soul was the price, should I be willing to pay it.

"If you do choose to go through with it, then it must be done before morning. There is only a small window before the chance is gone, lest his soul drift too far to be brought back in one piece." His tone was reassuring and gentle with no obvious signs of pressure from him. As much as I knew he cared for Rory and wanted him back as much as I did, he would be willing to let him go if I chose to not do this.

My heart leaped into my throat, and I had to swallow it down before I tried to speak again. "Give me some time." I had to have at least a few more hours, enough time for me to weigh the decision before I had to make it.

"When—if," he corrected himself again, "you're ready, I will wait for you in the spare room."

I turned and left silently as I sucked down breath after shaky breath. The air felt suffocating, and I closed myself in my room before I allowed my sobs to resurface.

# THIRTY-TWO

## AVA

My fingertips prickled as I approached the spare room, my heart racing. I stood outside the door for a long time and attempted to steady my breathing. The floor beneath my bare feet creaked as I rocked from side to side, and the silk fabric of the white robe slid over my skin with every movement.

I rested my hand on the cold metal handle for a few minutes, mustering the courage to enter. I didn't know if I was ready to see Rory's lifeless body again. But I had made my decision. I wasn't about to stop fighting for Rory, not after everything. I'd been fighting for him since we met—since I first saw pieces of myself in him. Someone who was a little broken, a little lost, but worth saving nonetheless.

With a deep breath, I pushed into the room. All of the furniture had been pushed to the walls. Every chair, table, rug, and even the four-poster bed was shoved aside, creating a large open space in the center.

Two perfect spell circles were drawn side by side on the hard-wood floor in white chalk. Thick black pillar candles lined both circles, each of them placed in a star pattern. A shallow gold dish sat in front of each candle, filled with the spell ingredients Vain had prepared—equal parts gold and silver dust to keep the channels of magic open, ash of an ancient oak tree to amplify the spell's power, thread spun from the purest silk for binding, lamb's milk bathed under the light of a full moon to lure a wandering soul, and a raw shard of black tourmaline crystal for protection.

The soft, warm glow of the candlelight cast long, dark shadows to the edges of the room. My eyes fell to the circle on the left where Rory's body lay in the center, a plush cushion set beneath him. The way his forearms had been dressed in bandages to cover the deep, gouging wounds made my chest cave in, and I had to tear my gaze away to keep my emotions from spilling out all over again.

Vain faced away from me as I shut the door, the candlelight canvassing his form in an almost-ethereal golden light. If I didn't know better, he could have easily been mistaken for an angel.

He was strikingly beautiful, as equally breathtaking as he was formidable. But as entrancing as he was, the temptation of him and what he was didn't escape me—a powerful archdemon, a creature born of darkness and domination. And yet, beneath his nature and the thrill of dread he spurred instinctively within me, he was...so much more.

Vain made me feel untouchable. Powerful. Wanted. And more than anything, I felt safe with him. It was a kind of safety I'd never known in my life. The kind where there was no fear of rejection, no desire to be anything other than who I was. The thought was equally as terrifying as it was bewildering.

The hem of my robe hissed along the floor as I padded barefoot across the room. Vain swung his head toward me when I approached, and his gaze pierced me over his broad shoulders. When I paused a foot away, he finally turned to face me, his eyes trailing up the length of my body, which was hidden beneath the shamefully thin fabric. There was none of his usual lustful, smug expression to be found. In fact, he looked somber as he shifted his attention down to Rory's body.

I might have once believed that Vain only wished to go through with this ritual to selfishly claim my soul. But it was clear to me how wrong I would have been. The truth stared me in the face, and there was no denying how deeply rooted Vain's affections for him were. How much he truly loved Rory.

We said nothing as we stared at each other. The only sound was the faint crackling of the candle wicks and the whisper of the sputtering flames that danced upon them.

"You are sure of this?" Vain finally spoke, his deep voice rumbling through the silence.

"Yes."

"And you understand the ramifications?"

"I do."

Rory had given his soul to save mine. There was no question of whether or not I would do the same for him. I was more than prepared to sacrifice my soul and bind myself eternally to Vain for a chance that Rory might live again.

"Then, we'll begin."

Vain tugged a small knife out of the pocket of his robe and lifted the milky white selenite blade between us. I offered my palm to him, and he did the same to me.

Expecting the cut didn't make the sting of it hurt any less. I couldn't stop the hiss from escaping through my teeth when Vain dragged the tip of the blade along the flesh of our palms, drawing his black and my crimson blood to the surface. We let our fists hover over each of the gold bowls around the ritual circle until our blood dripped over the offerings before ending at Rory.

"I offer to bind my soul in exchange," I uttered as red droplets splattered against his bare chest.

Vain's ichor spilled over mine. "I offer my immortality."

My head snapped up and Vain's eyes met mine. I had expected him to make an offering of great power as was required of both participants for the ritual to work, but nothing of that magnitude. I almost couldn't believe I'd heard him right.

"You would give up your immortality for him? For us?"

"I would give up—" Vain's breath hitched as he spoke, "*every-thing.*" Pain and immeasurable longing swam in the demon's ethereal eyes. "I have lived a long life, mellilla. And I wish for nothing more than to finish this life with the two of you by my side."

Vain took my hand and stepped over the chalk line into the empty circle, leading me with him. The moment we crossed over, the demonic runes hummed to life, glowing gold as they entwined themselves between our circle and Rory's in a figure eight pattern. Their power vibrated like a living thing, a thrumming heartbeat, and I could feel their warmth inches from my toes. Even the candles appeared to burn a little brighter around us.

My eyes didn't leave Vain's as he drew me in close, his hands gripping my arms just below my shoulders. He was so much larger than me in every way. Even his mere presence felt looming, like a dark omen cloaked beneath flesh and bone.

Vain leaned down, his head bowed low, to kiss me. It was a chaste gesture, meant only to soothe my nerves, which I had no doubt he could sense.

I chose to allow my emotions to pour from me without abandon. There was no point in keeping my mental shields up against him anymore, not when I was about to give myself to him more fully than I ever had before. The binding ritual was an intimate ceremony, the act of joining our bodies physically meant to ensure the seal of the soul bond.

He kept a hand on the small of my back while the other cradled my nape, his fingers laced through my hair. The kiss was the gentlest brush of his lips against mine. I could have sworn it was Rory's mouth when I closed my eyes. Or maybe I missed him so much that I *wished* it was Rory.

Vain pulled away, and I opened my eyes. His dark irises flickered, reflecting the golden flames around us with an uncanny iridescence. He brought our hands together between us, bloodied palms facing upward. My cut throbbed, a dull ache beneath the small well of blood that had pooled around it. Vain's had already healed.

He made another cut to his hand with the blade, then raised the edge of his palm slowly to my lips, and I mirrored mine to his. I readied myself to gag as I drank from him, but the feeling never came. Vain's ichor had the same bitter tang I had expected, but there was a hint of something sweet as well, making it palatable as it coated my tongue and trickled down my throat. He was careful not to allow me to consume too much, only enough to complete the ritual and nothing more.

After we had each taken the last pulls from one another, Vain sealed my cut with a kiss to my palm, and the flesh stitched together before my eyes. His wound had already healed as well, not a single mark marring the surface of his ivory skin.

Vain's ichor was pure, absolute, and unfiltered energy. The power of it rushed through me like a warm current of electricity running through every last nerve and synapse in my body. This power felt different than before—not like a curse, but more like a gift. There was a soft pull toward it, a craving for more, but Vain sated my hunger with a deep and demanding kiss.

The taste of blood and ichor mixed together, overwhelming my senses, and I groaned into his mouth, low and deep. I could feel the hard length of him pressed against my stomach through the fabric of our robes. He twitched against me, and my body shuddered in turn. He held himself back with so much more restraint than I expected from him.

He gave a sharp snap of his fingers, and I shivered against the cold air on my bare skin as both of our robes were glamoured away.

With strong arms holding me tightly to him, Vain lowered us onto the floor. I sat poised above his lap, chest to chest, our mouths locked in a careful entanglement. His hands roamed over my body, exploring every inch of me, slowly at first, and then becoming more insistent and desperate. He released a low hum into my open mouth, our tongues locked in a fevered dance, which left my core aching for him. I was more than ready to give him everything I had, and it didn't matter at all what remained of me when he was done.

He shifted his weight underneath me, positioning himself at my entrance and holding there. It took me a moment to realize the unspoken offer he was presenting me—a chance to change my mind before it was too late.

My choice.

But I had made my decision long before setting foot in this room. Maybe I even made it the moment I watched the light leave Rory's eyes.

I lowered myself down and Vain hissed in a sharp breath and groaned as he slid into me. The hard length of him sank deeper and deeper until we were fully flush at the hips, our bodies melded as one.

We each released a heavy sigh and stayed like that for what felt like minutes as I adjusted to the size of him. I winced slightly and Vain froze, his eyes widening. I never thought I would see a demon's face contort with such worry over a life other than their own. That look undid something within me, and I thought that it might have been the most wondrous thing I had ever seen.

I brushed a reassuring hand down his arm, and only then did he relax.

My hips rocked over him in a steady rhythm as we clung to one another. The air became hot, the flames burning radiantly as we moved as one, gasping in each other's breaths with each stroke.

Vain's mouth moved from my lips to my throat where he sucked and nipped at the sensitive skin until I was whimpering, desperate for everything he had to offer me. I sank my fingers into his icy-blond hair, the strands shining like ethereal silver in the candlelight.

The sound of our bodies coming together, slick and fast, echoed around the room, pulling me closer toward my impending fate. Vain's hands were everywhere, in my hair, trailing over my back and clasping at my collarbone, nearly at my throat. He was close, his thrusts turning more insistent each time I slammed myself down onto him.

Every moan I gave him felt like a promise. Every gasp, every shudder, felt like an offering, sacrificing the pieces of my heart to an arcane deity to do with as he pleased. Soon he would have it all. He would have everything—anything if it meant having Rory back. If it meant having them both.

Vain hooked his hands under my arms and clawed at my shoulder blades, pulling me against him firmly as if he could meld us into one. His fingertips dug hard into my flesh, deeper every second he climbed closer to his own climax.

With his lips pressed against the shell of my ear, Vain whispered, "From this day on, I will be the guardian of your heart. Your burdens are now mine. My strength is now yours. I will protect your soul till my last breath, and you may wield me as you please."

Vain's name erupted from me in answer as I shattered around him. At the same time, he came undone too, and the flames encircling us surged higher as a tremor of energy shook deep within my core.

My intuition prickled, and as if by instinct, I recognized the warm sensation coiling through every atom in my body as the bond worming its way into every crevice of my soul. I opened myself to it, throwing my head back as the last waves of my orgasm subsided until I felt the bond snap into place like a lock.

There was a cord, like a tether, wrapped around my heart, and I felt it pull taut. And at the other end, Vain's essence burned wild, bright and warm, sheltering my soul. It wasn't at all what I expected binding myself to a demon would be like.

He felt safe. He felt like home.

I collapsed against Vain, and when I sighed into him, every last flame winked out from the candles, leaving us in complete darkness.

Then a velvety smooth voice sung through the silence, a whisper inside my head.

*I am yours.*

# THIRTY-THREE
## RORY

In death, there was nothing but darkness—nothing but the familiar endless void.

And yet I was...breathing? The scent of smoke filled my lungs, and there was a split second where I decided I must be back in the confines of my subconscious mind again with Vain in the driver's seat. Only I couldn't feel him there. That space where I could normally sense his presence, that constant, swirling essence was...empty. And that realization only forced my heart to skitter to a halt. Because if Vain was gone, then I really must be dead. There was no way that I could have reasonably survived without him.

But I couldn't remember dying.

A heavy blanket of fog shrouded the corners of my mind, making it difficult to wade through my memories. The last thing I remembered was the sound of Ava's voice breaking as she screamed my name over and over. And that memory came with the most horrific pain I had ever experienced, like my body was being split in two.

"Rory?"

Her voice cut through the dark, and my heart beat against my ribcage so hard I thought it might burst.

"Is he breathing?" Ava sounded closer that time. A low, muffled voice responded from farther away, one I could almost place but didn't have enough of my senses to identify it.

My fingers twitched against something soft underneath me. My eyelids fluttered open apprehensively, half expecting that this was all just my mind playing tricks on me—like how when people died the synapses in their brains would still fire, causing them to experience what some thought was an afterlife.

That had to be it.

"Rory!"

Ava threw her body on top of mine, hugging us close together as she wrapped her arms around me. The scent of her was overwhelming...but it was her. I could *feel* her.

My limbs felt too heavy to move. The way that she clung to me, the way her hands traced every line and curve of my body as if I were some precious, fragile thing. It was almost as if she were trying to convince herself that this was real just as much as I was.

I pulled all my strength into my arms and tugged her down by the waist so that her body was fully flush with mine. I felt the smooth, warmth of her skin beneath my fingers and realized that she wasn't wearing a single shred of clothing. And neither was I.

I froze, knowing immediately what she had done and what it had cost her. What it must have cost Vain.

I knew Vain had prepared for the possibility of my death. But I had never expected Ava to pay that price for me. And that realization sat like a heavy weight on my chest.

Ava shook over me with gentle sobs.

"I'm here," was all I could manage to say as I tucked my face into the crook of her neck and the fall of her hair. I held her tighter than I ever had before.

From across the room, there was a whisper-like hiss along the floor, slowly edging further away. When I peered into the darkness, I could only make out the shadow of a tall dark figure, standing perfectly still as he watched us from the doorframe.

Vain slowly turned away and left the room. My eyes did not leave the empty space he'd left even long after he had gone.

It was bizarre to no longer have a demon pestering me in the back of my mind when I went to do just about everything. That space where Vain had once occupied was nothing more than a nagging phantom limb.

Soft morning light streamed through the windows of the empty kitchen. I was content in the silence. I hadn't realized how much I had missed it. My thoughts were my own. My *body* was my own. It felt alien and a little terrifying, but also a relief at the same time.

The sound of bare footsteps barreled down the hallway, and Ava flew around the corner, short of breath, eyes wide, and cheeks flushed. "What the hell do you think you're doing?"

Golden rays of morning light haloed her disheveled hair like she were a radiant sun. The faint smattering of freckles across her nose appeared brighter, her amber eyes clearer as they sparked at me. It felt like I was seeing her for the first time. And she took my fucking breath away.

I had to fight the urge to laugh as I tipped the end of the spatula down. "Uh... making pancakes?"

Ava glanced at the griddle on the stovetop and then back to me as she heaved a relieved sigh. "You're supposed to be resting."

"Can't I make you breakfast?" I said through a warm smile. It faded quickly though when I took in her pained expression and I realized that I'd left her to wake up alone. She hadn't left my side once since last night. "Oh shit, did I scare you?"

Her eyes flicked down toward her feet, and her cheeks flushed a rosy pink as she hesitated to meet my gaze.

I set down the spatula and stepped into her path. "I'm sorry. C'mere." I wrapped her into a steady embrace, and she eagerly folded herself against my chest.

"I'm okay. I'm right here," I whispered into her hair. "I'm not going anywhere."

They were the same words I repeated to her all through the night until we fell asleep in each other's arms in her bed.

I bent down to place a kiss on her forehead. When she looked up at me, I found myself lost in how soft her lips looked, the warm blush of her cheeks, and how her honey eyes glimmered with fresh tears. I caught them with the pad of my thumb before they had the chance to fall.

Ava turned her head to the side, glancing down at the stove. "Those don't look like pancakes," she mumbled against my chest, and I laughed, the sound lighter than I'd felt in a long time.

She was right. They were weirdly misshapen and none of them were the same size because of how sloppily I'd poured the batter. A distinct burning smell wafted off them from sitting too long on too high of a heat.

"Shit," I hissed and moved to try and salvage them as Vain rounded the corner.

"Don't you dare burn my penthouse down, mortal. Or are you trying to force my hand and make me possess you again just to show you how not to ruin a simple meal?"

God, that voice. It was almost unsettling to hear him speak outside my head. I couldn't help but stare at Vain after I had scraped the last of the ruined batch into the garbage.

He looked exactly as I remembered him from that day seven years ago when I had let him in. The day he saved my life. He was all sharp angles, and a cold, predatory stillness hung off him. His silver hair flopped to one side as his dark stare took me in. Ethereal and otherworldly were the only words that came to mind to describe him, and even they still couldn't fully encompass all that he was.

If Ava was the sun, then Vain was the moon, and I stood in a fixed orbit between them both.

We held each other's stare for a long moment, our eyes searching the other.

"I'm sure you could do a better job than me anyways," I said to him.

The demon rolled his eyes. It was such a human expression that it caught me off guard. Maybe I had rubbed off on him a little after all.

Vain yanked the spatula from my hand and pushed me aside. He worked in precise movements with the grace and skill of a tenured chef. Apparently, none of *those* skills had rubbed off on me.

I attached myself to Ava's side, drawn to close the distance between us. We moved to one of the dining room chairs, and she sat herself across my lap. I ran my hand across the smooth skin of her bare thighs, which poked out underneath the hem of an oversized T-shirt. Occasionally, I caught Vain shooting glances in our direction, yet he would always look away as soon as he noticed me watching him.

"What's wrong?" she asked as she smoothed a lock of hair out of my eyes. "You seem distant."

"It's nothing." The smile I gave her must not have been convincing because she pressed further.

"Tell me."

I sighed. "I feel...guilty. I think—you shouldn't have—" I struggled to find the right words to express all the thoughts I had about what she had done. How hard it must have been for her to make that kind of decision.

Ava laid a hand to my chest, silencing me before I could finish. "It was my choice, Rory."

"But was it worth the cost of your soul?" My voice cracked as I fought down the hard lump in my throat.

Her eyes bored into mine, full of golden light and warmth as she shook her head. "It's not quite like that. I didn't give up my soul. It's just tied to Vain now, like we're tethered, sort of how you were with him." She brought one hand up to my cheek. "Besides, you are worth everything, Rory. And we would choose you all over again. Every time."

I buried my face in her hair and allowed it to muffle the sounds of my cries as I finally broke. Ava cradled me in her arms, one hand cupping the back of my head while the other brushed slow circles along my back as I shook in her arms.

Without even having to look up, I could feel the demon's possessive eyes on me from across the room, his stare holding me with the same gentleness as Ava's did.

I'm not sure I had ever felt so unburdened and at peace before as I did in that moment.

It was a good thing Vain ended up cooking breakfast instead of me. The pancakes he made looked like they could have been straight out of a fucking cookbook, beautifully golden, fluffy and topped with some fancy mascarpone cream he was fond of. The bastard had even garnished them with fresh berries and mint. I wanted to call him a show-off, but the second I shoved the pancakes into my mouth, I almost melted. The insides were so light and airy with the edges crisped up just the way I liked them, and the berries exploded, tart and sweet in my mouth.

"I think you're drooling," Vain said, pointing his fork at me as I swallowed.

I furrowed my brows at him before wiping at the corner of my mouth with the back of my hand like a savage.

Ava was quiet as she ate. When she looked up from her plate, she gave the demon a long, hard look. "Vain, we should talk about that book."

His expression was nearly unreadable. "What is there to discuss?"

"The grimoire doesn't belong with us. It needs to be locked away."

"You don't think it's safe here?"

"I'm not sure it's safe anywhere. There's too much dark magic in that thing. I flipped through it, and I'm not sure if all of it is even real. Soul magic was one thing, but there's pages about forging seraphim killing blades, methods of spells for creating abominations, and Eldritch beasts—" She shook her head like she was trying to brush the remnants of the dark magic from the book off of her. "I...I don't want it anywhere near here."

Vain's eyes flickered to me for a split second and then back to Ava.

"We could destroy it," I suggested.

Vain shook his head. "It's a cursed tome. It cannot be destroyed. Any attempt to do so would only cause harm to us." Ava's lips drew into a thin line, but he continued. "I will admit the risks of keeping it here far outweigh our use for it now. Ghen may be banished back to Gehenna for the time being, but he will not stay there for long. Once he finds a rift to come back through, I have no doubts he will return whether it's for us or that book, and I don't particularly enjoy the thought of putting you both in danger again." He paused and looked back at Ava, then covered her hand with his. "Putting either of you into his path again is a risk I'm not willing to take. We'll get rid of the book however you see fit."

Ava struggled to dampen her surprise, unable to keep her lips from tipping upward at her small victory. My eyes remained transfixed to where their hands were joined over the table.

"I can find a way to get the book to the Council or maybe D.A.R.C."

"Not D.A.R.C.," Vain said sharply.

"Fine, the Council then. They should know what to do with it."

"Are you so sure they can be trusted with it?" I asked her.

Ava shrugged. "I don't know. But I just want it gone. It's not our problem anymore."

I found myself agreeing with her. Even I had sensed the ancient evil pouring from the book when I had first touched it. Hell, even the thought of being in its presence repulsed me. But the idea of anyone else getting their hands on it made me shudder. It seemed almost too dark to entrust to anyone, even the witch Council.

"How are we supposed to get it to them though?" I asked. "I mean, I doubt they're going to let a defected witch and an archdemon waltz into their compound and then just let you go free."

"I'll take it."

All three of us whipped our heads to the doorway where Nesera stood. The pair of space buns on top of her head wobbled as she bounced on her heels through the kitchen and snatched an extra pancake off the counter.

"What?" she said, her mouth full after tearing into a piece.

"And who will take you?" Vain asked.

She rolled her eyes, as if the answer were obvious. "Alastair, of course."

"I can't let you do that," he said, but Nesera just crossed her arms over her chest.

"Honestly, Vain," she said, "can't you just let someone do something for *you* for once?"

That caused Vain to smirk a little, his eyes blinking shut in quiet acquiescence.

"It might still be dangerous," Ava cautioned her. "Even for you. The Council works closely with D.A.R.C., whether they want to or not. Any unregistered cambion they encounter would automatically be an assumed threat."

Nesera shrugged. "Well, if the witches do try and turn me over to those priest pricks and their damn hounds..." She grinned, a promise of violence dancing behind the gleam in her eyes. "I'll make them regret it." Then, snatching up two more pancakes, Nesera swept out of the kitchen, her mind clearly made up on the matter.

Vain shook his head with a soft laugh. He pushed his plate away and stood, the legs of his chair scraping loudly against the hardwood. When I glanced up at him and caught his stare, he quickly looked away and set himself to work cleaning up the kitchen, leaving Ava and I at the table to finish.

It felt as if he were trying to put distance between us, and I couldn't understand why. But I also couldn't find the strength within myself to ask.

Ava pulled my hand into hers and gave it a squeeze, and I reciprocated a smile that felt too weak.

"Just give him some time," she said softly.

I could only nod in answer because my head was a jumble of thoughts all at once. He needed time? When my soul had been the one dragged from fuck knows where and back, *he* was the one who needed time?

Admittedly, it was confusing to figure out where he and I stood now. He no longer needed to possess my body, so did he even need—let alone want—me at all? I'm not sure why I doubted it, even after everything we'd been through. But I couldn't help the thoughts from swarming in when he was acting this reserved.

I did everything in my power to avoid turning to meet Vain's gaze, even when I felt it burn against the back of my neck. It was as if my body and mind were rejecting the lack of him, and there was no way to completely ignore how badly I wanted to close the distance that separated us, no matter how hard I tried.

I woke in the middle of the night with Ava's body still folded against mine, noting the soft pattering of rain against the windows. The light from the city cast the room in a soft orange glow, reflections of the raindrops trailing down the glass glittered on the ceiling like diamonds.

I couldn't be sure how long I laid there, content to listen to the rain and Ava's steady breathing as I inhaled the scent of her. But underneath the familiar tea and eucalyptus, was something new, a recognizable musk that reminded me faintly of charcoal and warm cloves—Vain's mark on her now that their bond was in place.

A dark, looming presence crept out from the shadows. When I looked up, Vain stood tall and rigid, a thin sliver of light scarring down one side of his face as he leaned against the doorway. With his hands dug into the pockets of his black pants, I fought to keep my attention from falling to his bare chest. He was so incredibly still except for the long trailing gaze he dragged along Ava's figure that hung halfway out of the covers until his stare caught mine.

His eyes flashed like opals, reflective and iridescent in the darkness, offering a glimpse of the otherworldly being that he was. But I couldn't find it within me to be afraid of him. Of course, I feared some of the things he could do, but I never feared *him*.

In that moment, he looked at me with a glint of hunger, and I swallowed hard as his gaze devoured me whole. But there was something about his stance that remained hesitant in the way that he clung to the shadows, and it took me a moment to realize why.

From our very first moment when he came to me and offered me a second chance at life, he'd always given me a choice.

And even now, he was allowing me to choose him.

Though we were no longer one mind, I liked to think he knew me well enough that he could read the silent invitation in my eyes. To my relief, he did.

He padded toward the bed, a slow prowl as Ava continued to sigh deeply against my bare chest. The mattress shifted under Vain's weight as he slipped beneath the sheets to curl himself along Ava's backside. Once settled against her, he released a low and satisfied hum, his soft warm exhale brushing my face.

"Are you angry with me?" he asked, his voice little more than a low whisper.

I managed to catch his gaze and my heart skittered in my chest. "Do you think I should be?"

"I asked of her what you could not," Vain said. "However selfish my reasons were, I could not lose you. I refused it."

My face warmed at his admission, and knowing he could likely see it even in the dark only made my whole body heat more. "I know. I *am* grateful."

"Truly?"

"Have a look in my head if you think I'm lying." That earned me a soft chuckle as Vain lightly shook his head. "I could never resent you for the choice you made for me. The choice you *both* made. But I'm still struggling to feel deserving of it."

I tore my gaze away, pressing my face into Ava's hair as she remained asleep between us.

"Rory, look at me."

I swallowed the ache in my throat as I did, finding Vain's eyes inches from mine. He blinked and his irises flashed iridescent again, beautiful and unsettling all at once.

"You are deserving of more than you realize. I have fought for you to see that since our first day, and even if it takes every day we have after for you to know it, then I will not stop fighting for you."

He reached across Ava and took my hand in his, bringing it up to his mouth. He brushed his lips over my wrist, my knuckles, to the pads of my fingertips, and every nerve in my body sparked with the itch to draw myself closer toward him. Vain may have no longer possessed my soul or shared my body, but having him this close felt right, like I was completely whole.

With the three of us wrapped up in each other, I wished I could stop time in that moment so I would never have to give it up, not when it felt this perfect. Not when I felt content for the first time in my life.

# THIRTY-FOUR

## AVA

I stirred awake with two warm chests pressed against me, one to my back and another at my front. The bond between Vain and I fluttered in my stomach, and a smile dragged across my lips. It was impossible to not feel happy with both men at my side. There was nowhere else I wanted to be but with them, together.

I felt a gentle tug from the other end of the bond, a shimmer of warmth that hummed through every nerve in my body. It was going to take a while to get used to that. When I opened my eyes, the demon lying in front of me nearly took my breath away.

Words could barely begin to describe him. He was by far the most beautiful demon I'd ever laid eyes on, which I supposed made sense seeing as he was an archdemon. Their beauty was as mesmerizing as it was terrifying—unmatched in every way—and Vain was no exception.

His eyes were closed, and I studied his thick lashes fluttering over the sharp structure of his cheekbones and watched the steady rise and fall of his broad chest. The pale ivory of his skin and his soft silvery hair contrasted his sculpted dark brows. Vain was crafted in facets both of light and dark, a juxtaposition of the cursed being that he was, and a demon with more of a soul than I once could have ever believed was possible.

Beneath my skin, flowing through every vessel in my blood and atom in my bones, I could feel Vain's power. It had settled within my core, a force like a thrumming well. Even though I'd only taken a small pull of his ichor during the binding ritual, it had contained multitudes—a universe of potential. My magic had never felt so free before. So alive.

The bond stirred in me again, and I caught the slight twitch of his fingers against my skin from the hand he held at my waist.

"I can *feel* that you're awake, you know," I said quietly.

The corners of Vain's lips flicked upward before he opened his eyes—black, but not all-consuming like when he had possessed Rory. Up close, it was as if every other color swirled and shimmered through his dark irises, a beautiful and mesmerizing galaxy.

"I thought you might find it unsettling if you woke to find me staring at you."

I let out a small laugh. "You're right. That would be creepy."

Vain skated his hand along the side of my face before trailing down my curves beneath the sheets. The pull of the bond was irresistible, even pressed so close together. It was like my soul couldn't stand the atoms between us. I wanted to spend hours studying this new man—this demon—before me. I wanted to learn every inch of him.

"I've been thinking," he said. "I want to take the three of us away from the city."

"Do you really think Ghen will return that soon?" I asked.

"I do. And I wish for us to be as far away from here as possible when he does. He may not have any way to track you anymore since you banished him, but knowing my brother, he will not stop looking." Vain stroked my waist, and his fingers circled my hip lazily. "I have homes across the world where I can take you both. Anywhere you would like to go."

I tugged my lower lip between my teeth before flashing him a small smile. "Anywhere?"

"Wherever you desire."

"Somewhere by the ocean then," I said. "I want to be somewhere where I can hear the waves and smell the sea."

The ocean had always calmed me. Growing up with my parents in their estate on the coast, I loved the scent of salt on the air and the sounds of the waves crashing against the rocks. Those memories would always feel reminiscent of home, and I liked the thought of replacing old memories with new ones now with Vain and Rory at my side.

Vain's mouth eased into a slow smile, warming me like the rising sun. "That can be arranged," he said. "Whatever you desire is yours."

"And can you teach me?" I asked.

"Teach you what?"

"I want to learn everything you know. I want to be stronger and be able to help people. If I can continue my studies as a demonologist, I'd rather do it without being held under the thumb of the Council or D.A.R.C."

Vain's eyes glinted with something akin to pride. "I would never dream of stopping you," he said.

"So, you will?"

He placed a chaste kiss to my lips. "For you, my love, anything."

The rhythmic rise and fall of Rory's chest against my back as he slept and the way his fingers twitched over my abdomen while he held me close made my heart flutter.

Vain brushed a lock of my hair aside, and I managed to whisper, "How can you love me?" His brows pulled together and my eyes twinged shut for the briefest moment before I continued. "I'm not a good person, Vain. I might not ever be."

"Ava." My name sounded so sweet coming from his lips. "You are allowed to forgive yourself."

I moved to look away, but he caught one side of my face in his hand, my cheek resting in his palm, and his voice was rich and deep as he said, "If I have learned anything in my life, it is that there is not a single person, human or otherwise, that can call themselves truly good. And you do not have to exist as anything different than what you are. Not with me. You are what the world has made you, and there is not a thing about that which you should wish to change. Whatever faults you may have—no matter what flaws—you are human. And to me, there is nothing more perfect than that."

A warm ache radiated down the bond, growing impossible to ignore with each passing second. I had no answer for him other than to pull his lips to mine and lose myself in his kiss.

I had never felt worthy of forgiveness. Never once had I imagined it was something I would ever deserve. If anything, I'd always believed that living in the misery of all my shame and guilt was a fitting punishment. A necessity. But for the first time in my life, I felt a weight start to lift from me, the beginnings of a bright warmth seeping in to take the place of old, fragile memories I'd clung to for too long. And even if they'd never fade completely, at least living with them would no longer need to feel like a burden. And that thought alone felt freeing.

A soft laugh escaped me when we broke apart. "And here I thought you only lusted after me."

Vain stared into my eyes as he cupped my face. His thumb ghosted across my bottom lip. "Would it help if you heard the words? If I were to debase myself before you with my most ardent affections? To whisper to you the ache of my desires and to call it love?"

I loved hearing him say that, more than I could ever admit.

"A demon cannot love," I teased.

His eyes narrowed, a soft smile playing at his lips as he sensed my game. "Have I not proven you wrong enough times, mellilla?"

"Say it again." My voice quivered as I eased closer to him.

Vain pulled my hand into his and placed it against his chest. His skin was smooth and warm underneath my palm, where I could feel the strong, steady beat of his heart.

"I love you." He traced a line down my cheek with the knuckles of his other hand before cupping my jaw in his palm. "I will say it again and again forever or as long as you need to hear me say the words. You've undone me, Ava. All of me. You *both* have. I've never been more certain of anything. This all-consuming desire will be the ruin of me. I knew it from the very first moment, and I will know it until my last."

Rory shifted behind me before he pressed his lips to the back of my neck. "You have us, Ava. You will always have us." His hands trailed over my backside as Vain dipped his head and pressed his lips to mine again, a gentle kiss, soft and exploring. Vain's tongue swept over my bottom lip, teasing the seam open in a silent request. I opened for him, and Vain's low groan of pleasure vibrated through my chest before he sucked my tongue into his mouth greedily. I wanted them both so deeply, my hunger growing by the minute to a desperate, aching point.

Vain pulled away, drifting lower to bring his mouth against the curves of my breasts that felt swollen and heavy under his touch.

Rory grinned against my skin and planted one soft kiss after another against the sensitive spot on my neck. "You fucking love this, don't you?"

I answered with a moan as Vain sucked and teased the sensitive peaks of my nipples, and I couldn't stop myself from arching my back and pressing my ass against Rory's hard cock, which throbbed in response.

My entire body hummed for them. Goosebumps prickled across my skin, which suddenly felt too hot and uncomfortable. The lack of them inside me had me squirming. Vain shot me a knowing grin with my nipple still caught between his teeth. He gave a slight tug as he pulled away, the bond between us pulsing with heady desire.

Vain leveled his darkening gaze on Rory behind me. "Fuck her," he ordered, before returning his mouth to my neck.

Rory's hand snaked between my thighs, and he guided himself toward my entrance, then slowly slid inside. His name escaped my lips through a breathless moan as I threaded my hands through Vain's short hair. Rory chuckled as he teased me, the head of his cock moving in and out of me painfully slow.

Vain's mouth felt as if it was everywhere at once, roaming from my breasts to my lips, then to devouring the hollows of my throat. One of his hands had moved down my clit, and he stroked and circled the tight bundle of nerves as Rory fucked me slow from behind.

A low curl of amusement traveled through the bond. Vain was relishing in my reckless desire as both he and Rory tipped me dangerously close to the edge. As soon as I neared the height of my climax, Vain lightened the pressure on my clit and left me whimpering at the absence of his touch.

Rory's thrusts turned unrelenting as he pumped into me, finally giving me everything I craved—all of him, fast and hard. The rhythmic sounds of our skin smacking together, our shaky, trembling breaths, the warmth of them on either side of me...I was truly lost in every sensation as they brought me to the brink of abandon.

"Please." I pleaded with Vain, clawing at his bare chest and begging him for mercy.

"Not yet," he said, his deep voice had a sadistic edge to it, which made my stomach flip. "I know what you truly want, mellilla." He flicked a knowing look to Rory, then narrowed his gaze back on me.

Rory grabbed a hold of me and then deftly maneuvered us both so I sat on top of him, his cock still deep inside as he pistoned upward. I threw my head back, a trembling moan hanging in my throat. His fingers dug firmly into my hips and his muscled arms trembled, the strain evident in the bulging veins running the length of them.

"Patience, mortals."

"*Fuuuck*," Rory shuddered through gritted teeth.

Vain smirked as he watched the two of us, his eyes trailing hungrily over our bodies as Rory fucked up into me. "Stop," he commanded.

I came crashing down on top of Rory's chest. His arms wrapped around me, pulling me close. I grinned against his lips as his cock throbbed inside of me.

"Fuck, you feel good," Rory whispered before capturing my mouth.

Vain caressed my cheek, and I opened my eyes to find him towering over me and Rory. His other hand gripped the base of his cock as he looked down at us, and I couldn't help my gaze from dropping and scanning the hard length of him, inches away from my face.

I parted my lips and flicked my tongue out for a taste. Vain was warm, smooth as velvet and slightly salty when I drew him past my lips and swirled my tongue over his head.

Rory looked up from beneath me while I took Vain into my mouth. "Please, Vain," he begged, voice straining. "Can I move again?"

Vain groaned as my mouth teased him before I increased the suction. "Yes," he said. His heated eyes didn't leave mine once.

I let out a smothered moan around Vain's cock as Rory started fucking me again, possessed with a newfound vigor.

Vain's fingers tunneled through my hair, drawing together at the back of my head. Holding me in place, he pressed his hips forward and slid deeper into my mouth. I relaxed into it so I could take more of him, as much as he was willing to give me. He inched forward slowly until he hit the back of my throat, holding himself there until I sputtered for air and drooled greedily around his cock and over my chin.

Vain's smile was nothing short of wicked when he popped himself free. He stepped back to watch Rory crane his neck up and drag his tongue up from the base of my throat to the underside of my jaw, licking at the glistening trail as if he was seeking a taste of Vain too. I met Rory's mouth with a hunger he matched in earnest. Sucking his lips between my teeth, Rory groaned my name.

"I fucking love you," he said between thrusts and then took my face in his hands. "You have no idea how much."

From the first moment I'd laid my eyes on him, Rory had always been mine to save. To fight for. To love. He looked up at me, gray eyes sparked with heady desire, and I wanted to give him everything.

"You will *always* have my heart." I pressed my lips to his softly and let him wind his fingers through my hair.

The mattress shifted behind us, and I peered over my shoulder as Vain prowled toward Rory and I, inching closer with a predatory gleam in his eyes. I watched with peaked interest as Vain wrapped his hand around the base of Rory's cock and pulled him out of me. Luckily, Vain didn't make me wait long before he eased his hips forward and drove himself into me, sating the ache left behind in Rory's absence.

Each long, hard thrust had my eyes rolling back while Rory stroked a hand through my hair as he gazed up at me from below. Vain plunged himself in and out a few more times before he pulled out and repositioned Rory to take his place.

Again and again, they took their turns, their cocks moving in and out. Every eager pump of Rory's hips had me melting further into his chest. And the stretch of Vain as he sheathed himself inside, his hips flush against my ass, had me arching for him. Rory's mouth was on mine the whole time, our tongues locked a ravenous frenzy. He hooked his hands under my arms and gripped onto my shoulders. His shuddering breaths fanned over my heated skin as our sweat-slicked bodies moved together.

I gasped against Rory's mouth and jolted at the sensation of the warm press of a finger to my tight hole. Whipping my head around, I was met with a devious smirk from Vain as he eased a single lubed digit inside. I moaned as it sunk deep, the stretch of it filling me with a torturous bliss. He knew what I wanted. He knew all of my unspoken desires, every one of them, as if they were his own.

Rory kept his rhythm slow and steady as I adjusted to the new sensation tightening inside me, until I became the one to drive the pace. But even with every rock of my hips backwards into them both, it still never felt like enough. And I wasn't above begging.

"Please. More," I whimpered as I tossed Vain a heated stare over my shoulder that I could only describe as being intoxicated with lust. "Vain..."

Vain let out a low, approving hum and inserted a second finger to push past the tight muscle and spread me wider. I immediately went rigid, caught off guard by the added size, and I gasped. The demon leaned forward and pressed his mouth to the small of my back, gently caressing my hips with his free hand to coax me still.

"It'll be much easier if you relax, mellilla."

I tugged my bottom lip between my teeth and nodded, releasing the tension held within my muscles. Rory slid in and out of me at a languid pace while Vain carefully and patiently worked me open.

The building pressure was unlike anything I'd ever experienced. It didn't take long for the initial sharp sting to ebb before giving way to the throbbing heat of pleasure. By the time Vain introduced a third finger, I was practically bucking my hips.

"Stay still," Vain said, speaking to both me and Rory.

We obeyed. I nearly cried out when Vain slipped his fingers from me and I squirmed in the absence of him.

"Patience." He chuckled and then Vain spread me wide with his large hands, forcing another gasp out of me as he eased his cock past the rim, replacing where his fingers had been. The three of us inhaled shaky breaths against each other's skin as Vain pushed deeper, every inch filling me with blissful anguish before he finally drove himself to the hilt, his hips flush against my ass.

"Fuck, Vain. I can feel you," Rory panted underneath me. "She's so tight."

"Yes, and she's taking both of us so well. Just like I knew she would." The smile was evident in his words, and my stomach fluttered restlessly as the knot in my core wound tighter. Rory smiled too as he leaned up to kiss me, his tongue teasing my lips apart before delving deeper into my mouth.

Each of them remained motionless to allow me to adjust to the stretch of them both filling me. I didn't realize I had been holding my breath until they began to move, their long strokes dragging a deep moan of pleasure from my chest.

They worked in tandem—when Vain drew himself out, Rory pushed in. Back and forth, they kept an even pace, driving me mad with lust. I was insatiable. Every thrust turned increasingly more demanding, and every snap of flesh against flesh sent me hurtling toward a wild peak of ecstasy. There wasn't a single muscle in my body that wasn't strung taut, and I felt ready to snap at any moment.

Vain leaned over to purr into my ear, "You know, you make the sweetest noises when you're about to come."

Rory clenched his jaw, his expression fraught with tension as if he were about to come undone himself. "Come on, sweetheart. I've got you," he panted. "Come with us."

"I'm right there." I gasped, shaking. "Oh god!"

They sent me over the edge with one more thrust from each of them, and I broke apart between them, clenching through wave after wave of the most intense pleasure I'd ever felt. I was soaring, falling, screaming their names as my orgasm tore through me, which coaxed both men to follow me in turn.

I held Rory's gaze, awed at the incredible way his mouth fell open, and how his features twisted into the most beautiful clash of pain and soul-gripping pleasure as he emptied himself into me.

Vain roped my hair around his fist and tugged, craning my neck back so I could watch as he succumbed to his release. To behold an archdemon's control unravel as he came undone, knowing he was mine—that *we* were his—it was like looking upon divinity.

Even after the last waves of my orgasm faded, Rory and Vain remained flush against me, then the three of us collapsed between each other in a tangle of limbs. For a long while, the only sounds filling the room were our heavy panting and the thrum of our heartbeats.

"Ava."

"Mellilla."

They whispered against the shell of my ear; the tremble in their voices, every shaky breath, every kiss against my skin felt like the act of them sealing a promise. That these men were mine. Vain and Rory held me, body and soul, and I would allow them both to seal a thousand more oaths, enough to last us a lifetime.

# EPILOGUE

## RORY

Vain's right hand was warm in mine. He gave it a small squeeze after shifting me and Ava to a cliffside outside of Edinburgh where his tall and ominous castle loomed above us. I don't think I had ever seen a structure so magnificent up close. The pale granite stones rose up and up, imposing and breathtaking like a palace set against the edge of the world with the sea stretching out to the horizon beyond. The breeze whipped up from the ocean and tousled my dark hair into my eyes and I fought to keep it back.

Ava breathed in deeply on the other side of Vain and smiled.

"It's perfect," she said to him.

"This place was in ruins when I found it," Vain said. "I rebuilt it from the rubble centuries ago."

Vain spoke of centuries the way a human might speak of days. It was a stark reminder of what he was, though it didn't bother Ava or me in the slightest.

He led us up a small hill toward the front gate, the long grass brushing against our legs as the three of us walked hand in hand. Scottish roses lined the narrow dirt pathway, eventually turning to cobblestones the closer we approached.

Entering the keep felt like stumbling into a different era. Vain lit the sconces with a snap of his fingers, every torch jumping to life and revealing a grand, gothic interior.

My gaze roamed up to the high ceiling and the intricate gold chandelier hanging in the cavernous foyer. Crimson rugs ran along the hallways like rivers of blood and enormous crushed velvet curtains cascaded from the tall windows. Dark furniture decorated nearly every wall and corner. A large skull that hung from one of the arched doorways caught my eye, and it was impossible to tell if it was from an animal or a demon.

Everything was so tastefully macabre.

"Cozy," I muttered, my voice echoing off the stones.

Vain swung his attention to me, his gaze settling on mine like a burning ember that warmed me from the inside out. My attention trailed along the sharp planes of his face, the fall of his platinum hair, which shadowed his dark eyes, and his sensuous, hard mouth. As if noticing where my focus had wandered to, Vain offered me a slight smile before leading us deeper into his castle.

He gave us a tour of the dozens of rooms and discouraged us from getting lost. "There are ghosts that roam this keep, and I can't promise that all of them are as benevolent as I am." Whether Vain was teasing or not, I couldn't suppress the shiver that ran down my spine.

Ava pumped her eyebrows as she passed me. "Scared, Masters?" Her smirk was sinful, tempting me to clamp a hand around her wrist and pull her against me.

"Careful. Don't be so quick to taunt me, sweetheart. I know just how to shut you up if I need to."

Ava's lips parted expectantly as her eyes flicked down to my mouth. I teased my thumb across her bottom lip and kissed the top of her forehead before following Vain into the drawing room where a great fire roared in the hearth, bathing the room in warm golden light. From the large bay windows looking out over the coast, the last remnants of dusk were drifting low on the horizon. Vain had already poured a decanter of red wine into three crystal glasses and set soft music to play on an old turntable.

When I took my first sip, heavy notes of cherry and oak bloomed on my tongue. Sinking low into the couch cushions, I swirled my glass in one hand, content to watch Ava fall into Vain's touch. She twirled around him, a laugh playing at the corners of her mouth, and I caught myself hypnotized in the movement of the hem of her dress—how it swished above her knees and flashed tempting glimpses of her thighs. Vain held her close, his hands dancing along her lower back, her arms, her wrists, as he spun her expertly around him.

The more wine I drank, the more I felt as if I were dancing with them. My body tingled with warmth from the alcohol, and the fire, and the happiness brimming in my chest. The room swam as I tilted my head up to the shadowed ceiling and stared into the darkened corners. For once, I no longer felt afraid at what might be staring back.

A small hand pressed against my sternum.

"Dance with me," Ava said, her voice low and husky. She curled her fingers into the fabric of my shirt as she leaned in close.

Reaching for her hips, I pulled her on top of me. I hummed at the weight of her in my lap and traced my fingertips along her jaw. Her cheeks were flushed, and her lips brushed mine with the softest caress.

"If I try to stand right now, you're going to have to hold me up."

Ava sank her fingers into my hair at the back of my head and pressed her lips firmly to mine. I parted her mouth with my tongue, tasting the wine and drinking in her moan.

"You're so drunk," she said when she drew back.

The way she bit her bottom lip between her teeth had me straining against the front of my jeans. "You taste incredible."

A smile lit up her face, her eyes sparkling in the firelight. "You do too." And then her mouth was on mine again.

✶ ✶ ✶

"*Rorrryyyy.*" I jolted awake to the hoarse rasp of my name snaking through the drawing room.

Ava jerked up from my chest at the same time, the ends of her hair brushing against my face as she scanned around us.

"Did you say my name?" I asked her. My tongue felt heavy in my mouth from the wine.

"No," she whispered. "I thought you said mine."

Ava peeled herself off me, and I sat up off the couch cushions.

"Where is Vain?" she asked.

I figured she ought to know, considering she was the one who'd bound her soul to him.

The embers in the fire appeared to have died hours ago, leaving the room cold and dark. A low, droning hum vibrated through the walls like a constant pulse, as if the castle itself were alive. It sounded otherworldly, and I felt drawn to it despite also being a bit wary. It tugged at my chest the same way the whisper of my name had before, like a summoning, coaxing my soul toward something I didn't understand.

"This way," she said and took my hand in hers. We stepped tentatively out into the dark halls. The shadows were everywhere, obscuring nearly all the light throughout the castle. I couldn't keep my thoughts from lingering on the idea of ghosts that Vain had planted in our heads earlier.

With every turn we made through the castle, a familiar, snaking tendril wormed itself tighter around my mind, luring me toward it. My palms became slick, and my heart skittered like a child lost in the dark.

"*Ssscared little mortalsss,*" the voice crept up on a whisper.

Stopping dead in our tracks, the hair on the back of my neck rose. My skin prickled with the understanding that something was stalking us through the dark corridors. Fear gripped me as three hollow clicks echoed off the stone walls, creeping nearer.

A soft hiss slithered against the shell of my ear. "*Run.*"

Ava and I launched forward, our instincts driving us into the darkness as we gave chase to whatever nightmare hunted us through the castle, nipping closely at our heels. Whether it be a ghost, a monster, or a demon, we didn't care as we ran.

I pushed Ava ahead of me, stumbling into the great hall behind her. An eerie, red glow welcomed us from an arched doorway at the end of the chamber. It was the only source of light, and we ran toward it like moths to a flame, eager to escape the shadows and the darkness on the hunt behind us.

Through the doorway, a tight, winding staircase snaked below the castle. We scrambled for purchase on the smooth stones. One slight misstep and we might topple down to the bottom. The creeping whispers dissipated the further down we went, and the red light grew brighter.

Upon reaching the base of the stairs, I pulled Ava close, keeping my hand laced tightly in hers as we scanned ahead.

A door standing at the end of the corridor had the same red glow seeping out from the crack underneath. The familiar tug in my core again edged me closer toward the light. I pressed one hand to the surface, my body humming with a powerful energy which gave me pause. Ava gave my other hand a tight squeeze, filling me with the courage to push it open.

The circular chamber was bathed in red light. My eyes immediately went to the enormous bed in the center, draped in silky black sheets. A St. Andrews cross sat in one corner, and hanging from a large iron gate at the other end of the room were a pair of leather restraints. I wasn't particularly eager to be bound and shackled, not after the weeks of being held captive by Ava's former coven...so why couldn't I stop my imagination from wandering to the idea of it and how it might feel?

"Don't worry, I have no plans of using those...yet."

Vain sat in a deep armchair across the room with a wicked smile gracing his lips, his iridescent gaze dark and assessing. He was a true demon of the shadows, filling our heads with powerful and dangerous desire.

Ava laughed beside me, and I jumped at the sound that broke the pointed silence.

"*This* is your dungeon?"

"So, you do remember..." Vain tossed one eyebrow up at her, his face settling into an expression of amusement and borderline temptation. "I realized that I didn't bring you two to the lower levels during our tour."

Vain stood, immediately towering over both me and Ava as he circled us slowly.

"Was this all some sick game you wanted to play with us for your amusement?" I challenged.

The demon stopped in front of me and tossed a smirk over one shoulder at my defiant outburst.

"Oh, Rory," Vain purred. "I've not even begun the fun part."

I swallowed hard. Beneath the sensual tone of his voice was something dark and forbidden laced between his words. If I were a careful man, I might have run from it. But I was far too reckless, and all too eager to give in to it—in to *him*.

Beside me, Ava crossed her arms over her chest and jutted her hip. "So, you lured us down here by scaring us—"

"Who's to say I had anything to do with that?" Vain said. Ava stilled, which spurred Vain's sharp smile and the unmistakable glint in his eyes. "Don't pretend that playing with your fears didn't arouse you though. You know it's useless to try and hide your desires from me, Ava. Now more than ever."

Knowing the bond that they now shared together, I had little doubt that what Vain said was true.

"Look at me, mellilla." He tipped his fingers under her chin, fixing his eyes on hers. "Undress him."

Vain released her and stepped back to admire us from a distance. Ava's eyes sparked with enthusiasm as she turned to me. She braced her hands against my chest, then pulled at the fabric of my shirt and drew my lips to hers.

She was so warm. So soft.

The taste of cherries still lingered on her tongue, and I drank it in as I tunneled my fingers through her hair. Her hands turned ravishing as she skirted down my abdomen and tore at the hem of my shirt.

"Slowly," Vain warned.

Ava's breathing came out shaky against my lips as she fought to control the pace of her movements. She peeled off my shirt slowly as Vain had commanded, her fingers trailing along my bare skin and leaving goosebumps in their wake. When she finally reached my zipper, her hands roamed across my hard length through the fabric of my pants, teasing me with her glacial pace.

My cock jumped a little under the pressure of her touch and I grinned at the tiny satisfied hum she released. She inched my pants to the floor, followed by my boxer-briefs. My gaze flicked over Ava's shoulder to Vain, who only nodded, as if to say, "hers next".

I slid the straps of her dress down, then trailed my lips over her collarbone. She dug her fingers into my bare hips, and I popped the small buttons of her bodice open until the dress slid off her frame and fluttered down to her feet, revealing the black lacy set she wore underneath. I wanted nothing more than to rip them off with my teeth, but Vain's voice wrenched me out of my fantasy.

"Sit," he ordered her, approaching from behind. To my surprise, he'd already glamoured his clothes away, and I stared at his naked form. Vain was immaculate, his body chiseled and hard like he'd been crafted by the hand of a god. I sucked in a sharp breath as he neared me.

Ava lowered herself to the edge of the bed, obedience glinting in her amber gaze.

"And don't you dare touch yourself."

Her eyes went wide, and she stared between us before Vain dragged my attention to him.

Cupping my jaw, Vain trailed his other hand up my chest, past my collarbone until he grazed the side of my neck and over the V tattoo. It felt as if he had stolen all the breath from my lungs from his simple touch alone. His dark eyes were brilliant, vibrant, and hungry as they searched mine, and my stomach turned over nervously under his unrelenting gaze.

Vain thumbed over my tattoo, admiring it with an approving hum before he leaned in to kiss me.

His first kiss was gentle and sent pinpricks of energy jolting straight down to my toes. Our mouths melded together in a careful entanglement. His taste was eternal. Spiced, dark, and heavy with want. This kiss was real. *He* was real.

Vain's hand traced down my abdomen, his fingers gentle and exploring as he seared a path toward my aching cock, and I gasped against his mouth at the touch.

A shiver shot straight through my body when he gripped me, hard and firm, and there was no stopping my hips from pushing forward into his touch, desperate for more. Our mouths parted briefly, and Vain pressed his forehead to mine, his dark eyes catching mine. "How does it feel to finally have my hands on you like this?"

Held completely at his mercy, all thoughts—any semblance of words—escaped me. I could have died of pleasure in that moment, content with knowing he would be the one to bring me back again, and again.

A small, restrained noise came from over my shoulder from the whimper caught in Ava's throat.

"So impatient," Vain said softly as he turned to her, still cupping my face with one hand.

Ava's thighs pressed together as she tugged her bottom lip between her teeth. She had removed the remainder of her garments, leaving her exposed and ready for us.

Desire for them both curled low in my stomach, twisting me up in the most indescribable bliss. Ava curled her hands into the sheets, and she leaned back slightly from the edge of the bed.

"Use your words, sweetheart. Tell us what you want."

Ava's eyes darted between the two of us. "I want both of you on your knees, between my legs."

I was sure Vain's smirk matched my own.

We lowered ourselves together, parting her legs wide to make room for us both. I kept my eyes locked on Ava's as I sank down onto my knees and inched my face close to her delicious heat, salivating for a taste of the sweet arousal that glistened, begging for our attention.

Vain swept his tongue through her first, eliciting a long, drawn-out sigh from her parted lips. He pulled away, and I took the opening to trail my tongue upwards, teasing her lips with long, languid strokes and smiling against her flesh when she squirmed around my face. I circled her swollen clit until she gasped, and I rewarded her by sucking it into my mouth, groaning at the sensation of her nails scraping against my scalp.

I drew back, and Vain was staring at me with hooded eyes, his lips parted slightly as he watched me watching him. An intense wave of desire came over me, and I wanted to wind my fingers through his soft platinum hair and have him drag me toward insatiable abandon. His eyes held a promise, and he fulfilled my wish before I had the chance to vocalize it.

Vain's lips were soft on mine, and he explored my mouth with a gentle hunger that stirred my desire into a savage frenzy. I nearly came apart at the taste of him mixing with Ava's arousal, heady on both our tongues.

Vain and I lowered our heads back to Ava's dripping cunt and swirled our tongues together, teasing each other. Teasing her. Ava's hands turned wild as she tunneled her fingers through our hair. Her whimpers became desperate and rasping while we gave her everything, and not nearly enough.

Vain cupped the back of my head, pushing me forward to take Ava fully. Digging my hands into the warm flesh of her thighs, I dragged her closer to the edge of the bed and pressed my mouth firmly against her. I stroked and lapped and sucked like a man starved. Like she was the sweetest thing I'd ever had the privilege of tasting.

"Flip her over," Vain said, his voice low and strained. He stood behind Ava at the other end of the bed, his eyes burning with desire. "On her knees."

My stomach flooded with warmth whenever he gave me orders and my limbs buzzed with an eagerness to obey. I would do anything for them, just as they had done for me.

I pulled away and settled my hands against Ava's hips. She watched me with rapt attention, her eyes bright as I swept my tongue out to capture her arousal painted across my lips before I turned her over at Vain's command.

"Crawl to me, mellilla."

Slowly, she crawled on her hands and knees, the sway of her bare hips sucking me into a trance as she moved to the other edge of the bed where Vain held his cock, thick and heavy in his hand.

Tilting her head upward, she took him into her mouth without hesitation, licking at the pre-cum beaded at his tip. The sound of her humming around him knotted my stomach, and when she took him deeper, Vain hissed in a breath through his teeth.

I was so hungry for her. I couldn't resist crawling across the mattress and settling in on my hands and knees behind her before dipping my face back into her soaking wet cunt. At the first touch of my mouth against her, she moaned with Vain deep in her throat and the sound made my cock throb for attention.

I brought my fingers up and dragged them through her pussy. *Fuck*, she was so wet.

I slipped two inside her and curled them forward. Ava tensed, her muscles clenching around me with every stroke. Nipping my teeth at the flesh of her thighs and her ass, every tender bite had her panting as she continued to take Vain deep down her throat. As I pumped and curled my fingers in a steady rhythm, I dragged my tongue upward through her crease and circled her perfect, tight hole which fluttered in anticipation at the touch.

Ava's body was a drug. I could taste every part of her and never be fully satisfied.

I kept the pad of my thumb pressed hard against her clit and dragged her toward the edge until her muffled moans grew feral.

Vain took her chin between his thumb and forefinger and marveled at her from above. "Should we let you come, mellilla?"

"Please, Vain," she cried. "Yes, please, yes."

Ava quivered, ready to come undone at our command.

"Does his mouth feel good on you, Ava?" he asked.

"Yes," she rasped.

"You sound so wet on his fingers. You know, if I told Rory to stop, he'd obey me."

Ava shook her head. "Please, don't make him stop."

Vain's gaze turned molten. "When I spill down your pretty little throat, I want you to come. Do you understand?"

"Yes. Yes, I will. Please, just let me come."

Vain smiled. "Good girl," he purred before easing his hips forward and shoving himself into Ava's waiting mouth. She was a trembling mess, barely holding herself together as I continued working my tongue over her hole and filling her tight pussy with my fingers.

Vain didn't make her wait long, only a few fast pumps before he tipped his head back and groaned as he came. It was all the permission she needed, and Ava clenched around me, her come soaking my fingers until she was dripping onto the sheets. Her thighs shook as she came down from her pleasure. She sunk into the mattress, breathless and limp.

I sucked my fingers clean and then reached underneath her stomach, flipping her onto her back. Crawling over her, I settled myself between her thighs, coaxing her legs open with my knees.

The last shreds of my patience had worn thin. I sheathed myself inside of her warmth in one hard stroke. I knew how sensitive she was, but I couldn't bring myself to be gentle with her. I wanted to pound her into the mattress until she forgot how to speak. I wanted her nails raking down my back until she drew blood. I needed to hear her raspy, shaky moans against the shell of my ear as

I sank my teeth into her neck, leaving behind a mark, a brand that was just mine.

Ava arched into me as I drove myself into her again and again. I seized her mouth with mine, and she tasted divine. Even the salty hint of Vain left on her tongue was like an addictive force that I couldn't get enough of.

I broke the kiss and pushed myself up, my arms braced on either side of Ava's head, and caught Vain's eyes from across the bed. The demon's eyes were half-lidded and burning with insatiable desire as he lazily stroked his still-hard cock at the sight of us.

"I want you," I said to him, barely a whisper.

Vain prowled forward, nothing but pure possession flaring in his dark eyes as he reached out and cupped my cheek in his palm.

"You are *mine*, Rory. And I'm going to fuck you like you're mine."

*Holy fucking shit.* I swallowed hard as I stared up at him.

"I'm going to fuck you while you make her come again." Vain said nothing else as he settled onto the bed behind me. His finger was cool and slick as he pressed into me, preparing me. I bit down on my lower lip to fight back my moan.

"Tell me if you want me to stop." His voice held an edge of worry, almost as if this powerful demon was afraid he might break me.

I peered over my shoulder to catch his gaze. "You forget this isn't my first time."

Vain smirked at me. He knew better than anyone. All my wants and desires. My past and my present were all his. They always had been.

One finger became two, then three, but I was tensing with anticipation for more. I needed *more*.

Removing his fingers, Vain then positioned himself at my entrance, and my mouth popped open silently when he pushed inside. Ava dragged her thumb along my lower lip, and I sucked it into my mouth to muffle my groan, my teeth scraping over her knuckle.

"Don't you dare hold back," Vain purred. "I want to hear how good I make you feel."

I gave into the pain and the pleasure and allowed my moans to break free from my chest.

Vain hissed when my muscles clenched and sucked him deeper, inch by torturous inch, until he finally bottomed out inside me. Ava's inner walls clamped around me, and I nearly came on the spot. Everything was so hot and tight and...*fuck* did it feel good. Better than good. I felt alive. It felt like all of me was on fire, fighting to hold myself together as they edged me toward the brink of blistering ecstasy. The heat, the pressure of them both at either end of me, taking and giving, I was already so close to breaking under the overwhelming pleasure.

Vain leaned over me, his mouth brushing along the curve of my ear. "Admit it," he said, low and dark, the unmistakable hint of a smirk playing at his lips. "You missed having me inside of you."

I couldn't even begin to equate this feeling to him possessing my soul. No, this was something else entirely, and somehow felt far more intimate. He had embedded himself into every part of me, in the marks he'd left on my soul, to now my body in the way that he ravished me like I was something to be worshiped, and I was completely captivated by him. I lost myself in his touch, his lust, his...everything that he was. Vain was always a force that I could not fight, and one I never wanted to. He'd claimed my soul all the same. And I was glad for it.

He dug his fingers into my hair and yanked my head back to expose my neck. It was hard enough that I yelped, but I softened into his touch the moment his shadows wound themselves around my throat, applying just the right amount of pressure.

Again, Vain thrust into me, driving me into Ava in turn. I moaned loudly and Vain chuckled.

"You're both such a beautiful mess beneath me."

"Rory," Ava breathed. "I'm close."

I already knew. Her legs shook as badly as mine did. We were both tipping dangerously close to the edge of something earth-shattering, and Vain was leading us there with every thrust and hard, measured stroke.

The three of us were a tangle of breath, limbs, and heat, with no beginning and no end. Enveloped in their frenzied touch, I gave into them both, and my orgasm rocked through my body like a fucking tidal wave. My muscles seized and my toes curled as I spilled into Ava. She cried out beneath me through her own explosion of pleasure. Vain was not far behind us, and he came inside me with a strained groan that melted my soul.

My arms shook as I propped myself up over Ava, and her eyes shone up at me, bright, dazed, and dreamlike. Her beautifully flushed face held a perfect balanced expression of amazement and reverence, all her love she had for me softening her delicate features.

I placed a chaste kiss to her swollen lips and sighed against her skin. I tossed a look over my shoulder to Vain, *our* demon, who stared at us with all the dominance he possessed in this world.

My voice came out heavy with lust, lacking any and all hesitation. "Again."


THE END

# ACKNOWLEDGEMENTS

In the nearly two years since this story began as nothing more than a mess of scenes frantically typed into my notes app in the ungodly hours of the night, I could have never expected it to grow into what it is today. But this fever dream of a book would have never been even remotely possible without all of the support and encouragement I've received along every step of this journey.

Firstly, to Jake, my incredible husband, my best friend, and my biggest supporter. Thank you for putting up with my venting frustrations, my tears, and all my anxious ramblings. Thank you for always being patient with me and being there for me even on my worst days when I was ready to give it all up and quit. I don't know what I did to deserve you, and I love you endlessly.

To Anna, for being the very first to read this story at one of its earliest stages and giving me the confidence that it was worth putting out into the world. You loved these characters as much as I did, and it encouraged me every day to know that there would be other readers out there someday who could love them too.

To Skylar, my Virgo twin, for all the wine and the whining, and every writing session which eventually devolved into chaos. You talked me out of a spiral more times than I can count, and I don't think I would have ever made it through my edits without you at my side!

To Julia, I still can't believe that my silly little book was your first introduction to the world of dark and smutty romance. I'm sorry I made you wait so long to read it but thank you for loving it, for pushing me to believe in myself and to put my all into this journey. Love you forever!

To my amazing editor, Brittany, I'm so grateful for everything you did to help shape this book into the version of the story that I wanted to publish. Thank you for understanding the story I wanted to tell and for handling my book with so much care. Without all of your invaluable feedback, this story would not be what it is now, and I'm forever thankful.

To all of my amazingly supportive and lovely beta readers, Lilliana, Akita, Faith, Reena, and those at E&A Editing for all of your feedback and encouragement. Thanks for taking a chance on me and this story. I appreciate every single one of you more than you know!

And finally, to any and every reader who picked up this book, who found something in this story they could relate to, who saw parts of themselves in these characters...There are not enough words to express my gratitude to you. As someone who has always dreamed of one day becoming an author and sharing my stories with anyone who would listen, just knowing that this book found its place with someone is an indescribable feeling and the greatest reward. So thank you, thank you, thank you.

*— Katia Black*

# About the Author

Katia Black is a paranormal romance and fantasy author who currently lives in Northern Virginia with her husband.

When not writing dark, haunting stories filled with magic, otherworldly beings, and pathetically obsessed men, she can be found devouring smutty books, attempting to wrangle her cat (demon), and failing to curb her addiction to blueberry Red Bull.

You can find her online on...

Instagram: @katiablackauthor
Substack: katiablack.substack.com

*Subscribe to Katia's
newsletter!*

www.ingramcontent.com/pod-product-compliance
Lightning Source LLC
Chambersburg PA
CBHW061901310726
48972CB00004B/1122